What people are saying

You Make Me Feel Like Dancing

"We have a winner here! *You Make Me Feel Like Dancing*, starring an endearing Boomer Babe, is a book for all ages. Its plot line carries some strong subjects—but with grace and without losing track of the fact that a novel is something people read because they love story. Dance on out and get your copy!"

Gayle Roper, author of *Fatal Deduction*

"Tangee lipstick, Dippity-do hair gel, Yardley fragrances, Bonne Bell cosmetics ... Donna Summer, The Bee Gees, and Barry White. *Sound familiar?* Allison Bottke embarks with her readers on a special journey from the Peace Train of the past to the Disco Inferno of the here and now. If you loved the night life and you still like to boogie, take time out for a novel written by *one* of us for *all* of us!"

Eva Marie Everson, author of
Things Left Unspoken

"Embrace your stroll through the '70s with Allison Bottke's boomer chick lit. It's about time someone who understands what it's like to be a boomer woman captured our lives, writing with candor, credence, and class."

Dotsie Bregel, founder of the National
Association of Baby Boomer Women and
www.BoomerWomenSpeak.com

"Dancing on the red carpet takes a plethora of steps of business savvy, courage, questionable relationships, hidden agendas, surprises, plans, and most of all faith. Allison Bottke takes us on a square dance of situations, circumstances, relationships, and adventures that lead us waltzing to success. If you want encouragement and inspiration as you seek your dreams, this is the book for you."

Thelma Wells, DD, president of A Woman of God Ministries, speaker, author, founder of the Ready To Win Conference

You Make
Me Feel
Like
Dancing

Also by Allison Bottke

Fiction:
One Little Secret
A Stitch in Time

Nonfiction:
Setting Boundaries with Your Adult Children: Six Steps
to Hope and Healing for Struggling Parents
I Can't Do It All: Breaking Free from the Lies That Control
Us (with Tracie Peterson and Dianne O'Brian)

Compilations:
God Allows U-Turns
More God Allows U-Turns
God Allows U-Turns for Women
God Allows U-Turns for Teens
God Allows U-Turns—American Moments
God Allows U-Turns—A Woman's Journey
God Answers Prayers
God Answers Moms' Prayers
God Answers Prayers—Military Edition
Journeys of Hope
Journeys of Love
Journeys of Joy
Journeys of Friendship

Youth:
Pastrami Project
Friend or Freak
Get Real

Children:
Laughter and Love
Jingles and Joy
Picnics and Peace

Va Va Va
BOOM
SERIES

You Make
Me Feel
Like
Dancing

A NOVEL

ALLISON BOTTKE

David C Cook®
transforming lives together

YOU MAKE ME FEEL LIKE DANCING
Published by David C. Cook
4050 Lee Vance View
Colorado Springs, CO 80918 U.S.A.

David C. Cook Distribution Canada
55 Woodslee Avenue, Paris, Ontario, Canada N3L 3E5

David C. Cook U.K., Kingsway Communications
Eastbourne, East Sussex BN23 6NT, England

David C. Cook and the graphic circle C logo
are registered trademarks of Cook Communications Ministries.

This story is a work of fiction. All characters and events are the product of the author's
imagination. Any resemblance to any person, living or dead, is coincidental.

Quotation in chapter 2 is from Rick Warren, *The Purpose Driven
Life* (Grand Rapids, MI: Zondervan, 2002), 25.

LCCN 2009902387
ISBN 978-1-4347-9949-4
eISBN 978-1-4347-0031-5

The Team: Don Pape, Anne Christian Buchanan, Amy Kiechlin, Sarah Schultz,
Jack Campbell, Caitlyn York, and Susan Vannaman
Cover Design/Illustration: Connie Gabbert, The Designworks Group

Printed in the United States of America
First Edition 2009

1 2 3 4 5 6 7 8 9 10

032709

For all my boomer babe sisters.

*We will survive, thrive, and dance
our way into midlife!*

Chapter 1

Susan Anderson yawned and mumbled an incoherent complaint. She tried to focus heavy-lidded eyes on the glowing chartreuse numbers of the digital clock. Six a.m. She rolled onto her side and picked up the ringing cell phone, wishing she'd shut it off the night before. This was her day off, the one day in seven she could stay ensconced in her luxurious bed, wrapped in Egyptian cotton like a mummy princess. The one day in seven she could snuggle with her hubby when he came home from working the night shift.

"I'm-sorry-to-wake-you-up-but-it's-an-emergency-and-you're-the-only-one-who-can-help-something-horrible-has-happened-to-Tina."

"Slow down, Karen," Susan whispered hoarsely. "I understand you haven't been to sleep yet, but I'm still waking up, okay? Now, start from the top. Who's Tina?"

Stretching like a limber feline, Susan propped her pillow against the headboard and slowly sat up, her eyebrows knitting together as Karen spoke. Her eyes opened more fully as she listened to Karen's amazing tale.

"… that's the whole story. I'm afraid she's going to do something drastic. Please, you have to help her. I know you don't work Mondays, but you're the only one I know who might be able to do something."

Susan leaned her head back and yawned again as she considered.

"Susan? Susan, are you there?"

"Still here. Sorry. Okay. I need coffee and a bagel, but you can tell her to meet me at the salon at seven."

"Seriously? Fantastic! You're a lifesaver!"

Susan hung up the phone, rolled onto her stomach, and buried her face in her pillow. Part of her wanted to go back to sleep. But the rest of her loved a challenge—and this was truly a challenge. Although dull moments were few in her world, so were new ventures these days—at least ventures of the dramatic magnitude Karen had just described.

She pulled back the covers and eased up on the edge of the bed. Absentmindedly tucking a strand of ash blond hair behind her ear, she considered her options for another minute or two before reaching for the phone.

"She works hard for the money, so hard—"

"Stop singing, Loretta—please. It's too early for Donna Summer, even for you. I hate caller ID."

"Heretic—bite your tongue! It's never too early for Donna. And you should love caller ID. It's the only reason I always answer your calls."

Susan laughed. More than a dependable employee, Loretta Wells was a good friend and a sister in faith. She was also the reason Susan could take Mondays off. Loretta was more than capable of handling things without the boss. In fact, she'd been Susan's right hand for almost twenty years.

Every Monday morning before opening the salon at seven thirty, Loretta had coffee at the Starbucks just off Tropicana Boulevard.

Susan knew she could depend on her to rise to this challenge, cut her Starbucks run short, and get things ready for Tina before she arrived.

Susan explained what little she knew about what she'd dubbed as Tina's Tragic Trauma. "You don't mind coming in early?" she asked.

"Are you kidding? Sounds utterly fascinating. Don't worry about me—what about you? I don't think I've seen you on a Monday in more than a decade. Think you can function?"

"Very funny. I'll be just fine. See you in forty-five."

She flipped the phone shut, grabbed a notepad and pen from the bedside table, and scribbled a note to leave downstairs for Michael on her way out. Her husband wouldn't get home until eight, about the time she was usually getting ready for work. He wouldn't be happy with her for taking off like this on their one day together, but what could she do? This young woman needed her.

She recalled the most recent argument she'd had with Michael about this very subject.

"You're a hairdresser, for crying out loud—not George!" he had shouted into the phone last week when she called him from the salon at two-thirty a.m.

George was their neighbor, a psychologist who was on call for police emergencies twenty-four/seven.

"You wouldn't say that, Michael, if you had seen her. The creep used a butcher knife to cut off her hair. I couldn't say no. Michael, you should have seen—"

"What if he had showed up at the shop? What then? He might be outside waiting for you right now. Maybe I should come over and follow you home—"

"No, Michael, I'm fine. I'm sure he's not waiting for me. He doesn't have a beef with me."

Susan didn't tell him she had worried about the same thing when the girl showed up, referred by a friend who ran a shelter for battered women.

"I'm sorry I called," she said with a sigh. What she had really wanted to share was her excitement at being able to pray with a young woman who was openly searching for an answer to the unexplainable emptiness in her heart.

"Me, too," Michael grumbled. "Now, get out of there and go home. I'll stay on the phone while you lock up."

That had been several days ago, and they had yet to talk about the situation again. She wasn't exactly eager to bring it up—not with the way Michael had been acting lately. His sixtieth birthday loomed on the horizon, and Susan was quite certain he was having a delayed midlife crisis. She was hard-pressed to feel sympathetic. She was turning fifty in April, and she wasn't snapping at everyone about every little thing.

Susan didn't start thinking about Tina's Tragic Trauma again until she was in the shower. What if she couldn't help Tina? *Lord, I'm almost embarrassed to bring this to You. I mean, I know it's just hair. But what if Karen isn't overdramatizing the situation? Surely someone wouldn't commit suicide over a bad hair day, would she? Please help me help Tina. Amen.*

Hurrying to get dressed, she pulled her thick hair back in a ponytail and wrapped a vintage Chanel scarf around her crown as a headband. She brushed her teeth, stroked on moisturizer, and applied her makeup in record time even though she'd been tempted to go without it, since her goal was to return home in a couple of hours and jump back into bed.

She quickly straightened up the bathroom for Michael, knowing he would take a shower as soon as he got home. When she finished, she sat down at her laptop and sent a quick e-mail to her online chat group. Then she checked herself one last time in the hall mirror and headed out the door.

—*mm*—

From: Susan Anderson (boomerbabesusan@ boomerbabesrock.com)

Sent: Monday, January 9, 6:43 a.m.

To: Patricia Davies; Mary Johnson; Lisa Taylor; Linda Jones; Sharon Wilson

Subject: You will NEVER believe this ... story to come later

Good morning fellow boomer babes!

I'm off to work early ... seems we have a Hair Emergency. I'll fill you in when I know more. Can't believe it's only week two of the new year. Things haven't slowed down at the shop ... we've been operating full tilt since before Thanksgiving. Guess I shouldn't complain ... business is good. Hope everyone is healthy and happy.

Suze

—*mm*—

Looking around the casino on his way out that morning brought Michael Anderson a bittersweet feeling. He liked his job, and every day yielded a new challenge. Yet, after thirty-five years, he was beginning to consider early retirement. The past night had been another busy one, and he was tired from walking the length of the property countless times as one mechanical problem after another surfaced. The Silver Spur was one of the oldest casinos in Las Vegas, and time was beginning to take its toll.

Of course, mechanical problems were easier to deal with than the inevitable people problems his wife seemed to encounter on a daily basis. He couldn't imagine what it must be like for Susan, standing in one area, doing the same thing day in and day out. It must drive her crazy. It drove *him* crazy sometimes, just hearing about it.

"I love it, Michael, really I do," she often told him. And he knew she was proud of her unique beauty salon, Disco Diva. But she had to be as tired of the daily grind as he was. They'd both been at it for so many years.

He couldn't wait to get home and tell her his news—and this was the day to tell it. Mondays were their only full days to spend together. Oh, sure, he saw her throughout the week, but not for long. Most days they were like the clichéd ships passing each other. He came home from the night shift just before she left in the morning, and she woke him when she returned from the salon in time for him to shower, get dressed, eat, and take off for work.

For years, though, they had enjoyed their evening meal together—Susan's dinner and his breakfast. It was a solid ritual. And there was always something to talk about. Communication wasn't a problem in their relationship. Having *time* to communicate was the problem. He'd once computed the time they'd actually spent together in the almost twenty-five years they'd been married; it was far less than the years implied.

And recently, it seemed, things were getting worse. More often than not during the past few months, Susan was already gone when he came home in the morning. And instead of waking him in person in the evening, she had taken to setting the alarm clock for him before she left for the salon.

This was all very unusual for her. He suspected she might be going through early menopause—not that he was an expert on such things. But she was certainly acting strangely these days. She spent more time at the salon than ever and seemed on edge a lot of the time.

That was another reason he'd decided to unveil his surprise a little early. It was time to free her from the growing responsibilities that were clearly taking away her joy.

Time for him to make their longtime dream come true.

Chapter 2

"You Should Be Dancing" by the Bee Gees greeted Susan on the state-of-the-art sound system as she opened the back door. It was most likely the soundtrack to *Saturday Night Fever*—one of Loretta's favorites.

Susan had no objection. She loved it too. Music—loud seventies dance music—had always been an integral part of her vision for the salon. She insisted that sound mixes be played throughout the day, and her collection of classics from the mid to late seventies rivaled that of some radio stations.

Disco might have officially waned in the late seventies, but Susan had never let it go. And although it had taken more than a few years for her high-concept salon to take off, she was now reaping the rewards of a risk-taking visionary. Disco Diva was fast becoming a Las Vegas institution.

Susan noticed the young woman already sitting in her chair, wearing a bright blue broad-rimmed hat, and staring at herself in the mirror. In her hands was a steaming Disco Diva mug. The aroma of hazelnut java filled the air.

Thank you, Loretta!

"Good morning," Susan called cheerfully from the back of the salon where she had entered. "You must be Tina."

"Yes, that would be me." She spoke with some kind of British accent.

"I'll be right there." Susan stashed her purse in the cupboard as Loretta emerged from the supply room with a stack of fresh towels.

At sixty-one, Loretta could pass for a forty-year-old fashion model. Cropped hair accented her chiseled features, and her light chocolate skin was flawless. Almost daily Jazzercise classes on her lunch hour helped her maintain the lean muscle on her six-foot frame. The sign above Loretta's station read, "Bodacious Boomer Babe," and that she was.

"Morning, Suzie-Q." Loretta leaned in to hug her friend and whispered in her ear, "She might look calm from here, but trust me—that sweet young thing is about as close to the edge of panic as anybody I've ever seen. She won't take off her hat. I gave her herbal tea—no sense ratcheting up her anxiety with caffeine. But there's coffee ready for you."

"I can smell it. Bless you!"

They looked over at the young woman, who now stood to the left of Susan's station, looking closely at the photos that lined her mirror.

"She's exquisite. A genuine natural beauty," Loretta said. "Reminds me of a young Liz Taylor, back when she was thin. Except this girl is much taller. I think her hair is jet black, or close to it. Hard to tell. See the tentacle hanging over her left shoulder?" Loretta nodded in the girl's direction.

"You mean tendril?" Susan craned her neck.

"No, I mean tentacle. You'll see."

"Apparently the folks at the Tropicana are grooming her for big things," Susan whispered. "Seems one of the owners discovered her singing and dancing in a club in South Africa and offered her a job on the spot. She's only been in town a few months."

"That explains the accent—couldn't place it. Yeah, well, apparently someone else was grooming her for disaster. I've never heard such a story."

"Karen wasn't sure if it was intentional or not. Did she come with her?" Susan looked around.

"No, but she'll be here for her ten o'clock with me. Think we'll be done by then? I have a full schedule today."

"Don't worry. I fully intend to be home snuggled up with my hubby long before your first appointment. It can't be that bad. Can it?"

"Hmm. No comment. But I'm sure you're up for it."

"Hello, Tina." The young woman jumped at the greeting. She'd been so wrapped up in perusing Susan's photo gallery she hadn't heard Susan approach.

"Sorry, didn't mean to scare you. Welcome to Disco Diva."

"Thank you for seeing me. I know this is your day off. I really appreciate it."

She looked up from under her hat, and Susan caught her breath. Tina was quite possibly the most beautiful woman Susan had ever seen—and many beautiful women had crossed the threshold of her upscale salon over the years. She had to agree with Loretta about the likeness to Elizabeth Taylor. Tina's light blue eyes—not quite violet, but close—were framed by a thick, dark fringe of lashes above delicate cheekbones, a sensual mouth, and a dainty pointed chin.

Except for a few long glitter-encrusted tendrils of dark hair somewhat resembling dreadlocks that peeked out, Tina's oversized hat completely hid the disaster that had brought her to the salon. Susan resisted the impulse to reach up and remove the hat.

"I've never seen a beauty salon quite like this." Tina looked around at the specialty decor that filled every nook and cranny. "This is amazing."

"Disco Diva is much more than a beauty salon—it's the Planet Hollywood of beauty salons," Loretta said, joining them and sitting in her chair. "We feature History with a capital *H*." She twirled around in her chair and winked at Susan.

"Like a museum?" Tina continued to look around.

"Exactly." Susan grinned as she watched the young woman's eyes dart from object to object.

Loretta wasn't joking about being the Planet Hollywood of beauty salons. Susan's priceless disco memorabilia collection made coming to Disco Diva an unmatched experience even in a jaded town known for unmatched experiences. Appointments were booked far in advance, and an unprecedented number of regulars maintained standing appointments. Today, showgirls from the Tropicana's famous Folies Bergere, the longest-running production show in Vegas history, had back-to-back appointments until closing. Tina's friend Karen White, who had been dancing in the Folies for years, would start the lineup at ten.

"What do you say we get started?" Susan reached for the bright pink rhinestone-embellished smock she used to cover her own clothes. "Have a seat, and we'll see what—"

"Who are these guys?" Tina pointed to a photo of Susan between two men. "The one on the right looks familiar. You sure look like Grace Kelly in this picture. Actually, you still look like her. Do people ever tell you that?"

"From time to time, yes," Susan said, nodding her head. The fact was, so uncanny was the resemblance, even at Susan's age, folks frequently did a double take when she ran errands. Yet any similarity stopped there. She might look like Princess Grace, but she behaved more like Bette Midler—a dichotomy she enjoyed more and more as she grew older.

Susan noticed that Tina's hands were shaking. In fact, it appeared that her entire body was trembling ever so slightly.

Poor thing, she's terrified.

Putting down the smock, Susan placed her hand on Tina's arm and leaned in to view the photo over her shoulder. "Those *guys* are clothing designers, my dear girl. That's Halston on the left and Calvin Klein on the right."

"You're having me on!" Tina exclaimed. "You know them?"

"I knew them. The picture was taken a great many years ago at Studio 54—on opening night, as a matter of fact."

"You were at Studio 54? In New York? Seriously?" Tina's eyes sparkled for the first time. "That is too cool."

"You're much too young to know about Studio 54." Loretta laughed, still lounging in her chair. "Or Grace Kelly, for that matter. What are you, all of twenty-one?"

Tina sighed. "I wish."

"When were you born?" Susan began straightening things on her station.

"In 1980. I'm twenty-five."

"And you wish you were younger? I moved to Vegas from New York City the year you were born."

"Is that where you're from? New York?"

Susan laughed. "Not a chance. Moved there from Ohio, fresh out of high school."

"Why would you ever want to leave? I'd love to go to the City." She breathed "the City" as though it were some sacred place like Jerusalem or Mecca. "The closest I've ever gotten to New York is the New York, New York hotel on the Boulevard. I have some friends in *Zumanity.*"

"I love *Zumanity,*" Susan said. "It's one of my favorite Cirque du Soleil shows." She reached for her mug and took a sip. "So you haven't been over to the MGM Grand yet?"

"Not yet." Tina shook her head. "No time."

"They've done a pretty good job recreating Studio 54 over there. It's not quite the same, but they have state-of-the-art sound, video and lighting, live dancers, and some pretty good dance music."

Although she seldom visited, Susan was quite familiar with this modern Studio 54. In fact, the manager of the hotel had been after Susan for ages to sell them some of her memorabilia. The MGM Grand nightclub offered four dance floors and bars, several semiprivate lounges capable of accommodating up to four hundred people, and an exclusive area on the second floor for invited guests. It wasn't quite the same as the VIP floor at the Studio 54 she remembered, and Susan was thankful they hadn't tried to recreate what the Studio regulars called the "Rubber Room"—a place that brought back memories she'd much rather forget. However, the MGM Grand did have something she wished was in her collection.

They had the original Studio 54 neon sign—the crescent moon face with the spoon. She had a much smaller prototype—one of only two in existence. But having the original would have been better.

"Okay, enough chitchat." She reached for her pink smock again. "Have a seat, and let's see what we can do for you today."

Tina reluctantly sank down into Susan's chair as Loretta jumped up to drape a bright yellow cape around her shoulders.

"Things sure are colorful around here." Tina pointed to Susan, smiling nervously. "I love your outfit."

"Thank you. It's one of my favorite ensembles."

The slacks were lime green, classic wide-leg trousers, and the Nehru blouse she had covered with the smock was a quilted blend of shiny satin with a vibrant floral print of yellow, orange, lime green, and white.

"Can I ask where you got it? I'd love to have something like that."

"Good luck. You won't see this suit unless you get lucky on eBay or manage to find a vintage shop I don't know about." Susan laughed. "The slacks are Halston, and the blouse is Bill Blass. Circa 1975."

"You mean they're originals? Not reproductions?"

"I do have a few knockoffs, but most of my clothes are originals from the seventies."

"Wow, they're in great shape for being so old … er, I mean, it's brilliant you can still fit in them … I mean, they look great for vintage … uh … I'm sorry." The girl waved her hands. "Your suit looks great, you look great, and this place is great."

"Don't worry, honey, I know what you mean. Thanks for the compliment."

Susan was accustomed to this kind of response. In fact, for a woman about to turn fifty, she was almost as well preserved as the priceless disco memorabilia she had been collecting for years. At five feet, five inches, she seesawed between a size four and a size six and, except for height, could hold her own against many of the showgirls who frequented her shop. Her mother had been Austrian and her father Swiss, so she came by her fair complexion and ash blond hair naturally. She liked to think her style came from her mother and her tenacity from her father, although memories of her parents were few. They'd died in a boating accident on Lake Erie when she was ten.

"But enough about me," Susan said. "That's not why you're here."

Still nervous, the beautiful young woman peered out from under her floppy-brimmed hat, gripped the armrests, and swallowed, trying desperately to maintain her composure. Tears pooled in Tina's eyes, cascading down her cheeks as she began to shake.

"I'm going to get you some more tea." Loretta disappeared without waiting for a response.

"They're going to fire me," Tina sobbed. "I know it."

"Oh, honey, why would they fire you?" Susan furrowed her brow. "Have you done something wrong?"

"No! It wasn't me! It wasn't my fault. It was the dresser. But I don't think she did it on purpose—at least I hope not."

"Then why would they fire you?"

Distraught, Tina grabbed one of the loose tendrils and shook it at Susan's reflection. The rope of matted black hair was about two feet long, covered with small shiny pieces that resembled octopus suckers.

"They hired me because of this!"

"Because of your hair?" Susan chuckled. "Who are you, Lady Godiva?"

"It's not funny!"

"I'm sorry, but I don't understand. Even if we have to cut your hair, it's not the end of the world. Let's put things in perspective, okay? The good Lord didn't bring you all the way to Las Vegas because of your hair. I'm sure He has a much bigger plan for your life than your fabulous tresses."

Tina looked at Susan in the mirror as though she'd sprouted a third eye in the middle of her forehead. "So you really believe that?" She pointed to a framed quote hanging above Susan's mirror that read, "There is a God who made you for a reason, and your life has profound meaning! We discover that meaning and purpose only when we make God the reference point of our lives."

"Yes, I really believe it. It's by a pastor named Rick Warren. My friend Lily gave it to me a couple of years ago. Do you believe it?"

The young woman tilted her head, casting her eyes downward. "I'm not sure what I believe anymore." A new flood of tears ensued.

Susan pulled up a stool, sat down next to her, and grasped Tina's hands in her own. "Honey, you could start pulses racing wearing dirty coveralls and a bandanna, and it has nothing whatsoever to do with your hair, okay? And from what Karen tells me, your singing and dancing gifts are already taking this town by storm. I'd say God has definitely made you for a reason. You're young, beautiful, talented, and single ... right?"

"Yes," she whispered. "I guess so."

"You guess you're single?"

"My fiancé moved here with me, but he didn't like Vegas. He went back to Cape Town last week."

"What's your last name, sweetheart?" Susan cupped Tina's chin in her hand and tilted her head up.

"Deitman."

"Well, Tina Deitman, I'm sorry about your fiancé, but God has still blessed you beyond measure. He made you for a reason, and He brought you here for a reason—to Las Vegas *and* to Disco Diva. I believe there are no accidents or coincidences—only what I call 'God-cidences.' So whatever happened to your hair under that big ol' hat is not the end of your world. It just might be the start of something new—something great."

Tina let the words sink in as she watched the hairdresser get up and move the stool away.

"Don't let the flash fool you," Susan said gently. "I know what I'm doing, and I know God is with us." She smiled as she placed her hands on both sides of the hat, preparing to remove it gently. "Now, let's see what we have here. I'll bet it's not that bad."

She lifted the hat and then held it in her hands, unable to speak.

It wasn't bad. It was much, much worse.

"Oh my," Susan murmured as tears began to course anew down Tina's cheeks.

Pretending to look from another angle, Susan swiveled the chair away from the mirror to save Tina the anguish of seeing her own reflection just as Loretta turned the corner carrying another mug of tea. Loretta coughed to cover her gasp, almost spilling the tea.

"Well … um …" she ventured, "it's got … possibilities…."

Placing Tina's tea on the counter, Loretta walked around the young girl so her face was visible only to Susan. She dropped her jaw in horror, grasping her cheeks in her hands.

"Karen said if anyone could help me, it would be you," Tina squeaked, using her feet to swivel the chair back toward the mirror and looking again at Susan's reflection. Loretta stood frozen, waiting to see what Susan would do.

Susan tried to recall exactly what Karen had told her on the phone that morning. The showgirls' costumes in the Folies Bergere consisted of elaborate headdresses and very little else—a fact Susan hated and often discussed with her clientele. The night before, when the headpiece for Tina's grand finale costume refused to cooperate, one of the apprentice dressers had the brilliant idea to simply glue it on to her head, assuming the spray adhesive she borrowed from the set crew would somehow wash out like hairspray.

Clearly, common sense wasn't so common anymore.

Tina stared miserably at her reflection. "We ruined the headdress—had to break it off in pieces. My boss doesn't know it yet—she's going to flip. And look at this." She picked at a tuft of hair close to her scalp. "Karen had to cut chunks of my hair to get it off."

They all stared at the remaining bits of wire mesh and glitter fabric stuck to the woman's head like the opalescent scales on an ornamental koi fish. Sick all over again, Tina bolted to the restroom. Susan and Loretta conferred frantically in her absence.

"What do you think?" Tina whispered when she returned, blowing her nose. "Can you help me?"

No way could she save the dancer's long, luscious locks. Susan feared everything was going to have to come off right at the scalp. She glanced at Loretta, searching for words.

"Looks like wig time to me," Loretta said, trying hard not to stare. "But that's not so bad. There are some fabulous wigs out there now."

"My hair won't fit under a wig," Tina protested, then did a double take. "Oh no. You mean cut it all off?"

What else does she think we can do?

"Sweetheart, the only thing that will remove this cement from your hair is a solvent so strong it would turn your hair to mush, burn your scalp, and blind you if it dripped." Susan didn't have the heart to tell Tina that most of the length was already gone. The matted tentacles—er, tendrils—that hung down over her shoulders were all that was left of what must have been elbow-length hair.

"I'm sorry," she said, "but there's nothing anyone can do to save the length. The good news is it will most likely grow back even fuller." She took a heavy bunch of Tina's matted hair in her hand. "Your hair is healthy. You won't have a problem growing this back."

"How much will you have to cut off?" Tina whispered.

"All of it."

"Like to my shoulders?" Tina looked hopeful. "I've always wondered what it would look like a little shorter."

This girl was in serious denial.

Susan shook her head and looked closer. There were sections in back where chunks of hair were only an inch long.

It must have hurt like the dickens to pull off the headpiece. And Karen must have been freaking out having to cut it off her head—no wonder she was in a panic on the phone. Then the question remained of what to do with the pieces of wire mesh and fabric still adhering to other sections of hair close to her scalp.

Still, none of it is actually touching the skin. Maybe … Susan launched into her most professional explanation of what would have to be done, then waited.

Several slow minutes passed before Tina was able to come to terms with reality. Her tears subsided. She took a deep breath and closed her eyes.

"Just do it. I can't look."

Susan began first by cutting off the remaining long strands of hair, quietly dropping them into the wastebasket Loretta held close by. This was only the beginning.

She looked into the mirror at the young woman's reflection. Tina's eyes were still closed and her lips were moving. Her pale, blue-veined hands were clasped tightly in her lap.

Even if Tina wasn't praying, Susan knew that she and Loretta were.

Chapter 3

As soon as she realized how much time Tina's haircut was going to take, Susan excused herself to call Michael and let him know she'd be late. She expected he wouldn't be happy, but the level of his irritation surprised her.

"I'm sorry, honey, but she needs—"

"I know, she needs you. You and only you. No one else in the entire salon can do what you do."

"It's not like that, Michael. Karen called me, and I—"

"Came to the rescue. I know. Wonder Woman strikes again!"

"That's not fair. You're called into work often enough when there's an emergency. What's really the matter, Michael?"

"Nothing's the matter. I'm just tired."

And grumpy. Susan didn't know what else to say.

"So when will you be home? This *is* Monday, you know."

"I know what day it is, Michael. Did you see my note?"

"I saw it. I'd rather see you."

"I know, honey. I'll be home as soon as I can. But this is going to take longer than I thought. You wouldn't believe—"

"I'm sure I wouldn't. Hey, don't worry about it, Susan. I have a few projects in the garage to attend to anyway. Don't hurry on my account."

"You're angry."

"I'm not angry."

"Yes, you are."

"Okay. I'm angry. What else am I, Susan? Since you're so keen a barometer on my innermost feelings?"

The conversation went from bad to worse, and within seconds he informed her she could feel free to stay the entire day if she so desired.

She hung up the phone, shook off her annoyance like hair clippings from her smock, and returned to her station.

—*mm*—

"What a blessing that you're here today," Loretta said to Susan later that morning.

"Tell that to Michael," Susan replied.

Their receptionist had called in sick while Susan was still working on Tina's hair. Since Michael was already in a foul mood, clearly indicating she wasn't wanted or needed to keep the home fires burning this particular day, she'd opted to stay at Disco Diva and play receptionist.

"He'll get over it when you have a chance to tell him the whole story." Loretta stowed away her blow dryer. "What you managed to do for that sweet little thing was nothing short of a miracle!"

Susan smiled. "It was pretty miraculous, wasn't it?"

The ideas had started to form as she was painstakingly cutting the remaining mesh pieces from Tina's hair. It would be an unusual cut—it had to be, considering what Susan had to work with. But with Tina's bone structure, it could work.

Disco Diva team members had begun trickling in that morning at nine. All were surprised to see Susan in the salon on a Monday. They'd have been even more surprised if any of them had seen Tina's hair when she arrived.

As it was, everyone who came in commented on what a fabulous cut Tina was getting. Not many women could wear such a short, edgy style, but she could more than pull it off. No one would have guessed that yesterday she had luxurious hair down to her elbows … and that a few hours earlier she had looked like something from a horror film.

The positive feedback buoyed the young showgirl's spirits. Susan could see her brighten with every comment.

By the time Shannon, the receptionist, called in sick, Susan was washing Tina's hair, and by the time Karen arrived for her appointment at ten with Loretta, a new Tina greeted her in the lobby of the salon.

"Oh my gosh!" Karen yelled as she opened the door. "Tina! Is that really you? Come here this minute and let me see you! I love it! This is fabulous! Do you love it? You must love it!"

They jumped around like schoolgirls, and soon Karen was hugging and kissing Susan. "I knew you could work a miracle! I knew you could do it!"

Susan had managed to save inch- and half-inch-long sections of hair all over Tina's head, spiking it into a trendy look that worked famously for Tina. In fact, the look made her big eyes appear even bigger and her chiseled features all the more exquisite. Susan had to admit she was, indeed, very proud of what she'd accomplished.

"Forget about Liz. Now you remind me of a young Liza Minnelli,"

Susan said. "She wore her hair just like this when she was younger. Follow me." She motioned for Tina to join her and went to the entrance of the salon, where the photo gallery was located. "See? Look here." She pointed to a photo of Liza Minnelli, Andy Warhol, and herself.

"You knew Liza Minnelli—and Andy Warhol?"

"I knew a lot of people back in those days."

"Wow, I'd give anything to have memories like yours. What was it like? If you don't mind my asking?" Tina ran her fingers over the framed picture.

That's a loaded question. "What exactly do you want to know?" Susan leaned against the wall and crossed her arms as the young woman continued to stare closely at the wall of photos.

"Was it as ... you know ... like they say? From what I've heard, it was pretty ... uh ..."

"Decadent?" Susan's eyes followed Tina's to a photo of Bianca Jagger sitting on Truman Capote's lap.

Tina nodded. "Was it?"

"In many ways it was. But there was so much more to it than that. There was this marvelous sense of artistic freedom. It was everywhere—in fashion, art, furniture, jewelry, music, dance, color—everywhere. I admit there were some crazy things going on, but they weren't the essence of the era. And most of the time I was more of an observer than a participant, thank God."

"But wasn't it difficult for you? I mean, you're a Christian, right?" Tina bit her lower lip. "I'm sorry. I shouldn't have asked. That's none of my business."

"No need to apologize, sweetie. I'm sure it would have been difficult for me had I been a Christian then—but I wasn't. I didn't wise up until years later." She stood behind Tina as they looked at a photo of Susan and a young man on a dance floor. His face was turned away from the camera, but Susan had stared straight into the lens and smiled, one arm held high in a dance move made famous by John Travolta in *Saturday Night Fever.*

"You look happy." Tina smiled.

"I thought I was. But someone once said there is a God-shaped place in our heart that only God can fill, and I wasn't smart enough to know that at the time. Unfortunately, I filled that place with things that left me emptier than when I started."

"It was Blaise Pascal who said that." Tina leaned in to peer closer at a photo.

"That's right—you're right. I can never remember his name. Do you know how it goes? The quote?"

Tina closed her eyes, pursed her lips, and drummed her lacquered nails against her temple as though shuffling mental Rolodex cards. Her words tumbled out first in French, leaving Susan speechless. Her dumbstruck look made Tina laugh.

"Sorry," Tina said before she repeated the quote in English. After a stunned pause, Susan laughed and applauded, shaking her head in wonder.

"Well, well. Beauty and brains … a lethal combination."

"Don't let the cat out of the bag, okay?" Tina smiled as she filled Susan in on her unusual education and the lifelong desire to sing and dance that had brought her to America.

"Your parents must be proud of you," Susan said.

"I wish." Tina lowered her head.

"Well, if you were my daughter I would be very proud of you,

Miss Tina Deitman." Susan reached out and hugged the young woman, who reciprocated as though her life depended on it.

"Thank you, Susan," she whispered in her ear, fighting back tears. "Thank you."

"You are most welcome, dear," Susan answered, pushing aside an unexpected bout of melancholy. Something about this young woman made her New York memories all the more poignant. But she had no time for memories at the moment. Disco Diva's appointment book was too full.

After Tina left, Loretta and the other stylists hit the ground running, their clients filing through the door like models on a cattle call. For the first time in, well, longer than she could remember, Susan got to spend most of the day up front—greeting clients, answering the phone, and offering assistance to the employees when she could. She enjoyed playing receptionist. It gave her a big-picture view of the salon she rarely got these days.

Along with the A-list showgirls, the clientele of Disco Diva consisted of some of the wealthiest socialites, philanthropists, and businesswomen in Las Vegas. Susan's longtime clients included Lily Peyton, Elaine Wynn, and—when she was in town—Melania Trump. But Susan wasn't the only person with well-known customers.

Susan and Loretta shared side-by-side stations near Disco Diva's front entrance—prime real estate, an arrangement they'd kept throughout every expansion the salon had experienced since Susan had been proprietor. The last renovation had brought them to twelve thousand square feet and enabled Susan to rent chair space to nine additional stylists. She now employed twenty-four people, including stylists, colorists, facialists, nail artists, and two massage therapists—and playing receptionist that day gave Susan the opportunity to see them all with a fresh perspective.

"We need more space," Susan declared midday. "Have you noticed how cramped the reception area is getting?"

"It's always been cramped." Loretta put her client under the dryer as another was escorted to her chair by one of the shampoo girls. "You're just never out front long enough to realize it." She pointed her finger and winked. "Now quit complaining and answer the phone like a good little receptionist."

"Maybe so," Susan whispered to herself as she returned to the front desk. "But I hadn't realized it was this bad. I wonder what we can do about it."

Her answer arrived an hour later. When the call came in, Susan rushed back to Loretta to share the news.

"Sam just called. Petite Pet is going out of business. We can have the space!" Susan whispered to her friend, not wanting the other stylists within earshot to overhear the news. "I can't believe the timing!"

Sam Cartwright was her landlord, a retired railroad worker who owned several older strip malls in the area.

"They'll be out by the end of February. Tell me this isn't a God-cidence!"

Loretta gave her a wry smile. "Why, honey, you know I'd never tell you that."

Chapter 4

The hours flew by, and the warm winter sun slipped behind the hills. As the city of lights awakened to its nocturnal utopia, Susan looked around the almost empty salon. It had been a long, albeit very profitable, day.

Loretta finished loading the washer with towels and began her Monday evening ritual of refilling the shampoo dispensers. Susan closed up the till, appreciating the work her receptionist did on a daily basis. Her thoughts once again returned to Michael.

Mondays had always been special for them, but it was the evenings she particularly treasured. They would usually have dinner together, go to a movie, or take in one of the shows on the Strip. Many of the theaters were dark on Mondays, but there was always a nightclub act or a cabaret show playing somewhere, or they would hang out at the Bootlegger Bistro on Las Vegas Boulevard, where Monday night karaoke reigned supreme and celebrities often stopped in unannounced.

Susan sighed. Even if she wasn't so tired, she doubted Michael would be interested in an evening out. Not in his present mood.

She had wanted to call him all day, especially when she got the news about the soon-to-be-vacated space. But she was still stinging from his unpleasantness on the phone earlier.

What did he expect her to do? God had delivered Tina right to Susan's door, and she wasn't about to slam that door in her face. Surely Michael could understand that if he gave it some thought.

She wasn't sure when she was going to approach him about renting the final space in the strip mall. According to Sam, Petite Pet had given their thirty-day notice, so she would need to act fast. And something told her this could be one more step toward making her dream come true.

Since Michael had rented the first corner unit for her back in 1981, they had systematically rented every unit as it became open. Sometimes they'd had to borrow extensively on their home to obtain the funds for leasing and expansion, though Susan always made sure the loans were repaid promptly. Susan had upgraded and updated at every opportunity, and every expansion had cost a great deal of money. The decor might be vintage, but there was nothing vintage about the services they provided or the equipment and supplies they used.

With this final unit, Disco Diva would occupy the entire building—and Susan wanted to do just that. In fact, what she really wanted was to make the owner an offer on the property. Then she would finally have space for her museum.

The truth was, the disco memorabilia displayed at Disco Diva represented just a part of her collection. Susan also had a huge collection at home and in several storage units. When time permitted, she attended estate sales and antique auctions to add to her cache, although space limitations meant she had to exercise significant discernment these days. And while Michael had never really understood her collecting bug, he'd always been supportive of her work and dreams. So she had worked and waited—knowing that one day God would open the door and the Disco Hall of Fame and Museum would become a reality.

"I've got to run," Loretta said, interrupting Susan's reverie. "It's after eight, and my babies are waiting to be fed. I'll see you tomorrow, okay?"

Loretta didn't actually have children. Her "babies" made up a menagerie of Doctor Doolittle proportions. She shared her home with several cats, a toy poodle, a parrot, and a half dozen colorful canaries—and doted on every one.

"Sure. See you tomorrow." Susan secured the cash bag in the small safe under the counter and followed Loretta to the door, locking it behind her. She watched her friend get safely into her car.

Loretta waved as she drove out of the parking lot, leaving Susan alone with her dreams for the future and memories from the past. The former made her smile with expectant wonder, but the latter brought a painful sadness she hadn't felt in some time. Young Tina, it seemed, had touched a nerve.

So young. So alone.

So much like me ... back then.

She put on her favorite dance mix and quickly went from sweeping the floor to whirling around the shop, allowing her body to respond to the music. Energetic dance numbers often erupted during the day at Disco Diva, and that frequent dancing always brought her joy. Yet dancing in private like this with wild abandon and unrestrained passion brought her something more—access to places in her heart and mind she seldom visited.

She had moved to New York from her home in Ohio the day after she'd turned eighteen, vowing to conquer Broadway as a dancer.

For three years she'd worked almost nonstop pursuing that dream. She'd had some success dancing in backup chorus lines for several productions, but her short stature had held her back. To supplement her sporadic performing income, she'd attended cosmetology school, even studying part time under the renowned Vidal Sassoon. Yet the dream of dancing never left her heart.

She was nearing twenty-one when she began to resign herself to the fact that dancing professionally was not her destiny. Then on her twenty-first birthday, her real destiny swept her off her feet—or so she thought. She fell in love with a man she met that night, and Mr. Perfect changed her life. She would have done anything for him—and often did.

Almost overnight, she entered a world where money was as plentiful as air—and immediate gratification was taken for granted. It was an exceedingly affluent world, where sex, drugs, and high-rolling glamour weren't merely things you read about in the gossip columns.

A world that had turned her life upside down and inside out.

The pulsating music came to an end, thrusting the salon into abrupt silence and jerking Susan back from a trip down memory lane she really didn't want to take. She sank into a nearby shampoo chair to catch her breath, willing herself to stuff back the thoughts that threatened her peace.

Looking around the salon, she was happy that she'd managed to keep so many good parts of the era alive for posterity. And the bad parts, the parts that used to cause her shame and humiliation, no longer controlled her. She controlled them.

Most of the time, anyway.

Susan looked at the clock, wondering what Michael was doing, and noticed the gentle blue light of the screen saver on the office computer.

She grabbed a towel to wipe away the sweat that cascaded down her face, hit Play on the CD changer, and then sat down at the appointment desk. She logged on to the Internet, accessing her private e-mail account with the password her tech wizard had set up specifically on this computer. Susan almost never used the salon computer for reading or sending e-mail, but it was nice to have the option. Besides, she had to cool down from her exercise, and she wasn't yet ready to go home—not when she wasn't certain what she would find.

What better way to end an emotionally charged day than with trusted friends. She smiled as her inbox filled.

~mm~

From: Patricia Davies (boomerbabepat@
           boomerbabesrock.com)
Sent: Monday, January 9, 7:08 p.m.
To: Susan Anderson; Mary Johnson; Lisa Taylor; Linda Jones;
           Sharon Wilson
Subject: RE: You will NEVER believe this ... story to come later

Must be a busy Monday for everyone. It's after seven my time and there isn't a single message from anyone but Susan. I talked to Mary on the phone—her hard drive crashed again, poor thing, so she'll be offline for awhile. Anyone heard from Linda? Should we be worried? And has everyone seen Lisa's latest YouTube video clip? Does anyone else think our youngest boomer babe looks great as a redhead?

Now that you have our undivided attention, sweet Susan, what's the scoop on your "Hair Emergency"? Inquiring minds want to know.

Love to all, Pat

From: Lisa Taylor (boomerbabelisa@boomerbabesrock.com)
Sent: Monday, January 9, 7:15 p.m.
To: Susan Anderson; Patricia Davies; Mary Johnson; Linda
             Jones; Sharon Wilson
Subject: RE: You will NEVER believe this ... story to come later

Redhead? What are you talking about? Check your color settings on your monitor, Pitty Pat. I was wondering about Linda as well. Haven't heard from her in ages. I think Sharon was going to visit her. Our two single boomer babes in one place ... very scary. Well, I'm not actually scared, but I *am* jealous! We should all plan to meet one day. Really. Not just talk about it.

From: Linda Jones (boomerbabelinda@
             boomerbabesrock.com)
Sent: Monday, January 9, 7:22 p.m.
To: Susan Anderson; Patricia Davies; Mary Johnson; Lisa
             Taylor; Sharon Wilson

Subject: RE: You will NEVER believe this ... story to come later

Why does everyone think something happened to me? Because I don't spend all of my available time online gossiping? Some of us have to work for a living.

Linda

P.S. SW is NOT here in AZ

From: Sharon Wilson (boomerbabesharon@
              boomerbabesrock.com)
Sent: Monday, January 9, 7:36 p.m.
To: Susan Anderson; Patricia Davies; Mary Johnson; Lisa
              Taylor; Linda Jones
Subject: RE: You will NEVER believe this ... story to come later

Ouch. Methinks we all just received a cyberspanking from the ever-loquacious Linda. Care to elucidate, LJ, on what you think WE are doing from sunup until sunset while YOU are slaving in the desert coal mines?—SW

P.S. LJ is correct. I am not in AZ. I'm still in sunny So-Cal, sitting on the beach sipping sangria and taking siestas. Ah, the charmed life of a single business owner who doesn't have to work for a living.

From: Lisa Taylor (boomerbabelisa@boomerbabesrock.com)

Sent: Monday, January 9, 7:43 p.m.

To: Susan Anderson; Patricia Davies; Mary Johnson; Linda
             Jones; Sharon Wilson

Subject: RE: You will NEVER believe this ... story to come later

Gossip? Someone correct me if I'm wrong, but isn't that what
people do behind someone's back? We made a vow long ago to
air all of our dirty laundry concerning one another publicly—at
least publicly within the confines of this group. It's what makes
us strong and invincible. It's what makes us powerful boomer
babe women! Oh no! I think I feel an attack of Helen Reddy
coming over me!

From: Patricia Davies (boomerbabepat@boomerbabesrock.
             com)

Sent: Monday, January 9, 8:05 p.m.

To: Susan Anderson; Mary Johnson; Lisa Taylor; Linda Jones;
             Sharon Wilson

Subject: RE: You will NEVER believe this ... story to come later

Linda, what's wrong? Did we say something to offend you? Talk
to us. We love you. Pat

—*mm*—

"Bravo, Pat!" Susan said aloud as her fingers quickly tapped on the
keyboard.

Normally, her Boomer Babes Rock group communicated
quite civilly. This rather testy round of e-mails was very unusual.

But since Linda got divorced last year, her messages had become increasingly terse, and Sharon had developed a short fuse. Susan wished they could talk in real time. But they had tried the chat room method, and it had become more trouble than it was worth. The most challenging hurdle was trying to get everyone online at the same time. So they'd agreed months ago to stick to e-mail, and it was working fine.

Judging from the times on this last string of messages, though, it seemed that everyone except Mary was currently online or had been within the past hour. Susan was dying to tell them about her day.

Well, about most of her day.

—*mm*—

From: Susan Anderson (boomerbabesusan@
              boomerbabesrock.com)
Sent: Monday, January 9, 8:24 p.m.
To: Patricia Davies; Mary Johnson; Lisa Taylor; Linda Jones;
              Sharon Wilson
Subject: RE: You will NEVER believe this ... story to come later

Greetings and God's peace! I'm still at the salon—can't believe this CRAZY day!

#1. Pat, I keep forgetting to tell you that I'm going to call to discuss the earrings you sent. I would love to sell more merchandise from Glitter and Bling—my ladies love your designs. Thanks for the update on Mary. For someone who operates one of the largest online travel agencies in the world, she certainly has her share of technology problems. And—now that Lisa has added credibility to what I have been telling you for months, would you PLEASE get a new monitor? Lisa's hair is NOT red.

#2. Mary, we miss you! Come back to the five and dime, Mary J., Mary J.

#3. Lisa, love your new SANDY BLOND hair color. Your most recent YouTube clip is amazing. Several of my girls have signed up for your dating service since we posted the flyer in our reception area. And I agree with you—we need to connect IRL. Say, there's a huge weekend flea market every July in Ithaca, NY. We could go antiquing! Anyway, let's seriously talk about a group trip, okay?

#4. Linda, how are things going at Pure Perfection? More important, how are things going in your life? I feel utterly confident in saying that I speak for all the boomer babes when I say we love you UNCONDITIONALLY. We know what we do here is not anything like gossip. We share from our hearts about our own lives. And we are not the enemy. All of us work for a living—you know that, and we know you know that. We also know that it's not you, not in the true sense of who you are, who has been showing up online lately. We want to help. Even if it's to let you verbally rail on us—as long as we know that you understand how much you mean to us.

#5. Dear sangria-sipping, nap-taking Sharon: You know Linda didn't mean to imply that none of us work. In fact, I think we all probably work too much. However, the beach fantasy sure sounds inviting!

Okay boomer babes, now I'm exhausted from writing you all. I wanted to tell you about my day—about the showgirl who had an elaborate headpiece glued to her head and the subsequent haircut that took me three hours to create. I wanted to tell you about the amazing news that I'm about to lease the final space in the strip mall and at last open my disco museum. I wanted to blow off a little steam about my midlife-crisis husband who is both exhilarating and exasperating. And I wanted to tell you about a host of other things heavy on my heart and soul that I can share only with you, my beautiful boomer babes who rock. Alas, I am too exhausted to do so. Therefore, I will bid you a fond adieu until we meet again.

Susan, the Official Disco Diva Queen

Chapter 5

Susan logged off the computer and smiled, knowing the gals would be feverishly typing responses to her message. They were a dynamic group of women who had been through more than a few emotional upheavals in their years together. It was hard to believe they had yet to meet in person, so close were their friendships.

Perhaps she could convince them to come out for the grand opening of the Disco Hall of Fame and Museum! The more she thought about the project, the more she wanted to share the news with Michael, to get started on making plans. This was a fabulous opportunity—occupying the entire building. Michael could oversee the expansion just as he'd done with the previous ones. And they could surely afford to buy the building if the owner agreed to sell. They finally had a little money saved and a great track record with the bank.

She began to shut off the lights, dancing her way around the salon like someone in an old RKO musical. All in all it had been a good day. It was nice to work a miracle once in a while. But she wondered if she'd ever see Tina again. You could never tell with some of these girls.

She reached the switch that operated the mirrored ball overhead, and on a whim she flipped it on—just as the CD player began one of her favorite songs. Slowly, the room began to glow with shots of jagged light as the revolving ball increased speed.

Once again, she let the music take over her body—unable, or unwilling, to restrain her passion. She was so immersed in Leo Sayer's hit "You Make Me Feel Like Dancing" that she didn't hear her husband let himself in, didn't see him standing quietly in the back of the salon, smiling, watching her every move.

She danced a full ten minutes before his applause interrupted her concentration and made her blush. Not that she was shy. But he'd witnessed something private, something that was hers alone.

After almost twenty-five years together, she and Michael shared a great deal, yet there was something about her dancing that he simply didn't get. Not that he didn't support her passion. In fact, without his help throughout the years, she couldn't have made her Disco Diva dream come true. Yet his total disinterest in dancing, combined with his two left feet, had always been a sore spot in their marriage. So for the most part she danced alone with her memories—memories that Michael didn't share.

"You can put any of those girls on the Strip to shame." He flashed a smile and kissed her sweaty forehead before sitting in Loretta's chair. "The girls dancing," he added, "not the ones walking."

"I'm glad you clarified that." She grabbed the broom and began to sweep.

"I want to apologize for being a jerk today."

She stopped sweeping and looked up. "Me, too. I wanted to call you all day. It didn't feel right, not being with you on a Monday. But, Michael, it really was crazy here today. I needed to be here."

"I know."

As she put away the broom and dustpan, one of her favorite songs by Earth, Wind & Fire began to play, instantly transporting her back in time. "Fantasy" conjured up two very distinct memories.

One was from their wedding reception, when the deejay somehow managed to jam the volume control and the song blasted most of the guests out of the ballroom.

The other memory she quickly put out of her mind.

"Great song," Michael said. "Makes me think of our wedding." He leaned back in Loretta's chair and grinned mischievously.

She shook her head at this gentle man who infuriated her with his practical nature and quirky habits yet still managed to make her heart skip a beat when he smiled at her that way. She thought of all they'd been through together. If he'd been acting a bit odd lately, perhaps it was because turning sixty affected him more than she realized. Maybe she needed to be more sensitive to this time in his life. Even if he was being a grumpy old curmudgeon.

"I like this haircut on you," she said. She turned the chair toward the mirror as she stood behind him, massaging his shoulders and staring at his reflection. "Look how sexy you are."

"Sexy?" He chuckled. "I don't know about that, but it's kind of growing on me. The guys say it makes me look younger."

The "guys" were Michael's crew at the Silver Spur Casino.

"See, I told you!" Susan playfully ruffled his hair with her fingers. She had been cutting her husband's hair since they met, but it had taken her until this year to convince him he needed a new look. No doubt his upcoming landmark birthday had something to do with his willingness to give her carte blanche with the scissors. When she was done he looked like Harrison Ford—or at least his hair did.

Staring at him afterward, she'd thought how attractive their children would have looked if they had been able to have any.

Blessed with good genes, he had aged well over the years. Truth be told, they both had.

"A penny for your thoughts," Michael said quietly.

"I was thinking about the day I met you."

"You can still remember that?" he joked, pulling her down onto his lap.

"You can't?" She looked him in the eyes.

"Like it was yesterday." He grabbed her hand and planted a kiss in her palm.

"Me, too." She stretched her legs over the armrest and laid her head against his shoulder as he spun the chair in slow, hypnotic circles.

She closed her eyes and remembered what it had been like the first time they met.

―――

"It's New Year's Eve, Susan!" her roommate had said. "And I won't go if you don't." She sat on the sofa and pouted.

"Fine," Susan said. "Then we'll stay at home and watch TV."

"Over my dead body!" Her roommate jumped up.

"Tempting …" Susan said. But then, reluctantly, she agreed to go to the party at the Silver Spur Casino.

She had been in Vegas only three months. Between getting settled in her new apartment and looking for work, she hadn't had much time for socializing—and that was fine with her. She'd had enough of the party scene in New York to last a lifetime.

Her roommate, a six-foot Amazon beauty who danced in the Folies Bergere, disappeared almost as soon as they arrived at the casino. Susan knew she could hold her own, but that didn't stop her from wanting to run as fast and as far as her dancer's legs would take her.

She could almost hear what her friends at the Manhattan Church of Christ would be saying to her: "You don't need to be afraid. You don't need to hide. You can be in the world, but not of the world." Since she was so new to her faith, it had taken her awhile to understand what that meant, but she was beginning to grasp the concept. She could mingle in settings like this New Year's Eve party without giving in to the temptation of sin. It might not always be easy—but it wasn't impossible.

What had been impossible, on many levels, was her ability to remain in New York City. Especially after she made her U-turn toward God.

The job opportunities in Las Vegas far outnumbered those on the Great White Way anyway, so when given the opportunity to move, she had quickly done so. All she had ever wanted to do was dance—and Vegas was a great town to dance in. She would put behind her the years the locusts had eaten, like she'd read in a recent Bible study, and become a new person … in a new place.

At the time, it hadn't occurred to her that the costumes for Vegas showgirls left little to the imagination—a fact that was becoming an issue with every audition. She was beginning to think she might need to do something else after all. She was also beginning to think of calling a cab to go home when her roommate reappeared with her boyfriend, a stocky young man Susan knew only slightly. With him was "a friend who worked at the casino."

As they talked, it dawned on her that this was a setup.

And she realized she didn't mind one bit.

Michael Anderson was ten years older and vastly unlike the men she'd known in New York. His utter lack of pretension instantly made her laugh.

"I've got seniority here," he told her proudly. "Been at the job almost a decade."

Did she know anyone who'd had steady work that long?

He was a big man, well over six feet tall. His hands were twice the size of hers. His eyes were the color of jade, and he had lashes longer than the ones most showgirls glued on.

He later claimed it was love at first sight. What she remembered most was how safe—how protected—she felt around him. They were married eight months later—and Susan realized she'd been blessed to be born again twice.

First, by the redemptive love and grace of the Lord.

And second, by the committed love and tenderness of Michael Anderson.

$\diamond\!\!\diamond\!\!\diamond$

"Sorry, babe, time to move. My legs are falling asleep." Michael gently moved her off his lap.

"No, I'm sorry." She stood and stretched. "Did I fall asleep?"

"You were out like a light. Were you dreaming about me?" He raised and lowered his eyebrows seductively.

"As a matter of fact, I was."

"Pray tell, what were you dreaming?"

"We can talk about that later, okay? First, I have something I want to discuss with you." She sat in the chair at her station and crossed her legs.

"I have something I want to discuss with you, too." He grinned, leaning forward in Loretta's chair.

"You first." She bent forward, happy to see him in such a good mood.

Clearly he had gone over and over what he was going to tell her, so concise was the pronouncement. She wondered how many times during the past several months he had practiced this well-rehearsed speech.

It took him fifteen minutes from start to finish to outline his plan.

"You can't be serious, Michael," she whispered as she fought back tears.

Chapter 6

Michael watched his wife melt like ice cream on a hot day. Her face, though relatively unlined for a woman about to turn fifty, morphed before his very eyes, contorting into expressions he was unable to decipher.

"Are those good tears or bad? Say something, Susan."

"I don't understand."

"What don't you understand?"

"We own how many acres of land?"

"Two hundred and forty."

"In Henderson?"

"Correct."

Of course she was flabbergasted at the sudden knowledge. He'd expected that. He'd gone over and over the surprise revelation for years—planning the right time to tell her.

"We've driven by it—through it, even—every time we go to the lake. I couldn't wait to tell you."

"You couldn't wait? You've waited almost twenty-five years!"

"Honey, it's my retirement present to you—to us. I've been planning this for years. It's for our dream home."

"Our dream home? How can it be our dream home when this is the first I'm hearing about it? And you're not retiring for years, Michael. You really aren't serious about this, are you?"

"Of course I'm serious! You know we've always talked about having more space!" He jumped up like an excited little boy. "I've got plans and drawings in the car. Don't move. I'll be right back. You're gonna love this, honey. I promise."

Susan watched him run from the salon, feeling as though she were watching a stranger. Yes, they'd talked about more space, but for the salon, not their home. She loved their home. Surely he was joking. He was going to come back inside and shout, "Punk'd!" or maybe, "Surprise!" and she'd playfully smack him as they laughed about this less-than-funny charade. But her heart sank when she saw him jaunt back through the door with a long cardboard tube in his hand.

"Come here. Check this out." He pulled out what appeared to be blueprints and began to open them on top of the reception desk. "I know this is a bit of a shock, but it'll grow on you. Look." He pointed. "I've even given you a room for your collection."

Susan walked slowly toward this stranger and peered down at plans that clearly indicated the layout of a new home—apparently their new home—complete with a room called "Suzie's Stuff" adjacent to the master bedroom.

"Suzie's Stuff?" she mouthed in true amazement.

"Yeah, that's what Roger named the room. He's the architect I've been working with for years. Look, it's got lots of built-in shelves and lighting for your things."

"You've been working with an architect for years on our dream home, and I'm the last one to know about it?"

"Come on—it's not a total surprise, honey. Anyway, you'll meet Roger at the party next month."

"What party?"

"Earth to Susan! My anniversary party, remember?"

Next month marked the thirty-sixth year Michael had worked for the Silver Spur Casino, and the owners were throwing a party in his honor. Susan knew this meant a lot to him—but this recent news had far overshadowed the celebration in her mind.

"Michael, this is a monumental thing you've just dumped in my lap, so forgive me if I'm not quite tracking with you. I'm still trying to wrap my brain around the land—let alone plans for a house. You've owned it how long?"

"I told you, my parents bought it before I was born. They left it to me in their will, and taxes have been paid on it every year from their estate. I always knew we'd retire there. I just never knew how valuable it would become. Who'd have figured Henderson would grow like it has?"

"Wait, is it that huge chunk of land just before you get to town? The one you always comment on?"

"Yes, ma'am, one and the same."

They'd often joked that the land was probably owned by Steve Wynn, Donald Trump, or maybe one of the Vegas superstars like Wayne Newton or Cher.

"What's it worth, Michael?"

"Millions. I figured we'd sell a few acres adjacent to the city limits to bankroll the house so we'll own it free and clear, honey. Just think. Look at this place." He gazed fondly at the blueprints. "This is a twelve-thousand-square-foot castle with acres of land everywhere you look. We'll finally have all the room we've ever wanted."

"I thought you loved our home."

"I do. But come on, honey—don't tell me you haven't felt the walls closing in. Our place is hardly the Taj Mahal."

"What do you know about the Taj Mahal?"

"It was built by a guy in honor of his wife."

"After she was dead—he buried her there!"

"It's a mausoleum?" He cocked his head.

"Precisely."

"I'll be."

"You'll be what, Michael?"

For the first time since he presented the surprise to his wife, Michael sensed her unhappiness.

"Aren't you excited about this? I thought you'd be ecstatic."

"Ecstatic? You thought I'd jump up and down like, what, a cheerleader? Oh goody, goody! My husband has kept a monumental secret from me for twenty-five years and has planned my life without asking my opinion!"

Susan began to empty the laundry hampers of towels as Michael stared.

"Don't look at me like I'm the one who's crazy! You waltz in here and tell me we've owned acres of prime property for years and you've had our dream home designed without considering my thoughts … or my feelings?"

"I did consider your feelings! I even had a room added for all your disco stuff—at least the main things you want to keep."

Susan stopped and turned.

"What do you mean the main things I want to keep?"

"We've talked about this, Susan—that when we sold the shop most of the stuff would go with it."

Sold the shop?

"When did we talk about that, Michael? I never agreed to sell one iota of my collection. And when did we talk about selling the shop?"

"Now you're kidding, right?"

"Hardly."

"Back when we bought it. This was something to keep you occupied after … after we decided you needed a hobby."

"A hobby? You think Disco Diva is my *hobby?*"

"Don't twist my words, Susan. You know what I mean." He began to roll up the blueprints.

"No, I don't know what you mean. Michael, listen to me. Please." She placed her hands on the blueprints, preventing him from continuing. "For years we struggled to keep Disco Diva alive. We had to practically beg, borrow, and steal to keep the doors open … at least for the first decade."

"It wasn't like that, Susan."

"It was like that! I cried myself to sleep more times than I care to remember, wondering how to keep things afloat."

"Are you serious?"

"Of course I'm serious! You were there! You know how many times we had to go to the bank to get loans. Why didn't you tell me we owned such valuable property? You could have made things easier on us."

She stopped trying to wipe the tears from her eyes and just let them flow freely.

"I think we should stop talking about this before one of us says something we'll regret." Michael gently moved her hands, rolled up the blueprints, and stuffed them inside the tube. "Let's go home—do you need help closing up?"

"No. I don't need your help. I'll be fine. You go ahead. I'll be along in a bit."

"Susan ..."

"I agree with you." She held up her hand. "I'd rather not talk right now."

He left without saying another word.

She locked the door behind him, leaned her forehead against the cool glass, and cried.

~mm~

From: Susan Anderson (boomerbabesusan@
              boomerbabesrock.com)

Sent: Monday, January 9, 10:32 p.m.

To: Patricia Davies

Subject: CONFIDENTIAL

Pat, this isn't a BBR group message—your eyes only, okay?
Chance to lease last space in strip mall, maybe even to buy
the building. Would make a good retail space or maybe disco
museum. Not sure what to do. Still at salon. Michael just left.
Had a BIG argument. I feel angry and sick to my stomach all
at once. Can 2 people live together for almost a quarter of a
century and not know one another at all?

From: Patricia Davies (boomerbabepat@
              boomerbabesrock.com)

Sent: Monday, January 9, 11:15 p.m.

To: Susan Anderson

Subject: RE: CONFIDENTIAL

Sweet Susan—ah, the vicissitudes of life! I just got home from the shop myself. John worked a few hours at the store today so I could spend some time in the studio. He brought me a cup of coffee. Black. We've been married for a gazillion years, and I've always taken cream and sugar in my coffee. Always. So, yes, I guess it is possible two people can spend time together and not know one another. Or could it be that men and women (more specifically, husbands and wives) don't retain the same things as important?

Sounds exciting about the building. Trust me, though, ownership is a whole different ball game. I sometimes wish we'd never bought ours.

What exactly do you mean by "BIG argument"? Call if you need to talk. I'll be up late.

Love you, Pat

Chapter 7

Michael was still sleeping when Susan left early for the salon.

Wake yourself up, buddy, she thought angrily. They'd argued most of the night, and she was worn out—and still ticked off. It was going to be a long day. Thankfully, her receptionist was feeling better and had called to say she'd be back to work today.

The morning passed quickly, and Susan was so busy she didn't have time to think.

It was late afternoon before she had any real break to speak of. Loretta had just finished a cut on one of the lead dancers from Cirque du Soleil when Susan walked by her station on the way to the ladies' room.

"I'll be right back," she said.

Loretta grinned. "I'll alert the media."

"You do that." Susan responded to the well-worn repartee as she had for years, minus the good humor that typically accompanied the routine.

Loretta was leaning into the mirror and touching up her lipstick as Susan returned, carrying a mug of steaming coffee.

"You must go through a ton of lipstick," Susan said.

"You must go through a ton of coffee. What is that, number seven?"

"What are you, the coffee police?" Susan snapped.

Loretta peered into the mirror at her friend, who wouldn't meet her eye.

"Sorry," Susan said quietly.

"Apology accepted." Loretta waited to hear if Susan would follow up with further explanation. When nothing appeared forthcoming, she put the cap on her lipstick and took a deep breath, speaking quietly so no one else would hear.

"I'm not going to ask you if anything is wrong. Because clearly something is."

"Nothing's wrong."

"Don't do that, Susan." Loretta turned around and faced her. "Don't pretend it's business as usual, okay? We've worked together longer than some folks have been married, so give me a break. You aren't yourself. You've barely said a word to anyone all day."

"It's been busy, in case you didn't notice."

"Really? Gosh, I didn't. Must have been lounging in my chair and eating bonbons, I guess."

Susan managed to smile but remained unusually silent as she cleaned and straightened her area.

"I have a new client about to walk out of the men's room, so I can't get into this now." Loretta wagged her finger. "But don't even think about leaving here today without telling me what's wrong." She fluffed her hair with a rhinestone-handled afro-pick and used her index finger to remove lipstick from her front teeth. "Can you at least try to look somewhat happy?" she whispered. "I'd like this fellow to be a return customer. He's more than easy on the eyes."

"I *am* hap—" Susan felt a strange tightness in her chest as she looked over Loretta's head to see the young man exit the men's room.

She fumbled with the curling iron she was cleaning and dropped it. "Oh my goodness."

Loretta turned to see her new customer walking toward her station, then glanced back to Susan, who appeared to be all thumbs as she bent down to untangle the iron from the cords. "Something wrong?" Loretta teased.

"Uh, no, just having a problem with these cords is all ..."

"Having trouble with that? Here, let me help you."

The stranger sidled between Susan and the cabinet that held her blow dryers and curling irons and bent down to retrieve the fallen iron, their hands brushing.

Susan had once been involved with a man whose physical attributes blinded her, and since then she'd grown a bit jaded when it came to pretty men.

But this was one pretty man.

Beyond pretty, he had the looks and stature that screamed virile, macho, and male. He was dressed with casual elegance—the understated look of someone who knew classic fashion and could afford the best, yet didn't want to overdo it. (There were a great many overdone men in Vegas.) She guessed he was wearing Armani. The day-old stubble on his olive cheeks couldn't conceal the deep cleft in his chin, and when he smiled, dimples creased his cheeks. His eyes were the steel blue of an Alaskan husky, and she felt certain Ralph Lauren would snap up this fellow in an instant if he saw him. She'd be surprised if he wasn't a model or an actor. And, she thought, he smelled familiar.

He chuckled warmly. "Cord control is a never-ending issue these days, isn't it?"

"Y-yes, it can be," Susan stammered. "Is that Green Irish Tweed?"

"It is. Wow. No one's ever guessed my cologne before."

"I, um, once knew someone who wore it."

She was surprised how quickly she'd recalled its brand name …
and how strongly the memories washed over her, leaving a strange
mix of excitement and melancholy.

"A fragrant Prince Charming to the rescue," Loretta said with a
soft laugh.

"Here you go." The young man held out the curling iron as
the corners of his eyes crinkled and a hundred-watt smile followed.
"Prince Charming, huh? If that's all I have to do to earn that title,
I'll come by any day of the week to untangle your cords. The name's
Power. Ryan Power." He extended his right hand to Susan before
sitting in Loretta's chair.

"Thanks for the help." Susan nodded toward the cords. "You're in
good hands with Loretta. Hope you enjoy your experience at Disco
Diva." Susan tried not to stare at the young man as she took off her
smock and laid it on her chair.

"Loretta, I have an unexpected break between clients." She reached
for a stack of envelopes propped between two cans of hairspray. "I'm
running to the post office." She smiled at her friend, who nodded.

"Nice to meet you, Mr. Power," Susan said. She picked up her cell
phone from the counter, hooked it into her rhinestone belt, and left.

"Was it something I said?" Ryan looked at Loretta in the mirror as
she draped a cape around his shoulders.

"I doubt it. She's got a lot on her mind these days."

"Is she the owner of this place?"

"Yes. Now, what can we do for you today?"

"This place is amazing. I don't know where to look first." His jaw gaped as he perused the salon like a hungry teen looks at a buffet table.

"How about starting here." Loretta gently turned his head to face the mirror as she ran her fingers through his thick, wavy hair. "You've got a beautiful head of hair. Who's been cutting it?"

"A stylist back home. Is that really John Travolta's vest?" He turned to stare at a framed shadowbox on the wall to the left of Loretta's mirror.

"It is. Stay focused, Mr. Power." She again turned his head toward the mirror, this time with a bit more firmness.

"Call me Ryan." He grinned sheepishly at her in the mirror.

"So, Ryan, where's home?" She combed his hair, studying the texture, cut, and natural wave.

"Southern California. I'm only here for a few days. A friend is scoping out the lay of the land for his wedding. I didn't realize how mangy I looked until I got here."

"Mangy? Yeah, right. Like that's a word you hear often."

"I don't let just anyone take scissors to it."

"Understandable. But I'm not just anyone."

"So I hear." He relaxed and eased back in the chair, keeping his head firmly pointed forward while allowing his eyes to dart around the room.

"So where did you hear about Disco Diva?" Loretta asked.

"One of the blackjack dealers at the Bellagio. I liked his haircut and asked."

"That would be Ernesto. Susan has been cutting his hair for years."

"Yeah, that's what he said. But is it true she's not taking new clients? Uh, not that you won't do a good job, it's just that—"

"Don't fret, sweetie pie, it's all good. But rest assured, I'll take excellent care of you."

"I'm sorry. I'm sure you will. I didn't mean it that way."

"Really, it's okay." She spun the chair away from the mirror so she wouldn't be distracted.

They discussed what he'd like in the way of a hairstyle. Loretta took notes on one of the customer cards she kept for all her clients.

"Alrighty, then, let's get you shampooed. May I get you some coffee or water?" She waved to one of the shampoo girls, who strutted over like a poodle in a dog show.

"Thanks. Black coffee sounds great."

"I'll have it waiting when you return. Adele, please see that Mr. Power gets the full treatment."

"Gladly." Adele giggled and escorted him away.

By the time he returned, Loretta had a steaming mug of coffee and a dark purple smock waiting. No rhinestones for the male customers at Disco Diva, even if some of them probably wouldn't mind the flash.

"Do many guys come here?" he asked. "I don't see any."

"About thirty percent of our clients are men. We have a section of the salon just for them. But Susan and I work up here. You want us, you get the girls' glam side."

"Anytime." He gave a thumbs-up. "Hey, is that an original?" He leaned forward to look more closely at a photo of Susan with Andy Warhol and Bianca Jagger.

"Yes, sir." Loretta gently moved his head back.

"She doesn't look a whole lot different, does she?"

"Susan's been blessed, that's for sure. We tease her that she's been preserved in that chemical that keeps flowers looking fresh. What's it called … silica gel?"

"Yeah, that's right. But surely she's had work done to look like that."

Loretta raised her eyebrows. "Young man, did you check your manners at the door before you came in?"

"I'm sorry. You're absolutely right. It's just that …"

"Yes?" She stopped cutting and looked at him in the mirror.

"I can't believe this place. It's like stepping back in time. I had no idea. Ernesto said it was wild, but I never expected this." He waved, staring at the room in awe. "I'm kind of into this stuff."

"Really?"

"Seriously. I'm not just saying that. I collect memorabilia from the sixties and seventies, mostly pop culture and rock-and-roll stuff."

"No wonder you're gawking."

"Am I gawking?"

"Since you walked through the door. Now, may I continue?"

"Sorry. Of course. Don't tell me no one else finds this fascinating."

"Most do, some don't. Some folks think it's a bit over the top—they don't quite get Susan's fascination with the disco era."

"What's not to get? It was an artistic movement, a subculture that proliferated a lifestyle that changed the way we think."

Loretta raised an eyebrow. "Susan's going to be sorry she missed talking to you. You're cut from the same cloth."

"Except from the looks of these photos, she actually got to

experience it. I'm living vicariously. So, what's her story? I mean, this is no ordinary—oh, man! Don't tell me. Is that …?" He stood up quickly to get a closer look at the glass-enclosed shadowbox holding a collection of twelve-inch records. "It is! She's got original Tom Moulton singles! Do you know how rare those are? Oh man."

"Take a breath, kiddo, before you pass out. They're only records." Loretta pulled him back into the chair. "Next time you jump up like that, I'm liable to stab you. Give me some warning, okay?"

"Sorry. But I have to know where she got them."

"I think the guy who made them gave them to her. I think that was his name—what you said, Tommy. That's his picture over there." She pointed.

"I'm giving warning," he said, jumping up to peer more closely. "Criminy! It is Moulton! And it's signed."

"Most of her photos are signed. She knew the photographer— some guy named Bob or something."

"Bobby Miller?"

"You know who he is?"

"Of course! He was the club photographer at Studio 54. His stuff is high on the food chain of desired collectables. I can't believe how many she's got."

"There's a room off the reception area filled with stuff. Make sure you check it out before you go—lots of photos and geegaws."

"Geegaws?"

"Yeah, stuff like ticket stubs, jewelry, menus, invitations … dust-collecting geegaws."

"Whose shoes are those?" He pointed to another display atop a square column in the corner of the room. Blue-glitter platform shoes ensconced in a Plexiglas cube.

"David Bowie's," she said nonchalantly.

"No way! Seriously?"

"As a heart attack."

"This is too much." He could barely sit still.

"What's too much is the time I'm spending on this haircut. How about we make a pact? You sit still and let me do my job, and when I'm done you can wander around the shop and check out the decor. Deal?"

"Deal."

"As for Susan's story, there's a flyer on the reception desk that gives a bit of history about Disco Diva. Wait. I've got one here." She opened her drawer and took out a glossy trifold brochure. "She's pretty private about her personal life, though." She handed him the brochure. "She'll tell you when and where the photos on display were taken, the occasion and all, and she's got some great celebrity stories, but you won't get much else out of—what are you staring at now?"

He pointed to the large mirrored disco ball hanging from the ceiling. "Does that work?"

"Attention, ladies!" Loretta shouted, startling Ryan. "Our new customer wants to know if that works." She waved her comb at the ceiling.

"Oh, goody!" said a customer several chairs down.

"Give me one minute," another hairdresser yelled, folding a piece of red foil on a shank of blond hair.

"It's been ages since someone has asked," one of the shampoo girls sang out.

"Did I say something …?" Ryan's eyes widened as Loretta nodded affirmatively.

"Honey, you have no idea." She placed her scissors and comb on the counter and spun Ryan around in the chair so that he faced away from the mirror with a bird's-eye view of the main area of the salon.

Ryan watched—and listened—in amazement as blow dryers and conversation stopped, stylists stepped back away from their chairs, and the cute little receptionist stood alert by the bank of stereo equipment and light switches.

"Ready?" she squealed.

"Hit it!" Loretta said.

The receptionist systematically flipped a series of switches and breakers on and off. The main lights in the room disappeared as the strains of Alicia Bridge's "I Love the Nightlife" blasted from what Ryan suspected were some mighty expensive Bose speakers. Colored lights began flashing from various points in the ceiling, and a spotlight focused on the mirrored ball as it began to spin, cascading twinkle spots around the room like flickering fireflies.

Ryan's jaw dropped. "This is amazing."

All around the salon women danced, some doing synchronized dances like the hustle, others enjoying freestyle movement. Some had towels draped around their shoulders; others wore brightly colored smocks. A few had multicolored foil pieces sticking up like space-age antennae all over their crowns, and still others had towels wrapped turban style on their heads. One patron a few chairs down, clearly a newcomer, sat stunned. Ryan caught her eye, smiled, and shrugged.

Lights flashed, and the pulsating music and expressive dance moves created a mood of nostalgia he wished he could bottle. He wanted to jump up and dance with them, yet he felt glued to his seat as though he were watching an elaborate production number. The singing and dancing waiters at Joe's Crab Shack couldn't hold a candle to this.

All too soon the song was over. Applause and shouts of "You go, girl" and "That was fun!" could be heard around the room as the salon returned to its original look. The gentle hum of blow dryers and conversation replaced the extravaganza, and it was back to business as usual.

Loretta spun Ryan's chair back toward the mirror.

"Yes, it really works." She grinned. "Any more questions?"

"Wow" was all he could say as she picked up her scissors and continued to cut his hair.

He couldn't believe his good fortune—to simply walk in on a gold mine of pop culture. A museum in the middle of a salon ... or was it a salon in the middle of a museum? Either way, it was mighty cramped. What this collection really needed was display space. He was glad, however, to see a security system on site with miniature surveillance cameras throughout.

The minute Loretta finished his haircut, he went looking for specific photos—photos that would tell him more of the story of the owner's life. He wished he had gotten a better look at this Susan Anderson before she'd left. All he could recall was that she'd looked like she'd stepped out of a 1975 issue of *Vogue*.

"Aha! There you are!" he exclaimed when he located the display room off the main entrance. The walls of the little alcove were covered with pictures of Susan with disco legends like Steve

Rubell, the co-owner of Studio 54, and music icons of the era such as Donna Summer, the Bee Gees, and Grace Jones. There was a particularly poignant photo, enlarged to eleven by fourteen, of Susan with Truman Capote, Andy Warhol, and, if he wasn't mistaken, the designer Halston. Everywhere he turned, the story of a fascinating life flashed before his eyes. How he wished he'd been born decades earlier.

He had to talk to this woman to find out more about her.

Who are you, Susan Anderson, and what's your story?

Chapter 8

It was a half hour before Michael was due home, and Susan didn't want to be there when he arrived. She'd been making excuses for almost three weeks, leaving him notes on the kitchen table.

> M:
>
> *Sorry to miss you again. Crazy week ... lots going on. Left a slice of spinach quiche in fridge. Nuke it for one minute. I've got a full day (as usual), but I'll call tonight when I get home. Sleep well. Love you.*
>
> S

It wasn't unusual for them to go for days without physically seeing one another—that was the price they paid for working opposite shifts. Until these past few weeks, however, they'd always managed to touch base by phone several times throughout the day. Lately, Susan found herself at odds with even that. The past few Mondays had seen them both busy with personal projects—the dentist, doctor, errands—which worked out fine for her. She didn't know what to say to her husband, what to think about his insane idea to build a mansion in the middle of the desert.

She had yet to tell him about the vacancy Petite Pet was

leaving—or that she'd made the decision on her own to lease the space, even though she was beginning to wonder if it offered enough square footage to house her museum. She had even asked Sam if he would consider selling her the building.

"I'll think about it and let you know," he'd said.

That's been our real dream, Michael—to make Sam an offer on the building when the time was right. Not to build some kind of cowboy castle in the desert, for crying out loud!

But Susan refused to start off another day with these negative thoughts. Instead, she prayed for the patience to get through this rocky time with her husband. They'd had their share of disagreements, but things had always smoothed out. She just had to give him some breathing room to see that the timing wasn't quite right for his crazy idea. Maybe in a few years when he retired they could talk about it, but not now.

She'd spoken with Pat on the phone several times since the argument with Michael, gaining a better perspective on the situation.

"It's different for men," Pat had said. "Their masculinity is all tied up with providing for us … wanting to feel needed."

"I do need Michael. I need him to be sensitive and get with the program."

"Ah, love with conditions, eh?" Pat asked quietly.

"That's not what I meant."

"I'm sure it wasn't. Just think about it, okay? Since John's accident, we've had to redefine virtually everything in our life—from personal to business. Remember, Scripture says love is patient and kind … not easy and agreeable."

Susan knew Pat was right. She just didn't feel like talking to her husband quite yet.

On her way out the door, she smoothed on an icy pink shade of MAC lipstick that reminded her of the Yardley Lip Slicker gloss she had loved when she lived in New York. But the Yardley line had been discontinued years ago. She stared at the tube of lipstick before tossing it into her Michael Kors handbag. She smiled broadly. The lipstick gave her another idea for increasing the salon's revenue.

mm

"Lily, I have an idea."

Lily Peyton was one of Susan's closest friends—a mentor, really. Perhaps even a substitute mother. Her opinion was worth its weight in gold to Susan.

"Good morning, dear. Are you in your car? I hear traffic. You know how dangerous it is to talk on a cell phone while you're driving."

"You call me from your car all the time."

"Yes, dear, but that's different. Franco is driving, and you know that."

"Okay. I'll call you when I get to the shop. Unless you have time to meet me today for lunch? I have an idea I'd like to run by you."

"Let me check my calendar and get back to you. I'll call you at the salon in, say, fifteen minutes?"

"Yes, ma'am. Over and out."

By the time Susan had talked her way out of the speeding ticket an officer was intent on writing her, it was well beyond fifteen minutes later when she arrived at Disco Diva. She turned off the alarm, flicked on the bank of light switches, hit Play on the stereo system, and sat down behind the reception desk to check the voice messages on the phone.

"I'm clear this afternoon any time after one," Lily's message said. "How about if I save us some time and have Franco run in to Bella Luna and get our special? We can have a car picnic! I can't wait to hear what you've got up your sleeve this time. Good-bye, dear. Call me to confirm."

mm

From the moment Loretta arrived at work that morning she could tell something was up. The salon wasn't open yet, but Susan had Donna Summer playing at a volume that practically screamed "party time!"

Loretta knew something was wrong with Susan. She'd tried on several occasions to get her to open up, to no avail. She thought it might have something to do with leasing Petite Pet and expanding the shop, but she couldn't be sure. Then again, something about young Tina had affected Susan as well.

Loretta didn't much care for the theory of letting emotions run their course. She liked to cut to the chase, deal with issues as they arose, and then get on with things. The slow, simmering *something* in the air had her nervous and on edge. But maybe the music meant Susan was finally ready to talk.

"Well, well, what are we celebrating?" she called out as she stowed her purse in the cupboard at her station.

"Life!" Susan came out from the supply room strutting to "Hot Stuff" and grabbed Loretta to join her.

"Better than Jazzercise any day," Loretta said as she danced. "So, what are we really celebrating? 'Hot Stuff' this early in the morning is like a neon sign. What's up?"

"Really?" Susan stopped dancing and cocked her head. "You know by the music I play what's going on in my mind?"

"Give me a break, girlfriend. Of course I know when something's up. Just like you know I'm down in the dumps when I play the Carpenters. Spill the beans before my eight o'clock gets here." She plopped down on her chair and spun around toward Susan, who had begun to rearrange items at her station.

"I have an idea, that's all." Susan shook an empty aerosol can of hairspray and tossed it in the trash. "It's still too new to talk about, but I promise I'll share it with you later if it comes to anything. Really. You know me—it could be nothing. I'm just having fun dreaming."

Loretta did know Susan, and she also knew her ideas were seldom nothing. In fact, they usually turned out to be big somethings. She admired her friend's vision and would stand behind her whatever she planned to do. But the past few weeks had been unusual, to say the least, and Loretta felt strangely discombobulated.

"Susan, hang on a minute and hear me out, okay? I've been worried about you. You haven't been yourself the past few weeks. You're working more, talking less, and you've lost some weight."

"Really?" Susan stopped to look at herself in the mirror.

"Really. And suddenly now you're dancing to 'Hot Stuff' and 'having fun' with some new ideas. What's up?"

Susan chewed her lower lip. "I'm sorry if I've been a bit moody."

"A bit?"

"Okay. A lot. But I'm better now. Honest. I just had to sort out some stuff. It's fine."

Loretta watched Susan strut back to the supply room and shook her head.

"Okay, Lord," she sent up in a fervent prayer. "Help me be ready for whatever You send our way!"

Chapter 9

"Brilliant idea, Lily. I love Bella's food."

It was lunchtime, and Susan and Lily were in the back of Lily's Rolls-Royce in the lot behind the salon, eating their favorite meatball sandwiches. Franco, Lily's driver, sat before them in dignified silence, thoroughly accustomed to such high-class picnics.

Susan, too, had grown accustomed to her friend's desire for privacy. As a fourth-generation Las Vegas native and a well-known philanthropist, Lily Peyton was frequently recognized when they ate out. No stranger to the community herself, Susan was also the object of many a table-side greeting whenever they tried to get away for lunch or dinner. So they'd taken to having meals at Lily's home or in the back of her luxurious automobile when time was short—which was typically how it was in Susan's world. They both enjoyed it.

"So, dear, tell me your idea." Lily picked up her sandwich and took a bite, leaning forward as meat sauce dripped into the Styrofoam box.

"Well, you know how much I love the cosmetics and fragrances of the disco era …" Susan dabbed away some red sauce from the corner of her mouth.

"And the clothing." Lily politely covered her mouth with her hand.

"Yes, and the clothing. Anyway, I was putting on lipstick this morning, and I remembered an article I just read about the Vermont Country Store. You know, that catalog place that has all the blast-from-the-past stuff from when we were young."

"When 'we' were young?" Lily smiled. "Like you remember horse-drawn carriages?"

"Very funny. You know what I mean. Like Tangee lipstick, Evening in Paris cologne, Dippity-do hair gel, Teaberry gum, Yardley fragrances ..."

"Yes, dear, I know the place you mean. I just ordered some Bonne Bell lip gloss from them."

"Yes! Bonne Bell! When did you last hear that name?"

"Longer than I'd care to recall. They must be manufacturing these products new, with licensing permission from the original companies. They couldn't possibly have actual stock left from years ago. Could they?"

"I wouldn't think so. All I know is that for the first time in years I can get some of the products I fell in love with back in the sixties and seventies! And I know I'm not the only one who fell in love with them. So what if we sold them at Disco Diva?"

"Makes sense to me, Susan. You have a strong customer base. You've done very well in retail sales." Lily took another bite.

"We have. And it's not just hair care products. Everything we offer sells—from books to CDs to jewelry."

"Speaking of jewelry—" Lily took a sip of San Pellegrino water— "have you been able to acquire another pair of earrings from your friend?"

"They're in the mail now. And that's another opportunity. I can get a Nevada exclusive on Pat's jewelry line. She's about to blast off in a big way. We can even be a distributor for Glitter and Bling—like a satellite store."

"I'm glad to hear Patricia is doing well."

"Her shop on Melrose has exploded. Did I tell you they bought the building?"

"Good for her." Lily smiled. "She needed more space. Which I assume brings us to your immediate dilemma. Where exactly do you plan to put all of this retail merchandise?"

"Well, that's the other part of my idea. What if instead of displaying more of my disco collection, we turned the Petite Pet space into a retail shop?"

"So you've decided to lease the last space after all?"

"It makes perfect sense, Lily. But I'm not just thinking about leasing it. I've asked Sam if he would consider selling us the building."

"What does Michael say about that?"

Susan's silence said more than words could.

"I see." Lily wiped her hands on the blanket-sized napkin in her lap.

"No, you don't. But I don't want to talk about that right now. I want to know what you think of the idea."

"So you've already done the market-trend studies to validate the consumer interest in such an endeavor?"

Susan smiled. She loved how business-savvy Lily was. That was one of the reasons she asked her advice and trusted her feedback.

"Not specifically," she said. "But I've been watching the fashion and music trends for years, and we live in the heart of one of the hottest entertainment capitals in the world. Disco is making a comeback—I always knew it would—and retro is hot. I just know this will work."

"What about the Disco Hall of Fame and Museum? You've always said that was your ultimate dream if you could occupy the whole building."

Susan leaned back and sighed. Her friend knew her dream while her own husband seemed not to have a clue.

"That was my initial thought when I heard about the vacancy. But there really isn't enough square footage. I did some rough calculations, and a museum would need much more room. Maybe someday that will be a possibility, but not now. I could bring a few more of my pieces out of storage and put them in the new retail shop for decoration—maybe even have a museum wall in one section—but I'm afraid my grandiose idea must remain an idea, at least for now. I'm excited about the idea for a retail shop, though. What do you think?"

"So you're no longer excited about a museum project?"

"It's not that I'm no longer excited, Lily. I just don't have the money or the space for it right now." She couldn't bring herself to tell Lily that Michael could fund the entire project if he wanted to, simply by selling a couple of acres of dirt. And that she was pretty sure he wouldn't want to—a fact that was beginning to fester.

Lily finished her sandwich in silence, gently folding her napkin and placing it on the seat beside her.

"I think the addition of a retail shop is a splendid idea, dear. Really, I do. I love Disco Diva. Seeing you and the girls is the high point of my week, and being able to shop at the same time would double the pleasure."

Susan laughed. Lily traveled in a crowd that included the Trumps, the Wynns, Mayor Oscar Goodman, and a host of celebrities and dignitaries. Her weekly appointment at the salon might be fun—but the high point?

"You don't believe me?" Lily smiled.

"Oh, Lily." Susan took the hand of her friend. "I believe that you enjoy the salon. But I hardly think that with your lifestyle, a trip to the hairdresser could be a significant occurrence."

"You have no idea what you have, do you?"

"What do you mean?"

"Sweetheart, do you know why those girls flock to your shop?"

Susan grinned. "I hope it's because we have some of the best stylists in Vegas."

"That's part of it. But Disco Diva isn't just about hair. It's a feeling you get while you're there—a feeling that you matter, that people care, that along with being pampered, you're loved, truly loved. By you, Susan, and by God. It's an anointed place, your unique little haven off the strip, and that's because you're living your purpose and your passion."

Susan looked at her friend and didn't know whether to laugh or cry.

"Sweetheart, you love those girls as if they were your own children, and for some of them, it's the first time they've experienced that kind of unconditional love. Where else can Vegas showgirls hear about the Lord from someone who walks the talk?"

"That's not fair. A lot of showgirls are believers. More of my clients than not go to church, and you know that. I'm not telling them anything they don't already know."

"Oh, but you are, dear. How many of them have left shows where they wear less and get paid more for shows where they wear more and get paid less?"

"That's hardly a claim to fame." Susan sighed.

"Oh, my darling, you are so wrong. You are speaking the truth in love—truth very few people in this town are sharing with these girls."

Susan swallowed back the tears that threatened to overtake her. Lily understood.

"It's true," she said. "Many of your customers, especially the showgirls, come to your shop because you do have state-of-the-art services. And yes, the whole disco scene is great fun. But the real reason they return to Disco Diva is that they feel safe under your roof. They feel protected and loved. And quite frankly, the environment many of them inhabit instills very little of that.

"Susan, the business you've created is so much more than just a business, and I think you're selling yourself short to give up on the idea of your museum so quickly. God is able to do exceedingly more than we could ever imagine when He wants to. If we let Him."

"Oh, Lily." Susan's throat tightened.

"Just think and pray about it some more, okay? And talk to Michael. I don't know what's going on with you two, but something's not right. Your Michael is a good man. Don't take for granted the time you have together. Don't wish you had done things differently when it's too late."

Lily glanced at her gold Patek Philippe watch and jumped.

"Oh my, look at the time. I've got to run. Thank you for lunch, dear, and thank you for sharing your idea with me. I really do think it's a splendid concept if that's the way you decide to go."

She leaned over and hugged her friend, gently kissing her on the cheek and whispering a short prayer before Susan exited the car.

Susan watched the sleek vehicle pull out onto the street and walked around to the front of the building. She looked out over the desert landscape, breathed in the crisp January air, and wrapped her sweater around her.

Tomorrow was February 1, Michael's thirty-sixth anniversary at the casino. He would turn sixty in late June, and she would reach the big five-oh in April. Topping it off was their twenty-fifth wedding anniversary in August. A year of monumental milestones.

There were other milestone dates this summer as well—dates wrapped in melancholy and loss—but she always tried to push through the sadness into gratitude. She had so much to be thankful for. It just didn't make sense to mope over what couldn't be changed.

She was daydreaming in front of the salon when a Jaguar convertible screeched into the parking lot. Three leggy blondes unfolded themselves from inside it.

"Wow, great outfit!" the tallest one chimed, commenting on Susan's Calvin Klein pantsuit.

"And your jewelry matches perfectly," her friend added with a grin.

The third young woman remained silent, and her air of disapproval wafted like sour perfume as they passed. Her words floated back to Susan from the salon entrance.

"What the heck was *that*—something from Ripley's Believe It or Not? Get a life, lady."

Chapter 10

Susan prepared for her next customer with a smile on her face, singing and dancing to "Heaven Knows" by Donna Summer. Loretta would have joined in, but it was her morning off. Had Susan paid better attention to her calendar, she'd have seen that Lily was scheduled to come in today and would have spared her the visit yesterday, although their car picnic had been fun. Talking to Lily about the retail space concept had helped her. She needed a sounding board, and clearly Michael wasn't it.

Elegant as always, Lily arrived wearing a powder blue St. John Knits suit with matching shoes and earrings. Lily was petite in stature yet regal in stance. Her delicate appearance belied her real strength.

"Just a bit of a trim today, dear," Lily said as they walked back to the shampoo area. "I rather enjoy the way my hair is framing this poor, tired old face."

"*Poor, tired,* and *old*—three words I'd *never* use to describe you, my friend." Susan leaned Lily's head gently back into the shampoo bowl and began to wash her hair. For most clients, this was a step handled by one of the shampoo girls, but not for Lily.

"So, have you decided what to do about the expansion?"

"Not yet … not exactly."

"It's not like you to sound so confused, dear. What's really the matter?"

"It's Michael. He wants to build the next MGM Grand. And I'm trying to get over being angry with him about it, but I can't seem to do it."

"Your husband wants to build a casino?"

"No, he wants to build what he calls our dream home, but the plans he has are almost as big as *your* place, for crying out loud!"

Lily's seventeen-thousand-square-foot house sat on eight and a half acres, with a breathtaking view of the Vegas skyline. The guest suite by the pool was almost the size of Susan's entire home.

Susan wrapped a towel around Lily's head, and they walked back to her station.

"But it's sweet of Michael to want to build you a house."

"No, it's not sweet. It's selfish—he didn't even consult me. He didn't ask what I wanted." She left out the news about the land they owned.

"So what do you want, dear?"

"I've told you what I want. I want to buy this building and add a retail shop and later find space for my museum."

"Sweetheart," Lily said, her eyes sparkling, "what do you *really* want—if money wasn't a consideration?"

Susan combed through Lily's hair and then picked up her scissors. "Now that's a loaded question."

"It is, and I'm asking it."

Susan thought a minute. "Well, if you really want to know the truth," she said, "I've always wanted to own—now don't laugh—a restaurant and dance club."

Lily raised her eyebrows and looked at her reflection in the mirror as Susan continued to cut her silver hair.

"There's quite a bit of competition in this town already for that kind of thing, don't you think?"

"Sure, if all I wanted was a typical restaurant and dance club. But that's not what I'd want to do."

Lily's eyes gleamed as Susan continued.

"I'd love to open a disco-themed restaurant and dance club, modeled after Studio 54, but without alcohol. I know Vegas is known for twenty-four/seven drinking and partying, but I also know not everyone who wants to have a good time needs to drink in order to do it. And, here's the icing on the cake: I'd love to have the museum as part of it too."

Lily nodded and grinned. "The Disco Hall of Fame and Museum."

"Yes. All under one roof. Maybe even a banquet room folks could rent for receptions and special events. Oh, and a gift shop, too. The entire place would need a killer sound system throughout and … well, that's my dream. A disco-flavored entertainment complex."

"A grand idea!" Lily was beaming.

"Do you really think so? You don't think I'm crazy?"

"Oh, darling, I would never call anyone with a dream crazy. People thought I was crazy when I built the FAITH Project years ago, but look at it now."

Located on the outskirts of the Vegas city limits, the FAITH Project had been conceived by Lily's late nephew, Colt Peyton, a visionary artist. The acronym stood for Finding Art in the Heart of God. Dedicated to preserving the art of people who were inspired by

Jesus Christ, the multimillion-dollar project was primarily an art museum and gallery. However, it also included a conservation lab, artist studios, shops, study areas, and educational facilities. Lily had been almost single-handedly responsible for its development.

"Is there a disco museum in the country?" Lily asked. "Have you googled it to find out?"

That Lily would even think to google something amused Susan. "I have," she said, "and there isn't. Not officially, at least not like the Rock and Roll Hall of Fame in Ohio. And I can pretty much bet that no one has the collection of disco memorabilia I have—between what's here in the salon and in storage. You have no idea." She finished the haircut and began to set Lily's hair on large Velcro rollers for the sleek pageboy look she enjoyed.

"I really think it's a splendid idea! Where would you build it?"

"Lily, it's crazy. There's no sense even talking about it."

"What does Michael say?"

"About what?"

"About everything. The expansion, your dream—everything."

"We haven't discussed it. All he can think about is building his dream house, and he thinks he's doing a great thing, setting aside a little room for my stuff. My hobby, he calls it. Frankly, I don't know what to say to him these days."

"Shame on you, Susan Anderson." Lily shook a finger at her in the mirror.

"Why?"

"You're telling me you are angry at your husband for not consulting you about the dream home he wants to build for you, and you haven't talked to him about your dreams. You haven't even let him in on the potential salon expansion or the possibility of buying the entire building. Seems to me that for two married folks, you live pretty separate lives."

Leave it to Lily to hit the nail on the head. During all twenty-five years of their marriage, Michael had worked nights and Susan days—their only times together were their days off and an occasional three-day vacation. It had been years since they had taken any extended time off together. Lily was right. They lived like single people.

"Time for the dryer." Susan pushed aside the cart containing hair rollers and put her hand on Lily's elbow to help her up.

"I didn't mean to sound judgmental, dear." They walked to the bank of hair dryers, and Lily sat. "I just don't like to see you this way."

"I know, and you're right. I do need to talk with him." Susan turned the switch to fifteen minutes, placed the dryer bonnet over Lily's head, and smiled, mouthing the words, "Thank you."

She would talk with Michael tonight at his party—if the timing was right.

"Mrs. Peyton is on the phone and wants to know if you're free for lunch."

Susan jumped. She was just finishing up a color weave on one of the dancers from *O,* the show at the Bellagio, but she'd been working on autopilot all morning, her thoughts far away.

"Your one o'clock cancelled," Shannon, the receptionist, informed her. "And your next appointment isn't until three."

Susan glanced at the wall clock. "Find out where she wants to meet and tell her I've got to be back by two forty-five. I'm cutting out early to get ready for Michael's soiree."

Shannon saluted and snapped her heels crisply, turning on her three-inch Jimmy Choo knockoff sandals to head back to the reception desk.

"Okay, time to put you under the dryer for a few minutes." Susan ushered her gorgeous client to the bank of pink leather chairs under the hair dryers. She turned the knob to high, set the timer for fifteen minutes, and lowered the dryer over the foil antennae sprouting from the showgirl's crown.

"Can you put on that Barry White CD I like?" she asked Susan in a throaty voice, crossing long, tanned legs.

"Sure, but you won't hear much under the dryer."

"That's okay. I won't be under here long." She picked up a dog-eared copy of *People* from the side table.

Susan was placing new CDs in the multidisk changer when Shannon found her.

"Lily, er, Mrs. Peyton said she'd come by to pick you up in a half hour. She'll wait out back—said to take your time."

"Thank you, Shannon."

Susan wondered what Lily wanted to discuss. Only a few hours earlier Lily had sat in her chair scolding her for not communicating better with her husband. Susan knew she was right, but did she want to hear about it again?

She sighed. For years she had looked up to this amazing woman of faith and courage. If Lily intended to counsel her again on her marriage, well, that was a small price to pay for the dividends of her wisdom.

Besides, truth be told, Susan could use all the help she could get.

—*mm*—

"Do you miss driving yourself?" Susan stretched out her legs in the roomy backseat of Lily's Rolls, which was headed west on Tropicana. "No offense, Franco." She grinned in the rearview mirror at the chauffeur-slash-butler, who had been with Lily as long as Susan had known her. The smoked glass panel separating the front and back seats was hardly ever closed.

He smiled back. "None taken, ma'am."

"Goodness, no," Lily said. "Not at all. I know very well I'm not as quick as I once was. Old biddies my age have no business behind the wheel of an automobile."

"You are not an old biddy. Stop that negative self-talk, you'd be telling me."

"Touché!"

They drove in silence for a few minutes before Franco slowly turned into a vast parking lot. Foot-high weeds sprouted up through the cracks in the cement.

"Is this sufficient, madame?" Franco asked as he coasted to a stop.

"Perfect. Just keep it running. Excuse us, please." Lily reached over and touched the button that quietly closed the window, sealing them off from the driver.

"Okay, what's up?" Susan stared at her friend.

"Do you know where we are?"

Susan looked out the window to see what the locals had dubbed the White Elephant. The three-story white-brick building had once served as the western headquarters for a large ready-to-wear company. Years ago that company had been gobbled up by an even larger one, leaving the vacant building tied up in legal purgatory. It sat on several acres of prime real estate near Chinatown, not far from the Palace Station Hotel and Casino.

The huge parking lot had been the site of a community protest several months back when it was discovered that drug dealers and addicts had been using the building as a haven. Almost overnight, new doors and windows had replaced the broken ones, and, from what Susan could see, a perimeter fence was going up around the huge parking lot.

"Of course I know where we are." Susan peered out the window. "Looks like she's getting a face-lift."

"At least someone is." Lily laughed.

"That's one heck of a lot of windows to replace. Must be costing someone a small fortune."

"One hundred twenty windows and eight main exit doors, to be exact. And it's not as expensive as I thought it would be—a small price to pay to keep our community safe."

Susan's eyebrows arched. "You own the White Elephant?"

"No, I own the future Disco Hall of Fame and Museum, Restaurant, and Dance Club. What do you think of it?"

Susan was speechless—until she wasn't, at which time the two women began to cascade ideas and plans, falling over one another in a Niagara of creativity.

Chapter 11

"If I didn't know better, I'd say you and Lily tied one on at lunch," Loretta said with a smirk.

"We didn't have lunch." Susan plopped into her chair and spun around.

"Really? When I got in, Shannon said you were at lunch with Lily."

"That was the plan, but we got sidetracked."

"Where at, a hookah lounge?"

"Very funny." Susan laughed. "But wait till I tell you …"

By the time Karen and Tina arrived for their simultaneous appointments, the festive atmosphere in the salon was approaching Mardi Gras proportions.

"I love this place!" Tina relaxed in Susan's chair.

"Different from the last time you were here, eh?" Susan said, securing a neon orange cape around Tina's shoulders. Although she no longer accepted new clients, she occasionally made an exception. She was glad the young woman had returned.

"Oh heavens, yes! That was a nightmare."

"Look how much your hair has grown in less than a month!" Susan exclaimed, running her fingers through the short, lush locks.

"I know. Can you believe it?" Tina grinned, her elegant face aglow. "That's why I'm here. It won't stand up like it used to. Cut it short again. I loved it."

"Really?" Susan had figured the young woman would be focused on growing back her once-long tresses.

"Yes, really. I've never felt so free, and it's really easy to take care of."

"Maybe I should go shorter too," Karen mused.

Loretta did a double take. "Seriously?"

"Well, I was thinking about it. This other girl in the show, she ..."

The hair discussion quickly segued into the typical banter about their love lives and the relationships of some of the other girls in the Folies chorus. All the while, Susan tried to deflect the conversation from unkind gossip, encouraging the young women to talk about themselves and what they were doing and asking them about their families.

Susan detested gossip, though it tended to be a staple of salon conversation. Whenever possible, she encouraged her clients not to fall into what she called the "sin of the tongue." In fact, she'd read a new book about taming the tongue that she was recommending to her clients.

Along with music and memorabilia, Susan believed in sharing books with her customers, and every month she featured a new book available for sale in the reception area. That was another reason she felt a retail shop adjacent to the salon would be a good idea. And the more she thought about it, in fact, the more convinced she was that the shop was the way to go. Lily's idea of converting the White Elephant into Susan's dream business had been exciting to discuss and had buoyed her spirits all afternoon, but she knew she could never afford a project of that magnitude. Lily often forgot, bless her heart, that not everyone was in her socioeconomic league.

Still, it sure was fun to fantasize.

"Is that your husband?" Tina pointed to the photo Susan had recently stuck on the edge of her mirror.

"Yes, it is."

"He looks familiar." She tilted her head.

"He works at the Silver Spur."

"Really? We were just there the other night. A bunch of us went out after the show. Is he a pit boss?"

"Goodness, no. Michael works in the maintenance department."

"Oh." Tina blushed. "Sorry."

"Don't be sorry, honey," Loretta put in. "Suzie-Q loves laying that line on folks—as if he cleans toilets or something. But the truth is, Michael's a bigwig at the Spur. Been there thirty-six years today! He's in charge of the entire maintenance and landscaping department."

"Wow," Tina said. "Thirty-six years? My uncle was with the Ford plant that long. They gave him a gold watch when he retired, and you'd have thought it was a gold Cadillac."

"Actually, the Spur is giving him a party tonight," Susan said.

"Think he'll get a gold watch?" Loretta asked.

"Who knows?" Susan took another careful snip at the hair over Tina's right ear.

"What are you wearing?" Tina asked. "I love what you have on today, by the way. Looks like Oscar de la Renta."

Susan nodded. "Very good."

"Brownie points with your hairdresser." Karen grinned. "What exactly does that get you?"

"Gosh, I don't know." Tina laughed. "What does it get me, Susan? A free deep conditioner or something?"

"At least."

"I love fashion, so sue me." Tina stuck out her bottom lip at her friend.

"Play nice, girls." Loretta pointed her comb like a ruler aimed for the knuckles.

"Well, what *are* you going to wear?" Karen asked.

"I have a few things in mind, but I haven't decided yet." Susan frowned. "Michael's wearing a tux."

"The Forum Shops have a big sale going on," Tina said. "Have you been there yet?"

"Oh, I doubt they'd have anything there for me," Susan said.

"Why?" Tina furrowed her brows. "They have amazing things."

"I'm sure they do, but not in my style."

"Susan, you'll have to forgive Tina," said Karen. "She doesn't fully understand."

"Understand what?" Tina inquired.

"Yes, do tell." Susan reached for her blow dryer. "What doesn't your friend understand?"

"That you have a certain style, a reputation, a definitive brand, as it were. You're the official Disco Diva of Las Vegas, so your public expects you not to let them down. You can't show up at any public function looking normal."

Susan and Loretta both stared at Karen's reflection in the mirror.

"Don't look at me like that," she said. "You know what I mean."

"That people expect me to look *ab*normal?" Susan began to dry Tina's fresh haircut, using her fingers as a comb.

"That's not what I'm saying at all. Your makeup and hair are always perfect for your look. You have a fabulous wardrobe. We'd kill to have the clothes you have and the style you have. I'm just saying that you're kind of a historic icon in town."

"An icon, huh?" Susan pulled Tina's hair into little spikes.

"Yes." Karen smiled. "An icon."

Susan couldn't decide if she'd just been insulted or not.

When they had opened Disco Diva back in May of 1982, she had worn one of the gowns she'd brought with her from New York. After all, it was a disco-themed salon, and she felt the dress would be appropriate for the gala celebration. It was a hit, so she'd decided to continue the style. She certainly had enough clothes from the era—good clothes, clothes that would last.

It had never been her intention to become a brand or an icon. It had just happened. But now that she thought about it, she didn't mind at all.

"Oh well." She smiled as she reached for a jar of high-gloss gel. "At least you didn't call me a fossil."

Chapter 12

Tonight was Michael's big night. Thirty-six years with the same company was almost unheard of these days. Yet he prided himself that many of his team had been with the Spur for twenty-plus years and his top two guys had more than thirty years each under their belts.

"It's because of you, Michael," his boss had told him at the company Christmas party in December. "You're the reason this department has almost no turnover. Wish I could say the same for housekeeping and food service. Are you sure I can't convince you to take over those departments?"

Michael had laughed at the joke, knowing it wasn't totally a joke. He knew the Spur was having trouble keeping help, but so was everyone lately. Cliff, his boss, was as high up the management chain as you got before reaching the casino owners—and he was the seventh general manager Michael had worked for during his tenure. The owners had offered Michael himself the job time and again, but paper pushing and politics weren't for him. He liked it where he was just fine, thank you very much—even if the daily grind was beginning to make him look forward to retirement.

"Yeah, the old work ethic sure isn't what it used to be." Michael had set down the glass of eggnog that appeared to have been spiked with brandy. After all this time, it seemed someone would have caught on to the fact that he didn't drink.

"That's why we've decided to celebrate your anniversary in February." Cliff had slapped him on the back as though they were old friends. "We're going to throw you a party."

"Well, that'd be nice. But it's not necessary …"

"It *is* necessary! Couldn't believe they let the last one slip by. No excuse, no excuse. That won't happen under my watch. No, sir."

And sure enough, shortly after the new year, an invitation to celebrate employees who had been with the company more than ten years began to circulate. Eighteen employees would be honored, twelve from his team. He held the top spot for the person employed the longest by the Silver Spur.

Tonight would be his night.

He should have waited until tonight to tell Susan about the plans for their new home. He realized now that laying it on her a few weeks ago at the salon like that, after a long fourteen-hour day, hadn't been fair. No wonder she was mad at him.

So instead of bringing it up again, he'd simply moved ahead on plans to subdivide the land and apply for the permits to begin building. He'd met again with the architect and asked him to make the changes that Susan had brought up in their discussion, including an increase in square footage for her collection of disco memorabilia. They wouldn't be able to keep all of it in the house—there was just too much—but she could make the decision to continue to store it or sell it at an auction.

Throughout the years, she had been approached by numerous collectors offering her a pretty penny for the stuff she had in those dusty storage units off the strip. She always refused. As they said, one person's trash is another person's treasure—and he knew his wife treasured her things. At least she didn't have a thing for dolls, like the wife of one of his coworkers. He wasn't sure he could live with hundreds of eyes staring at him all the time.

He adjusted the bow tie on his tux, nodding approvingly in the bathroom mirror. If things continued to move smoothly, they should be able to break ground on the house in early fall—a perfect time to start construction in the Nevada desert. Now all that was left to discuss was what to do with the salon. He had some exciting ideas to run by Susan later that night after the party, and hoped she would agree to at least one of the options he had in mind.

"Susan, are you just about ready? We need to get going," he called to his wife.

"How do I look? Is this okay?"

"Va-va-va-voom!" Michael wolf-whistled as Susan pirouetted slowly in front of him.

She wore a light pink satin floor-length gown sashed at the waist with a wide swath of black moiré taffeta. The boatneck style accented her collarbone perfectly, and the black satin elbow-high gloves were set off by rhinestone cuff bracelets on each wrist. She reminded him of a photo of Marilyn Monroe he'd once seen. Not disco—but definitely gorgeous.

"It's a Valentino," she told him. "I got it from storage last week and had it cleaned. Jackie wore it to a state dinner at the White House."

"*The* Jackie?" Michael gulped. "As in Kennedy?"

"One and the same. We got it at an auction at Sotheby's. I've only worn it once."

Who "we" referred to, Michael knew better than to ask. He'd learned long ago that his wife loved sharing the history of her clothing and other disco bric-a-brac, but discussing the person or persons who'd bought the items in question was strictly off-limits. Perhaps she'd been involved with one of the many celebrities in her photos—in which case, he'd rather not know. He knew there had been at least one very wealthy man in her past and that she preferred not to discuss him. Michael had a few ghosts in his own closet from the years before he met Susan, and it was fine by him to let both their pasts remain buried.

"Honey, I just thought of something," he said. "Do we have enough insurance on those units? I know the shop and this house is costing us a fortune to insure, but isn't the stuff you still have in storage kind of valuable too?"

"Kind of? Michael, I've been telling you for years that what I have in storage is priceless—there's no way to place a value on most of it. But don't worry about the insurance." She said it curtly, as though she were peeved. "We have six more months before it's due again."

"Did I say something wrong? Are you angry? I didn't mean—"

"No. I didn't mean to sound short. Let's get going. We don't want to be late."

—✐—

The night was a smashing success. In fact, Susan hadn't anticipated that the Silver Spur would pull out all those stops. She was surprised to see a host of Vegas dignitaries at the party—including the mayor, several councilwomen, and many local area business men and women. And Lily, of course.

"You could have told me you were coming." Susan playfully pinched her friend.

"Wanted to surprise you." Lily batted her eyes dramatically, and they both laughed.

"He looks dashing in his tuxedo." Lily nodded toward Michael, who was mingling nearby.

"I agree. That's only the second time I've seen him in a tux. The first was at our wedding."

"My Harry used to complain bitterly every time he had to put on what he called his penguin suit. There always seemed to be some kind of soiree that required formal attire."

"You still miss Harry, don't you? Even after all this time?" Susan placed her gloved hand on her friend's arm.

"Every day. I talk to him all the time—but it's not the same. You look absolutely dazzling yourself, my dear. Wherever did you find that breathtaking frock?"

The change of subject was clear, and Susan had just begun to tell Lily the history of her dress when Michael interrupted.

"Excuse me, ladies, but the boss wants to see me in his office. Says he has something he wants to share. I'll only be a few minutes or so. Are you okay here?"

"We'll be fine, sweetie." Lily patted his hand. "You run along and have a good time."

Susan and Michael smiled at the fact that Lily answered a question intended for Susan. But they had grown accustomed to her habit of thinking she was the center of every conversation, a well-earned quirk they chalked up to her social position and stage of life. Michael kissed his wife on the cheek and planted an elegant kiss on Lily's outstretched hand before walking away.

"Precious man." Lily grinned. "Susan, I was thinking about our lunch today."

"So, you don't want to hear who owned my dress before me?"

"I do, but before Michael returns I'd like to talk with you about something."

"Me, too," Susan said, quickly rushing on. "Look, I really appreciated that you thought of me for the White Elephant. And I won't lie, it sure was fun talking about it … but there's no way I can afford—"

"Let me go first, dear. Age before beauty. I think having a retail shop combined with Disco Diva is a strategic idea."

"Thank you."

"I mean that. I'm not agreeing with you because it's what a friend does. I even talked to Carter about it after I dropped you off." Carter was Lily's nephew, Colt's twin brother, and handled a great deal of her financial affairs—along with a team of accountants at some firm with eight surnames attached to it. "He thinks it's a stellar idea as well."

"A man thinks another retail specialty boutique for women is a stellar idea?" Susan shook her head. "I would think he'd say it was overkill. As if there aren't enough shops in this town."

"Why do you sound so negative, dear?"

"I'm sorry, Lily, but it's just that everything is so darn expensive. I do have a lot of ideas and I think they would work, but I need to be realistic. When I stopped to get this dress out of cold storage, the manager told me the rent is going up when my lease expires. Plus, my insurance agent informed me the other day that I now have to supply individual appraisals for every item in my collection worth more than five hundred dollars, and that alone will cost a fortune. I'm not sure what adding the retail shop will cost." She sighed. "I'm just so tired of thinking about all of it. But I had another idea tonight when I was getting dressed. Maybe instead of continuing to pay for off-site storage units, I should use Petite Pet as storage space for the time being. That would cut down on some of the expenses for awhile. Security could be a problem, but we could figure that out."

"No retail shop?"

"I'd love to have the store. I'd love to have a lot of things, but ..." Susan sighed again and played with her bracelet.

Lily leaned back and daintily crossed her legs at the ankles, holding her hands in her lap. "Susan, I applaud you for trying to be a wise businesswoman, but you've totally missed the mark in this case. Have you forgotten I have more money than I could ever hope to spend in what little time I have left?"

"Don't talk like that! You've got a lot of years left. And I know you've got money, but what does that have to do with me?"

"Let me put it this way—you're a hairdresser, correct?"

"Correct."

"As your good friend I avail myself of your profession—of your gifts, correct?"

"Correct ..."

"If I went to someone else to have my coiffure cropped, you'd be pretty upset, correct?"

Susan laughed. "Correct."

"All right then, dear child. You're a cosmetologist, but what I am is a venture capitalist. Folks are always asking me to fund their harebrained ideas—you have no idea the proposals that come across my desk. Only last week I was asked for 2.4 million dollars to partner with three old geezers on an Internet dating service for wealthy senior citizens. Seems there are more than a few old biddies like me who are single and have considerable pocket change."

"People really ask you for that kind of money?" Susan could only shake her head.

"All the time. That's what a venture capitalist does. We invest in ventures that create capital."

"I guess I hadn't thought of it that way."

"Now you do, and I think your idea has merit."

"You want to invest in a retail shop in an outdated strip mall?"

"No, dear, you aren't listening. I want to invest in renovating the White Elephant from top to bottom. The top floor will house a disco dance club—as well as the Disco Hall of Fame and Museum. The second floor will be home to a lovely restaurant with banquet rooms for special events, and the main floor will house the new home of the Disco Diva salon, day spa, and retail boutique. If we're doing it, we might as well do it all. What do you think?"

Susan could only stare at her friend as tears filled her eyes.

"Oh, dearie, don't cry," Lily soothed. "You'll get mascara all over that beautiful dress. Here, take this." She handed Susan a lace handkerchief from a beaded purse shaped like a Fabergé egg.

"Pretty purse," Susan said with a sniff.

"Thank you, dear. It's a Vivian Alexander. But don't change the subject. I've been thinking a great deal about this, and trust me, it isn't a whim. I'm old, but I'm nobody's fool. I think you're on to something here. And the timing is right. Your current salon is lovely—you've done a fabulous job over the years—but it doesn't make good financial sense to keep putting money into that particular piece of real estate. Susan, you've got the clientele and the reputation. You can take the step up."

"But ... the cost. It's—"

"You still aren't listening to me, sweetheart! I have more than enough money to take care of myself even if I outlast Methuselah, although I doubt that will happen. Carter is all I have left, and he's well taken care of. The FAITH Project is endowed for decades, and I'm not getting any younger. I want to do something fun! I bought the White Elephant on a whim—I had no idea what I was going to do with it. It's already paid for, just sitting empty waiting for something grand to happen to it! And I think this qualifies. In fact, I think it qualifies as a God-cidence! Come on, Susan, let's do it!"

Lily leaned over and took Susan's hands in hers. "I understand how awkward the money thing can get, so we won't let that happen. We'll draw up a contract that will give you majority ownership, along with a dollar-figure investment you and Michael are comfortable making—let's say something between ten and twenty thousand dollars. However, I can well afford to handle the bulk of the project, so you won't have to cut corners in any way. Please, Susan—I want to do this more than you could know."

Susan fought the urge to crumple into Lily's arms, weeping tears of joy and disbelief at the offer that had just been made.

"Let's talk more about this next week," Lily said. "Give it some time to sink in. But write down all of your ideas as they come to you, okay? All of them, no matter how crazy you think they are. This is the time to be creative."

Susan was laughing and crying when Michael returned.

"What's wrong? You okay?" He pulled up a chair and sat next to her. "What happened?"

"She's fine," Lily told him. "I just gave her a little present that made her happy, that's all. She'll be okay in a bit, won't you, honey?" Lily held Susan's chin in her left hand and used the handkerchief in her right hand to wipe her eyes. "There, there. Now don't spoil Sir Michael's night with puffy eyes, do you hear me? What did your boss have to share with you, young man?"

"You're never going to believe this, honey. Look." He held out his wrist to show off a striking gold Movado watch. "It's the real deal, not a knockoff. And look at this." He pulled an envelope from his inside jacket pocket. "It's a bonus check for thirty-six thousand dollars—one thousand dollars for every year I've been at the Silver Spur."

"Oh my." Susan hiccupped. "Sorry. That's wonderful, honey. Really it is."

"I want you to have half of it to do anything you want—anything. Eighteen thousand dollars just for you." He kissed her cheek as Susan looked at Lily and once again began to cry.

"Does that mean she's happy?" he asked Lily. "Honey, are you happy?" He peered into Susan's moist eyes, confused as only a well-meaning husband with an overemotional wife can be.

"Oh yes, Michael, I'd say she's very happy." Lily patted her hand. "Very happy, indeed."

Chapter 13

Susan managed to pull herself together just as Michael's boss joined them to congratulate her on having such a successful husband. It was as though he were a prizewinning racehorse she owned. She knew he meant well, but he was such a ... well, a dork.

"You don't mind if I steal our man of the hour, do you?" the general manager asked, grabbing Michael's elbow and pulling him away without acknowledging Lily or waiting for Susan to reply. Michael winked and mouthed, "I love you" as he was dragged away.

"Was that horribly rude, or am I just getting old?" Lily shook her head.

"I'm sorry, I should have introduced you. That was the GM of the Spur. I can never remember his name."

"Ah, so that's Clifford Jenson." Lily nodded. "George and Jean have talked about him. They say he's rather good at what he does, in spite of his less-than-genuine personality."

Susan always managed to forget how well connected Lily was to the Vegas community. Her parents and grandparents had been some of the first residents to settle in the desert. They had been railroad tycoons. In fact, Lily was distantly related to John C. Fremont, who led an overland expedition to Vegas in 1844. Her family held a place of significant distinction in the town, and

George and Jean Cohen, the longtime owners of the Silver Spur, ran in the same circle.

"Well, dear, I'm afraid I need to bid you a fond adieu." Lily stood and discreetly straightened the folds in her Oscar de la Renta gown.

"But ... the party only just started."

"I've congratulated your dear husband, delivered exciting news to my favorite friend, and my need to press flesh is several decades behind me, dear one, so there really is no reason for me to remain. Plus, I'm far too excited to keep quiet about this project. I'm afraid I might say something untoward, and you still need to talk with Michael about everything."

"Yes, I do." Susan looked across the crowd at her beaming husband.

"It's a rather lengthy process, applying for permits and such." Lily smiled, following Susan's gaze. "We'll want to get started as soon as possible on the paperwork. I do so abhor this stage, but I'm afraid it's a necessary evil. A first order of business will be to hire someone to manage the project. I'll place a call to Lyle Decker in California. He managed the FAITH Project, and he was the best project manager I've ever worked with. If he's available, we'd be foolish not to hire him. Would that be okay with you?"

Susan looked at her blankly. Lily was already making plans, and she was still trying to figure out how to get through the rest of the evening.

"Lily, I don't quite know what to say yet. This is all a bit overwhelming."

"I understand, dear. Take time to talk it over, but not too much time, okay? There really is a great deal to do. Oh, one more thing—you wear Valentino far better than Jackie ever could." Lily excused herself with a gentle kiss on the top of Susan's head, promising to connect early the next week.

Leave it to Lily to have recognized her gown. Her steel-trap memory always amazed Susan. But Lily's recent announcement amazed her even more. This was no small undertaking—they were talking about millions of dollars. Did Lily actually believe enough in her dream to fund the majority of the project? She'd never considered that option—never even thought about building a new salon from the ground floor up. Her mind began to spin with possibilities.

The more she thought, in fact, the more excited she grew.

Surely Michael would be just as excited as she was.

—*mm*—

"I thought that was you. Hello."

Susan was deep in thought when the handsome young man tapped her on the shoulder, startling her.

"Sorry. The name's Power. Ryan Power. We met at your salon a few weeks ago." He extended his hand.

"Oh, yes, I remember. Bond, James Bond."

He laughed. "One and the same." His inquisitive eyes quickly traveled over her and she noticed his Adam's apple move as he gulped. "You look utterly exquisite."

"Well, thank you, sir. You look rather … comfortable yourself."

He was dressed in what the girls at the shop called shabby chic—expensive, but messy. A casual Ralph Lauren look with open-necked shirt, suede sport coat, and loafers that most likely cost a small fortune. Once again, his scent left her unsettled.

"Clearly I'm not part of this soiree. I'm here with some buddies for a bachelor party. We took a wrong turn, and I saw you when we passed through on our way to the other side of the tracks." He laughed. "What's the occasion?"

"My husband works here. It's an anniversary party."

"Wedding?"

"Employment. He's been with the Spur thirty-six years."

"Wow. I'd say that deserves a party." Ryan whistled. "So, where is the good man?" Ryan looked out over the crowd. "He's mighty brave to leave a treasure like you all alone. May I?" He pointed to a nearby chair.

"Uh, sure. But what about your friends?"

"They won't miss me for a few minutes."

Susan pointed out her husband, who appeared to be deeply involved in a conversation with a group of men. They all looked rather uncomfortable in their formal attire as they fidgeted with ties, adjusted cummerbunds, and shrugged their shoulders. She smiled. "They don't look very at home in their finery, do they?"

"Unlike you. I'm serious, Susan, you look fabulous. That is an amazing dress. Looks like a Valentino original."

Susan's eyebrows rose. "It is. I'm impressed."

"And your hair. You look like you've stepped off a *Vogue* cover from the seventies."

She laughed. "What would a young whippersnapper know about *Vogue* in the seventies?"

"*Whippersnapper*—now, that's a word you don't hear often these days. My mother was a fashion photographer, and she loved *Vogue*. I grew up around beautiful women—and paid attention."

"Good for you." She smiled.

"Your salon is incredible," he added. "And your disco collection is mind-boggling. When did you start acquiring it?"

They were deep in discussion when Michael interrupted them. "Excuse me, honey, but they want to take some photos." He extended his hand to the young man, who quickly stood. "I'm Michael Anderson, Susan's husband. And you are …?"

"Power. Ryan Power. Congratulations on your anniversary. Your wife is very proud of you, and rightfully so."

Michael nodded and gave a half smile.

"I'm afraid it's time for me to get back to my party," Ryan added. "It was a pleasure to visit with you, Susan." He reached for her hand and gently kissed the back of it before turning to Michael and extending his hand. "And congratulations again. Have a pleasant evening, you two."

They watched him walk away as Susan shook her head.

"What?" Michael unbuttoned his jacket and placed his hands on his hips as he watched Ryan walk away.

"He surprised me, that's all. He's a collector too."

"Yeah, I'll just bet he collects."

"What's that supposed to mean?"

"I see his type all the time. Chick magnet—I think that's what guys like him are called. He collects women."

"Oh, please, Michael, how would you know? You talked to him for what, two minutes?"

"I watched him before I came over to rescue you."

"Rescue me?"

"Exactly. Who is he?"

"A customer. He came to the shop a few weeks ago."

"Yours?"

"No, Loretta got him. Everyone was jealous." She smiled, remembering the comments made throughout the day after he left.

"Everyone?"

"Michael Anderson, are you jealous?" She crossed her arms and grinned.

"Should I be?"

"Don't be silly. He's young enough to be—oh, this is silly!" She picked up her purse and patted his arm. "I'm going to touch up my face before I get in front of anyone's lens. Tell me where to meet you. I'll be right there."

<center>~~~</center>

She made her way through the crowd and down the corridor toward the ladies' room, startled to find Ryan Power leaning against the wall.

"I figured you'd visit here before posing for any photos."

"Good instincts."

He grinned. "I was born at night, but it wasn't last night."

"What can I do for you? I really have to get going ..."

"I know. I won't keep you. It's just I was hoping we could set up a time to talk more about your collection. Where you acquired some of your pieces, the history behind them—things like that."

"Why the interest?"

"I told you. I'm kind of a collector myself. I do some freelance work for a few museums, scout out things that might be of interest."

"I thought you looked familiar when I first saw you! You're the guy who acquires pieces for the Rock and Roll Hall of Fame, aren't you?"

"One of many."

"Don't be modest. I read the article in the *LA Times* last year. You brokered the deal for Janis Joplin's Karmann Ghia."

"Wow, that's some memory you've got."

"Ryan, let me make your job easier, okay? I'm not interested in selling any of my collection. I'm flattered you would consider inquiring, but nothing I have is for sale."

"Everything is for sale. For the right price." He leaned back against the wall and crossed his arms. For some reason, his cocky look infuriated Susan.

"I once knew someone who used to say those exact same words. It's as untrue now as it was back then." She took a step in the direction she'd been going when she encountered him. "Now, unless you're planning to follow me into the ladies' room, I'm afraid I'm going to have to excuse myself. Have fun at your bachelor party, Mr. Power."

She patted him on the cheek as though dismissing a child.

By the time they got home, it was too late to share anything with Michael—even if Susan wanted to, which she didn't. Not yet. Not after the "discussion" that began in the car.

"I still don't get it." Michael tossed his keys into the dish on the table and pulled off his bow tie. "It's a soup can, for crying out loud—not the Sistine Chapel. Give me a break."

"That's not the point." She turned around so he could unzip her dress. "Thank you."

"You're welcome. Then what *is* the point?" He held out his arms, wrists together so Susan could unhook his cuff links. "Thank you."

"You're welcome. I don't want to discuss this anymore, Michael."

"You never want to discuss anything anymore, do you?"

"What's that supposed to mean?" She hung her gown on a pink satin padded hanger and watched as her husband struggled with the small black enamel studs on his shirt.

"Let me do that." She unbuttoned his shirt, placing each tiny button in his outstretched hand. "Make sure you put those studs in the little bag they came in, or they'll charge you a fortune."

He looked down at the buttons in his hand. "Never could figure out these things."

"Michael," she said quietly, "when it comes to art and fashion, we're like that political couple—what're their names? Carlin and Mataville or something like that. I love you, but we're never going to agree. What Andy Warhol was doing with the Campbell's Soup can was more than meets the eye … he was elevating the ordinary to the extraordinary. That man was a visionary, a cultural phenomenon! He almost single-handedly birthed the entire pop art movement."

"He was one weird dude, and you know it." Michael grinned. "And what about that hair?" He wrapped a white towel around his head as though portraying the artist's signature towhead locks and began to strut around the room in an exaggerated effeminate manner.

"Shame on you, Michael Anderson!" She tossed a pillow at him. "Andy didn't walk like that at all."

"Sorry. Didn't know you were so close." He raised his eyebrows in mock surprise.

She had photos with Andy Warhol all over the shop—and a custom portrait by him hanging in the living room. Did he think she'd had her image inserted somehow?

"I don't know why I let you get my goat every time." She got into bed and pulled the covers up to her chin. "Let's not argue. It's been a great night, and we're both tired. What do you say we hit the hay and agree to disagree about pop culture and the seventies?"

"Okay." He crawled in next to her and wrapped her in a big bear hug.

They went to sleep snuggled together … without discussing either the Henderson property or the White Elephant.

Chapter 14

Susan sat in a high-backed Chippendale wing chair in Lily's living room, looking out the expansive wall of windows at the huge swimming pool, hot tub, waterfall, and a backyard barbecue area that never failed to make Michael green with envy.

But Michael wasn't here today.

It had been two weeks since his party, and she had been unable to approach him about the offer Lily had made. She was waiting for the right time, but the time never seemed to be right. After the Valentine's Day rush, things had been unusually calm at the salon, a fact that enabled her to spend time thinking about Lily's generous proposition. She had taken this Friday afternoon off to meet with her.

"Thank you for taking some *time off* to meet with me." Lily poured herself hot tea. "I know you have a great deal to accomplish on a daily basis, and *time off* is a luxury. It must be challenging to handle the ownership of the salon, take care of a home, spend *time off* with your husband, and have a life of your own with very little *time off*. I give you credit, dear."

"Okay, Lily, I get your drift. You're trying to tell me something." She took a sip from her delicate Limoges cup. "So spit it out."

"Spit?" Lily smiled.

"Sorry, I forgot that isn't in your lexicon." Susan grinned. "So spill the beans, bare your soul, let it all hang out … your choice."

"Silly girl. Okay, so I do have something to share with you."

"Share away."

Lily gracefully added a spoon of honey to her tea and stirred. She appeared to be choosing her words carefully.

"Please, allow me to finish this thought before you say anything, dear. I've been thinking and praying about this since we spoke at Michael's party. I reviewed my notes from when I began working on the FAITH Project, and I remembered how important it was that I be fully involved in the early stages of the project—to precisely convey my concept and ideas from the start. As things progressed, I was able to spend less time on the daily management and entrust more and more of the project to my experienced team."

"That makes sense," Susan said.

"That's why I want you to consider something." She put her teacup on the end table and moved to sit in the chair across from Susan. "I need you to know that while I fully intend to fund this project and guide you on the journey, I have a great many things on my plate and this can't be my full-time concern. However, it needs to be *someone's* full-time concern, and that someone needs to be you. I'd like you to think about cutting back your hours at Disco Diva for the next few months. Strictly on a temporary basis, you understand. Loretta is perfectly capable of handling things—you know that, dear. And I can't see how you are going to be able to do it all."

Lily's suggestion didn't come as a surprise to Susan. She had, in fact, been praying about this very thing only that morning.

"I agree with you," she said.

"You do?" Lily was startled. "I thought you'd bristle at the idea. I know how much you love your work."

"I do love my work, but you're right. If we're going to do this, someone needs to be in charge."

"Exactly! Oh, my dear, I am so glad you understand."

"But that's just it. I'm not sure I do understand. With Michael's help, I've coordinated the construction renovation on every expansion we've done at Disco Diva, but it was nowhere near the size of what we're considering. I'm not sure I'm capable of handling it."

"Sweetheart, you won't need to handle all of it. Even I don't get all of the rigmarole involved in these things. But I surround myself with talented people who do—that's the key. All you have to do is be clear on the concept, the theme, the vision you have for the project. Then you just make sure your team is following that vision."

"My team?"

"Yes. We must assemble a team. We cannot do this on our own. I spoke with Lyle Decker, and unfortunately, he's unavailable. But he highly recommended the owner of an established firm. Lyle said the fellow is "seasoned," in his late sixties and semiretired, but we might be able to convince him to take on the project if it interests him. I've already placed a call and scheduled a meeting. I hope that's okay with you?"

"Lily, I'm excited about this—really I am. It's just that I'm feeling things are moving too fast. We haven't even discussed the terms or the expenses or anything legal yet. Shouldn't we do that first?"

And then there is the issue of my husband …

"Of course, dear. My apologies—I'm afraid I've gotten ahead of myself. I've never funded a project as exciting as this, but I have been involved in dozens of developments that cost triple what this will most likely cost, so I have something of an edge on you as to what to expect. Please, bear with me if I get on a tangent and lose you—stop and ask questions whenever you need to, okay? Now, let me share with you how I see the next few weeks, and you tell me if we are on the same page."

They spent the next two hours discussing the arrangements Lily had in mind—terms, timelines, logistics, expense categories, and a host of things that made Susan's head spin.

"But I don't know a thing about the restaurant business, or how to run a dance club, or the expenses required for—"

"My dear child, haven't you been listening to me? You don't need to know about those aspects, at least not in-depth. That's why we hire a knowledgeable team. But my guess is that you and Michael will learn a great deal in the coming months. Take it one step at a time and enjoy the experience! It's going to be quite exhilarating!"

Michael, Susan thought, gazing out the window.

Lily referred to notes in front of her. "Our first order of business is to hire the project manager—he'll help us nail down a definitive timeline and develop our expense projections. After that, we need to begin looking at architects to design the space. You'll work closely with the PM, and it will be his job to begin to put all the pieces together. An experienced PM will know what we have to do every step of the way, so you won't have to worry about anything falling through the cracks. Your job will be to make sure he fully comprehends your vision."

Lily could see Susan's look of fear. "Don't worry. I'll still be around. But I have confidence you'll get into the groove much faster than you think. You know what you want, you know what this can become, and you've been living the Disco Diva dream for years—it's as natural to you as breathing. So, here's a question … how do you want people to *feel* when they walk into the museum?"

Susan cocked her head and bit her lower lip as she thought.

"I'm not talking about the restaurant, the store, or the salon," Lily added. "Let's begin with the museum."

"Well, I always thought it should look like—"

"I didn't say 'look,'" Lily interrupted. "I said 'feel.' Close your eyes, take a deep breath, and tell me how you want your visitors to *feel*."

"Happy. Joyful. Excited. Young."

"What makes people feel happy, joyful, excited, and young?" Lily whispered. "What memories do you wish to conjure up?"

"Memories of love," Susan said quietly.

"How so?" Lily leaned back, jotting notes on a pad of linen stationery attached to a gold clipboard.

"You know … love. The love of music, fashion, art, dancing … oh, how we loved to dance."

"Yes, but in that era people also loved things far less pleasant— more destructive."

"That may be true, but not everyone. There was so much about the time that was good. It wasn't all horribly dark and decadent."

"I know." Lily folded her hands on the clipboard. "However, a great deal of it was. We can't change that aspect of history. I've spoken with someone at the PR firm I use, and they've given us some advice for how we can best combat any negative perceptions." She stood, walked over to the window, and looked out, then turned back to

Susan. "We're going to need to address the sex and drugs and such in a way that leaves no doubt we do not advocate that part of the era."

"I don't," Susan said. "I say that all the time when people from the press visit the salon—I've always made that clear."

"I know, dear. That's why I brought it up. It's a topic we are going to have to address more than once as we proceed. I'd rather we plan proactively for all contingencies, rather than reactively. Agreed?"

"Agreed."

"Now, the firm is working on some public positioning statements for us to use in our materials. We'll be talking about this more than a few times, but I wouldn't worry about it now." She picked up the clipboard again and sat down. "Okay, you want people to *feel* love. Now, what do you want the project to *look* like, the first impression visitors will get?"

"I think the entrance needs to be outfitted with black lights. You know, the lights that make neon colors glow—"

"Yes, dear, I remember black lights," Lily said. "From what I recall, they were quite popular in the sixties."

"Yes, but a lot of the clubs in New York used them in the seventies. The effect was always stunning. We could have the entrance to the museum as a kind of wide corridor, with black lights and posters of the era—you know, music posters, film posters, artwork, things that depict the time."

"Brilliant!"

"Lighting effects in tandem with music was a big thing too. Do you know what a lighting Translator is?" Susan asked.

Lily chuckled. "Most likely not what I think it is."

"It's a piece of equipment designed by an artist named Ron

Ferri." Susan's eyes sparkled. "It coded music into electrical pulses that activated a flashing light system. It was all very technical … and very cool."

"Am I to assume from your excitement that we have a … Translator?" Lily asked.

"We do!" Susan exclaimed. "I found one at an auction years ago in Greenwich Village. I hope it works … it's been packed away for a long time. If it doesn't, we could still have strobe lights, mirrored globes, and smoke machines. And lots of neon."

Lily once again began jotting notes on her clipboard as Susan continued. "The entrance music needs to be chosen carefully as well. It'll set the tone for the rest of the museum experience. The sound system needs to be state of the art. And I think music needs to be a part of every display. Have you been to the Rock and Roll Hall of Fame in Cleveland?"

"I visited last week."

"Last week?"

"I was in Cleveland on business and, knowing of this impending project, I made time to see it. They did quite an amazing job on the facility, don't you think?"

"I do. I like the way every artist is highlighted in a specific scene that depicts the era and their music. I just don't see how that will work for my collection. At least I can't quite wrap my brain around it yet."

"You will, dear, in time. The more we discuss it, the better. We'll probably have to take an inventory of your entire collection as well." She jotted a note. "Unless you already have that?"

"I do, somewhat … for insurance purposes."

"Brilliant!"

Brilliant was becoming Lily's word of the day.

They discussed the layout of the Rock and Roll Hall of Fame and compared it to their vision for the new Disco Diva.

"We keep calling it 'the new Disco Diva,' but it's going to be much more than the salon," Susan said. "Do you think we need a new name for the entire facility, or should every entity have its own name?"

Lily looked at her watch. "I think that's something we should continue to think and pray about, but for now we need to table this discussion and prepare to meet a potential team member. The gentleman Lyle recommended as our project manager is in town on business, and I never overlook what I clearly see as a God-cidence. I've invited him for coffee so we can check him out."

"Today?" Susan hadn't expected to be meeting anyone.

"Any minute, actually. Lyle says he's 'old-school'—right up my alley." She grinned. "Which means he should be buzzing the intercom right about—"

Franco entered the room with the flamboyant flourish that always made Susan smile.

"Excuse me, madame, but your guest is at the gate."

"Please buzz him in. We'll take the meeting in the den."

"I'm going to freshen up." Susan reached for her purse. "You're something, Lily Peyton. I can't believe you." She pecked her friend quickly on the cheek before making a beeline for the guest bathroom.

"You can join us in the den," Lily called after her. Then she stood and walked majestically out of the room.

Chapter 15

A man was talking to Lily when Susan entered the den, his back to her. She could see Lily smiling over his shoulder—laughing, in fact. A good sign.

"Hello, dear, I want you to meet Mr. Power. Ryan Power. This is Susan Anderson, the owner of Disco Diva."

Once again Susan found herself face-to-face with the man whose dashing good looks and familiar scent left her speechless. Today he wore a suit she would almost bet was Hugo Boss. He sure knew how to accentuate his positive features.

"Pleased to meet you, Susan." He extended his hand warmly. "But I'm afraid I've slightly misled you, Mrs. Peyton. Susan and I have met before—twice, actually. I had my hair cut at the famous Disco Diva last month, and we ran into each other at one of the casinos a few weeks ago."

"You've met?" Lily tapped her index finger against her cheek. "Interesting."

"If this is Lyle's idea of 'seasoned,'" Susan said, "someone needs to call him a doctor."

Ryan laughed. "The seasoned guy is Charles Carrington. He started the firm, but his son and I pretty much run it. He called me a couple of hours ago when he realized he couldn't make the meeting.

As soon as he described your project, I knew he had to be talking about you and your salon."

Lily was still trying to make connections. "You ran into each other again where …?"

"At the Silver Spur the night of Michael's party—right after you left, as a matter of fact. You most likely crossed paths," Susan said. "You were at a bachelor party, right?" she asked Ryan. "How did that go?"

"Fine. We had a good time." He laughed. "I think."

"Someone is getting married?" Lily asked.

"Yes. Phillip Carrington, the owner's son. He's getting married this weekend at the Bellagio. That's why we're all in town. We've been driving back and forth a lot these past few weeks, getting things set up." He chuckled, shaking his head. "It's morphed into quite an event."

"Back and forth from where?" Lily sipped her tea.

"California. Malibu, to be exact."

"I see. So, tell us about your business."

"Actually, Phillip and I own a few businesses together. Our fathers are friends, and we kind of grew up together. Mostly, we travel around looking for retro artwork and memorabilia."

"Like antique dealers?" Lily asked.

"Kind of, but not really. We don't look at much of anything made before 1950. We're mostly interested in pop culture, music, fashion, film stuff—things like that. It keeps me busy between development projects. But my wandering days may soon be over, at least for a year or two. I've been asked to oversee a new Andy Warhol museum being built in New York."

"New York?" Susan asked. "There's already a Warhol museum in Pittsburgh."

"I know, but there's a contingency of New York aficionados who want to fund another one." Ryan smiled. "I'm still deliberating over the project."

"I have several of Andy's original sketches in my collection," Susan said. "He was far different in real life than what has been written."

"I saw some of your photos with him." Ryan edged closer to her. "How well did you know him? I'm not sure I've ever heard anyone refer to him so familiarly."

"We spoke often. We had mutual friends. He was actually quite shy. He'd sketch on anything available so as not to look you in the eye. You know—napkins, menus, even clothing. He once drew a cartoon figure on the breast pocket of a new Calvin Klein blazer I'd bought only just that day."

"Do you still have it?"

"Of course. I have everything from my years in New York." She looked away. "Well, almost everything."

"I can't believe it."

"I have no reason to lie to you."

"Mr. Warhol did Susan's portrait," Lily offered. "It's a huge thing—hanging in her living room."

Ryan stared as though he were seeing Susan for the first time.

"A commissioned portrait?"

"Yes." Susan glared at Lily.

"Don't look at me like that, dear. He needs to know what he's dealing with. This isn't your typical collection, Mr. Power."

"I would agree. What took you to New York?" he asked Susan. "Were you in the theater? Did your family live there? I would love to see the rest of your collection."

"Mr. Power." Lily raised her hand as though to silence him. "I can appreciate your desire to know all about my dear friend and the history behind her collection—trust me, the items you saw in Disco Diva are merely icing on the cake. However, we don't have a lot of time to spend reminiscing at this stage, so let's cut to the chase, shall we? We're talking about much more than a museum—you know that now. We want to develop a multimillion-dollar complex."

Ryan stared at her like a young boy looking at a Red Ryder BB gun at Christmas.

"If you have the time now, I'd like to invite you to walk through the proposed building with us so we can share more of our vision with you. Then, if you find our unique project more intriguing than a second Andy Warhol museum, perhaps you can tell us why you're the best person for this job and why we should hire you."

Walking through the cavernous belly of the White Elephant once again exhilarated Susan. She'd been through it several times with Lily, and seeing it now through Ryan's eyes caused her blood to pump even faster.

"This space is phenomenal!" he exclaimed, running ahead as they entered the main floor.

"I've been saying that for months," Lily called out, "but it wasn't until I heard Susan's vision that I knew what to do with it."

"Do you have stats on the structure?" he asked.

"I've assembled everything you'll need to make a thorough assessment for your bid."

"My bid?" Ryan stopped in his tracks. "You're getting quotes?"

Lily smiled. "Isn't that the way it's done?"

"Yes, it is, but I guess I figured since Lyle recommended our company—"

"Mr. Power, while I fully trust my dear friend Lyle, I'm no fool when it comes to business. I may be an old woman, but don't confuse being around the block a few times with being at the end of the road."

"I'm sorry. I didn't mean to imply that. It's just—"

"What, Mr. Power?" She cocked her head. "You're not used to competing for a job?"

"Trust me, Mrs. Peyton, there is no competition. I'm the man for the project."

"Then you'll just have to convince us of that, won't you?"

Susan was already convinced. The man was young, yet he possessed a wealth of knowledge not only about pop culture but also about construction, project development, and particularly about museums. The fact that he used a blank *Andy Warhol Idea Book* for keeping notes wasn't lost on her. She'd bought many throughout the years from an online store and used them for her journals.

It seemed, at least to her, that they would be hard pressed to find someone better. Still, she trusted Lily to know best. It would be Lily who paid Ryan's salary for the duration of the project—or the salary of whoever they hired.

"When were you born?" Susan asked him.

Ryan laughed. "I don't think you're allowed to ask that."

"Oh. I'm sorry, I'm not? Uh ..."

"It's an equal opportunity discrimination thing, dear," Lily explained. "We can't ask his age, religion, political stance, or any number of things."

"I agree with you, it's ridiculous." He continued to inspect the building, jotting down notes all the while.

"I didn't say it was ridiculous."

"No, but your voice and body language screamed it loud and clear. I was just giving you a hard time. I was born in New York City on June 6, 1981. I'm a card-carrying member of the young Republicans, and I'm not sure what I'd say for the religion category—agnostic, I guess, or maybe on the fence." He laughed. "Is that a denomination these days?"

Susan stared. "You were born in New York City?"

"Yes." He began to walk the width of the room, placing one foot in front of another.

"How fascinating," Lily said. "But we already have the exact measurements, Mr. Power."

"I know. I just want to check out something. And call me Ryan, please."

"Did you grow up there?" Susan followed along beside him as he measured.

"For a few years. We moved to Los Angeles when I started high school."

"Excuse me, but I'm going to wait in the car while you folks travel down memory lane," Lily said. "Susan, will you walk me out? Take your time, Mr. Power."

"Who else are we considering?" Susan asked when they were out of Ryan's earshot.

Lily grinned. "No one, dear."

"So you're faking him out?"

"Keeping him humble, that's all."

"Do you think he's right for the project?" Susan asked when they reached the Rolls. "He's pretty young."

"Pretty and young … a lethal combination for certain."

Susan giggled. "Shame on you, Lily Peyton."

"Old does not mean blind, dear. I think he's exactly what we need, and contrary to what I said back there, I trust Lyle's recommendation implicitly. But what do you think of the young man?" With Franco's assistance, Lily slid carefully into the backseat of her luxurious automobile.

"I'm not sure yet, but he seems to know what he's doing." Susan stared back toward the building. "We'll see."

"Go and spend some time walking through the building with him. Pick his brain, share more of your vision, and see how he responds. Ask a lot of questions about his experience, what he would do in specific cases. I'm fine out here."

"I'm not sure I know what to ask. You're the pro when it comes to—"

"Stop this instant!" Lily raised her voice, startling Susan. "We've already had this discussion. You know what you want—what you see in your mind's eye. Simply convey that to him. But there's no need to tell him we aren't looking at anyone else. Let him put together a solid proposal for us. I want to see what he brings to the table."

Susan stepped back as Franco closed the car door. She gave a mock salute to Lily as she turned to head back inside.

They'd spent almost an hour inside the White Elephant, going from floor to floor, discussing how Susan envisioned the project. She was particularly gratified that Ryan paid attention to the views from each level as well as the direction of the sun. His attention to detail was impressive, and the more they talked the more certain she felt that he was their ace in the hole.

"Enough about me," he said, suddenly stopping to lean against the wall. "When did you live in New York? I'm assuming with your knowledge of the City that you lived in Manhattan?"

"I did, for six years or so. I moved there right out of high school in '74. And I left before you were born—fall of 1980."

"Ah, the height of the disco era. That explains a lot. I can't wait to hear more of your stories. What a rush that must have been—to be in the heart of it all, where it all started."

"It didn't actually start there."

"I know, I know, but Studio 54 made it famous in New York. From the photos in your salon, I'm assuming you were there a time or two?"

A time or two? How much was she willing to tell this young man?

"Yes," she said. "I've been to the Studio."

"Incredible! I am truly jealous! I think my dad was there once with some folks on business, but he's totally clueless about what a historic place it was."

"I have quite a bit of Studio 54 memorabilia in my storage unit."

"Like what?" He was practically hyperventilating. "This is so cool … I can't believe it."

Susan smiled, enjoying his interest. Michael never expressed much interest in the things she had brought with her from New York. In fact, he'd visited her storage units only a few times throughout the years to help her swap out pieces of furniture. He still thought she was keeping a lot of useless junk.

"I don't want to leave Lily in the car any longer than necessary," she said, "so perhaps we should head out. Do you have enough information to develop your proposal? I know the sooner we can get it from you the better. We'd like to make our decision soon."

"Susan." He faced her. "I'm sensing Lily holds the purse strings on this project, and that's okay. She's a savvy chick—er, woman—and I like her. But this is your baby, right?"

"My … baby?"

"Yeah, the vision—it's yours, right?"

"Yes, it is. But without Lily I—"

"I understand. You don't need to tell me your arrangement. That's not what I'm fishing for. I just want you to know something." He put the notebook under his arm and gently held her by the shoulders. "I want you to know that I can do this. I'm not blowing smoke. I'm not a hotheaded … what did you call me?"

Susan grinned. "Whippersnapper."

"Exactly—I'm not that. But I'm the best person for this job. I love the era, and I grew up around this music. It was my mom's favorite kind of music when I was a kid—until she got into jazz in my teens."

He smiled and stepped back from her, gripping the notebook. "Also, I know what I'm doing. I've been the project manager on a half dozen developments."

"But nothing this big."

"No, nothing this big. But I know I can do it."

"What about the Andy Warhol museum?"

"Anyone can do that. This is a once-in-a-lifetime experience—and I want it, Susan. You're not going to find anyone who has a better appreciation or understanding of pop culture—or of the era. I mean, this was a time that absolutely defined today's culture, and it's worth preserving." He faced her like a lawyer making a closing argument, finishing with a passionate plea. "I understand this, Susan. *I get it.* Let me do this. Give me a chance."

It had been a long time since someone had so clearly articulated what Susan had been trying to do for so many years. He *did* get it. He was quite a gifted young man.

"Your parents must be proud of you." She reached up and tucked a piece of his hair behind his ear as though he were a little boy and was surprised when he grabbed her wrist.

"We're not talking about my parents. We're talking about us. From the moment I walked into your salon I felt some kind of connection to you. I know you felt it too. I'm not one to believe in what you and Lily call God-cidences, but there's a reason for us being thrown together like this." He waved the hand with the notebook in it. "I can feel it in my bones. Tell me you don't."

"Uh, I ... I'm not sure what to say."

"Say what's on your heart. Say you know I'm right for this job."

God help her, she wasn't certain about much these days, but she had to agree with him.

Chapter 16

"Are you going to tell me what's up, or do I have to do something drastic—like go on strike or threaten to quit?" Loretta tore open the packet of Paul Newman salad dressing and ended up squirting it all over the table. "Oops ... sorry."

"Nothing's up." Susan grabbed a container of yogurt from the refrigerator and sat next to her friend at the supply room lunch table. "It's a busy Saturday, that's all."

"Give me a break. I'm not just talking about today, and you know that darn well. The pet guys are moving out at the end of the month. Did you or did you not lease their space? You go from talking about expanding the salon to not talking at all. You're like a schizo."

Susan sniffed. "I've been talking."

"Yes, but not about anything important."

"Gee, thanks a lot."

"Look, don't make me spell it out. You took yesterday afternoon off—a Friday afternoon. When did you last do that? I'll tell you when—never! Something's up."

"Puh-leeze!"

"It's true. Are you and Michael okay? I haven't seen him for awhile."

"We're fine. It's not Michael."

"So you admit it's something."

"Don't put words in my mouth, Loretta. I simply said Michael is fine. We're fine. Don't worry."

Loretta picked at the salad in front of her, not making eye contact. "Susan, if you're planning something that's going to affect the salon—and my livelihood—don't you think I deserve to know about it? We've been together a long time. I'm not just one of the girls … am I?"

"Of course you're not," Susan assured her. "Loretta, I'm sorry; I just can't talk about it yet. But I can tell you it's a good thing—a very good thing."

"Then why can't you tell me? Don't you trust me?"

"That's not it at all." She placed her hand over her friend's. "Please don't think that. I just have to do something first, before I can share my exciting news with you. I promise, we'll talk soon."

"You're sure everything's okay?" Loretta ate a few more bites of salad before getting up from the table and tossing her bowl into the trash can.

"More than okay. Really."

As soon as Susan told Michael her plans it would be okay. She was still waiting for the right time to let him know, but things were moving fast and she was running out of time. Decisions needed to be made, decisions she knew needed to be made with her husband.

Tomorrow was Sunday. She'd be meeting with Lily in the afternoon to finalize some things on the project. And Monday was her day to spend with Michael.

She'd tell him then.

She had to.

After their brief lunch break, Loretta and Susan returned to their stations just as a frantic Shannon emerged from the reception area.

"There was a water pipe break at the Carlyle," she shrieked. "They just called to see if we can handle any of their appointments today. The phone is already ringing off the hook. What should I tell them?"

"Slow down, Shannon," Susan said. "It's going to be okay."

The Carlyle was the main salon at one of the biggest hotels in Vegas—and their main competitor. Susan was friends with the salon manager and empathized with him for the havoc this situation would cause.

"Call Zachary and tell him we'll take as many of his clients as possible, but he's going to have to send us only those who *must* have service today. Not those who *want* service today—those who *must* have service."

Shannon gulped. "Uh, how do we know the difference?"

"Zach will know the difference. Let him prioritize. Call Carla. See if she's feeling better and can put in a few hours, and I'll call a few of my regulars I know can rebook for next week. That'll open a few slots."

"I can think of three or four of mine that could rebook," Loretta offered.

"Thanks, Loretta. Go with Shannon and show her what she can open on your schedule. And, Shannon, please call my house and leave a message for Michael. Fill him in on the emergency and tell him I'll be late. And, Shannon …"

"What?" the girl said, swallowing hard.

"Calm down. You're doing a great job."

—*mm*—

Loretta put her arm lovingly around Shannon's shoulder and walked her back to the reception area of the salon.

"Honey, don't let this stress you out, okay? It's part of the territory from time to time. We want it known around town that we may be called Disco Diva but we are not divas. We are here to serve our community, and we can be depended on, especially during emergencies. Okay?"

"I understand." Shannon smiled and saluted dramatically.

"I'm serious. This isn't a game. Emergencies like this are remembered for a long time, and I know Susan wants us to be remembered as people who care enough to help."

"I'm sorry. I didn't mean to laugh. I know Susan cares. Especially about showgirls—she's really got a thing about showgirls."

Shannon took her seat at the reception desk. Loretta stood behind her, looking at the names booked.

"Thank God she does. Some of those gals are out here all alone. They're hungry for someone to listen to them, to give them good advice, and to care without expecting anything in return."

"And sometimes even pray with them. I've seen her when she thinks no one is looking," Shannon whispered. "That's pretty cool, you know?"

"It is. We might have a lot of fun here, but Susan takes this all very seriously. This is more than a beauty salon. It's her ministry outreach to young women in the Vegas community. She thinks of them as her children, and it breaks her heart every time one of them comes to her in pain."

"Last Sunday in church the pastor was telling the story about the woman who washed Jesus' feet," Shannon mused as Loretta put check marks next to the names of customers she thought could be rescheduled. "He said we should look for times when we could do something unselfish like that for someone else. Fixing hair might not seem like a big thing to some people, but it's kind of like washing the feet of somebody in need, isn't it? Kind of?"

Loretta couldn't answer. She prayed the hearty bear hug she bestowed on the young woman said what she couldn't.

The last client left Disco Diva at nine that night, followed by Loretta and three other stylists who were scraping bottom.

"Don't worry," Susan told them. "I'll lock up. Go home and take a hot bubble bath."

"Whew. That was a rush," she said aloud as she transferred clean towels from the washer to the dryer and reloaded the washer. She had turned on both machines and picked up a broom to sweep when she heard a knock on the back door. She checked the surveillance camera screen—Tragic Tina. She really had to stop referring to her like that. One day she might actually say it out loud.

"Coming," she shouted, moving to unlock the door.

"I was driving by and saw your car and the lights on, and … oh, I'm sorry. It's late." Tina turned to go. "I'll come back later."

"No, wait. It's okay. Come in." Susan ushered Tina in and

pointed toward a chair. "Do you want a cold soda? I was just about to have one."

Tina nodded, head bowed, as Susan opened the refrigerator and removed two cans of diet soda.

"Need a glass?"

"No, this is fine, thanks."

The sound of two cans being opened … *pop* … *pop* … echoed in the silence.

It was Saturday night, a prime time for Vegas production shows, and Tina's position in the Folies was significant. She should be on stage at the Tropicana right now, not at Disco Diva. Something was wrong.

"What's the matter, honey? Shouldn't you be at work?"

"I, um, took a sick day."

"You're sick?"

"No. Well …" Tina's lips trembled as tears filled her eyes. "I went to an abortion clinic today."

Susan's heart leaped to her throat as she put down her soda and grabbed Tina's available hand.

"Oh, honey, I am so sorry … so sorry."

She'd suspected Tina might be pregnant the first time they met. Getting sick that first day hadn't been just about her hair trauma. They had talked a great deal about children the second time she came back, just a couple of weeks ago. In fact, Susan had shared about losing three babies early in their marriage—how hard it had been on both her and Michael. She and Tina had also talked briefly about abortion. Tina had asked what she felt about it. And Susan had told her what she told every young woman who sat in her chair.

"I don't feel abortion should be an option. No matter how you spin it, abortion is taking the life of a living being. It's okay if you're not ready to be a mother—but allow someone who is have the opportunity to raise the child."

She could recite those three sentences in her sleep, she'd said them so many times. If the conversation continued, she was always ready to share Scripture and stories she had from years of counseling young women. She tried to share as much information as possible and always kept a supply of business cards on hand to distribute.

"If you know someone who has to make a choice, please give this to them." She'd placed a card in Tina's hand. "The Hope Pregnancy Center is owned by a good friend of mine, and it's not far from here. Thelma Vick does pregnancy counseling from a Christian perspective."

"Very pro-life then." Tina looked at the card.

"Yes, she is. But she's also very pro-information and very nonjudgmental."

"Thanks. I'll pass this on."

Tina had placed the business card in her jacket pocket and changed the subject.

That had been two weeks ago. Now Susan's heart was breaking—not only for Tina, who would be forever changed because of her choice, but for the child of God who would never experience life.

"Should you be up?" Susan fought back tears. "Did you drive here? Shouldn't you be lying down? I can take you home."

"No. I'm fine." Tina gently pulled her hand from Susan's and took a sip of soda. "Before I left my apartment this morning, I went to the Web site on the card you gave me. I couldn't believe what I saw." She put her hand on her stomach and continued. "At eight weeks, like I am, a baby actually has fingers and toes and looks like … a baby."

She began to cry. "I couldn't do it. I went to the clinic, but I couldn't go through with it. I've been driving around all day. Then I saw your lights …"

Susan took the can of soda from the young woman and set it on the floor, leaned over, and wrapped her arms around Tina. She whispered in her ear, "You did the right thing, honey. It might be confusing right now, but you'll work it out. I know you will. And I'll be here if you need me."

Tina wept like a little girl being held by her mother as Susan patted her back and rubbed her hair, gently crying along with her and silently thanking God.

———

It was almost midnight by the time Susan made it home. Michael was already at work. She'd hoped to have some time to talk with him this evening before he left, but Tina had needed her and she was glad she'd been there to help. As a next step, Tina had agreed to meet with Thelma, and for that Susan was thankful. Thelma was a good woman who would be able to guide Tina through the next few weeks and months, no matter what decision she eventually made.

Michael had stuck a note on the refrigerator with their signature message magnet, a silly pair of three-dimensional red rubber lips.

Sweetie Pie:

Sorry to have missed you again. This is getting to be nuts, don't you think? We haven't seen each

*other in days. I'm sorry I've been so busy—and I
know things have been crazy at the salon. What do
you say we hang out together tomorrow? I'll take a
sick day (i.e., night). Let's do something out of the
ordinary—like sleep together at the same time (and
I do mean sleep, although hanky-panky would be
welcome if I could remember how to do it). Maybe
we can go to church and catch a movie later or do
something normal for a change. What do you say?
I'll see you in the morning at eight—same bat time,
same bat channel.*

Love you,

M

Susan smiled at the note, then frowned in confusion. Michael never
took a sick day. Even when he was sick, Michael never took a sick day.
The fact that he actually suggested it frightened her. She prayed he
was okay, that he wasn't really sick … and that he hadn't found out
anything about her project with Lily before she could share the news.

His note didn't sound angry, though. Perhaps this was a God-
cidence—the "right time" she'd been looking for.

She sighed, both hopeful and apprehensive.

It was time to get this show on the road.

Chapter 17

Susan was pulling hot cinnamon rolls out of the oven when Michael walked in the next morning.

"I could smell those outside!" Michael put down his lunch box and took off his jacket.

"Gosh, I hope not!" Susan grinned. "If that's true, we need to replace those rubber thingies around the door."

"I'm surprised you're up," he said. "Figured I'd find you under the covers, snoring."

"I don't snore."

"Fine, you don't snore." He wrapped his arms around her and kissed her head. "What time did you finally get in? I got Shannon's message—sounds like a mess. I was running late myself. Didn't walk out the door until quarter to eleven."

"I just missed you, then." She squeezed him gently and pulled away. "Coffee's fresh. Pour us a couple of mugs and have a seat. I'm going to put icing on these rolls while they're still warm."

She cut the tip off the clear plastic bag containing the powdered sugar icing and began to squeeze it atop the bubbling cinnamon rolls.

"Man, oh, man, that should be a perfume. Eau de Cinnamon." Michael breathed deeply as he picked up the coffee carafe.

"Funny you should say that. I was reading something the other day where they conducted a survey of scents and found men were more attracted to the scent of hot pizza than the top five perfumes available today." Susan placed a hot roll in front of her husband and smiled.

"I rest my case." He took a bite. Icing dripped down his chin.

"Be careful, honey, they're still hot." Susan dunked a piece of roll into her coffee.

"So, tell me about the emergency." Michael kicked off his shoes and put his feet up on the chair opposite him at the table.

They sipped coffee, ate three cinnamon rolls each, and discussed her crazy day at the salon, including her late-night visitor.

"I don't know what she's going to do. I'm just glad she didn't go through with it."

"Suze, you've got to be careful what you tell those girls. They're big enough to make their own decisions. I hate to see you get involved where you don't belong. One of these days …"

"What? One of these days, what?" She got up to pour herself another cup of coffee.

"I don't want to argue, kiddo. I'm just saying, one of these days your meddling might have an adverse reaction."

"Michael, I don't meddle! These girls ask my opinion. Some of them don't have anyone who will talk truth into their lives."

"I'm sorry, Susan. Don't be angry with me. Did you see my note?"

"I did."

"So, what do you think?"

"About?"

"About spending the day and night with your husband, that's what!"

He got up and walked behind her, rubbing her shoulders as she slowly relaxed. "I have an idea. Let's hop in the car right now and head out of town. We have today and tomorrow—and how about if you call in sick on Tuesday? That'll give us three full days together. I can't remember the last time we had three days together, can you?"

Susan thought about that. Michael was right; they needed time together. But she had planned to meet with Lily around two that afternoon to discuss whether to hire Ryan Power and to finalize the verbiage on their contract. Monday was the day Tina would be going to see Thelma Vick, and Susan had promised to go with her. Tuesday she had a full schedule of clients ...

"You know I can't call in sick," she said. "I own the place, remember? And Tuesdays are busy for me since I have Mondays off."

"Okay, then, I'll settle for today and tomorrow. Go pack an overnight bag, and let's hit the road. I say we drive for a few hours in any direction and stop at the first hotel with a pool and hot tub. We'll pretend it's a second honeymoon." He playfully kissed her ear while pulling her toward the bedroom. "Come on, let's be spontaneous—throw a few things in a bag and—"

"I can't, Michael. I'm sorry. I'd love to. It sounds like fun. But I've got other commitments. Maybe next week?"

"Next week I won't be off on Sunday."

"Well, we could go away next Monday, spend the day doing something fun."

Michael sat down at the table, ran his fingers through his hair, and sighed.

"Susan, we hardly see one another anymore. We used to spend time together in the morning before you left for the shop, but you've been gone before eight every day for weeks."

"I know, I know. It's been busy. But I see you at night before you leave."

"When? When do you see me at night? Look at the calendar, Susan." He pointed to the one on the wall. "See the red dots? They indicate the nights you came home in time to see me before I had to leave. How many red dots are there?"

"Two." She lowered her head.

"Exactly. Two. In the last month." His eyebrows gathered and he crossed his arms. "Now, are you going to tell me what's up or continue the charade?"

Susan chewed on her lower lip. She didn't want this to be the mood when she told Michael about the new Disco Diva. She wanted him to be as happy as she was about it.

"You're right," she said. "I have been working too much. Let me make a few calls and clear my schedule for today and most of tomorrow. But, Michael, I really want to be back tomorrow afternoon to take Tina to Thelma's, okay? This is a human life we're talking about—and she's all alone out here!"

"She's not alone. She has dozens of fellow chorus girls in the Folies."

"That's not the same, and you know it. Please. She needs me."

"I need you too, Susan."

She wrapped her arms around him. "I know, Michael."

He pulled back and looked into her eyes. "So you're saying we can head out now ... as long as we're back by tomorrow afternoon?"

"Yes. For points unknown. Let me pack us an overnight bag and make a call or two and we'll be on our way. Is there gas in the car?"

"I'll go fill up the tank and get the cooler from the garage. We can stop on the way out of town for ice and car munchies."

Susan embraced her husband again, holding him close, smelling his aftershave, and appreciating the blessing he was in her life. Then she laughed as he swung her around and then bounded out of the kitchen.

He was right—they did need more time together. Time to relax, to laugh, to have fun. And to talk.

This little trip could be just what they needed to get them back on the same page.

—*m*—

As soon as Michael left, Susan called Lily and explained the situation. "I'm sorry to cancel our meeting today."

"Canceling isn't a problem. But I am upset that you've waited so long to tell Michael."

"I know. I'm sorry. I'll tell him today. I promise."

"It's not me you have to make promises to, dear. Michael is your husband. I should have known by the way you were acting that you hadn't told him. I feel somewhat responsible."

"Don't! None of this is your fault. Besides, I'm sure it will be fine. Michael's going to be as excited about this as I am—especially when he hears I'm cutting back on my hours at the salon. He's been after me to do that for a long time."

"Hmm," Lily said.

"I've got to hang up now. I'll talk to you tomorrow when we get back."

She was standing at the kitchen sink washing her hands, their overnight bag on the floor by her feet, when Michael returned.

"Ready?" He smiled like a kid on his way to Disneyland.

"Yes, sir! We're off to see the wizard!" She laughed, genuinely happy to spend time with her husband and share the good news with him. It wasn't every day that someone funded a multimillion-dollar project like this—an endeavor that could earn them considerable income in the coming years and help them prepare for their retirement. Maybe by that time they could discuss Michael's dream to build a house on the land his parents had left them.

Chapter 18

They took off north on Interstate 15, turning off on U.S. 93 and then taking the famous State Route 375, a ninety-eight-mile stretch of road unofficially dubbed the Extraterrestrial Highway. The entire highway was a popular gathering place for UFO enthusiasts because of its proximity to Nellis Air Force Base's top-secret location, known as Area 51, near Rachel, Nevada. Susan and Michael liked the drive because it was a smooth road and a straight shot out of town.

"Oh, look!" Susan shouted after they'd been on the road awhile. "A yard sale. Pull in, Michael."

He dutifully maneuvered the car into the driveway.

"I can't believe we found these," she said fifteen minutes later, sliding back into the car with a pair of lemon yellow, glitter-encrusted platform shoes.

Michael laughed. "I can't believe we found a yard sale in the middle of the desert that had disco memorabilia."

A few hours later they were lying by the pool at the Pinecrest Motel in Rachel, holding hands and enjoying the silence. Not the most scenic of getaways, it was a small new roadside motel. They had chosen it because it had a clean pool and very few cars in the lot—an indication they might have some privacy. They'd been right. They had the place almost to themselves.

"Yum," Susan murmured, half asleep. "This is nice."

"Told you so," Michael mumbled behind the magazine folded open on his face.

"I love you," Susan said.

"Love you more," Michael responded.

"Do *not*," Susan whispered, falling gently into slumber.

"Do too." Michael moved the magazine off his face and rolled over onto his side to look at his wife. She was stretched out on the chaise lounge, wearing a one-piece cobalt blue bathing suit, a neon floral caftan draped across her legs. She had the body of a woman half her age. He thought that was most likely due to the fact she worked at a place where periodic dance exercise kept her moving throughout the day. She sure did love to dance.

And she was a remarkable woman, really. She'd had a vision for Disco Diva, and now she'd built the salon into a Las Vegas landmark, a destination location on more than one tourist map. Her vision had been realized, her dream achieved.

Years ago she'd had another dream—to dance on Broadway. Michael suspected she wasn't focused enough—or ruthless enough—to do what it took to make that dream come true. Instead, she'd moved to Vegas in September of 1980 with several friends who had been hired to dance for the Folies Bergere at the Tropicana. It was hard for him to feel bad about her failed dreams … because it had brought her to him.

The fact that there was ten years' difference in their ages had never seemed to bother either of them. Neither of them had been married before. And though he'd suspected right off that Susan had been involved with someone in New York, she hadn't talked about it.

What she did talk about that night was disco, which seemed to flow through her veins like lifeblood.

For all Michael knew back then, the Village People were a group of itinerant farmers. He didn't really understand her passion—but he was passionate about her. They were married eight months later.

They agreed their past relationships didn't matter. What mattered was their future together, and Michael wanted nothing more than to take care of his beautiful dancing princess. He wanted to give her the dreams of her heart, including a half dozen or more children. Susan eagerly wanted to be a mother, and Michael felt he would make a good father. Alas, that wasn't to be. Losing the last baby had left Susan deathly ill, necessitating a full hysterectomy—and leaving her heartbroken.

Michael wasn't totally oblivious to the psyche of his wife. He knew that, on some level, the young women who came to the salon were like surrogate children to Susan. Through the years she had opened her heart and their home to countless young showgirls who were in transition or crisis. He knew this gave Susan added purpose in her life.

He knew a lot more than she gave him credit for, in fact. But it had taken him awhile to learn—especially when it came to disco.

When they'd started planning Disco Diva over two decades ago, for instance, he wasn't convinced the sound system needed to be as extensive, or as costly, as Susan envisioned.

"Honey, it's just a beauty salon, not a dance club," he remembered saying. He also remembered it was the first and the last time he had called Disco Diva "just a salon."

He'd quickly learned her vision for the business was much bigger than he'd anticipated, this inkling coming on the heels of the first of many disco-era history lessons she would give him year after year.

"*Disco* is short for *discotheque*," she'd informed him. "It comes from the French words *disque*, which means 'record,' and *bibliotheque*, which means 'library.' And, sweetheart, what good is a library of records if the equipment you play them on is tinny? When we play 'I Will Survive' or 'The Hustle,'" she continued, holding up records with colorful jackets and waving them in the air, "I want patrons to feel the heavy bass and the electronic rhythms. Disco music is all about the beat. It's positive energy personified. It's fun. We need a sound system that can handle heavy-duty four-on-the-floor beats."

"But a built-in sound system will cost thousands of dollars, honey," he said gently. "Can't we wait for a few months to see how things go and maybe add something later? We could pick up a nice little stereo and some speakers at Sears."

"Sears?" She stared at him. "You're kidding, right?"

"No, I'm not. Suze, don't you think this is being a little bit obsessive? I understand this hobby is important to you, but—"

"No, you don't understand—not at all. This is going to be a full-time business—a phenomenally successful full-time business. And I'm no more obsessive than you are! You don't think it's obsessive to know verbatim the number of touchdowns or home runs some players have made in their entire career? Or that jersey number eighty-five belongs to Joe Schmo or car number one forty-two is Mario Ferretti's?"

"Andretti, dear." He smiled, pinching his wife lovingly on the cheek. "I'm sorry, kiddo. I didn't realize it meant so much to you."

"I'm sorry I raised my voice." She cuddled into his bear-hug embrace. "But it's much more important than you realize, Michael. It makes sense to put in the system now, while we're adding walls and installing electric. The wires need to be inside the walls, not strung all over the outside like an afterthought. The speakers can be built-in—there and there." She pointed to locations on the walls already marked with big red *X*s. "Maybe we can use less expensive speakers at first, then replace them with better ones, but the holes need to be cut now, while we're designing the space—not later, after it's done."

"Let's not argue over this ever again, okay?" He kissed the top of her head. "I've leased this space for three years, so we might as well go for it and give it all we've got. If it doesn't work out, at least we tried, right?" She kissed him back, and he added, "If we budget wisely, I think we can afford to do everything you want from the get-go. I trust you, honey. I trust you know what your Disco Divas are going to want. You have my full support."

He'd meant it. They had invested in a state-of-the-art sound system for the salon. And Susan had been right—the music and the lighting she'd also convinced him to install made Disco Diva instantly popular. Financial success took considerably longer.

But they'd made it. It had been a successful run, a phenomenally successful run, just as Susan had predicted. After twenty-five years, though, Michael was ready for a new chapter in their lives. He needed it, and his wife needed it too, maybe more than he did. She seemed to be getting more and more preoccupied with business and making money. She smiled less, brooded more—just wasn't herself. She clearly needed a change.

Looking at his wife lying in the sun, seemingly without a care in the world, made him feel certain she would embrace this new chapter as well. She had to be tired of the countless hours she put in at the salon—and the toll it was taking on their marriage. After this time together today, she would be able to see more clearly how right he was to take the initiative to make changes in their life.

"Sweetheart," he quietly asked, "are you awake?"

"Mmm?" she murmured. "Kind of. What is it, baby?"

"Wouldn't it be great if we could do this more often? Take time like this?"

"That would be nice." She sighed.

"I was thinking …"

"Yes?" With no response forthcoming, she opened her eyes. "What were you thinking?"

"I have an idea. Instead of waiting four more years, I was thinking of taking my retirement early. There's talk George wants to sell out, and I think the timing is right. I want to spend time with you, honey."

"Really?" She took off her sunglasses and rubbed her eyes.

"Yes."

"Totally retired, as in having lots of time available?" She leaned up on her elbows.

"Yes. And I have an idea. I want us to work together to build our dream home. I want to make the ranch a reality, Susan."

"The ranch?" She sat up fully, shielding her eyes from the sun.

"The plans I showed you … our home in Henderson. I've gone ahead and had the land subdivided into four parcels. Don't get upset. We can sell off one parcel and use the cash to bankroll the entire project. You won't believe what that land is worth. We'll have enough money to build the house, furnish it from top to bottom, and add a pool if you want. We can even get a few head of cattle, maybe a horse or two."

"Cows?"

He laughed. "Yes, cows, city girl."

"But the salon … our home?"

"We can sell our place—that's a no-brainer. And, Susan, I'd like you seriously to consider selling the salon, or at least cutting back on your hours so you can work with me on this. I'm not sure how soon I can cut myself loose from the Spur, but I want to get started on the house right away, and I'll need your help. There's a ton of stuff to do. We'll be project managers together. It'll be fun, I promise. What do you think?"

Chapter 19

Susan didn't know what to think. But in one crystal-clear moment she understood how people could divorce after years of marriage and sit in a courtroom espousing diametrically opposing thoughts. She didn't know this man, and obviously he didn't know her. How could she ever tell him what she needed to tell him? Was there even a chance he would understand?

The ache in her heart was so intense she couldn't put it into words. But Michael apparently misinterpreted her silence as speechless excitement. As she sat there, at a loss for words, he just rambled on and on about his plans.

When he'd finished, Susan sat up on the poolside lounge chair and took a deep breath.

"Say something, honey." Michael reached over and grabbed her hands. "I guess we don't really have to sell the salon—that was kind of crazy of me to suggest—but Loretta is perfectly capable of taking over. She can handle things if you decide to work less. You know that."

"Yes, I do." She twisted her husband's wedding band around his finger. "Are you losing weight? This never used to be so loose."

"Yeah. Just a few pounds, not so anyone would notice. Guess I've been kind of preoccupied—not knowing how to tell you and all. The last time …"

"I know. I wasn't very receptive, was I?" She pulled her hands away and used the beach towel draped over her chair to wipe the sweat off her face.

"No, can't say that you were." He smiled, shaking his head. "I'm sorry I went behind your back and split the land anyway." He looked down. "But it had to be done, and it's usually a pretty lengthy process. They're pretty stoked about developing those parcels, though."

"I'm sorry too," she said. "But not for the same reason."

He furrowed his brow and cocked his head.

"I need to tell you something, honey." She clasped her hands together and leaned forward. "But I need you to hear me out completely before you say anything, okay?"

"What do you mean?"

"I mean, no matter how crazy this sounds, let me get through what I have to say before you interrupt me. Can you do that, Michael?"

"I think I can. But can I run back to the room first?" He stood.

"Michael, this is important."

"So is mother nature." He leaned down and kissed the top of her head. "I'll be right back, I promise. Hold the thought, or rehearse your words, or pray, or do whatever you need to do, but I really need to go."

She was sitting on the side of the bed when Michael emerged from the bathroom a few minutes later.

"I followed you," she said. "It's cooler in here anyway."

"You can say that again." He sat next to her and kissed her neck. "But we could warm things up."

"I'm sure we could, dear." She smiled and stood, sitting across from him on the second bed. "But I have something I want to tell you. Remember?"

"Sorry. That's right." He reached over and fluffed up the bed pillows, putting them against the headboard. He lay back, put his hands behind his head, and crossed his ankles. "Shoot," he said. "I'm all ears."

"Don't fall asleep, Michael," she warned.

"Wouldn't think of it." He listened as she launched into Lily's offer and the plans for the new Disco Diva entertainment complex, reading notes from inside the fat file she'd brought with her.

By the time she was done talking, he was no longer lounging on the bed.

"You're kidding," he said.

"No, I'm not. Isn't it exciting? Say something, Michael."

"That'll cost millions of dollars."

"We know. She knows. It was her idea—well, offering the White Elephant was, after I told her about my dream to have a dance club. It's a fabulous opportunity, honey. Don't you agree?"

Michael stood and walked around the room a few times before reaching into the ice chest for a cold diet soda.

"Want one?" He held out a can.

"No, thank you."

He opened the can, took a long swallow, and burped.

"Sorry."

"No problem."

"Honey." He put the can of soda on the nightstand and reached for her hand. "I can appreciate that Miss Lily may have more money than sense, but now I need you to hear me. Can I talk now? Are you done?"

"Yes. I'm done. Thank you for letting me get through it all at once. I've been trying to tell you for ages. I don't really know what stopped me."

"Susan, I've watched you build Disco Diva into an amazing place—and I've supported your dream for more than twenty years. Haven't I?"

She nodded. "Yes. You have."

"I understand that you want to leave a legacy, that it's more to you than just a salon. But you've got to understand that this is more to me than just a house."

He looked her square in the eyes. "I've worked at this job day in and day out for years, missed very few days. I've watched you pursue your passion, and I know you love what you do." He took her face in his hands and got close. "But, Susan, when is it my turn? When do I get to do something I've been dreaming of? I want to do this—more than you can imagine. And I don't want to do this project alone. I want you by my side."

He released her face and stood, crossing his arms. "I gave my notice at the casino."

"You gave notice? As in, you're retiring now … already?"

"Yes, honey, don't you see? I'm serious about this. This is our life, our future, our home. I'm not talking about a job."

"But—"

"No buts. I know Disco Diva is important to you. But basically it's still a job … a profession. It's not us. It's not who we are, not our future, not our respite against the storms of life. I want to grow old with you, honey, in a big house with a big yard and some big pets and—"

"You have big dreams too. That's what you're saying." Susan looked up at her husband. He gazed back at her with a love and longing that pierced her heart and opened her eyes. She felt like the blind man who could suddenly see—an analogy she'd never fully understood until this moment.

"I guess I didn't understand what this meant to you," she whispered, swallowing hard.

"Honey," he said softly. "I really want to do this. I want *us* to do it. To make this dream come true together—like when we built Disco Diva. Remember how much fun we had?"

Though he didn't actually say that it was his way or the highway—he would never say something like that—Susan sensed this issue wasn't up for debate. Yet instead of feeling anger or confusion, she felt her heart breaking with the conviction that she had been wrong. That if she continued on her own path, her selfishness might cost her her marriage.

"I understand," she finally said. "I do. I'll let Lily know tomorrow that it was a great offer, but I need to decline."

"You mean that?" He sat down and put his arm around her.

"I mean it—even if I'm not sure I'll make a very good co–project manager for you. But I'll need more than a room called 'Suzie's Stuff,' okay?"

She fought back tears as Michael pulled her close. She didn't want him to see how conflicted she truly was. She knew this was the right thing to do—that her place was beside her husband as they built their home. Yet she couldn't help but feel a sense of loss over what could have been.

"You've got it, sweetie!" He showered the top of her head with kisses. "We'll build you an entire wing, okay? We'll call it 'Suzie's South Forty.'"

He held her close, rocking her gently as his excitement bubbled over. His plans tumbled out like puppies running wild as she listened quietly, wondering how she was going to tell Lily and trying to wrap her brain around this new journey.

Chapter 20

By the time they returned home on Monday afternoon, Susan barely had enough time to shower and get dressed before meeting Tina at Thelma's office. Michael had gone straight to bed, apologizing for being unusually tired. They were both exhausted from talking practically all night. Susan pulled into the parking lot of the Hope Pregnancy Center at the same time as Tina. They got out and hit the buttons on their car security systems, laughing at the simultaneous *beep-beeps.*

"How are you feeling?" Susan asked.

"Better. That trick about eating crackers at night before going to sleep really works. Thanks."

"You're welcome." Susan smiled. "But you'll have to thank Thelma, 'cause that's her secret. She's a wealth of information."

"Susan?" Tina stopped when they came to the door of the center. "I want to thank you for what you're doing. I really do appreciate your support, but …"

"Yes?"

"I need you to know that I haven't made my decision yet. I respect your position on abortion, I really do, but I'm not sure I share it. I don't want you to hate me or to think I'm a bad person or anything."

"Oh, Tina." Susan embraced the lovely showgirl. "I won't hate you. Just as Jesus won't hate you—He loves you unconditionally, no matter what choice you make. I just want you to be aware of every option you have, okay? And the consequences of those options."

Susan stepped back and held her at arm's length, hands on her shoulders. "I don't want you to do anything you don't fully embrace. The decision must be yours alone. But I can encourage you to get all the information—*all* the information—before it's too late."

They entered the clinic holding hands, and Susan said a silent prayer. *Lord, please, be with Tina. Help her make the right choice and do the right thing, even if it's hard. Amen.*

She thought about her own hard choice too. She believed it was the right one. Things might not be great between her and Michael right now, but she was committed to making them better, making things work. And she couldn't blame Michael for wanting to experience his dream—she'd been living hers for many years. She still had a lot of uncomfortable feelings to work through, and that would take some time. But she was filled with a sense of peace she hadn't experienced in quite awhile.

Lord, keeping secrets doesn't work. I'm so thankful there are no secrets from You. Forgive me for not trusting You enough, for not trusting my husband enough to be truthful from the start. Help me and Michael get through this time. Help me want to do it. Help us grow closer ...

She was still praying an hour later when Tina exited Thelma's office, her eyes red and puffy. Thelma followed her, holding out a Jessica Simpson handbag. "You forgot your purse."

"Thank you." Tina slung it over her shoulder.

"You okay?" Susan asked gently.

"She's more than okay." Thelma smiled broadly. "You didn't tell me what a special young woman she is." Thelma reached over to hug

Tina. "I would be mighty proud to have you for a daughter—no two ways about that."

"As would I," Susan chimed in, patting her on the back as the tears began again.

"I might as well give up wearing makeup." Tina straightened up and wiped her eyes with a crumpled tissue. "I cry at the silliest things."

"Emotions aren't silly, dear," Thelma counseled. "You're bound to run the gamut of them, especially during this period when you have some serious decisions to make. Now, you have my card, I think. I want you to call me if you have any questions or concerns, no matter what time. There's an answering service on call twenty-four hours a day if I don't pick up, but I try to answer when I can."

"Thank you," Tina whispered again.

"No, thank *you* ... for caring enough to make an informed decision. I'm proud of you. We both are."

Susan and Thelma exchanged glances, knowing anything could still happen.

"Honey?" Thelma placed her hand on Tina's arm. "Remember you need a checkup and blood work, just to make sure everything's okay. And prenatal vitamins right away are a must, no matter what you eventually decide. Right?"

Tina silently nodded.

Susan walked out with Tina the way they'd walked in, holding hands ... and silently praying. She waved as Tina drove away, thankful the young woman had felt comfortable enough to come to her with the news of her pregnancy. She hadn't lied when she said she would be proud to call Tina her daughter.

She eased into her car, resting her head on the steering wheel.

Now she had to meet with Lily to give her the news that she was backing out of the project.

She reached for her cell phone just as it rang. Caller ID indicated it was Michael.

"I'm surprised you're up," she told him. "You looked beat."

"How did it go with Tina?"

"It went well, I think. I'll tell you when I get home. Thanks for asking."

"No problem. I was praying for her—and you. What you did for her, it was important. I didn't mean to imply that it wasn't."

"I know you didn't, Michael. Thank you."

"Susan?"

"Yes?"

"I've been thinking."

"Yes?"

"I don't know how it will work—I haven't figured that out—but maybe we can do both our projects at the same time. Maybe it doesn't have to be either/or. What do you think?"

Susan was thankful she was still in the parking lot and not driving. She held her breath for a long minute, then let it out. "I think I'd like very much to try."

"Then get your beautiful little disco-diva derriere home and let's talk about it, okay? I don't want to lose you—or us—over this. It's not worth it. We'll figure out how to make it work."

She flipped her cell phone closed and pulled out of the parking lot with a lightheartedness she hadn't felt in a long time.

Thank You, Lord. Thank You!

Chapter 21

"You're sure you can live with this schedule?" Susan took a bite of her steaming burrito, the spicy aroma overpowering the usual smell of bleach and other chemicals.

"I'm sure I can, but can you? That's a lot of juggling." Loretta gave up using chopsticks as they were intended and stabbed her California roll. "Never could figure these things out."

Susan had filled her friend in on the plans for the new Disco Diva and was encouraged by her enthusiasm. Loretta hadn't commented much when she heard about Michael's plans for the Henderson Ranch, just nodded. Now they were poring over the schedule, a detailed plan that had Susan spreading her time between the salon and the two major building projects. Almost every waking hour was taken up with something for her to do.

"Michael and I went over it a half-dozen times before we came up with this." Susan's mind was going a mile a minute. "I'm not sure that two full days here will cut it—we'll have to see how that goes. We can go over my client list later to see who I'm going to let go, and you can decide if you want to take any of them."

"Michael is really behind this?" Loretta nodded at the list while shaking soy sauce on her lunch. "I mean, he does know about *all of it*, right? Exactly what you're planning over at the Elephant? It's going to take a lot of work."

"Yes, he knows. This was his idea!" Susan waved the paper. "I was ready to give up Lily's offer. Seriously. He's the one who had second thoughts. Thank You, God!" She glanced upward, clasping her hands together.

"Okay, so let me be sure I've got this straight." Loretta took the paper from Susan's hand, peering closely at the notes. "You're here two full days from seven until seven, and the other four days you're working with Michael every morning from eight until one and afternoons at the White Elephant from two until …" She squinted down at the list. "What's this mean?" She pointed to a grouping of three little stars.

"That means until nighttime—or whenever." Susan laughed as Loretta shook her head. "So sue me—I'm a visual person. Anyway, Michael will be at the casino all night, so I can stay at the White Elephant construction site office as long as I need to."

"Looks like Monday is your only day off. Are you giving up church?"

"Uh, no. We actually talked about that. I'm going to try to make Saturday night services, and I'll record programs for Michael. It'll all work out." Susan waved her hand dismissively. "Besides, this is only for three months—until June. We'll come back to the table then and readjust the hours and days." Susan took the list from Loretta and jotted some notes in the margin.

"I can't believe Michael's actually retiring. That blows my mind almost as much as the idea of having a new salon—oh, listen." Someone had turned up the volume on Vicki Sue Robinson's "Turn the Beat Around." Loretta put down the chopsticks and snapped her fingers to the music. "I love that song."

"You love every song." Susan laughed. "Yeah, I know. I can't believe it either. I thought we had at least three more years until retirement, but this is important to him …" Susan's voice trailed off. Loretta stopped rocking out to the music and leaned back in her chair.

"But not to you?"

"I didn't say that. The more we talk about the Henderson Ranch, the more excited I get. Kind of."

"Kind of. Now that's convincing."

"Well, it was all kind of a shock, you know? I had no idea we owned hundreds of acres of prime real estate. I guess I figured we'd grow old and die in our house. I'd always hoped for a bigger salon, more space for a museum and all, but I really hadn't thought much about moving into a bigger house." Susan got up and tossed her take-out container in the trash. "I'm getting into it, though. Really. And I can't help it that I'm more excited about the new Disco Diva. Tell me you're not."

"I'd be more excited if I could work with you on it, but I guess someone has to stay here and hold down the fort. Do you want this?" She held out the last two pieces of sushi on her plate.

"Nah. Thanks. I'm stuffed. Put it in the fridge—someone will eat it."

"So, what are you doing about the pet store? In case Sam calls again."

"You're going to love this. It was actually Michael's idea, and I think it's kind of great. We're not going to break ground on the Henderson

Ranch for quite awhile. First we have to decide on the plans, get price quotes from vendors and such, and there's still the matter of working with the city on permits. It's a lot more work than I thought. Anyway, we don't have room at home for an office, so we're going to lease the pet store for the ranch-house office. What do you think?"

"Well, that's actually kind of cool, I guess. You'll be close by if I need you."

"Oh no you don't." Susan scrunched up a napkin and tossed it at her friend. "If I'm putting in twelve-hour days here on Tuesdays and Wednesdays, you're not getting me any more than that."

"Hey, twelve-hour days are a walk in the park for folks like us." Loretta got up and started to move with the music. "Okay, fine. I'll leave you alone in your ranch office to play house with Mighty Michael. But it will still be nice having you close. Just in case."

Susan watched her friend dancing and smiled. "I love you, Loretta."

"Yeah. I know. Me too, you." Loretta stopped dancing and placed her hand on Susan's shoulder. "I really can handle things here. You know that. Don't worry about me."

"I know I can depend on you. I wouldn't be doing this otherwise." Susan placed her hand on top of Loretta's.

"Now don't get mushy on me." Loretta moved away, reached into her smock pocket for her lip gloss, and peered into the mirror, applying the gloss in two expert strokes. "So, tell me more about the White Elephant. I've got ten minutes before Clara's appointment." She sat down, put her elbows on the table, and rested her chin in her hands. "What kind of stations are we going to have in the new salon? I want a window this time around—if you have any pull with the owner." She grinned as Susan told her more of the plans she and Lily had discussed.

—*mm*—

From: Susan Anderson (boomerbabesusan@
            boomerbabesrock.com)
Sent: Tuesday, February 21, 10:49 p.m.
To: Patricia Davies; Mary Johnson; Lisa Taylor; Linda Jones;
            Sharon Wilson
Subject: REQUESTING PRAYERS! New Salon, House, Life!

Just said good-night to Loretta and locked up the shop. Long day, exciting day—been ages since I've checked e-mail. I promise to read through all of the outstanding messages and get caught up soon.

You know I was talking about leasing the pet-shop space for a disco museum. Well, that has all changed—and in a big way! I'm going to partner with my friend Lily (you remember Lily, she's my friend/client with all the money?) on a NEW DISCO DIVA! Yes! You heard right! She owns an old warehouse that we're going to renovate. And it's gonna be way more than just a salon—we're talking restaurant, dance club, boutique, banquet rooms, and day spa! And Pat, we have to talk about the boutique—I would LOVE to sell your jewelry!

I'm so excited about all of this! It's going to take ages to finish, but we're starting right away. And that's not all! Michael and I are going to build a new house in Henderson—way bigger than anything I ever imagined. So, I've got TWO building projects starting. It'll be a tad crazy until Michael retires.

Oh! I forgot to tell you ... Michael is retiring early! More later— need to head home and get some sleep ... if I can. I'm so wired I can't see straight. Then again, that could be because of all the energy drinks I've started to consume. I'm hooked on the coffee ones!

More later—promise. Suze

Chapter 22

"Here's to the first Tuesday in March." Lily held up a Waterford Crystal goblet. "We're going to have many dates to celebrate as we take this journey, but this one today is significant."

Susan took a deep breath, picked up the Montblanc pen Lily had provided, signed two copies of the agreement making their partnership official—and handed Lily a check for eighteen thousand dollars to seal the deal. It was the money Michael had given her as a gift from his anniversary bonus.

Lily had given Susan a first draft of the agreement shortly after Michael's anniversary party. Susan had carefully read the document numerous times during the following weeks, waiting for the right time to share it with Michael. They had now looked over it together and requested a few slight changes. But not many. Lily had been more than generous regarding the terms. She asked to be involved in the deliberation process for expenditures over five thousand dollars, and she requested hands-on involvement in three specific projects: hiring the project manager, coordinating the on-site office trailer, and handling the grand-opening festivities. Otherwise, she was merely "along for the ride," as she'd said when first presenting the contract to Susan.

"I've chosen to invest these past years in what some may call risky ventures, and I've yet to be dissatisfied. What I'm offering is not a loan. You won't be tied to a payment schedule that will put you into the poorhouse in case things don't go as anticipated. Which, I might add, is highly unlikely, in my estimation."

The contract stated that Lily would fund the entire project to the tune of a maximum dollar figure that made Susan gasp. She didn't think there was any way they could possibly spend that much money, but she trusted Lily and her team of legal advisors to know what they were doing. Certainly, a budget like this would enable them to develop a state-of-the-art entertainment complex. There were payback stipulations that would eventually have a percentage of profits being distributed to the Peyton Foundation.

All in all, it was an amazing offer, and Susan thanked God for bringing this incredible woman into her life. She also thanked God for Michael's new willingness to support the project.

They celebrated the signing with chilled glasses of sparkling juice, a peach flavor that reminded Susan of the Bellinis she used to drink years before in New York.

"I'm sorry Michael couldn't join us." Lily set down her glass, placed one copy of the signed agreement in her folder, and handed the other to Susan.

"Me, too. He was planning to come. But since he told them he was taking early retirement, they've been freaking out. They don't want him to go. It's like they're inventing emergencies to keep him busier than usual." Susan laughed. "I have to give the general manager credit for this strategy. He knows my husband. He's been calling personally, telling Michael they need him to do things that only he can do. They're on a campaign to puff him up like a peacock. It would be pathetic if Michael didn't know exactly what they're up to."

"Do you wonder if he's going to miss it? Thirty-six years is a long time."

"I don't think he will—not now that he's got the ranch on his agenda. He's going to have more than enough to keep him busy. We both are."

"Well, what do you say we get started and make our first official decision as partners?" Lily waved a thick file in the air. "You've read young Mr. Power's proposal. What do you think—should we ever let him know he was the only one to submit a bid?" Lily giggled, pulling out the fifty-six-page bound proposal Ryan had sent them less than one week after their meeting.

"He must have stayed up round the clock to put this together." For the twentieth time, Susan paged through the impressive document.

"I would hope so." Lily nodded. "It shows he wants the job—was willing to do the work to get it. I'm especially impressed that he has factored in the possibility of the project extending into multiple years. That he's willing to commit to the project long-term."

"I couldn't begin to guess how long this will take. Michael's timeline for the Henderson ranch is two years. I can't imagine taking two years to build a house, but I'm going to leave that in his capable hands."

"A wise decision." Lily removed Ryan's business card from the clear pouch on the inside cover of his proposal. "I have every confidence our Mr. Power will have a good sense of our timeline within a few months. I say we hire him, but what do you say?"

"Ditto." They shook hands and then hugged.

"Now," Lily said, "shall we make the call?"

Lily put Ryan on the speakerphone when she called him a few minutes later, offering him the position for two years at a salary that made Susan catch her breath.

"We both know it may take more or less time to complete," Lily added. "I am guaranteeing your salary for two full years, with an agreement to renegotiate in the event it takes longer." They talked briefly about timeline possibilities.

"I know you'll be worth every penny of this, Mr. Power," Lily said. "If you'd like to consider our offer, I'll have the contract sent within twenty-four hours so you may review our terms. If they're acceptable, can you begin by the first of next month?"

"That's April Fool's Day," Susan whispered.

"Superstitious?" Lily whispered back.

"It's also a Saturday. Let's make it Monday, April 3," Susan suggested.

"Mr. Power, my partner has pointed out that the first of the month is April Fool's Day."

"Well now, that would certainly be an auspicious day to begin a new project." Ryan laughed heartily, after which a long pause ensued.

"Mr. Power?" Lily leaned forward. "Are you still with us?"

"Absolutely. But I'm sorry, ma'am. I don't think I can even look at your contract unless you accept my main term."

Susan's jaw dropped as Lily smiled.

"And what might that be, Mr. Power?"

"That you call me Ryan. I keep thinking my father is in the room every time you call me Mr. Power."

"I will do my best, Ryan, but please have patience with me. You know what they say about old dogs and new tricks."

"Perhaps so, but I don't see any old dogs in this scenario." They all laughed. "I'm sure your terms are going to be more than acceptable, but I promise to look the contract over carefully. And I'll most likely come out sooner to find an apartment and get myself settled. This driving back and forth is getting wearisome."

"If I may make a suggestion, *Ryan* ..." Lily placed considerable emphasis on his name. "I would like you to consider something. The development director for our FAITH project worked with us for about one year, and she stayed in the guest quarters on my estate. I would like to offer you the same opportunity. However, before you say yes or no, please come out and spend a few days at Cedar Ridge. If you feel comfortable here, you'd be welcome to use it as your Las Vegas home headquarters while you are here. If not, you'll still have somewhere to hang your hat while you search for an apartment."

"That's very generous of you. I'll take you up on that offer."

"Okay, then, it's settled. I'll get this contract to you. In the meantime, I'll be arranging for the on-site office trailer. You'll find this is one of my terms, that I handle this part of the project myself. Therefore, if you would begin to think of specific pieces of equipment and supplies you'd like and send me a list, that would be beneficial."

He laughed. "Aye, aye, cap'n!"

"You have that look on your face, Susan," Lily said as she hung up the phone.

"I do? What look?"

"That disapproving look. Did I say something untoward? I thought that was a stellar conversation!"

"No, it's just that … well, we really don't know anything significant about this man, and you've asked him to live in your house. I just worry about you, that's all."

"*Au contraire,* my dear friend. We know a great deal about Ryan Power." She held up a large manila envelope. "This is a complete background check on our new project manager. He's everything he says he is and then some. In fact, did you know his father was a foreign ambassador? And his mother was far more than just a fashion photographer. She was one of the top photographers for Paris *Vogue.*"

"You had Ryan checked out before you even knew I was on board." Susan pursed her lips in mock anger.

"Forgive me, dear, for my premature exuberance. I simply couldn't wait for you to make the decision I knew you were inevitably going to make—or at least I prayed you were going to make."

"Oh, you …" Susan shook her finger at Lily as they laughed at the adventure they knew was only just beginning.

m

From: Susan Anderson (boomerbabesusan@ boomerbabesrock.com)

Sent: Tuesday, March 7, 11:36 p.m.

To: Patricia Davies; Mary Johnson; Lisa Taylor; Linda Jones; Sharon Wilson

Subject: We're off and running!

Well, I did it! I signed the papers today. I'm now officially the co-owner of the White Elephant (henceforth known as the WE).

We hired the project manager today—a very cute young man, not that I noticed. He starts April 3. You know I've been talking about this project for weeks, boring you all to tears, no doubt. Now that it's happening, things seem to be moving quickly.

Loretta will be taking management of Disco Diva during the project (PTL!), and I'm officially cutting back my hours, starting right now. You can reach me at the salon Tuesdays and Wednesdays from sunup until way past sundown. ☺ The other days I'll be shifting my time between the WE and working with Michael on the Henderson ranch. (Might as well call this HR to be consistent.) Did I tell you we leased the pet store to use as the HR office? I thought briefly about asking Lily to make room in our WE construction office, but then I figured it might be better to separate the projects. Not sure I'm ready to jump into a 24/7 life with the DH.

Hugs and blessings to all. Suze.

Ryan Power's signed contract came back within a week without a single change to the terms. An attached sticky note read:

> *Dear Miss Lily:*
>
> *No time to visit before starting. Like the April Fool that I am, I'll arrive on Saturday the 1st and start work first thing Monday the 3rd. Thank you for the offer to stay at Cedar Ridge while I deliberate*

my long-term living arrangements. Your gracious
hospitality is appreciated. See you on the 1st.

Ryan Power

Lily had jumped right in the day Susan signed the contract, and in record time a new double-wide, three-bedroom, two-bath modular home was delivered to the parking lot of the White Elephant. Although two portable restrooms had been delivered and set up outside the building for when the work crews began, Lily made sure those inside the mobile home were functioning as well. This was no easy feat considering they had to be connected to city sewer and water. But Lily had both money and influence to make that happen.

"I'm flexible," she said, "but when it comes to porta potties, I draw the line."

The two smaller bedrooms were turned into private offices: one for Ryan and one for Lily and Susan to share. The master bedroom became a state-of-the-art conference room, and the living room was the reception area, with adequate space for an assistant if they eventually needed one. One entire wall in the conference room was outfitted with a fancy kind of corkboard on which to mount blueprints, plans, and task lists. The kitchen remained as such and would come in handy for long days.

By the end of March, the mobile home had been equipped with everything needed for a temporary on-site office—phones, computers, fax machine, photocopier, PowerPoint projector and screen, the most exquisite office furniture Susan had ever seen, and all the desk supplies imaginable. Susan watched in awe as Lily orchestrated this entire phase with detailed precision.

The day before Ryan was scheduled to arrive, the installation of the security surveillance system was completed in both the office trailer and in the White Elephant, with monitors in Ryan's office showing round-the-clock views of all areas of the property. Plus, Lily had hired an outside security service to be on site twenty-four hours a day.

"Isn't that a bit much?" Susan asked when she saw the security guard parked in the lot one morning. "We have perimeter fencing around the entire place. It looks like Fort Knox here."

"Not at all. This is a big empty building right now, and the more activity we have, the more interest it will bring. During early construction it's going to be difficult to secure the building fully. We need someone on site. Trust me on this."

Trusting Lily wasn't Susan's problem. Trusting that she herself could juggle both projects, work at the salon, and take care of her home was beginning to concern her. Moreover, she had to factor in time for luxurious stuff like grocery shopping, washing clothes, showering, and maybe a little Bible study. Oh, and there was eating, too.

Dear Lord, just get me through the next few months.

Chapter 23

"This is our office?" Ryan's eyes bulged as he took in the homey building, complete with a bit of southwestern landscaping around the entrance.

"Close your mouth, dear, before sand blows into it," Lily joked.

"This is a house ... not a trailer," he stammered.

"Actually, it's both." Lily clapped. "It's a trailer house! Do you like it?"

He stood speechless as she continued. "I know most construction projects have dirty little shanties with long tables and folding chairs set up inside, and scarcely anything else. I've worked in my share of those in my time, thank you very much. How they expect people to work productively in a shack is beyond me!"

Lily gently took the young man by the arm and walked him up the steps. "Come inside and see what we've done while you've been gone. Then we'll take a jaunt over to Cedar Ridge and see if you can handle my hovel while you're here."

"Why do I think Cedar Ridge is hardly going to be a hovel?"

Susan winked. "Good call, Ryan."

"Don't you two even think about forging an alliance against me." Lily playfully pinched him as they entered what would soon become their home away from home for a good, long time.

―*mm*―

"I'm stunned." Ryan leaned back in his elaborate black leather desk chair and put his feet up on his desk. Lily and Susan sat across from him in two luxuriously upholstered wing chairs, enjoying his reaction.

"Turn around and hit enter on the keyboard," Lily instructed.

He'd been so enthralled with the exquisite furnishings and attention to detail, he hadn't noticed the new laptop on the mahogany credenza behind his desk. Clearly, they had opened a window on the computer and prepared something they wanted him to see.

He jumped at the sound behind him when he clicked enter, spinning around to see Lily's image on the fifty-two-inch plasma TV screen mounted opposite his desk.

"It's networked to your computer," Lily said from on-screen as the camera panned back to reveal Susan.

"Look how cute you are," Lily said to Susan.

"Shh, watch the movie." Susan furrowed her brow as their on-screen performance continued.

"We thought this would be a good way for you to share presentations to vendors or conduct virtual tours of the building so folks won't have to go traipsing through the construction site," the on-screen Susan said, clearly reading from a teleprompter.

The real Susan and Lily were squirming in their seats with excitement watching him watch the high-tech video presentation.

"Now, listen up, boss." Lily leaned in to the camera and wagged her finger. "We've had a host of equipment installed in this office as well as in the White Elephant, and it wasn't for our own edification.

You're going to need to get up to speed on all the software, equipment, and especially the surveillance system." Ryan's eyes widened. "So I've hired a young fellow to train you on everything. He's coming in every day from eight to four for the next week. Okay?"

Now, the camera zoomed in on Susan. "We're thrilled you're here, and we can't wait to start work on this dream project. I want you to know I was impressed with your proposal. I also want you to know that while Lily plans to hover around in the background, I plan to be more hands-on. I intend to let you do your job, but I do want to be involved. I've got a lot of ideas, and it's my prayer we'll be able to combine them with yours and Lily's to develop an amazing entertainment complex. Welcome to Las Vegas, Ryan Power. Now let's git 'er done!"

He was momentarily stunned when the video came to an end and the TV screen turned a gentle blue. He looked across the desk at Lily and Susan, who were grinning from ear to ear and holding out a gift-wrapped box.

"What's this?"

"A little something to commemorate the occasion," Lily said. "Open it."

He lifted the lid to find an exquisite glass statue of a white elephant.

"We know the name won't stay with the project, but this building has been called the White Elephant for ages. When we saw this, we felt it was a perfect way to begin our partnership." Susan swallowed back tears. "It's where we started."

"Who knows where we'll end … but here's to a grand beginning!" Lily extended her hand. Susan did the same, with Ryan adding his to the mix. Like the Three Musketeers, they began their journey together.

—✍—

Two hours later they were still talking over one another like politicians at a debate. But everyone agreed with Ryan's assessment of priorities.

"One of the first things we need to do is review the inventory of your collection. I've been thinking about this for the past few weeks. You don't build a museum without knowing exactly what you have to put on display. Plus, we have three separate entities on three separate floors—all with the same overall theme. We need to know what we have available and begin to identify additional items we may need to acquire."

"Just what you need, dear." Lily patted Susan on the back. "An official reason to continue antiquing and yard sale-ing."

"As if I've ever stopped." She jumped up and ran to her office, returning with a plastic grocery sack she handed to Ryan. "Look what I found last month at a yard sale in the desert."

He pulled out the almost-new yellow platform shoes and whistled. "These shoes would look great next to the blue ones you have at the salon." He put them on his hands and walked them around the desktop. "Did they really belong to David Bowie?"

"Yes, sir."

"The displays are going to be key to every area." His voice was unusually high, and in his excitement he sounded like a young boy. "This is going to be so cool!"

"Say, maybe we could take a trip to Washington DC and check

out some of the Smithsonian collections—they have some fabulous display concepts," Susan suggested. "I've always loved the inaugural-ball-gown display. Maybe we could highlight some of my fashions like that."

"Brilliant!" Lily shouted.

"I agree," Ryan said. "Let's do that after we get a thorough assessment of what we have." He wrote "Smithsonian" on a neon blue sticky note and stuck it on the cupboard above his credenza.

Lily sighed. "Lovely. I spend a fortune on corkboards, whiteboards, computers, and all those high-tech thingamajigs, and you revert to the note-on-the-cupboard system."

"Uh, I'm sorry. I didn't mean to ..." He reached for the reminder note as Lily let out a boisterous laugh.

"Don't touch it! I was only pulling your leg, young man. Use whatever system works best for you, just as long as you get the job done."

"You'll have to forgive my partner," Susan said with a laugh. "She gets a bit punchy when she's excited."

"I'll remember that," Ryan promised. "So, let's see the list." He rubbed his hands together.

"What list?" Susan blinked.

"The inventory of your collection."

She dropped her head. "Well, I don't really have a complete list. I have appraisals on a lot of the larger pieces, but there's tons of other stuff in crates. I'm going to have to spend some time going through boxes to get a full written inventory."

"You don't have everything documented," said Ryan, his eyebrows arching, "for insurance purposes?"

"Afraid not. When we moved everything into storage, all they asked for was the total amount we wanted to insure. Things were more lax back then."

"May I ask how much you have your collection insured for?" Ryan picked up his pen.

"I've got about a million in coverage on the things in my storage units. But now my agent has informed me I need to have everything worth over five hundred dollars itemized, appraised, and documented. Not just the big items. I've been trying to recall everything I have packed. I think I've underestimated the number of items as well as the value."

"Did you say 'storage units'—as in plural?"

"Yes. I have two, and it's going to take forever to tackle this project. I may need to get some help."

"How much stuff do you have?" Ryan's eyes got wide. "What kind of big items?"

Susan grinned sheepishly. "Remember that scene in *The Silence of the Lambs* when Jodie Foster crawls under the door to get into the storage unit?"

"No way! That much?"

"Times two. But my stuff is much neater—very organized." She chuckled. "And you won't find any body parts in my car."

"A car?" both Lily and Ryan blurted out.

"What kind of car?" Ryan whispered.

"A Shelby."

"Unbelievable!" he yelled. "What kind of Shelby?"

"A cotton-candy pink one," she teased, enjoying the suspense.

"Susan—give me a break!"

"My goodness—no need to get testy. My girl is a 1967 427 Semi-Competition Cobra Roadster. I call her Marilyn."

He stared at her as though she'd morphed into Medusa before his very eyes. "You are totally kidding me, right?"

"Is that something special?" Lily removed her reading glasses and leaned forward.

"Beyond special." Ryan gulped. "Priceless."

"That's what I was afraid of." Susan's demeanor changed as she began to pace.

"What condition is she in?" He tried to appear back in control.

"Pretty good," she assured him, "but that's not the point. Now that I'm thinking about it, between the storage units, Disco Diva, and our home, I don't think I have nearly enough coverage. Plus, the policies I do have in place have gone through the roof during the past few years—that's kind of why Michael has been encouraging me to sell some of it."

Ryan remembered meeting Susan's husband at the Silver Spur back in early February. It was hard to believe how far they'd come in two months. He wondered how involved Michael Anderson was going to get in the project. He didn't have time to deal with a meddling husband.

"So, how hands-on will your husband be with all this?" Ryan rocked back in his chair.

"Not very, unfortunately," Susan said. "He's still working full time, but he retires at the end of June. We're going to build a new home in Henderson, and we're already pretty involved in that project. Which reminds me—we'll be furnishing our new place in a Spanish cowboy kind of style. That means we'll have a house full of things we can use in the museum. We'll have to reupholster some of the pieces, but we don't have cats or kids, so most everything is in pretty good condition. There are dozens of vintage retro pieces, including chairs, sofas, and tables by Saarinen and Florence Knoll and a ton of stuff by Heywood-Wakefield. The house won't be ready for awhile, but we can still identify the pieces to use."

"This is amazing." Ryan was jotting notes as fast as he could. "What possessed you to begin collecting disco memorabilia in the first place? It's not a common hobby, by any stretch of the imagination."

Susan pursed her lips. "It's not a hobby."

"Uh, sorry," he responded hastily. "I didn't mean any disrespect."

"You'll find our dear Susan takes this era very seriously." Lily leaned back and crossed her legs. "It's one of the reasons I agreed to partner with her on this project. She believes in keeping the historic era alive—preserving what it meant to the generation of people like her who lived it, breathed it, experienced it. Don't underestimate her level of commitment."

"Thank you, Lily," Susan said. "Don't think I'm not aware there are people in town who call me eccentric at best and loony at worst. You'll find I have a reputation for being somewhat … odd."

"Odd?" He cocked his head. "How so?"

"I look like I stepped out of a time machine, for crying out loud. You think I don't know that? I love my clothing—my style, this look. It's my brand as much as Dolly Parton's wigs or Tammy Faye's eyelashes. So I'm sure as word begins to spread about the project, you're going to find many people who will initially respond with negativity. I hope you won't let that sway you."

"You wouldn't believe the folks who thought it was insane to build the Rock and Roll Hall of Fame on the shore of Lake Erie.

Trust me, I don't pay much heed to naysayers. They're the bane of visionaries the world over. Plus, I don't see anything odd in being passionately committed to something, and people spend tens of thousands of dollars for brand recognition. The way I see it, we already have that in platinum!"

Susan smiled.

"Okay, then," Lily said, standing. "I'd like to show you the security system. I think you'll be pleased."

"I have no doubt." He stood and stretched.

Susan stood too. "You know, if it's okay with both of you, since we're talking about it, I think I'll run over to the bank and get the appraisal forms and photos out of my safe-deposit box." She grabbed her purse and headed for the door.

"I don't mind." Ryan extended his hand to Lily. "Do you?"

"Not at all. A stellar idea. But remember, it's Saturday." She looked at her watch. "They close early. Why not let Franco drive you, dear? He gets bored just sitting there, and he can navigate traffic like an Indy 500 driver."

Chapter 24

"Lily said you could drive me to the bank. Would that be okay, Franco?"

"My pleasure." He began to get out of the car.

"No, that's okay. I can get it myself—please." She opened the back door and was about to climb in when a familiar car pulled into the lot.

Tragic Tina.

"I thought that was you." Tina nodded at the sleek Rolls-Royce. "Is this your other life?"

"I wish. It belongs to a friend. I'll be right back, Franco." Susan got out and walked to the driver's side of Tina's vehicle. "What's up, sweetie? How are you doing?"

Tears welled up in Tina's eyes. "I've been driving around thinking, trying to figure out what to do. Then I saw you. Must be a—what do you call it?—a God-cidence. What is this place?" Tina peered out her window toward the White Elephant.

Susan ignored the question. "Tell you what. I have to run an errand. How about you hop in the back of that rattletrap buggy and take a spin with me? We'll be back in less than an hour."

"Really?" Tina's eyes grew wide. "I've never been in a Rolls before. That's what it is, right?"

"Correct."

"And I wouldn't be making a pest of myself or anything?"

"Not at all. Come on. I've got to get to the bank before it closes."

Susan introduced Tina to Franco and told him where she needed to go.

"Very good, Miss Susan." Franco smiled in the rearview mirror. "You know how to open this if you need anything." He winked at Susan and closed the partition between them, allowing Susan to talk privately with Tina.

As soon as the glass went up, the troubled young woman began pouring out her heart. "I took your advice and called him."

"I didn't advise you to call him, Tina. I merely stated that as the father of your baby, he has a right to know."

"I know, and after thinking about it I had to agree. I wanted to give him the benefit of the doubt … that maybe he would be happy."

"Was he?"

"Not even close."

"I'm sorry, honey."

"He doesn't care one iota. Didn't even offer to pay for the … clinic … if that's what I decide to do. I can't believe I was so blind."

They discussed Tina's situation and her options, and Susan continued to pray silently that she wouldn't say too much or too little. They pulled into the parking lot of her bank a few minutes before closing.

"Hang tight. I need to get something out of my safe-deposit box." Susan bolted from the car as soon as Franco opened the door.

"Franco, why don't you tell Tina something about your buggy. This is her first time inside one."

"A pleasure, Miss Susan." As she disappeared into the bank, he launched into the history of the Rolls-Royce.

The drive back to the White Elephant was less emotional. Susan asked Tina about her life before coming to Vegas.

"This is only my second job in my whole life. My parents own an antique store in Cape Town. I started working for them when I was in high school, mostly office work. You know, filing, correspondence, and what all. I didn't want to go to university right out of high school like so many of my friends were doing, so I stayed home and worked in the family business."

"I think that's fascinating … the antique business. What type of antiques?"

"Papa loved clocks, and Mum loved anything from before the 1800s. Nothing contemporary or American or even African—mostly European. They had quite a collection. It took me two years to inventory everything."

"Inventory?" Susan's eyes widened. "Did you say you do inventory?"

"I convinced them to buy a computer and let me bring them into the twentieth century. I set up a catalog and inventory system and entered every piece they had." She rattled off a list of some of the items in their store.

"Oh my, that sounds like a daunting project."

"It was, but I had a blast. They kept horrible records. Papers in shoeboxes and such. I developed a data system to inventory every piece—where they acquired it, date of origin, materials, if it had a signature stamp or not. By the time I got done, they could conduct sorts and searches by any number of criteria, including the bottom-line dollar of inventory on hand."

Susan shook her head and grabbed the young woman's hands. "You are like a gift from God."

"I am?" Tina squinted her eyes in confusion. "Well, thank you … I think."

"I'm serious. I might have a project for you if you're interested. A job—part time on the days you're not working." She reached over and pressed the button, and the partition window quietly whirred open.

"Franco, you are never going to believe this amazing God-cidence!"

—*m*—

The car pulled into the lot of the White Elephant just as Lily and Ryan were walking out the front door. Lily was hurrying to an appointment.

"Please forgive my abrupt departure." She kissed Susan on the cheek and pointed at Ryan as Franco helped her into the Rolls. "Susan will give you directions to Cedar Ridge—come by anytime after four. And, Susan, I'd love to meet your young friend later. Now, bye!"

Franco closed the door smartly, nodded toward the group, got into the car, and drove away.

"I think that's the most elegant lady I've ever seen," Tina whispered.

"That she is." Ryan extended his hand. "But then, so are you, if I may be so bold. I'm Power. Ryan Power."

"Oh," whispered Tina as she turned around. "Hello …"

"Forgive me." Susan shook her head. "I forgot my manners." She introduced them and watched as the two young people shook hands, their eyes fixed on one another.

Well, now, she thought, *this could be interesting.*

"You are never going to guess what Tina did before moving to Vegas." Susan proceeded to tell Ryan about Tina's background. "So what do you think?"

"Uh, I think that's wonderful." He couldn't stop looking at Tina.

"Wonderful? That's all you can say? Ryan, it's perfect."

He looked at her somewhat blankly.

"Ryan. Read my lips." She pointed to her face and spoke slowly, every word precise. "She's experienced in cataloging antiques … inventory control … hello!"

"Oh … oh!" His head snapped up with understanding. "That *is* fabulous!"

"What's so utterly fabulous about inventory control?" Tina asked. "And what is this place?" She looked toward the White Elephant and back again at Susan and Ryan, who were grinning like Cheshire cats.

"What time do you need to be at work, Tina?" Susan pushed her Kate Spade sunglasses up on top of her head and looked at her watch.

"I'm off tonight," the girl said quickly.

"Tina is one of the lead performers in the Folies Bergere at the Tropicana," Susan explained to Ryan. "She sings *and* dances."

He whistled. "Wow. That's a great show."

"You've seen it?"

"Not recently. A couple of years ago."

"I'll get you tickets." Tina blushed.

"Thanks, that'd be great."

"Are you in a hurry?" Susan asked Tina. "Can you stay for an hour or so?"

"I guess so. Why? What's this all about?"

"You don't need to be at Lily's for an hour, right?" Susan asked Ryan.

"That's correct."

"What do you say we take a little drive, and I'll introduce both of you to Marilyn."

Ryan's face lit up. "I'll drive. Let me get my keys and lock up. Be right back." He vaulted up the trailer steps two at a time, slamming the screen door behind him.

Chapter 25

On the drive to the storage facility, Susan filled Tina in on the project.

"You only just arrived today?" Tina asked Ryan breathlessly.

"A brief four hours ago."

She gave him a big smile. "Welcome to Las Vegas."

Susan could actually feel the electricity between them … there was no mistaking it. She felt surprisingly like a voyeur and was glad when they arrived at the storage facility.

"You have the whole thing?" Ryan gawked at the large unit Susan had directed him to.

"Two, actually—remember?" She pointed to another full-sized unit. "That one's mine too. Help me out with this, okay?" She inserted a key in the padlock, and Ryan lifted the heavy garage door as a blast of cool air spilled out.

Ryan blinked. "Climate-controlled?"

"Yes. Otherwise nothing would have lasted in this heat."

Ryan and Tina stared at the floor-to-ceiling boxes, the wooden crates, the furniture pieces covered in white sheets, and an array of items hanging on the south wall. Narrow walkways separated the rows.

"Told you it was organized." Susan leaned against the garage wall and crossed her arms.

"May I?" He pointed inside.

"That's why we're here," she said. "Knock yourself out."

"All of this needs to be cataloged?" Tina stammered, and Susan nodded.

"What kind of code is this?" Ryan asked, looking at numerals, letters, and years written on many of the containers.

"Some crazy system I dreamed up when I packed it in New York." Susan sighed, reaching into her handbag for an envelope. "Here, I just got this from my safe-deposit box. It's the code—a treasure map, if you will."

He laughed, taking the envelope from her and quickly opening the document. Then he practically hyperventilated as his eyes darted over the page.

"Tina! Check this out." He grabbed her by the hand and led her down one of the aisles. "Guess what this stands for?" He pointed to the letters *SNF* on the corner of a large wooden crate.

"Uh, Single Narcissistic Female?" She jokingly shrugged her shoulders.

"Very cute." He playfully hit her with the list he held. "*Saturday Night Fever!* One of my favorite movies of all time! So ..." He stared at Susan. "What's inside?"

"You really like that movie?" Tina whispered.

"Yeah ... why?" He stopped, as though they'd reached a pivotal moment in their fledgling relationship.

"Last Halloween I went to a costume party at Caesars Palace. My date was Tony Manero and I was Stephanie Mangano." She said the name of the movie's lead characters with a thick Brooklyn accent as they both struck the famous one-arm-in-the-air "Stayin' Alive" pose immortalized by John Travolta. "I've watched it so many times I wore out the videotape and had to buy the DVD," Tina exclaimed as they launched into their mutual admiration for a movie that had been released before they were born.

"One of those boxes," Susan said, pointing, "is filled with clothing John gave to me for my collection. We had some friends in Brooklyn who hosted parties two or three times a week after shooting wrapped for the day. I sat and visited with John many a night. He was surprisingly humble—rather soft-spoken, actually."

"John Travolta gave you clothing?" Ryan's voice once again did that high-pitched thing that reminded her of a young boy.

"He found out I collected stuff. I was in the right place at the right time one night when he was tired of the mess in his trailer. He just grabbed a couple of pillowcases and started dumping things into them for me—clothing, old script drafts, receipts, all kinds of stuff. It was kind of funny now that I think back on it."

Tina and Ryan continued to stare at her, shaking their heads, and she grinned, enjoying the moment. She searched her memory for more tidbits she could dangle for effect.

"I was at a charity benefit in 1979 when Gene Siskel outbid Jane Fonda in an auction for John Travolta's white disco suit. He got it for two thousand bucks. I read somewhere that it's now valued at a hundred thousand. It's in the Smithsonian now."

"What's in this one?" He tried to lift off the lid and noticed it was nailed shut. "We're going to need a crowbar to get these open. What the heck were you preparing for—Armageddon?"

"Just protecting my assets." He jumped as she came from behind him.

"I guess so! Really, what's in it?"

Susan stared at the container and cocked her head, thinking. "Um, I think that one has movie posters, photos, albums, one of the earlier Wexler scripts … signed."

"No way!"

"Yeah way. And I'm not sure, but that box might also have a stack of *New York* magazines. The June 1976 issue with Nik Cohn's article, the basis for *Saturday Night Fever.*" She shook her head. "Or maybe they're in that one?" She turned and pointed to another box with *SNF* written on the side. "Oh, I can't remember."

"This is nuts!" The veins were popping out on Ryan's neck. "Sorry, no offense."

"None taken." Susan bit her fingernail. "I really should have written down what was inside all of these. I just didn't think …" Her voiced trailed off as she recalled what it had been like to pack up her collection, her heart, and her dreams all at the same time.

Ryan continued to rush around the large garage, pointing out codes and quizzing Susan to no avail. There were boxes identified as BG for the Bee Gees and BM for Bobby Miller, the house photographer at Studio 54. GR stood for Gossip Rags; CL was Clubs; DRS was Disco Roller Skating; MV was Movies; CEL was Celebrities … and the list went on. The entire back wall of the unit was filled from floor to ceiling with wooden crates all identified with the same code: S-54.

"I know that one!" Tina squealed. "Are they all filled with Studio 54 memorabilia?"

"They are." Susan sighed. "I'd forgotten how much of that I had."

"I can't believe you thought to make this." He held up the code list. "But you didn't record anything you put inside?" He shook his head.

"Give me a break. I was twenty-four years old. You're lucky I categorized them in boxes."

"So where's Marilyn?" Ryan craned his neck.

"Next door." Susan nodded toward the other building. "Want to see her?"

"I don't know. Let me think about it." Ryan tapped a manicured finger against pursed lips. "Nah, I think it's getting late," he deadpanned. "We've seen enough for now."

"Okay, then," Susan said, calling his bluff. "Let's hit the road. Help me pull down this door, would you?"

"Very funny. Of course I want to see her. Lead the way." He pulled down the door and replaced the padlock as Susan crossed the drive to the other large corner unit and inserted a key in a second, much sturdier, padlock.

"She's all yours." Susan motioned to the handle as Ryan took a deep breath and raised the heavy door.

Chapter 26

"Gene would love this car." Ryan ran his hands around the steering wheel as he sat inside the pristine roadster.

"Gene?" Tina asked.

"My old man. Do you know there were only fifty-three of these ever made?" He opened and then closed the small glove box.

"Not quite." Susan used the edge of her sweater to wipe a spot off the door. "The original fifty-three were competition cars. Only thirty ended up as street rods like this."

"You call your father by his first name?" Tina asked.

"Sometimes. Okay, thirty. This is worth a fortune. Does she run?"

"She did when we parked her back in 1980."

"What's your mother's name?" Tina asked.

"Gloria. But she passed away a few years ago. You haven't taken her out since? Man, I'd be driving this baby around every chance I got."

"I'm sorry." Tina gently touched his arm.

"Thanks," he said, placing his hand gently atop hers.

"Get in." He pointed a hitchhiker thumb toward the passenger side as Tina looked to Susan for permission.

"Absolutely." Susan nodded as the young woman slid into the sporty automobile. "I'll bring the keys next time. You can see if she turns over, though I highly doubt it."

Ryan and Tina pretended they were cruising down the highway, joyfully laughing. In between queries about Susan's collection, they asked each other question after question and traded compliments. It was sweet to watch. Susan wondered if they were even aware of the magic manifesting itself around them.

She recalled when she first met Michael. How he had exhausted her with questions, wanting to know all there was to know about her. She had never lied to him, but in retrospect, the CliffsNotes version he'd received on her life wasn't without holes. Thankfully, he had never pressured her for more than she could give.

"Uh, folks, I hate to break up the mutual admiration society, but I'm afraid we have to call it a day. Now that you've seen the scope of the project, Tina, is this something you think you could handle?"

"Oh, yes! I'd love to have the opportunity." Tina stepped out of the sleek machine, gently closing the door behind her. "But I could only work part time—around rehearsals and shows. Would that be okay?"

"Yes," Susan answered quickly, catching Ryan's eye. "But let me talk to the boss man, and we'll get back to you."

"I understand." Tina smiled. "Are you planning to move everything to another area? I'll need space to unpack, sort, run inventory, and catalog things. I have a suggestion for how to identify each piece, a numeric system I developed for my parents' store … if that's okay with you?"

"Oh my, you really are a gift from God! But I hadn't thought about the need to move things. You might be right. What do you think?" She turned to Ryan, who was gazing at Tina.

"I had no idea your collection was this extensive," he said when she got his attention. "And you said we'll most likely have large furniture pieces as well, correct?"

"Yes. From our home."

She couldn't believe she was saying this. Michael had been after her for years to buy new furniture. When they'd married, she'd thought he enjoyed the lovely furnishings she brought into their union. As the years went by, however, she'd come to understand he hated the style. "I want something I can actually relax in, Susan, not just admire," he'd complained. "None of this is really comfortable. It's like living in a museum."

Eventually he'd stopped asking her to change. And after several years she'd acquiesced when he brought a large leather La-Z-Boy recliner into the living room.

Well, he would be getting his wish. They would have entirely different furnishings in their new home. Susan's head was spinning just talking about the changes that would be occurring.

"We'll have to take a look at the furniture another day," Susan said. "But what do you think is the best way for Tina to begin the inventory?"

"I have to agree with her." Ryan winked. "I think it would be best to have everything down at the site. What are you paying for two climate-controlled storage units? I'm thinking we might be able to lease one comparable-sized temporary aluminum storage building and have it placed on site near the office trailer."

He gasped when she told him the yearly price of the current units.

"Tell me about it," she said. "Multiply that by twenty-five years. Kind of stupid now that I think about it—we could have bought a building for what we've paid."

No wonder Michael was always harping on her to get rid of some of her stuff.

"Oh, but that price also includes cold storage for my clothing in the building over there." She pointed to the adjacent four-story enclosed storage facility.

"Clothing?" Ryan stared. "How much clothing? What kind?"

"Well, I have several costumes worn by Donna Summer from a couple of her tours and a fabulous sequin jacket from Gloria Gaynor. I have four sky blue tuxedos The Temptations wore when they appeared on *The Ed Sullivan Show*, and I have the dress Liza Minnelli wore in that photo I have in the salon, the one with Andy Warhol and Truman Capote. And there are my own clothes. I have everything from evening gowns to pantsuits to bell-bottoms from Oleg Cassini, Valentino, Calvin Klein, Versace, Pucci, Adolfo, and my favorite pieces from Halston and Fiorucci. I pretty much know what I have over there," she said, pointing, "because I periodically come down and swap out my clothing. I can't fit it all in my closet at—what are you two staring at?"

"Susan, I'm flabbergasted. All of this changes the whole thing." Ryan took a small notepad from his inside jacket pocket and began to write notes.

"Changes what whole thing?" Susan looked at Ryan, then at Tina, who shrugged.

"I have no idea what he's talking about," Tina said. "I only just met him."

"No wonder your vision was—is—so stupendous! You've known all along the magnitude of this collection. I had no idea."

"But I told you …"

"Not really. At least not so I fully understood. Does Lily know what you've got here? Has she been inside?"

"No."

"She'll flip."

"Lily doesn't flip," Susan said. "Ladies of her ilk do not flip, trust me."

"Sorry. She'll bust a gut?"

They all laughed at the visual picture.

"Here's what I think," Ryan said, moving into take-charge mode. "I'm going back to the office to make a few calls and put pencil to paper. I'll get back to you early next week with a recommendation. Just put it out of your mind for now and let me do what you're paying me to do."

"Sounds good." Susan reached down and picked up a snow globe sitting atop an open box. The liquid inside had long since evaporated. She felt a familiar melancholy wash over her.

"Are we heading back now?" Tina whispered to Susan as Ryan continued to jot notes. "I need to find a restroom."

"Listen, would you mind going back with Ryan alone if I stayed awhile? He's trustworthy ... I think." She smiled as Tina blushed.

"Uh, sure, okay. He seems sweet."

"Sweet on you, I'd say." Susan winked.

"Bad timing." Tina frowned.

"One never knows, my dear. Don't discount the power of God in any situation." She hugged the young girl and called out to Ryan.

"Say, boss man. Would you mind taking Tina back to her car? I'm going to stay here for a bit and lock up. I'll grab a cab back to the office."

"Sure, boss lady." He walked Tina toward his car, smiling back at her. "You have paperwork on the dimensions and cost of these units and the stats on the cold-storage unit, right?"

"Yes." Susan nodded.

"If you can leave them on my desk, that would be great."

"Not a problem."

She followed them over to Ryan's car as he opened the door for Tina to get in. "I need my purse." She reached into the backseat to grab it. She stood back as Ryan closed Tina's door, then extended her hand.

"Thanks for accepting our offer. I think we made a wise choice."

"Thanks for believing in me." He took her hand. "Susan, you're trembling. Are you okay?"

She nodded quickly. "Just thinking about all the work we'll need to do to unpack this."

"I have to tell you, I'm a bit overwhelmed myself. But give me a few days to comprehend it all, and I can guarantee you we'll have even more to be excited about. See you a bit later?"

"Yes … no. On second thought," she mused, staring back at the building where Marilyn was housed, "I think I'm going to head over to the salon. I left the directions to Lily's place on your credenza, and you have a set of office keys, right?"

"Correct."

"How about we call it a day here and you get yourself settled at the Cedar Ridge hovel?"

"That's all right by me."

"One more thing …"

"Yes?" Ryan walked around the car to his side.

"Take good care of her." She nodded at Tina, who was writing something in Ryan's *Andy Warhol Idea Book*. "She's a special young woman."

"I can see that," he said sheepishly.

"Ryan," she said quietly, "I hope it's okay that I kind of hired her without first consulting you."

"Kind of?" He raised his eyebrows. "It's okay." He smiled as he opened the door and slid into the front seat of his car. "Just don't let it happen again."

Susan waved as the two young people drove away. Then she walked back over to Marilyn and slowly lowered herself into the driver's seat. She ran her fingers over the dashboard, recalling the significance of this beautiful car. It was the first gift she had ever received from Jean-Claude—the gift that set the tone for their life together.

He had given her keys to a car.

And she had given him the keys to her heart.

Chapter 27

"Happy twenty-first birthday, gorgeous!" Jean-Claude handed her the keys, which were tied together with a pink satin bow.

"But my birthday was last week," she squeaked, staring at the cotton-candy pink Shelby Roadster sitting in front of his Fifth Avenue apartment at the Sherry-Netherland.

"Jean-Claude, I'm flattered, but I barely know you. I can't accept this kind of present from you."

His accented voice was smooth as honey, his eyes dark and mysterious. "Ah, don't be a foolish bunny, of course you can! This is a special birthday, you are a special woman, our meeting was a special occasion, and I want you always to remember it." He picked her up and twirled her around, hugging her close and kissing her hair.

"What do you think, Leonard?" he asked the stern-faced doorman who stood quietly nearby, like a guard in front of Buckingham Palace. "Would you accept it?"

"Pink isn't my color, sir," the man said. He bent at the waist and tipped his hat. "I'll be inside if you need me, sir." Then he disappeared inside the luxurious lobby of the elegant Sherry-Netherland Hotel.

The young pair stifled their amusement at the uniformed doorman's serious demeanor until he was safely inside—at which time they doubled up in laughter.

It was April in New York, and Susan was in love for the first time.

They had met the week before, on April 26, 1977, at the grand opening of Studio 54, a new Manhattan establishment co-owned by her friend Steve Rubell, known as "Lord of the Disco." That had been her real twenty-first birthday. "How thoughtful of you to open the Studio on my behalf!" She'd pinched Steve on the cheek and followed her friends to the dance floor, where they began to dance to the pounding beat of Donna Summer's "I Feel Love."

Opening night at Studio 54 had started slowly. Even at eleven that night the cavernous disco was only semicrowded. But that left more room on the dance floor, an occurrence that would seldom happen in days to come. At one point, Susan found herself in the VIP upper balcony looking down on Cher and Margaux Hemingway dancing, strobe lights flashing, and music pulsating. She'd just been introduced to a rather odd-looking man named Donald Trump and his new wife, Ivana, when someone tapped her on the shoulder.

"Would you care to dance?" The most handsome man in the entire world reached for her hand and brushed warm lips over the back of it. His dark eyes never left hers.

As lame as it sounded, once Susan looked into those eyes, she was lost.

That she had ever found herself again was nothing short of a miracle. And sometimes she wondered about the parts of herself she left behind.

A shaft of afternoon sun had found Susan as she sat in her Shelby in the open storage building. Flushed from the heat that was squeezing out the cool air, she climbed out of Marilyn and stretched.

She shouldn't be surprised that the car had stirred up memories of her first love. She had been thinking more about Jean-Claude recently—a fact that bothered her considerably. She thought she'd left all that behind. But she was wrong. The dreadful ache was still there.

But she did have one thing to thank Jean-Claude for, she reflected. She doubted she would ever have met Jesus Christ if not for him.

After Jean-Claude left, Susan had met a group of young people who belonged to the Manhattan Church of Christ. Had it not been for the love and support of those nonjudgmental brothers and sisters, the last months in New York before she moved out west would have been unbearable. They'd showed her what faith meant in the flesh, though they hadn't been able to extinguish her lingering grief.

The first few years she'd been married to Michael, her most fervent prayer had been that in moments of intimacy she wouldn't call out the name of her lost love. And when she quietly wept in her husband's arms after lovemaking, she hadn't had the heart to tell him why. She'd merely let him think she joined him in the utter heart-fulfilling happiness of the moment.

In time, though, the gentle love she felt for Michael had grown into something far stronger and more committed than she'd ever believed possible. A good man, a gentle man, he had been her lifesaver, her anchor in the storm. For that she would be forever grateful, forever loving.

She switched off the light, pulled down the heavy overhead door, and secured the padlock on a storage room that held years of memories, wondering what the coming months would bring as she journeyed into the future by unpacking the history of her past.

From: Patricia Davies (boomerbabepat@
boomerbabesrock.com)

Sent: Saturday, April 22, 9:53 p.m.

To: Susan Anderson

Subject: I'm Concerned About You

I won't beat around the bush. You don't sound like yourself. Your
past few e-mails have me concerned. Should I be? I trust you
know that whatever you share will remain confidential. How can
I help? Love, Pat

From: Susan Anderson (boomerbabesusan@
boomerbabesrock.com)

Sent: Monday, April 24, 2:11 a.m.

To: Patricia Davies

Subject: RE: I'm Concerned About You

Bless your heart. Don't know what I'd do without your friendship.

Plans for the new DD are progressing rapidly. I still want to talk
with you about the possibility of opening a branch of Glitter and
Bling inside the WE, or maybe a franchise, but we can discuss
that later, okay?

As for the Henderson ranch, Michael and I have been working
together on the plans. Truth be told it's his dream house, not

mine. It's all getting rather Spanish and Zorro-esqe, if you get my drift. But there's going to be a room for some of my collection, so I will be able to keep at least some of my stuff close by. ☺

We closed on the sale of the three development parcels—I can't believe we made so much money on that desert land. Michael said the ranch and everything in it would be paid for in full before we even moved in. In fact, we could build FIVE houses this same size with what we made.

I suppose I should be happy. But the truth is, I'm just so cotton-picking angry at Michael I can't see straight! You know how difficult it's been over the years, keeping Disco Diva alive. The past few years have been easier since we've been getting all the media attention, but money's still a concern. Last year when the lease came up on my two storage units, I had to sell one of my Andy Warhol sketches to pay for it. And all this time we've been sitting on land that is worth a fortune. We could have sold off even one parcel years ago and made enough for Michael's dream house AND my Disco Diva overhead. How could Michael just sit there and let me struggle? I would never do that to him if I had money and he needed it.

I guess I'm just tired, Pat. And menopausal. Can't believe my fiftieth birthday is this Wednesday. How did I get so old?

From: Patricia Davies (boomerbabepat@
             boomerbabesrock.com)

Sent: Tuesday, April 25, 6:45 a.m.

To: Susan Anderson

Subject: RE: I'm Concerned About You

Heading out the door to get to the shop early, but I had to respond to you. What were you doing sending e-mails at two in the morning? Do you ever sleep anymore?

As for what you are feeling ... I can understand why you might be angry. I know the money thing has always weighed heavy on your heart. What does Michael say?

You know, I've never met him. But unless you are a pathological liar, which I doubt after five years of cybercommunication, you've always indicated that he's a good guy. In fact, you hardly ever speak negatively about him—something I've always admired about you. You wouldn't believe how some of my customers talk about their husbands.

Suze, this marriage thing isn't easy. Since John's accident, we've had to redefine what we thought was true ... every step of the way. God has used this time to mold us into different people, individually as well as a couple. Perhaps that is what God is doing to you and Michael—moving you into a new space (including a new home and new furnishings). Then again, what do I know? I sell glitter and bling in Hollywood. Anyway, back to my original question ... what does Michael say about how you are feeling?

FIFTY! I keep forgetting how young you are (ha-ha). Planning anything special? Love, Pat

From: Susan Anderson (boomerbabesusan@ boomerbabesrock.com)

Sent: Tuesday, April 25, 10:45 p.m.

To: Patricia Davies

Subject: RE: I'm Concerned About You

Still at the salon. just locked up—long day. I'll be back at 6 a.m. tomorrow, I really should put a sofa bed here!

Forgive me for getting so caught up in my drama that I've neglected to ask you about John. How is he doing? He started with a new physical therapist last month, right? I don't know how you do it all, how you juggle everything and take care of him, too.

Okay, gotta sign off. My eyes are crossing. Guess I'm dealing with the mean reds or the bitter blues, or whatever the heck color applies. I know God has a plan, just wish He'd e-mail it.

P.S.: I think Michael has been planning a surprise birthday bash. I've noticed some telltale signs—like my address book was moved, little things like that. I'll let you know.

From: Patricia Davies (boomerbabepat@ boomerbabesrock.com)

Sent: Wednesday, April 26, 7:00 a.m.

To: Susan Anderson

Subject: HAPPY 50th BIRTHDAY TO YOU!

Click on the link below to hear John and me singing. What are you doing tonight for the big five-oh?

No need to apologize, Suze. You've got a lot going on yourself. John's doing well, spending less time in the wheelchair and using the walker more. Having him around full time isn't as tough as I thought it would be, at least not now that he's feeling better.

But you didn't answer my question. What does Michael say about how you are feeling? My gut tells me you haven't talked with him, and that's not good. Please know I love you and I'm here for you. Send a birthday photo, okay?

From: Susan Anderson (boomerbabesusan@
             boomerbabesrock.com)

Sent: Thursday, April 27, 7:05 a.m.

To: Patricia Davies

Subject: RE: HAPPY 50th BIRTHDAY TO YOU!

Thanks for the birthday song! Forgive me for not answering all your questions in much detail. I want to get out of the house before Michael gets home from work ... because I'm so mad at him I could spit. Maybe *mad* isn't the right word. *Hurt* is more like it—or *disappointed*, maybe?

I got all dressed up last night for our "dinner date." I was certain he'd planned a surprise party for me. I mean, it's my fiftieth birthday, for crying out loud! Well, it was a surprise all right—just the two of us at Bradley Ogden's in Caesars Palace. Just us, no one else. It's a nice place, and we had a splendid meal, and M gave me a beautiful strand of Mikimoto pearls. But then—get this—he informed me we had to get home by ten so he could change and go to work! Do you think he could have taken off one night? He's retiring in two months anyway.

He doesn't know I'm upset, and I wouldn't think of hurting him. That's why I need to get to the salon before he comes home—so I can cool down and not say something I'll regret. I keep asking God to soften my heart, yet the more I think and pray about it, the yuckier I feel.

It's just that I love parties, and Michael knows how much I love parties. How could he be so "off" on this? I guess I wonder about our communication in general—we've been "off" for quite awhile. Not sure what to do about that. I know I'm a lucky woman. Michael's a hard worker, a good provider, honest, ethical, dependable, etc. Just not very sensitive or romantic. Guess you can't have it all, eh?

Chapter 28

"I can't believe it's already the middle of May," Ryan said to Lily as they had coffee on the patio outside the guesthouse.

"If you think time flies, you should see it from an old lady's perspective. I go to sleep and wake up and a decade has gone by." She reached for a croissant as Ryan chuckled. "Don't laugh, it's true. *Carpe diem* takes on new meaning as one gets older."

"You are too much, Lily. I'm so glad you invited me to stay here at Cedar Ridge. Not only is this better than a sleazy apartment off the strip, but I get to enjoy your company, and that is indeed a pleasure."

"Something tells me any apartment you would have procured would be far from sleazy, my dear boy. But I'm glad you're here too." Lily took a bite of her croissant and smiled at him as they enjoyed the coolness of the quiet spring morning.

Ryan smiled back. He had never been this happy, this content, or this busy. The progress they had made since his arrival last month was mind-boggling. He had a trio of dynamic women working alongside him, and together they made a formidable team.

Susan was putting in considerable hours at the construction office and was eager to assist Ryan in following the timeline he had developed. Her energy was contagious, and her passion for the disco era surpassed anything he had ever experienced. It was funny, though.

The more he got to know her, the more of a mystery she became. She would be telling him all about a particular conversation she'd had with someone like Andy Warhol, then clam up to a simple question about her life. He was learning there was a great deal more to Susan Anderson than met the eye.

The same could be said for Miss Lily, although the sense of mystery he felt from her came more from the lifestyle she lived and less from things she didn't want to discuss. In fact, she loved talking about herself, though she did it in such a self-deprecating way that Ryan could never be offended. A generous and benevolent dictator, she ruled quietly from a distance, pretending not to rule at all. Her influence in the community opened doors for them in ways Ryan had never imagined possible.

Then there was Tina, the surprising fourth member of the White Elephant team. From the day they met, he'd been a goner. He had yet to admit that to a single person, though, including Tina, and he still wasn't sure how she felt about him. Fortunately, time was on their side. They could take things easy—one day at a time. That he got to see her daily was a wonderful bonus.

"Now, tell me how the inventory project is going," Lily interrupted, and Ryan jumped. "I'm sorry, dear, did I wake you?"

"Very funny. I was just thinking. What did you say?"

"I asked about the inventory project. What is the status of the temporary storage building—will it be here soon?"

He gave her an update on the plans to move Susan's entire collection from the two off-site storage units to the grounds of the White Elephant. He'd been working on the inventory plans with Tina since the day they met.

"Very good." She made a small check mark on a list she had pulled from her pocket. "Now, do we need to hire someone to help Tina? I know she can only work part time—less than part time, actually—and that's probably fine during this stage. But don't you think once we move the collection to the site we'll need someone full time?"

Ryan felt his face flush and struggled to keep the idiotic smile off his face as he thought of Tina. He thought he'd succeeded in looking merely professional at the thought of Tina, but Lily was not fooled.

"Oh, dear boy, methinks the cat is out of the bag." She crossed her arms, sat back comfortably in her chair, and tapped her index finger on her chin.

"What do you mean?" Ryan reached for his coffee and knocked a spoon off the table.

"I mean the love bug has bitten. I suspected as much."

"No one says 'love bug' anymore, Lily. And I haven't been infected with an insect-carrying disease."

"Oh, pish-posh." When Ryan didn't offer further explanation, Lily folded up her list, stuck it in her pocket, and pushed back her chair, preparing to stand. "Mark my words, young man, we will return to this enchanting subject soon." She looked at her watch. "But right now I have an appointment."

"About Tina's hours …" Ryan quickly moved toward Lily to pull her chair out as she stood. "What do you think we should do?"

"Thank you, dear." Lily brushed invisible crumbs off her skirt. "I think we should hire additional help. I'm not suggesting we replace Tina with someone who is able to work full time. Don't even think about that. She needs to remain in charge of the inventory project."

Ryan's shoulders visibly relaxed. "When she walked into our lives it was a God-cidence if ever there was one."

"But?" Ryan said. "I feel a *but* coming on."

"But this is going to be a huge project, and as much as I know you want to work with her every minute she is on site, you have other tasks on your plate. Once the collection is relocated, we need someone focused on the project a minimum of eight hours every day, five days a week."

"Yeah, I know. Tina knows it too. She knows that working a couple of hours every night before curtain isn't going to cut it." What Lily didn't know was that lately he and Tina had taken to working a few hours every night after the show as well. They'd grab takeout from one of the many nearby restaurants, go back to the office, and work. And talk into the wee hours of the morning.

"Then think about hiring a helper or two," Lily was saying. "They can work under Tina's capable direction. Now, I must be off. Have a good day."

Ryan leaned over and planted a light kiss on her cheek. "Thank you, Lily."

"For?"

"For being you—just for being you."

She dismissed him with a wave, and he returned to his chair, watching the elegant way she carried herself as she walked to the main house. Franco dutifully opened the door as she approached.

Ryan's cell phone rang, the first of the dozens of calls he would receive or make that day. Caller ID indicated it was Tina, and he felt the silly grin spread over his face again.

"Ryan Power. Can I help you?" Serious and businesslike, his

typical phone greeting always made Tina laugh. Lately, she had taken to responding by saying things like, "No, sir, I'm the one who can help you," or "Tina Deitman. Your wish is my command." But now her voice sounded strained. "C-can we talk?"

"Tina, what's the matter?" He sat at attention, his senses on high alert as he strained to listen, unable to make sense of what she was saying. So he said, "I'll be right there. Give me fifteen minutes."

He worried all the way over, replaying their conversation. Her words had been cryptic, disjointed even. What was wrong? Was she about to give him the boot?

When he got to her apartment and saw that she had been crying, he didn't know what to think. Especially when she told him the reason for her distress.

"You're telling me they placed you on temporary suspension just because you've put on a little weight?"

She nodded.

"But you look fabulous."

"I do not. I am getting fat." She began to cry again.

"You are not fat." He put his hands on her shoulders. "This is crazy! Somebody needs their head examined."

"That may be so, but I still need to lose eight pounds before I can go back to work."

He couldn't believe how ready he was to march over to the Tropicana and punch the artistic director in the nose. He'd never felt this protective of any woman in his life. When she told him the suspension was without pay, he grew even angrier.

"Can she really do this?" He clenched his jaw. "I mean, is it … legal?"

"She can and she did. And, yes, it's legal. It's in my contract. I agreed to it and signed it."

He stared at her in disbelief. He thought she looked better than when they first met. She had an amazing body, a dancer's body—but not like one of those stick-thin, flat-chested dancers.

"Tina, this is my fault. We've been eating way too much late at night, and it's always carbs like spaghetti and pizza. I'm sorry. I'm a bad influence. I'll stop, I promise."

"Oh, Ryan, it is not your fault." She reached for his hand. "I'm not sure there is anything you can do right now to help, but thank you for offering. That means a lot to me." She squeezed his hand. "I don't know right now what I'm going to do. I'm wondering if this singing and dancing thing is really for me."

Ryan was taken aback at her resignation.

"She's only the artistic director, not God," he said seriously. "Don't let her steal your dream."

She sighed. "I won't. She isn't. It's just … now that I've been here a few months, I'm not really sure this is right for me, that it's what I want to do with my life."

He couldn't imagine her doing anything else, now that he'd seen her perform. He'd first sat in the audience two nights after they met and had been blown away by her talent. Since then, he'd seen the show about a half dozen times and thought she was looking more beautiful every day. And the more time he spent with her, the more he liked what was on the inside as well.

Lily was right. He had been bitten.

"Whatever you do," he said, "I think you're the most beautiful and brilliant woman I have ever met."

"Tell that to my boss."

"My pleasure." He reached for his cell phone. "What's her number?"

"1-800-IMA-JERK." She spelled it out, sniffling.

"Tell you what." He pulled a clean monogrammed linen handkerchief from his trouser pocket and handed it to her. "I've got the perfect exercise plan for you. If you can temporarily readjust your internal clock to let you work during the day and sleep at night, I'll offer you a full-time gig."

"Are you serious? You'll give me a job?"

"Tina, you've had a job. You've done more in developing this inventory project than you give yourself credit for. But the next stage is going to require a lot more work. Lily told me to hire someone full time. And it looks like that someone is going to be you. Even if you work full time for only a few weeks, it'll be worth it. What do you say?"

Tina's lip quivered as she fought back tears.

"Don't cry." Ryan reached for her hand. "With all those boxes you'll have to schlep around, those eight pounds will be gone before you can blink an eye."

Ryan wasn't sure how to interpret the new flood of tears that ran down Tina's face as she buried her head in her hands.

Chapter 29

"So, this is where you hide every morning." Tina handed Susan a Starbucks Cinnamon Dolce Latte.

"I'm hardly hiding. Thanks for bringing this." Susan took a sip and rolled her eyes. "Heavenly! I've been drinking that horrid stuff Michael bought at Sam's Club all morning, and I hate it." She pointed to a Mr. Coffee machine on the counter of the Henderson Ranch office.

"No problem. Where is Michael?"

"He's meeting with someone in Henderson … the city planner I think."

"This is a nice office." Tina sipped her iced decaf, looking around the space that used to be the Petite Pet shop. "Cozy. I wondered what it looked like. It's a lot quieter here than at the White Elephant."

They discussed how plans were progressing on the ranch, and Susan showed her the latest architectural drawings.

"Wow, that's a lot of house." Tina peered closer at the blueprints. "I didn't know it was going to be so big."

Susan shook her head. "It gets bigger every day."

"Like me."

"Well, not quite like you. But since you mentioned it—what exactly are you going to do?" Susan rocked back in her office chair. "Ryan called last night, told me all about your weight-gain dilemma."

Tina sat bolt upright. "You didn't say anything to him, did you?"

"Of course not. I wouldn't do that, Tina."

"I know. I'm sorry."

"I'm sorry too, about the Tropicana. But having you at the site full time is going to be a blessing—for us at least."

"I love being there." Tina put her cup on the edge of Susan's desk and paced slowly around the office. "I know I should tell Ryan about the ba— about my condition. But I don't know *what* to tell him. I still can't decide what to do."

"You don't think he suspects at all?"

"I don't think so. Not even my boss suspects. She just thinks I'm getting fat. Do I look fat? I mean, can you tell?" Tina stood sideways and pulled her blouse tight to her frame.

"Not at all, and that blows me away. You're just over halfway through your second trimester, and other than maybe a little more fullness in your beautiful face, I don't see the slightest difference. How did your boss find out?"

"We have a mandatory monthly weigh-in."

"You're kidding."

"No, I'm not. Her scale says I'm up eight pounds, but it's really eleven."

Susan was careful not to pressure the distraught young woman in any way about her pregnancy. She knew that Tina was still in weekly counseling with Thelma and that she continued to weigh all of her options. She was cutting it close, though. In Nevada an abortion was illegal after twenty-four weeks. Susan prayed that wouldn't even be an issue.

"Well, dear, you're going to have to come to some decision soon, because Ryan is taking personal responsibility for feeding you too much. He's determined to help you lose weight. But personally, I think he's conflicted."

"What do you mean?"

"You know darn well what I mean. I think he'd feed you pizza and spaghetti every day if it meant he could have you with him at the office full time. He loves having you around. We all do. But Tina ..."

"Yes?"

"This isn't a game, sweetie. I think Ryan is head over heels in love with you. Why are you afraid to tell him the truth?"

"For that very reason!" Tina raised her voice. "As soon as he finds out, he'll drop me like a hot potato or feel some sort of pathetic obligation to take care of me. And that's not what I want."

"What do you want?" Susan crossed her arms and sat back in her chair.

"I don't know anymore. Back home, all I ever dreamed about was coming to America and performing. But now that I'm here and ..." She put her hand on her tummy and looked down, fighting back tears. "Now I don't really know."

"Come here, honey." Susan walked her over to a leather sofa Michael had recently bought, pulling Tina down next to her. "Let's sit and talk about this, okay?"

They spent the next hour and a half talking about Tina's options, about her future, and about Ryan. By the time she left the ranch office, Tina had decided she wasn't going to tell Ryan until she was completely certain what she was going to do about her pregnancy.

Although Tina voiced indecision, Susan felt in her heart that

Tina had already made up her mind. She watched from the doorway as Tina drove out of the parking lot. Susan would be seeing her at the White Elephant construction site office in a couple of hours when she finished up here.

Dear Lord, help me keep my big mouth shut ... or else open Ryan's eyes soon.

―*mm*―

"I'm very pleased with the progress, young man," Lily said a scant week later, gently closing her notebook. "Well done."

"Thank you," said Ryan, "but it's been a group effort. Everyone is giving a hundred percent."

The two of them had been going over preliminary budget estimations, and it had been a good meeting. Ryan cleared his throat and continued.

"My father is passing through Vegas on business the beginning of next month, and I'd like to show him the White Elephant if that's okay. When I told him about the project, he got very excited. He's never excited about anything I do."

"Give him a chance, son. Parents go through stages."

Since coming on board, Ryan had told Lily a lot about his relationship with his father; they discussed a great many things. Lily was not only a good listener, but she also gave wise advice.

"I'd like to introduce him to Tina as well."

"Things are going well in that department?" Lily sorted through pages in the file.

"Which department? Personal or professional?"

"Which would you care to disclose?"

"Well, the personal department is pretty darn good. That's why I'd like my old man to meet her." Lily bristled at the slang reference for *father* as he continued. "As far as professional goes, I knew she was good, but she has exceeded my expectations. Having her full time the past week has been a big plus for the project. But I'm afraid it's going to be short-lived. The way she works, she'll have those few pounds gone in no time, and we'll lose her back to the Folies."

"Then perhaps it would be wise to hire help now so she can train them while she's still on suspension?"

"We're on top of it already. Susan is interviewing people from a local temp agency."

"Good. Are we finished with our meeting then? Is there anything else you need?"

"Yeah, maybe." He slid a pencil over his ear. "Can I ask you something, Lily?"

"You may ask me anything." She smiled. "Whether I choose to answer is another thing entirely."

"It's about Susan."

"What about Susan?"

"I've been watching her. The way she takes care of everyone, like a surrogate mother. She found out Tina had a doctor's appointment today—nothing's wrong, just a basic checkup—but she insisted on going with her. It's like all those showgirls who walk through her door are her children. And it's not just the girls—she treats me like I'm a son. Heck, there are times I catch her mothering *you!* She's a born nurturer. I just wonder why she and Michael don't have kids of their own."

"They tried. When they were first married, she lost three babies. Carried them almost to term. They're buried out at Woodlawn Cemetery."

"Oh, man ..."

"Yes, that about sums it up."

"What happened? I mean, what was wrong?"

"It's called placental abruption. Happens in one of every one hundred pregnancies, with chances increasing in future pregnancies. The third time just about killed her, literally and figuratively. I'm not speaking out of school. She would tell you if you asked."

"I guess I didn't want to pry."

"But it's okay to ask me?"

"Criminy, Lily. Give me a break! I'm just trying to figure her out, that's all. She ..."

"What?"

"She confounds me."

"Is that good or bad?"

"I don't know what it is. One minute I feel like a professional businessman, maybe even a peer on some level, and the next minute I feel like I'm a kid who should be sent to time-out. She's kind of all over the map emotionally, if you know what I mean?"

"I'm not sure I do."

"That's because you're a woman. You're accustomed to fluctuating emotions. Come to think of it, Tina has been rather high-strung lately too. I figured it was being out of her element and all, but now I think it's the sisterhood of the traveling estrogen. You're all conspiring against me."

"What exactly are you saying about Susan?"

"I don't know. I just feel a weird connection to her. I can't explain it. It's like we're kindred spirits on some kind of strange level."

"Weird connection?" Lily cocked her head.

"Don't twist my words. I don't mean weird as in *weird*. Just odd. You know?"

"Oh, of course." She smiled. "That clearly explains it."

"Now you're patronizing me."

"No, dear, I'm trying to understand you."

"And I'm trying to understand Susan. For instance, why doesn't her husband ever stop by? I mean, I've been in town since April. It's almost June, and I've yet to see the guy. What's up with that?"

"You'd have to ask Susan."

"I wasn't asking you to gossip, Lily. I know you and Susan get hot under the collar about that—and I admire it. Really. I guess I just wondered if there was anything you could tell me that would help me understand her better. She's kind of closed off in a lot of ways."

Lily shook her head. "Susan has a great deal on her mind these days. Working on two major building projects is quite a feat any way you look at it. Plus, she's putting in two very long days every week at Disco Diva. I'm amazed how well she is managing to juggle everything … and work with a cocky whippersnapper like you on top of it." She playfully bopped him on the head with the file folder she held in her hand.

"I suppose so. Look, I'm sorry I said anything. This job is the opportunity of a lifetime, and I'm not going to do anything to jeopardize that. I'm just trying to sort out all the—"

"Weird feelings?" Lily interjected, smiling.

"Yes, weird feelings. They're flying all over the place." He gave her a crooked smile. "Like I said, I've never been around this much emoting. It's a whole different ball game working with three beautiful women day in and day out."

"Poor boy."

"I know. It's a tough job, but someone's gotta do it."

"Just remember," she said, "life is a never-ending journey to gain wisdom and knowledge. Contrary to popular belief, the two are not one and the same." She paused. "Now, why don't you just invite your father for a visit, and let's talk about how we can show him a good time while he's here."

From: Susan Anderson (boomerbabesusan@
boomerbabesrock.com)

Sent: Thursday, June 1, 2:13 a.m.

To: Patricia Davies; Mary Johnson; Lisa Taylor; Linda Jones; Sharon Wilson

Subject: hi all

its late—gotta tryto catch some Zs but wanted to say hi. lots going on with micheal and the WE and such. more later—i'm fried!!! G'night. Suze

From: Patricia Davies (boomerbabepat@
boomerbabesrock.com)

Sent: Thursday, June 1, 11:22 p.m.

To: Susan Anderson

Subject: Can we please talk?

Susan, sweetie—

When you told me back in February that you were going to be building a new Disco Diva AND a new house, I kept my mouth shut. It sounded completely crazy to me, but what do I know? I live in Hollyweird.

In March, when you signed the official contract with Lily and told us about this elaborate schedule you and Michael worked out so you could be all things to all people, I wanted to fly out and grab you by the lapels, get right in your face, and yell, 'What the heck are you doing?' But still, I kept my mouth shut.

In April, when you and Lily hired the Wunderkind from California, and then later that same month when you flipped out (rightfully so) about your neglected fiftieth birthday party, I once again executed my right to be a silent observer. After all, good friends listen and observe and offer opinions only when asked—and you never asked.

But by May, I was fielding dozens of e-mails from the entire Boomer Babes Rock contingent—begging me to conduct an intervention. They want me to fly out there and meet with you in person to see if you're okay, because all of us are worried. You aren't making any sense whatsoever in your messages. They are being sent to us at all hours of the morning—disjointed, full of typos, no punctuation. Who are you? e. e. cummings?

Susan, this isn't you. Are you eating? Sleeping? Going to church? Praying? We are surely praying for you, and we're all concerned. Please, Susan, do you need help? I can come out for a week or so. Just let me know, and I'll be there in a heartbeat.

Love, Pat

From: Susan Anderson (boomerbabesusan@ boomerbabesrock.com)

Sent: Friday, June 2, 3:24 a.m.

To: Patricia Davies

Subject: RE: Can we please talk?

Dearest Pat,

Appreciate your concern, but I have everything under control. (See, no more e. e. cummings.) Lots going on, but I'm managing—really. I'm eating, sleeping, working, and praying—no need to worry. Please tell the gals I'm fine. In fact, I can fit in clothes that were a tad tight, and that's a good thing. Michael is ecstatic that he retires at the end of the month, Lily is having a blast with Ryan living at Cedar Ridge—and Ryan's father is here for a visit. (Haven't seen him yet, will be meeting him later.) Loretta is blossoming with the added responsibility. My clients who were mad at me for letting them go have stopped calling to complain (another good thing). And even though it's getting hotter every day, I am keeping my cool. Most of the time. No need to worry, my dear friend. All is well.

Regards, Susan

From: Patricia Davies (boomerbabepat@boomerbabesrock.
               com)
Sent: Friday, June 2, 10:35 a.m.
To: Susan Anderson
Subject: RE: Can we please talk?

Regards? What am I, your elocution teacher? Call me after you meet Ryan's father and your schedule frees up for the weekend. We still need to talk. I love you. Pat.

Chapter 30

"Traffic is terrible!" Lily dropped her purse onto the table and sat down. "I forget what it's like on a Friday afternoon in the real world—so many vehicles! Doesn't anyone carpool?"

"Oh, now that's rich." Susan placed a document in the photocopy machine. "When did you last carpool? For that matter, when did you last live in the real world?" She pushed the start button on the machine as Lily broke into peals of laughter.

It did Susan's heart good to see her friend feeling so happy. Although Lily was involved in a great many service projects and philanthropic events in Las Vegas, Susan knew that at the end of the day she went home alone to that rambling estate. Having Ryan nearby in the guest quarters and now having his apparently charismatic father staying for a few days as well had given Lily a new glint.

"So, are you impressed with daddy dearest?" Susan joked as she walked to the supply closet for a fresh ream of paper.

"Very much so. He's quite dashing—you'll see for yourself when they come by today. He seems charming, too—not at all the self-centered man I expected from Ryan's comments."

It was true. During the past months as they were all getting to know one another, Ryan had shared that his father had been less than involved in his life. There were even a few hints that he had been unfaithful to Ryan's mother. Susan sensed a great deal of resentment in Ryan, along with a deep desire to show his father that he could succeed at something grand.

Maybe that was one reason he'd been working so hard the past few weeks. He had supervised the delivery and assembly of the temporary aluminum building for storage and moved mountains to get the electric service connected to the building. He'd also worked with Tina to design and set up the office and inventory areas for her to use. On Monday, the movers would transport Susan's entire collection from the two off-site storage units to the temporary building. Then Tina would get started on the next phase of the massive inventory project.

Although still in its infancy stages, this entertainment complex would indeed be a feather in Ryan's cap, and Susan prayed his father would be positive and kind during his visit.

"Did you sense any jealousy or anger between them?" Susan began to empty the wastebaskets in their office into a large plastic bag.

"Not at all. In fact, Gene seemed interested in the project. He asked a great many questions about the salon, your collection, the White Elephant, and what we proposed to do with the building. He wanted to know all about you. Ryan was superb—you'd have been proud of him. He gave the presentation with as much passion and purpose as you would have. His father was clearly impressed, especially when he mentioned Marilyn." Lily smiled. "Ryan was right. His dad almost jumped out of his chair when he learned you have a Shelby named Marilyn."

"Typical guy," Susan mused, securing a twist tie on the plastic bag. "But I'm really glad he was impressed by Ryan's presentation. He needs his father's approval, even if he won't admit it. Well, I guess we all do. I'm glad Mr. Power took the time to visit."

"Actually, he's decided to stay a couple of extra days. I think we should insist that Ryan take the entire weekend off, spend it with his dad."

Ryan's contract had him officially working Monday through Friday and on weekends only during critical times. However, since starting the project, he could be found at the White Elephant for at least a few hours every weekend. Since Susan worked with him Thursday through Sunday afternoons only, the weekend hours were often necessary.

"I agree. He needs some time off." Susan took a big gulp from the can sitting on her desk.

"Is that one of those energy drinks?" Lily asked.

"Yes, ma'am." She took the minivac from the closet and began to go over the office carpet, raising her voice. "Can't say that I'd mind taking the weekend off, at least from the ranch office. You wouldn't believe how cramped that office is."

"Susan?" Lily said.

"Not at all like this office. I can't believe I ever thought of expanding the salon into that space. I had no idea how small it was."

"Susan," Lily said again, a bit louder.

"The office is the only thing that's small in that project." She pushed the vacuum faster. "Michael has decided to expand the house some more. Seems he's always wanted a wood shop. Funny. I've been married to Gepetto for twenty-five years, and that's the first I've heard of that dream. God forbid he should decide that he's always wanted to play basketball. We'll end up with an indoor court ... or maybe a—"

"Susan!" Lily yelled, at last getting her attention. "Turn that off!"

Susan turned off the vacuum and pushed back the hair that had fallen into her eyes.

"Yes?"

"You haven't stopped moving since I walked in that door." Lily pointed. "I'm exhausted from watching you."

"Well, someone's got to clean the—"

"Someone does clean it, Susan. You know we have a service that comes in every Monday." Lily took the vacuum from Susan's hand and noticed she was shaking. "Something is wrong. What is it? Honey, please sit down. You're scaring me."

"Don't be silly!" Susan pulled away, laughing. "I'm fine." She grabbed the minivac from Lily, wrapped the vacuum cord on the handle, and looked around the office. "I think that's about it, at least in here. I'm going to check on the conference room."

"You don't need to do that. It's fine. Why don't you take a break until our guest arrives?"

"I don't need a break." Susan began to sort the paper clips and rubber bands on the work-station counter.

"Susan. You aren't listening to me. You need a break. After Ryan finishes giving his father the tour, I want you to go home as well, and I don't want to see you back here until next week. You get some rest."

"But—"

"No buts!" Lily said firmly. "Enough is enough. You need some time off. Look at you."

"What's wrong with me?"

"You've lost weight. You're working too much and not eating enough. And that stuff is poison." She pointed at the energy drink.

"It's hardly pois—"

"It is when it's all you live on. I'm serious, Susan. Just take a few days. Relax. Put things into perspective. We have a long way to go on this project, and it's going to take time to build that dream house of yours as well."

"It's not my dream house."

"Whatever!" Lily snapped. "What I'm saying, Susan, is that all of us need to be fit every step of the way if we're going to accomplish our goals."

"Aye, aye, sir!" Susan joked, standing to attention.

"I'm not kidding."

"I know you're not, and I'm grateful for your concern, but I'm okay. Everything is fine."

They heard car tires crunch on the gravel outside the office.

"Sounds like they're here," Lily said.

"I'm going to run a comb through this mop. Be right back," Susan promised, practically running from the room.

They were in Ryan's office when she returned, everyone laughing and talking at once. Ryan sat majestically behind his desk, and Lily and Gene Power were sitting in the high-backed wing chairs that sat opposite his desk, their backs to her. Susan smiled and gave a thumbs-up at the pride she could see on Ryan's face, and he rose from the chair like a proper gentleman when she entered the room.

"Susan, I'd like to introduce my father."

When Gene Power stood and turned to face her, the laughter died in her throat. It was as though a powerful sledgehammer had come down from above and knocked the wind clean out of her. Everything looked hazy, and she couldn't breathe.

"Hello, Susan," Jean-Claude said as he extended his hand.

Susan's heart leaped to her throat as her knees buckled and she fell to the floor.

Chapter 31

She awoke to find people kneeling over her as her head swam with a woozy feeling that reminded her of a bad hangover, something she hadn't experienced in many years. It took time for her to remember where she was ... and what had happened.

"I've called Michael, sweetheart. He'll be here any minute," Lily said, tears running down her cheeks. She turned to a paramedic. "What's wrong with her? Did she have a heart attack? Is she going to be okay?"

"Lily." Susan reached up to grip her friend's hand. "I'm okay."

"Oh, sweetie, you scared me."

As her vision cleared, Susan saw strangers, and she could read the EMT insignia on their shirts.

They had called the paramedics? What happened? The last thing she remembered was walking into the room and seeing ... seeing Jean-Claude. But surely she had to be mistaken. What kind of fool had she made of herself? Lily was right. She needed a rest.

An EMT leaned over her. "Mrs. Anderson, look at me. Can you see me? Try to focus on my finger. Can you follow the movement of my finger with your eyes?"

"Susan!" She heard Michael's voice, followed by the slamming of a door as her husband rushed into the room and knelt on the floor beside her.

"Honey, are you okay? What happened? Talk to me."

"Your wife is fine, Mr. Anderson," said a blond paramedic. Susan watched him remove the blood-pressure cuff from her arm in slow motion.

"It appears she fainted," said a dark Latino paramedic. He smiled at her. "Can I help you sit up?" He gently pulled her to a sitting position, propping her up against Michael's chest. Michael held her in his arms, planting kisses on top of her head and rocking her gently.

"You might not want to do that," the blond paramedic said. "Might make her dizzy."

"Oh, I'm sorry, babe. Did I hurt you? Are you okay?"

She felt bad for Michael. He was clearly distraught, as was Lily, who was sitting on the arm of a chair wiping her eyes as Ryan rested his hand on her shoulder.

Where was Ryan's father? How was she ever going to apologize to him? How foolish she had been.

"I'm not sure I've ever had that effect on a woman before." That unmistakable honeyed voice filled the room as she craned her neck to see him.

No doubt about it, the man sitting on the corner of Ryan's desk swinging his leg was her former lover in all his sartorial splendor.

"Oh, dear Lord," Susan said, turning her head into Michael's chest.

"We're going to head out now," the paramedics said, grabbing what looked like toolboxes and talking to Lily, who had clearly taken the role of the person in charge.

She followed them to the door. "Will she be okay? Is there something we should do?"

"Her vital signs are good. Sounds to me from what you said that she's been working too hard. Just get her home and to bed, let her have a good night's sleep. But you might encourage her to visit her family doctor, just to make sure."

"Thank you, gentlemen." Lily shook their hands. "Thank you for coming so quickly. I'll be certain to tell Mr. Santorini you were exemplary professionals."

They were surprised she knew the name of their boss and stood a little straighter as they said good-bye.

"Michael, what do you say we get her up off this hard floor and onto a chair where she'll be more comfortable?" Lily said.

They each grabbed an arm and lifted her to her feet, where she swayed a bit unsteadily. They helped her sit in one of the high-backed chairs as her eyes locked with Ryan's.

"I'm sorry," she said to him.

"For what?"

"For him." She nodded to his father.

"Now, that isn't very nice, is it, Susan?" Ryan's father took his son's chair behind the desk, leaned back, and crossed his arms.

"What's this about?" Ryan asked, utterly flabbergasted. "Do you know each other?"

The quiet was deafening as Susan stared at Jean-Claude, each waiting to see what the other would divulge.

"Susan," Michael said, his voice firm, "what is going on? Who is this man?"

She said nothing.

"Susan?" He reached for her hand, and she gripped it tightly. The sound of her weeping broke the uncomfortable silence.

"Honey, talk to me. What's going on?" He stared at Jean-Claude, who just smirked and said nothing.

"Do you know Gene?" Lily asked Susan as everyone continued to stare.

"I used to," she whispered, "before he was Gene. He was the guy who bought most of the clothes I wear, the furniture in our house, and a great deal of the memorabilia in my collection, including Marilyn."

"Marilyn?" Ryan choked, staring at his father.

"I can't believe you kept her." Jean-Claude grinned. "From what I hear, you kept almost everything. Wise girl. My son says we have a fortune in our collection."

He picked up the snow globe sitting on the desk. "I remember this. We got it in London, didn't we? You and Bianca bought matching ones, right?"

"You went to London?" Michael asked. "Together?"

"Bianca?" Ryan stared. "As in Jagger?"

"Oh, Sexy Suzie and Bianca were great friends. They drank the same scotch."

Michael glowered. "My wife doesn't drink."

"She did back then—like a fish."

"Shut up, Jean-Claude." Susan began to regain her composure.

"Jean-Claude? What's *that* about?" Ryan asked his father.

"My real name. Americans mangle French—it got rather cumbersome."

"Like me." Susan swallowed.

"Not at all like you, Sexy Suzie. You were never cumbersome, just a bit young. We met on her twenty-first birthday," he explained to Michael, who only stared. "I can't believe you haven't told your husband about us, Suzie. Shame on you. But then again, there was a lot to be ashamed of, wasn't there?"

"What's that supposed to mean?" Michael clenched his fists.

"Miss Pollyanna here wasn't so pure back then."

"How can you say that?" she whispered. "I trusted you."

"You used me, and you know it. It was my money you cared about, not me. I bought you a lifestyle you loved."

"That's not true." She looked beseeching at Michael. "Please, take me home. Please."

He helped her up from the chair, glaring at the man Susan so obviously loathed. "I have no idea who you are, but I want you out of our life now."

"I'm not sure you're in any position to tell me what to do."

"I'm not?" Michael struggled to lash out at the stranger who had caused his wife such pain, but she was clinging to him as they stood, urging him to move in the opposite direction.

"I'm not sure what I expected from you, Sexy Suzie, but it wasn't this," Jean-Claude said. "You were always the life of the party. What happened to you?"

"Michael, ignore him. It was a long time ago. I'm not the same person."

"You really do know her?" Ryan slammed his hand on the desk. "You liar!"

"Slow down, son," he said. "I never lied to you."

"Pardon me, sir," Lily interjected, "but you sat in my dining room last night at dinner asking question after question about Susan and the project and our plans, all the while knowing her? You don't call that a lie?"

Jean-Claude looked at her. "No. I call it a sin of omission. I couldn't be certain. The woman you were both describing sounded like Mother Teresa, a far cry from the sexy spitfire I knew. I suspected, but I had to be sure."

"Of what?" his son demanded.

"That, indeed, this was the woman who killed my unborn child."

Susan wilted back into the arms of her husband, fighting the urge to pass into the blank oblivion she had entered earlier. But no sooner had the urge to retreat raised its ugly head than the stronger urge to defend took precedence.

"You filthy vermin," she spat at him, lunging forward and taking Michael by surprise. She flailed at Jean-Claude like a madwoman. Her nails raked the skin on his face as she knocked him to the ground.

"Whoa, there, baby." Jean-Claude grabbed her wrists.

"Don't call my wife baby!" With Ryan's help, Michael pulled her off the man as she screamed incoherently, kicking, punching, and gnashing like someone possessed.

"Oh, dear Lord!" Lily cried, unable to move.

Jean-Claude stood up and touched his face, cursing at Susan for drawing blood. That only made her angrier. She broke away from Michael and pounced on Jean-Claude's back.

"Get off me, you crazy—ow!" Susan had wrapped her legs around him and was pummeling him with her fists.

"Susan!" Michael yelled. "Stop it—stop it, honey. Please, you're scaring us. Please, Suze!"

It took all three of them to pull her off. The struggle left Lily crying, Ryan fuming, and Michael holding his wife in his arms as she struggled to get free.

"Well, I think that warrants a call to my attorney." Jean-Claude straightened his slacks, reached for a tissue, and began wiping the blood from his face. "You'd best pray this doesn't leave scars."

"Shut up!" Ryan and Michael yelled simultaneously.

Michael held Susan tightly until she quieted down, crying like a baby on his chest. Too weak to stand, she collapsed on the chair as he cradled her in his arms.

"What did you do to her?" Ryan demanded of his father.

"Oh, sure, blame me. It's always the man who gets blamed—the horrible man who drives the woman to her desperate choice. Well, *I* didn't walk into the clinic to abort my child! She did that with her own two feet. Ask her if I forced her to do that. Go ahead. Ask her!"

Susan was in no condition to be asked anything. She was incoherent, almost catatonic, as her husband carried her out of the trailer and placed her onto the front seat of his car.

"Honey, I'm taking you home. It's going to be okay. I promise you. It's going to be okay."

But the haunting whimpers of his wife dispelled any assurance that things would ever be okay again.

Chapter 32

"You've got to get some sleep," Lily said sternly the next morning as Michael poured another cup of coffee. "Let me stay with her while you get some rest." She put her hand over his. "Michael, you're no good to her if you collapse from exhaustion. Please let me help. That's why I'm here."

Michael opened the cupboard, grabbed a large bottle of aspirin, and shook several into his hand, swallowing them with a slug of coffee.

"Get it off your chest, Michael," Lily urged. "What do you want to say?"

He felt a wave of anger, stopped short of slamming his fist on the counter, and said with quiet restraint, "What's going on, Lily? That's what I want to say. I don't understand any of this." He sank into the chair and rubbed his hand over his eyes.

Lily just looked at the slightly ajar bedroom door. "How is she?"

"She's been sleeping on and off since last night. Kept waking up crying—I'd hold her until she fell back to sleep. I've never seen her like this."

"Has she said anything? Is she talking—coherent?"

"She's a mess!" He stood, almost knocking the chair out from under him. "I don't know what to do—what am I supposed to do? She hasn't said a word, just cries. I got her to drink some water and walked her to the bathroom this morning, but it's like she's sleepwalking. I don't know what I'm supposed to do!"

"You've been up all night?" Lily put her hands on his shoulders.

"I'm always up all night." He pulled away. "I'm fine. She's not!"

"Look at me, Michael." He focused swollen eyes on Lily.

"I will tell you everything I know—that's a promise. But you need to get a couple of hours of sleep first. Don't argue with me. It won't work." She pointed toward the guest bedroom. "Go lie down, and I'll sit with Susan."

"But ... but ..." he stammered, all energy gone.

"No buts. This is a noncontingent offer. I sit, you sleep, and I'll tell you what I know when you're rested. Go. I'll be right here."

He shuffled down the hallway, taking one last look toward where his wife was sleeping before entering the guest bedroom, where he fell exhausted on top of the covers.

He didn't even bother to take off his shoes.

"Michael? Wake up."

The gentle knocking startled him as he looked around to get his bearings.

Where am I? He sat on the edge of the bed, trying to focus as the events of the past twenty-four hours returned. The knocking continued. It was Lily calling to him.

"I'm up. Is she awake? What time is it?" He looked at his watch and jumped up, running a hand through his hair. "Criminy, Lily, it's after three!" He jerked open the door to find her standing in the hallway.

"Shh, she just got back to sleep."

"What happened?" He started past Lily as she grabbed his arm.

"Wait. Listen to me." She held his arm and walked him toward the living room. "You were out like a light as soon as your head hit the pillow—I checked on you." She pulled him down on the sofa to sit next to her. "I sat in the kitchen for awhile and read, maybe an hour or so. About then I heard her call out."

"Did she talk to you?" he whispered.

"I tried to get her to talk, but all she does is weep. She appeared to know who I was. She let me hold her, and I prayed for her. But ..." She fought back tears.

"What?" He put his hand on her arm.

"It's like some hidden dam has broken, letting out years of sorrow. I've never heard more painful sobbing in all of my life. That poor child—I had no idea." Tears fell gently down Lily's cheeks as Michael rocked forward and put his head in his hands.

"I think I've read about this," Lily went on. "They even had something on Oprah awhile back—trauma from a sudden shock."

"What do you think I should do?" he asked desperately.

"I have a good friend who is a doctor. I could call him. He would come here as a favor to me. He's a psychiatrist."

"A shrink?" His eyebrows arched. "You think that's what she needs?"

"I'm not sure what she needs, but it would be a start." She picked up a pad of paper from the coffee table and handed it to Michael. "I started this when she went back to sleep. Look." She pointed. "You brought her home at about nine o'clock last night, right?"

"I guess so."

"You said she slept intermittently from nine last evening until late this morning, when she drank some water and you took her to the bathroom?"

"Yes." He looked at the chart in his hands.

"That means she slept for twelve hours. I got here at eleven, and she woke up about noon. I tried to get her to eat something, but she wouldn't. She took a few sips of tea and fell back asleep by one o'clock. She's been out ever since."

"She had the flu awhile back and slept a lot until she beat the bug. The doc said sleep and fluids were the best thing."

"She doesn't have the flu, dear." She took Michael's hand in hers. "Clearly something traumatic happened to Susan a long time ago—something none of us knows about." She couldn't bring herself to say the word *abortion*. "That … *impostor* must have dredged up the memory that set off the reaction."

"Like post-traumatic stress?" Michael said.

"Exactly—at least I think so. Oh, I don't know. I mean, I'm no expert on this by any stretch of the imagination. That's why I hope you'll let me call my friend."

"What's going on, Lily?"

"I don't know. That's why I want to call a doctor."

"I don't mean just with Susan. I mean with everything else!"

"You'd know that if you'd ever shown your face at the White Elephant. We've been working there for months. Why haven't you come by?"

"I should have, I know. But I figured you folks had it under control; Susan said everything was fine."

"We do have everything under control, and until last night everything was fine. That's not the point."

"What are you saying—that it's my fault?"

"Don't take that tone with me, young man," she said quietly. "I didn't say anything was your fault. I asked why you didn't think it was important enough to at least pay a visit to the place where your wife is working her fingers to the bone to make her dream come true … while doing her level best to help make your dream a reality as well. If you'd shown a lick of interest, you'd have known exactly what was going on."

"You're right." He rubbed his eyes. "I should have stopped by. I don't know why I didn't."

"I have a pretty good idea, but now isn't the time for me to share the amazing wisdom of my years." Her sarcasm surprised him.

"So what should we do?"

"Our priority must be to help Susan."

He nodded.

"I can't help but be alarmed at this pattern." Lily tapped on the chart she had developed. "If she continues to drink only water and sleep, in a few days she'll be dangerously weak. We can't let that happen."

"No, we can't." He swallowed. "Call him. Call the guy."

"I'll see if he can come over right away. Where's my phone? Oh, I think it's in the kitchen." She stood and hurried out of the room.

"Lily," he said as she was leaving the room.

She turned. "Yes, dear?"

"When you get back, can we talk some more?"

She nodded affirmatively and left Michael alone to piece together what little information he had.

—*mm*—

"Greg will be here early this evening—around five or six, he thought," Lily said as she returned to the living room. "Dr. Greg Allen is one of the best in his field." She handed Michael a glass of soda.

"Thanks."

She nodded. "I took the liberty of calling Franco after I spoke with Greg. He's bringing over something for us to eat from Camile's. You need to keep up your strength."

Camile's was a well-guarded secret among the locals—an authentic Italian restaurant off the strip. Michael hadn't realized he was hungry until Lily mentioned food.

"I looked in on her. She's sound asleep," Lily said. "I opened the door a bit more so we can hear her in case she wakes up." She sat in a bright red Eero Saarinen chair across from him and placed her hands in her lap. "So, what do you want to know?"

"Everything." He took several long gulps of the soda, quickly belching. "Uh, excuse me," he said sheepishly.

"Of course." Lily smiled demurely. "However, 'everything' is rather broad. Let's see what you do know so I won't be redundant, okay? You know about the new Disco Diva, about our project. Correct?"

"Yes." He sighed. "You know I know that."

"Fine. Just making sure. Let me continue. You know Susan's cut back her days at the salon, that she sometimes works fifteen hours a day on Tuesdays and Wednesdays so she can see as many clients as possible. You know that, correct?"

"Uh, I didn't know it was—"

"Didn't know what? That it was that many hours? Okay. Now you do. Let's move on. What else? I'm sure you know that she's at the ranch office—is that what you call it, the ranch office?—four days every week from eight in the morning until one in the afternoon, in order to help make your dream project come true."

"Hang on. The Henderson ranch isn't just my dream project. It's going to be our home."

"Of course it is, dear. Let's see, where was I? Oh, right. She works with you until one o'clock sharp, at which time you go home to sleep so you can be fresh for your night shift, correct?"

"I'm not liking where this is going."

"I'm almost finished. Then, while you are in dreamland, Susan leaves the ranch office and comes to our office, where she works from two until the wee hours of the night—sometimes early morning. You know that, correct?"

"I get the point, Lily."

"I'm not sure you do. Do you know that she's most likely getting about four or five hours of sleep every night? That in between all of this running here and there she's also personally mentoring and ministering to several young at-risk women who emotionally and spiritually depend on her support and encouragement?"

"I said I get the point."

"That's good. Then I'm sure you also know that she's pretty much stopped eating and lives mostly on liquid energy drinks. Have you noticed her nails? When did she start biting them until they bleed? I'm certain you also know that she's got almost every perimenopausal symptom ever recorded, correct?"

Michael stared at her.

"Didn't notice the hot flashes? The irritability? The sleep deprivation? Michael Anderson, do you know your wife has been running herself ragged trying to juggle it all?"

"Lily, give me a break! Don't make me feel worse than I already do."

"It is not my intention to make you feel worse, but I most certainly will not give you a break! I've been watching this from afar for months. I'm not saying Susan is an innocent waif without choices. But you, Michael, are the head of your household, and it's time you opened your eyes to 'everything.'" She leaned back and crossed her arms. "You did ask me to tell you *everything*, correct?"

"Correct."

"Well then, that's everything as I see it."

Michael felt like a sacked quarterback … the wind forced from his lungs.

"I thought things were going great. I really did. We've had a blast working together on the ranch. And Susan seemed happy."

"Happy?"

"Yes. Happy."

"She seemed increasingly stressed to me." Lily leaned forward and placed her arms on the table. "In fact, I was arguing with her just before Ryan and … his father arrived. I insisted she take some time off. I was worried about her."

"How could I miss all of this?" He fought back tears. "What's wrong with me?"

Lily patted him on the back as she stood. "Nothing that some good old-fashioned honest communication won't cure. You two need to get reconnected. That's all."

They continued to talk while Susan slept, Michael pouring out his heart and Lily pouring out her wisdom.

"There's only one more thing I need to know," he finally said. "What can you tell me about this Gene character? How did this piece of garbage find my wife?"

Chapter 33

"We had no idea Susan knew Gene until she laid eyes on him. Even Ryan was in the dark, poor boy." Lily set down her napkin after finishing the dinner Franco had brought them. They had been talking for more than an hour and a half. Susan slept on.

"You want me to believe that the kid is innocent?" He grabbed another piece of fresh bread and began mopping up the thick spaghetti sauce from his plate.

"He *is* innocent! Ryan is a fine young man, Michael."

"Yeah, well, you know what they say about the apple and the tree." Michael toyed with a lone mushroom on his plate. "Should we try to wake her up? See if she'll eat anything?"

"Why don't we wait until Greg arrives?" Lily looked at her watch. "He should be here any minute." She stood and began to remove the plates from the table, motioning for Michael to stay seated. "I can't tell you why Susan has never told you or anyone else about him, but she must have had a good reason. You'll have to ask her yourself."

"That doesn't appear to be an option right at the moment, does it?"

"Michael, Susan has a big heart. She's been knocking herself out trying to do it all, trying to keep all of us happy, and I don't think any of us realized what it was doing to her. Plus, I think because we've only seen the glamour and glitz that she wants us to see, we've all assumed her memories from the disco era were basically good. But there was obviously something painful, too, and digging through her collection the past few months must have dredged it up. Then there was the shock last night—I think she hit a wall."

"Yeah. A wall with a name. Did you know anything about him?"

"Gene? Er, Jean-Claude?" Lily continued to rinse the dishes, her back to him.

"Yes."

"No, I didn't."

"I knew there was someone in her life back then, but I figured ..." He paused. "I don't know what I figured. She never talked about him—never talked much about her life in New York. I had no idea about—"

"I didn't either, Michael." Lily wiped her hands, stood behind him, and put her hands on his shoulders. "She never told me about the ... the abortion," she murmured. "The poor child. I can't imagine the pain she's been enduring all these years."

He sighed. "I know, but I can't understand why she never told me."

"It's not always easy to communicate with the people we hold dearest."

A knock sounded at the door. Lily looked up. "That must be Greg."

"I'll get it." Michael stood. "Lily?"

"Yes, dear?"

"I'm sorry. I should have been more involved. I should have seen—"

"Put all of that out of your mind this instant. I understand fully, and so will Susan. Now, go let in the good doctor so he can take care of our girl."

He smiled and kissed her on the cheek before leaving the room.

—————

"So, does she have some kind of post-traumatic thing?" Michael stood as Dr. Allen joined them in the kitchen after seeing Susan.

"It's hard to say at this point, but I'm not sure I'd call it post-traumatic stress disorder. More like what we used to call a nervous breakdown—only now we've dropped the 'nervous' part. From what you've told me, she experienced a shock at seeing this gentleman." He placed his bag on the floor and leaned against the counter, crossing his arms.

Michael bristled at the word *gentleman*. "Did she talk to you at all?" he asked. "We haven't been able to get a single word out of her since yesterday. All she does is cry."

"And rightfully so," the doctor said. "She's hurting."

"So she did talk to you?" Michael's eyes widened.

"She did."

"Thank God," Lily said.

"I wouldn't expect her to say too much right away. She's got a lot to process. But my guess is that she'll talk to you when she's ready."

"What should we do in the meantime?" Michael tried not to yell.

"I'd prescribe an antidepressant, but I'd rather wait a few days." He pulled out a chair. Michael and Lily joined him at the table.

"I have a theory regarding cases like this," the doctor said. "When I was a boy, my parents owned a neighborhood restaurant. Nothing fancy—a mom-and-pop place. We lived upstairs. Mom was known for her pies. Every evening she would make pie from scratch, and in the morning, pie slices would show up in the refrigerated glass display case that sat next to the checkout counter."

"Sounds like a great memory," Lily said.

"It was. My job after school was to keep the case full and to make sure the slices all faced the same way. Dad was a funny guy, said the symmetry was important, that 'pie balance' was important."

Michael noticed the doctor eyeing the basket of Camile's Italian bread on the table. He nodded. "Help yourself."

"Thanks, don't mind if I do." The doctor reached for a slice.

"Can I get you something to drink, Greg?" Lily stood. "Water, tea, soda?"

"Water is fine."

"Sorry, Doc." Michael started to stand but Lily gestured for him to stay put.

She poured the doctor a glass of water. "And this pie story is somehow connected to your theory about Susan's case?" she asked him.

"It is. My job was also to let mom and pop know when the pie was all gone. Simple things, but I can't tell you how many times I'd get sidetracked." He laughed. "Thank God I had merciful parents. But I grew up hearing, 'Greg, your pies aren't balanced' or 'Greg, your pies are all gone.' I can still hear their voices in my head, and they've been gone a good many years."

Michael sighed and shifted his weight impatiently in the chair.

"Long story short," the doctor said, leaning back, "is that either your wife's pies aren't balanced, or they're all gone. We have to discover which it is."

Michael and Lily stared.

"However, I don't think it's the latter," the doctor continued. "If her pies were all gone, or even if some of them were gone, we'd have cause to be concerned. Not that having your pies out of balance isn't a problem, but it's my experience that straightening out the slices is a whole lot easier than replacing them."

He took a long sip of water as Michael looked at Lily and raised his shoulders in confusion.

"Greg ..." Lily began.

"Hang on, Lily. This will make sense, I promise." He stood, explaining as though teaching a class. "Humans are made up of four pie flavors, as it were—or maybe you can relate better to the working of a four-cylinder engine." He looked at Michael. "Those four flavors, or four cylinders, are physical, intellectual, emotional, and spiritual."

"Ah." Lily nodded. "P-I-E-S."

"Exactly." The doctor noticed a blank white message board on the refrigerator with a marking pen beside it. "May I?"

"Be my guest," said Michael.

"My initial observation is that Susan's four PIES aren't balanced— her four cylinders aren't firing properly." He flourished the pen.

"She's physically worn down from working too much and not eating right." He printed the letter *P* on the board. "Now, although I would say from the brief communication we shared that she is quite intelligent, I can't really comment on her intellectual pie right at the moment." He printed an *I* with a question mark next to it. "And from what you've indicated, her emotional pie is a total mess … sorry." He printed an *E* with several exclamation points next to it. "As for her spiritual pie"— he printed a big *S*—"you've told me Susan is a woman of faith, but has she been an active participant in her relationship with God these past months?"

Michael was once again embarrassed to say that he didn't know. He couldn't recall the last time they'd been to church together. He tried to recall if he'd seen her Bible or any Bible-study resources lying on the table or near her chair lately, but he couldn't.

"I'm sorry." Michael shook his head.

"Susan is strong in her faith." Lily placed her palms on the tabletop. "But she's been going through a rough patch lately. Her *S* pie may well be out of balance."

"I see. Well, all that said, I think once we get her PIES balanced, she'll be good as new. I would hazard to guess she'll be feeling better in a couple of days. Keep her hydrated. Get her to drink fluids when she's up, but don't grill her."

"Huh?" Michael furrowed his brow.

"Now isn't the time to ask her what happened, to ask her anything whatsoever about the situation that triggered this collapse. Instead of questioning her, I want you to make her feel safe and protected. When she's awake, tell her how much she is loved, how much you appreciate her. Discuss things that make her happy, things that would typically make her laugh—bring her joy. But you don't have to talk a lot. She doesn't need every second of silence filled with noise. Just let her know when she is awake that she is loved unconditionally. Offer her food—something light. And make sure she drinks something—water or juice or herb tea. No caffeine. Call me on Monday to tell me how she's doing."

"If there's no change?" Michael asked.

"Let's cross that bridge if we come to it, okay? She's had a shock and, from what she told me, she has a great deal of unprocessed grief and anger. I'd very much like to see her in my office if she'll come."

"Greg, please don't patronize us. I will attest to Michael's ability to handle the truth. If she's the same on Monday, what's the next step?" Lily asked.

"I would recommend hospitalization if she's still the same, but I don't think she will be. Stay with her and keep doing what you're doing. I feel confident she'll come around."

Lily escorted her friend out of the house while Michael checked on his wife. She appeared to be sleeping peacefully, with no outward indication of the shock that had sent her over the edge. He kneeled by the side of the bed and held her limp hand against his cheek.

"I love you, sweetheart. Please let me help you."

"Are you certain there's nothing else I can do?" Lily asked. Michael walked her out into the warm summer night. At the curb, Franco held open the door of her car like a hotel doorman.

"I'm certain. You've been here all day. Time for you to get yourself home. We'll be fine. You've done more than enough." He bent down and wrapped her in his arms. She smelled like his grandmother.

"Are you wearing Youth-Dew, by any chance?"

"I am." She took Franco's hand and slid into the backseat of her car. "Please don't tell me your grandmother used to wear it." She chuckled and winked. "Good night, dear. I'll see you tomorrow." As Franco began to close the door, she called out, "Wait! I just remembered something." Franco opened the door, and Michael leaned down to look at her.

"Have you called Loretta?" she asked.

"Not yet. I thought about it off and on all day, just not thinking straight. I'll call her in the morning."

"Oh, and you might want to send an e-mail to Susan's group, those boomer babe girls. They're strong prayer warriors."

He reached in the car and hugged her briefly. "Thank you, Lily."

"That's what friends are for. Now you get some sleep. I'll see you tomorrow."

~~~

From: Michael Anderson (MA@sscasino.com)
Sent: Saturday, June 3, 9:52 p.m.
To: Patricia Davies; Mary Johnson; Lisa Taylor; Linda Jones; Sharon Wilson
Subject: FROM MICHAEL ANDERSON—No Need to Worry.

Boomer Baby Ladies:

Michael Anderson here. Didn't want you gals to worry, but Susan's going to be offline for a little while. Not feeling well, been working too many hours and needs a rest. Lily said I should let you know. (I'm assuming you gals know who Lily is, right?) Susan will be back online soon. Prayers requested.

Regards, Michael Anderson

From: Patricia Davies (boomerbabepat@
            boomerbabesrock.com)
Sent: Saturday, June 3, 11:25 p.m.
To: Michael Anderson
Subject: RE: FROM MICHAEL ANDERSON—No Need to Worry.

Dear Michael,

If I'm wrong please let me know, but I'm reading between the lines and I'm worried there is more to this than you're letting on. Please let me know if there is anything I can do to help. John can hold down the fort here for a few days if you need me to come out. I know I've never met Susan IRL (in real life) but she's one of my closest friends nonetheless. I want you to know I am praying for her and you, and that I'm here if you need me. You can reach me here 24/7: 323-555-5550.

God Bless, Patricia Davies (Pat)

P.S.: I will retain as confidential anything you share unless instructed otherwise.

Chapter 34

The next morning, Lily and Michael were once again sitting at the kitchen table, this time dunking fresh-baked chocolate chip cookies into mugs of cold milk when Loretta came out of Susan's room.

"That looks good," Loretta whispered.

"You don't." Michael pulled out a chair. "Sit down."

"I've never seen anyone like that." Loretta reached for a cookie. "She's been like this since Friday night and you wait until Sunday to call me?"

"I'm sorry." Michael rubbed his eyes. "It's been scary. When she wakes up it's only to cry, go to the bathroom, and have a sip of water."

"It's like she's a little baby." Loretta shook her head as Lily and Michael stared at her.

"That's it!" Lily said. "That's exactly like what she is—a newborn baby, waking only to do the three things babies know to do when they don't feel well. I hadn't thought about it that way. That's why Greg said all we could do was to show her love and care and be here for her. I sat on the side of the bed for a half hour and held her." She gulped. "I've never heard a grown person cry like that. Well, that's not quite true. When Colt died, I think I cried like that."

Loretta and Michael were silent, not knowing what to say to

that. Lily picked up a paper napkin from the table and began tearing it up into little pieces.

"I did get her to drink some juice this morning," she finally said. "She had almost an entire glass."

"Thank you, Lily." Michael breathed deeply. "She's got to pull out of this."

"She will!" Lily slapped her hand on the table.

"I want to pray," Loretta said. "Is that okay?" Without waiting for an answer, she took their hands and started a prayer for Susan to be healed.

———

"I'm sure she'll be fine in a few days," Michael insisted. "It's only Sunday, she'll snap out of it." He paced the kitchen, mumbling, running his hands through his hair.

"I agree," Lily said. "But until then, how about we set up a schedule so Susan isn't alone?"

"Good idea." Loretta nodded.

"Just what I was thinking," Michael agreed. "Loretta, can you do something else for her—for us?"

"You name it." Loretta put her hand on his arm.

"I know you're already managing things at the salon, but could you do something with Susan's clients—the ones scheduled for the next few weeks? I don't know for how long, but I don't want anyone to know what's going on. Can you do that without making a big thing out of it?"

"Put it out of your mind. I'll take care of everything."

"Thanks. I don't intend to go back to the Spur. My retirement was to begin officially at the end of the month anyway. What are they going to do—fire me?"

Loretta headed out shortly after they developed a rudimentary schedule for taking shifts with Susan. Michael saw her out, then returned to where Lily sat at the kitchen table.

"Okay. So, now how do we want to handle the White Elephant project?" Lily slid a pencil behind her ear. "And what do we do about … Jean-Claude?"

Michael clenched his jaw, and his eyes narrowed. "I've been trying not to think about him."

"I know. Ryan has been calling since Friday night."

Michael twirled a loose button on his shirtsleeve until it came off in his hand.

"He asked about Susan," Lily continued. "And, Michael, he apologized for his father. He had no idea about their prior history."

"You believe that?"

"Yes, I do. He's mortified—doesn't know how he'll ever be able to face Susan."

"That's easy. He doesn't have to. He can leave town the same way he came."

"Ryan's not the villain—honestly. He's thoroughly ashamed of his father and wants nothing whatsoever to do with him. I knew their relationship was strained. He'd intimated as much, the poor boy."

"Why poor boy?"

"Oh, Michael, you should have seen him. He was deliriously happy that his father was showing some interest in what he was doing out here. The young man is a hard worker—graduated with honors from Harvard Business School. He's no slouch. You'd like him."

"I doubt that."

"I can understand the feelings you have."

"Like I said, I doubt that."

She looked at him and put another cookie on his plate. "You need more chocolate." She took another cookie and dunked it into the mug, dribbling milk on her chin. Michael reached over with his napkin and gently dabbed it off.

"His father has a suite at the Bellagio."

"I thought the old man was staying at your place."

"*Was* being the key word," Lily said firmly. "I had Franco remove his things Friday night when you took Susan home."

"And the kid? Is he still there?"

"I told him he was welcome to remain at Cedar Ridge until we decide what the next step should be, but he said he didn't feel comfortable. He took a room at the Palace Station."

"Not with his father?"

"Michael, are you listening to me? Ryan is disgusted with his father right now. I don't know all of their history, but I would hazard to guess this might have been the final coffin nail." She daintily picked up a loose chocolate chip from her plate and popped it into her mouth.

"So, what do you think I should do about this character?" Michael pushed away the cookie plate.

"Ryan? He's not a character, Michael. He's really—"

"No, I mean the old man. Gene, Jean-Claude, whatever his name is."

Lily got up, put the milk carton in the refrigerator, and carried their cookie plates to the sink. "Frankly, I don't know," she said. "I don't know what his purpose is for coming—what's his motive? Did you hear him say, '*We* have a fortune in *our* collection'?"

He looked up suddenly. "I didn't hear that. Are you sure that's what he said?"

"I'm pretty certain."

He thought a minute. "I'm going to the Bellagio to talk to him—if you can stay with Susan?"

"Do you think that's a wise move?" Lily sat. "We don't need you to do anything rash. Susan needs you here, not in jail."

"I'm not intending to do anything rash. But I think you're right. We need to find out what he's up to."

"I want you to take Franco with you."

Michael chuckled. "What is it with that guy? He's a driver, chef, butler, bodyguard, and security agent?"

"Don't laugh. You shouldn't go alone. I don't trust this Gene character."

"I'll be okay," he said sternly. "But you trust his kid? Tell me more about him. What's he accomplished since coming on board?" He finished off the milk in his mug in one big swallow as she launched into details about progress on the White Elephant project.

Chapter 35

"You expect me to believe that Susan stole your entire collection?" Ryan stood in front of his father, who sat in a gold brocade upholstered chair in his elegant hotel suite wearing his trademark Brooks Brothers casual suit.

"I have no reason to lie to you, son."

"And you never went looking for her? You just let her take off with a collection of memorabilia worth tens of thousands of dollars without a fight?"

"It's worth millions."

"Not then it wasn't." Ryan glared. "So it's about the money?"

"No!" Jean-Claude stood and grabbed his son by the shoulders. "It's not about the money. I don't need the money, and you know that. I was worried about you."

Ryan pulled away from his father's clutch. "Give me break. You never worry about anyone but yourself."

Jean-Claude rubbed the day-old stubble on his chin and shook his head. "You know that's not true, Rye-O." He sighed, then picked up the hotel phone and called room service. "Send a basket of croissants—and a pitcher of Bloody Marys."

"Bit early even for you, isn't it?" Ryan fell back on the sofa.

"Contrary to what you might believe, son," Jean-Claude

continued, ignoring the comment about his drinking, "I was worried. I still am. The Susan Anderson you know is not the Susan Phillips I knew."

He reached for his pack of Gauloises and lit one, inhaling deeply. "An abomination that I can't buy my brand here in the States," he groused, looking at the box of cigarettes in his hand. "No wonder I live in Paris."

He tossed the box on the coffee table and sat down. "When I met your Mrs. Anderson, she was in the upper VIP room of the Studio. You only got there by being somebody or by knowing somebody. Turned out Sexy Suzie knew a great many somebodies."

"You met at Studio 54?" Ryan raised his eyebrows.

"On opening night. Matter of fact, her twenty-first birthday. She was quite a beauty. Still is—that's kind of eerie. Wonder what kind of preservation work she's had done."

"None." Ryan glared as his father shook his head and smiled.

"My, my. Don't tell me you've fallen for her too?" He laughed. "Like father, like son."

"I haven't fallen for her, and I'm not at all like you. But you admit you had feelings for her?"

"I never said I didn't. Fell head over heels, matter of fact. Moved her in with me at the Sherry a week later."

Ryan didn't know what to believe.

"You lived at the Sherry-Netherland?"

"Yes, sir. We had quite a time. Those were the days."

Ryan knew his grandparents had been wealthy. They had owned vineyards all over Europe, and his father had grown up as a trust-fund baby. By the time Ryan was born, however, they'd sold their business and his father's trust fund had been seriously depleted. Ryan had grown up financially comfortable, but nowhere in the same league as his father had.

"How long were you together?"

"I don't know. Not that long. Maybe two, three years, I can't recall—it was a long time ago."

"So what happened?"

"Nothing happened. We had fun, that's all. She knew going in that I wasn't interested in anything permanent. We had an open relationship."

"An open relationship?" Ryan grimaced.

"Hey, it was the seventies. We were young. There were no secrets. Sexy Suzie was along for the ride and enjoyed every minute of it. I gave her a lifestyle most girls only dream about."

"Apparently you gave her more than that." Ryan stood up to answer the door, and room service wheeled in a silver cart with a crisp white linen tablecloth and a single white rose in a crystal vase. The crystal pitcher of blood-red juice gleamed in the morning sunlight.

"Thank you." Jean-Claude signed the room-service ticket and handed the man a twenty-dollar bill.

"Care for one?" he asked Ryan, pouring himself a drink.

"No. I don't drink."

"Really? Since when?" His father took a big swallow.

"Since never. You know that."

"Hmm, do I?" He cocked his head. "Well then, good for you." He walked to the window and looked out at the Las Vegas skyline.

"Did you know she was pregnant?"

"She said she might be." He turned to face his son. "Dropped the bomb on New Year's Eve, 1979 … about the same time the crystal ball was dropping on Times Square. Very theatrical."

"What's that supposed to mean?"

"Thought you were a disco expert. New Year's Eve, 1979? Ring a bell?"

The closing night of Studio 54—the end of more than an era.

"Yeah, it does," Ryan admitted.

"That sure was one wild ride. Stevie and Ian were a couple of characters. Everybody knew they were skimming—it was only a matter of time before they went down. Anyway, Suzie waited until just after midnight to share her big news." He shook his head and sat down. "Don't know what was going through her crazy mind. It's not like I promised her anything. We were having fun, and we did have some fun. I'm the one who gave her the collecting bug. We traveled all over the world looking for disco junk. Folks thought we were nuts. Your old man knew better."

"How so?"

"Gut feeling. Figured one day the stuff would be worth something. Not that I didn't pay a pretty penny for some of it back then. Especially the Warhol stuff. What a sick jerk he was. Anyway, I showed Sexy Suzie a darn good time, and what thanks did I get? She skipped with my collection and disappeared into the night."

"So, let me get this straight." Ryan leaned his elbows on his knees. "You innocently party for a couple of years, live at the Sherry, travel all over creation collecting disco memorabilia, and then she tells you on New Year's Eve, 1979, that she's pregnant. And then what—she disappears the next day with all of your belongings? When did you find out about the abortion?"

"I'm not sure I like the tone of your voice, son."

"I'm not sure I like the way you're portraying Susan."

"Well, get used to it!" Jean Claude went to pour himself another drink. "Because the truth hurts. And the truth is, she wasn't an innocent babe in arms by any stretch of the imagination. Heck, I don't even know for sure if the kid was mine. But I told her I'd give it a go if that's what she wanted. I had to go home on business the second week of January. I told her that when I got back we'd figure out what to do. But when I returned, she'd already cleaned me out. Not just the collection, but the furniture, linens, clothes, everything. Even my car, for crying out loud!"

"The Shelby was yours?"

"Of course Marilyn was mine! What did she tell you—that I gave it to her? Preposterous! I went looking for her, but she'd disappeared. Turns out she moved to Vegas, got married, and changed her name."

"And the baby?" Ryan whispered.

"One of her sleazebag friends told me she'd had an abortion. They were easy to get back then, especially in the City. Well, no skin off my nose. Like I said, I wasn't even sure it was mine."

Ryan thought he was going to be sick. How could this man—his father—be so coldhearted? And could Susan really be the person he was describing?

"So, other than worrying about me—" he turned to his father—"why are you really here? What do you want?"

"Only what's mine." Jean-Claude buttered a croissant and bit into it. "*Magnifique!*" He smacked his lips. "Almost as good as home."

Ryan's eyes narrowed. "And what do you feel is yours?"

"Pretty much everything in her collection. And I say *her* loosely, since it's really *my* collection."

"You'll destroy her … it's her life." Ryan ran his hand through his hair.

"Time to face reality, son," Jean-Claude insisted. "It's a collection of priceless memorabilia—historic artifacts, to be more precise, and it's all mine."

"But what possible use could this stuff be to you?"

"Sotheby's will be more than happy to help me out with 'this stuff.' In fact, they were ecstatic when I called."

"You're going to auction it off? You can't do that!" Ryan stood eye to eye with his father and stared. "Listen to me, you don't know what this will do to Susan. I understand she may have been a different person back when you knew her, but people do change, and the Susan I know is a good, honest person. She has a heart of gold. Please don't do this."

"When did you become so altruistic?" Jean-Claude patted his hand against Ryan's cheek, and Ryan flinched at his touch. "I'm meeting with the good Mr. Anderson this afternoon to discuss the plan of action." He looked admiringly at his Rolex watch. "He'll be here within the hour. Care to stay for the meeting?"

He poured another drink, finishing off the pitcher. "If you'll excuse me, I'm going to freshen up a bit, so help yourself to a croissant. Or call room service and order whatever you'd like. I'll be back soon."

He turned and walked into the bedroom of the plush suite, closing the door behind him.

Chapter 36

Michael knocked on the hotel room door, unsure what to say to the man who had turned his world upside down. He was surprised when Ryan Power opened the door.

"Mr. Anderson, I can't begin to say how sorry I am for all of this," he said quietly. "Lily told me Susan is having a hard time. You have to believe me—I didn't know a thing about my father's involvement with your wife. And listen—before he joins us, I want you to know that I don't believe his story, what he's going to tell you." The young man paused, looking over his shoulder, then added, "I know that sounds horrible, but I don't. Please believe me."

"Did I hear someone at the door, Ryan? Is that Mr. Anderson?" Jean-Claude's voice boomed behind them. Ryan waved his arm for Michael to enter.

"Ah, it is you." Jean-Claude sauntered out of the bedroom with a smile on his face. He extended his hand toward Michael, who kept his hands to his sides.

"I see. Well, then, please have a seat." He nodded toward the sitting room and strode deliberately over to the high-backed wing chair closest to the mirror. "I take it you know my son."

Michael nodded and sat on the edge of the sofa.

"Please make yourself comfortable, Mr. Anderson."

"I didn't come for tea," Michael said curtly.

"I should hope not." Jean-Claude laughed. He glanced at the serving cart with the empty pitcher. "I've ordered some more refreshments, sans tea. Room service is very prompt in this hotel. I expect it'll arrive momentarily."

Ryan sat in a chair opposite both men. "Um, how is Susan?"

"I'd prefer not to discuss my wife."

"Then what should we discuss, Mr. Anderson?" Jean-Claude leaned back and crossed his legs at the knee. "The weather?"

"Don't get smart," Michael warned.

"I would caution you with the same edict, since we both know the very premise of this encounter, as it were, has everything to do with your wife."

Michael kept repeating Lily's words over and over again in his head. *Stay calm, Michael. Nothing infuriates a pompous fool more than a calm adversary.*

Ryan wiped sweaty palms on his pant legs and looked at his father, whose grin had faded considerably. He wasn't used to dealing with men like Michael.

"As I told my son earlier, I want only what is rightfully—and legally—mine."

"Which is?" Michael asked.

"Pretty much everything in your wife's possession that was acquired when we were together. It was my collection. Let's just say she fraudulently appropriated it."

"You're accusing Susan of stealing?"

"In a word, yes."

There was a knock on the door. Ryan jumped up to answer it,

admitting the same uniformed waiter. Everyone watched silently as he moved aside the first serving table and pushed the elegant cart into position by the fireplace, flamboyantly removing silver lids from plates of fruit and cheese, vegetables and dip, and more flaky croissants. Four bottles of beer lay chilling in a silver ice bucket, and another crystal pitcher of Bloody Marys, this one slightly larger, took up considerable space on the crowded table.

Jean-Claude once again tipped the waiter, then poured himself a drink, stirring the tomato juice with a stalk of celery. "Would you care for a beer, Mr. Anderson? Or may I dispense with the formalities and call you Michael? You are welcome to call me Gene."

Greeted with silence, he walked to his chair and placed his drink on the end table. "I can see this isn't going to be easy. I was hoping we could communicate as gentlemen. It is a rather awkward situation, I'll grant you that."

"Awkward?" Michael barked. "My wife is in a state of shock—and you call that awkward?"

"Goodness. A bit dramatic, aren't—?"

Ryan interrupted. "Let's just stop playing cat and mouse and cut right to the chase, okay? Yes, this is awkward. Yes, there are emotions involved. And yes, it's going to be difficult to discuss this. But discuss it we must."

"Ah, my son the arbitrator." Jean-Claude returned to the food table and picked up a plate. "Please help yourselves, gentlemen. I ordered enough for all of us."

"I don't think Mr. Anderson came for Sunday brunch," Ryan said disgustedly. "Now, tell him what you told me. But have some respect for his wife." Ryan stared at his father.

Jean-Claude finished filling his plate and took it back to his chair before speaking. "I can appreciate, Michael, that the Susan you know is not the woman I once knew. I'm sorry if it causes you pain, but we didn't call her Sexy Suzie for naught. She was a good-time girl who had a good time. Unfortunately, she had it at my expense."

"I asked what you want." Michael raised his chin and looked Jean-Claude in the eyes.

"I told you. I want what is mine."

"And you're saying Susan's entire collection is yours?"

"Correct." Jean-Claude dipped a strawberry into a dollop of whipped cream and popped it into his mouth.

"Can you prove that?"

"Don't insult me! Do I appear to be an imbecile? Every purchase I made was through my trust-fund checking account. I have detailed records of everything I've purchased for most of my life. A blessing and a curse, I must say." He grinned. "My mother and father harped endlessly about my collection, not understanding it any more than Susan did. She only got into it to please me, to stay on my good side. It wasn't her thing."

Wasn't her thing? Michael thought. *What is this lunatic talking about? It's her* only *thing.*

"You don't know my wife," he said.

"Ah, but that's where we disagree. It's you who doesn't know your wife." Jean-Claude had gotten up to pour himself another drink when Michael stood and grabbed his arm.

"Be careful, Mr. Anderson," Jean-Claude said in a hostile whisper.

"Don't worry about me. I have no intention of giving you what you deserve, any more than I have any intention of handing over my wife's collection to you. Last I heard, possession is nine-tenths of the law and, from what I can see, my wife has possessed her things for more than twenty-five years. You're going to need to do more than wave empty threats."

Jean-Claude exhaled loudly. "So be it. I was hoping to remain stateside to spend time with my son, but it looks as though I'll need to return home to gather paperwork." He pulled his arm away and brushed it off. "In the meantime, I suggest you cease further action on your development. What good is a Disco Hall of Fame and Museum without any disco memorabilia?"

"You'll need some kind of a warrant or a cease and desist order or whatever the legal mumbo jumbo is before we stop doing anything. You don't tell us what we can and cannot do."

"Don't toy with me, Mr. Anderson." Jean-Claude sneered. "I said to *abort* the project, and I mean it."

The emphasis on *abort* wasn't lost on Michael. Ryan had to hold him back, pulling him out of the room before he could pummel Jean-Claude to death with his bare fists.

Chapter 37

"You look like something my cats wouldn't even drag in," Loretta said as she dropped her handbag on a kitchen chair the next morning. "Have you been up all night?"

Michael looked up, bleary-eyed, and nodded. "Couldn't sleep."

"It shows."

"Gee, thanks."

"No problem. Is she any better?"

"No need to whisper," he said. "She's sound asleep."

"Still?"

"Yeah, but I think she's coming out of it. I got her to eat some scrambled eggs this morning. Only a bite or two, but it's the most she's had since Friday night. And she's not crying as much, not like she was."

Loretta remembered yesterday's mournful wails.

"Oh, Michael, I am so sorry." She put her hand on his arm. "I just can't believe I didn't know any of this."

"Don't feel bad. She's my wife, and I didn't know about it."

They talked awhile about what he'd learned from Jean-Claude the day before.

"He's lying," Loretta said. "Susan isn't a thief. I don't care what proof he says he has."

"I want to agree. But I'm going down to the White Elephant to look at some insurance appraisal papers Susan got out of her safe-deposit box before this slimeball showed up. Maybe they'll help."

"I hope so." She followed him into the kitchen, where he showed her the chart Lily had developed.

"Lily's got us keeping track of when she gets up, what she drinks and eats. There's even a column if she goes to the bathroom."

"Leave it to Lily." She grinned. "But that's smart. Kind of like a hospital chart."

"Exactly. I'm only going to be a couple of hours at the most. Uh, who's minding the shop?"

"Don't worry, I've got it handled."

"Okay then. You have my cell number if you need me."

"Not to worry. I'll be fine." She pointed to the dishes on the counter. "Mind if I tidy things up a bit? Make myself useful?"

"Be my guest." He bowed gracefully. "Remember what the doc said. If she wakes up, don't talk about what happened. Just be supportive and—"

"I know, and encouraging and loving. I understand."

Like heck she did. If Susan woke up on her watch, she would be kind and loving, but she was darn well going to talk about what happened. All of this hiding-their-heads-in-the-sand malarkey didn't sit well in her craw. No, sirree.

"This puts our ranch office to shame." Michael looked around the White Elephant office and whistled. He had been so focused on Susan his last time here that he hadn't noticed much about it.

Lily smiled and handed him the papers he'd come for. "I believe in the power of comfort and atmosphere."

He walked to the bank of miniature television screens and stared. "How many cameras do you have running?"

"One for every screen."

He counted fourteen screens and whistled again.

He could see inside the cavernous belly of the White Elephant, where the majority of the cameras appeared to be focused. The grounds outside the building were being scanned by moving cameras. "What's this?" He pointed at a screen that showed a large building packed with boxes.

"That's the temporary storage building we bought to hold Susan's collection while it's being inventoried."

He stared at the screen. "That's a lot of stuff."

"It arrived only this morning—the movers just left."

In the far corner of the building, a tarp covered what was clearly a car. "Ah, that must be Marilyn," he said. "Haven't seen her in awhile. Forgot all about her, in fact."

"Michael, are you aware of the value of that automobile?" Lily looked at the screen over his shoulder.

"Not a clue. I'm not even sure I remember what it was … a Mustang, maybe?"

"It's a Shelby, and from what I gather, it's some kind of derivative of a Mustang. My insurance agent practically had apoplexy when he saw it. We've taken out a policy on the vehicle alone for over one and a half million dollars."

Michael gasped. "Seriously?"

"As a heart attack." Lily nodded. "Come with me, Michael, and

I'll show you exactly how serious we are. You need to see what you should have seen months ago." She grabbed him by the arm and walked him out of the office and over to the White Elephant.

Michael knew Lily was an astute businesswoman. He and Susan had often talked about her various projects, and in years past he'd attended a few fund-raising events for her FAITH Project. However, he'd never before heard her speak about feasibility studies, trends, budget projections, and project development with such intelligence and passion. She took him through every floor of the building, describing the overall plans with broad strokes, her voice alive with excitement. By the time she'd finished communicating Susan's vision for the project, Michael was speechless.

"So you see, Michael, this isn't just the whim of a junk collector. Susan has a priceless collection that needs to be in a museum, preserved for future generations. I know you read the contract Susan and I have, you've seen the project proposal. Why do you appear surprised?"

"I had no idea it was going to be like this. I mean, I knew you were planning an entirely new salon and a few other things, but I guess somewhere in my mind I saw it different ... smaller."

"Smaller? In the White Elephant?"

"I don't know what I thought! I didn't think, okay? There, I said it. Are you happy?"

"Seeing you uncomfortable doesn't make me happy, Michael."

"I don't know where my brain was. I just saw how hurt Suze was when I pressured her to get on board with my project and give hers up."

"You asked her to give this up? I didn't know."

"She didn't tell you?"

"Susan doesn't talk much to anyone about her personal problems—that's one of the reasons I suspect she's where she is now. You can only bottle up so much."

"But give me some credit, okay? I got to thinking that maybe we could do both projects. That's when she showed me your proposal and we read it over, made a few changes, and you guys got started."

Lily shook her head.

"What?" he said.

"How could you read it, know the building, and not grasp what we were doing? Were you in denial?"

"Heck, I don't know. Maybe. I was thinking about the ranch. Darn it, Lily, we've lived in a cramped, tiny home for over twenty-five years with furniture I can't sit on, and I never got to see my wife, and all I could think about was giving her the space she's always talked about."

"I've known Susan for years, and the only space I've ever heard her talk about was space for her collection. She loves her home. She feels safe in her home. She's going along with the Henderson ranch because you want it, Michael. But frankly, the way it's been growing has her scared silly."

"Yeah, well, not half as scared as I am about all this happening to her. What if she doesn't get better? What if she ends up hating me?"

Lily sat quietly next to him and patted his shoulder.

"Susan could never hate you. You are the love of her life. You've both just kind of lost your way for a time, going separate paths. But things are turning around—you're coming back together. It won't be easy, but it's going to work out. I believe that, Michael. You need to believe it too. Don't give up—not on her, not on yourself, and not on your marriage."

He gazed at her in admiration. "No wonder Susan loves you."

"Ditto." She patted him gently on the arm.

He glanced back at the security camera focused on his wife's vast collection. "I helped her unload all of this into storage years ago, but I don't remember there being so much."

"Michael, the entire collection is worth a tidy fortune. That's why we need to get it inventoried as quickly as possible. None of us knows what your wife has here."

"Apparently Gene Power does. He claims it's all his."

"That's ridiculous!"

"That's what I said. But I have a feeling we're in for a fight." Michael ran his hand through his hair. "Says he has receipts for all of it, even the car."

"That's what he meant by 'our collection'! The swine! I should have guessed. Don't tell Susan—it will kill her. What can we do?"

"I don't know yet. Any suggestions?"

"I suggest we go on the offensive and prepare our own strategy. I'll be talking to my lawyers—if that's okay with you."

He yawned and rubbed his fists into his eyes. "It's more than okay with me."

"In the meantime, do I have your permission to continue with the project? Business as usual … until Susan returns?"

"Do you need my permission?"

"Not legally, but there's more to life than the law."

He looked at her with increasing respect. "You have my permission."

She nodded. "Thank you, Michael." After a pause, she spoke again. "You know, I used to think there was more to Susan's obsession with this era than met the eye. But she never appeared wounded—not like some people who live in the past. So I finally decided her enthusiasm was the kind that makes historians passionate about whatever it is they're passionate about. Now I think I was wrong. We were all wrong. None of us realized what she was really trying to preserve."

"What do you mean?"

"Don't you see? She made the painful choice to end a life. Maybe she's managed to live with it by keeping another alive for years … the life of an era."

"You mean all this stuff somehow represents the baby she …" He couldn't bring himself to say it.

"That's exactly what I mean. And that's why we can't let anything happen to it. Michael, she's been keeping the memory of her baby alive for years. We can't let him take this one from her too."

He heard Loretta's voice when he opened the door. She was reading the Bible out loud.

"Bless your heart," he said quietly, wondering if Susan could even hear the powerful words of the psalm Loretta was reading. He walked down the hallway and into the kitchen and was stunned to see his wife sitting at the table with a cup of tea in front of her.

"H-honey?" Michael stammered.

"Hello, Michael." Susan's eyes began to fill with tears.

"Oh no you don't, missy." Loretta wagged her finger in front of her friend. "Remember what we talked about? Now, drink your tea.

And you promised to eat something." She kissed Susan on the cheek, picked up her purse, and turned to Michael, who was still staring. "There's a mashed potato casserole in the oven. Take it out in fifteen minutes. She's had a bath, we washed her hair, and I changed the linens on the bed. Put them in the dryer when the wash cycle ends, okay?"

She snapped her fingers in front of Michael's face, startling him. "Walk me to the door. Good-bye, Suzie-Q, I'll stop by tomorrow. Love you."

"Love you, too," Susan whispered, as Loretta walked out of the kitchen with her husband.

"What happened?" Michael grabbed Loretta's arm when they were out of Susan's earshot.

"Nothing happened. She woke up, and I told her it was time to get with the program. Almost three days in bed without so much as a sponge bath? Good heavens, Michael! What were you thinking?"

"What was I thinking? You saw her. She was a basket case. She was—"

"I know what she *was,* but she's not anymore. Listen to me. I know what you said about not rocking the boat, and that made sense at first. But I'm sorry, my mama didn't raise no ostrich! When she woke up, I sat on the side of the bed and told her it was time to get up and face the music. We had us a hearty girl-to-girl talk."

She opened the front door and turned. "I'm not making light of the situation. She's in a bad way, I'll grant you that. But I don't happen to agree with avoidance therapy. When someone's teetering on the edge, the worst thing you can do is pretend she's not gonna fall. I made the choice to grab hold and pull her back, that's all."

She hugged him, kissed him on the cheek, and walked out the

front door. "I'll be back tomorrow. Remember to put those sheets and towels in the dryer, and don't let that casserole burn." She winked and closed the door behind her.

"She's something, isn't she?"

Michael jumped at the sound of Susan's voice, surprised to see her leaning against the archway between the living and dining room. He hadn't heard her approach any more than he heard the sob in his own throat as he strode quickly to his wife and wrapped her tightly in his arms.

"I'm sorry, honey. I'm so sorry," she said as he showered kisses on her head, her face, and her neck.

"No, I'm the one who's sorry. I didn't know."

"You still don't know. Can we sit and talk? I'm a little shaky on my feet."

"Of course. Do you want to lie down? Should I carry you?" He started to pick her up and she smiled, pushing him away.

"I'm not an invalid. I can walk. And I've been in bed long enough, don't you think? Is it really Monday? Tell me Loretta was pulling my leg."

He shook his head as he helped her to the sofa. He pulled up a nearby ottoman and lifted her feet.

"Thank you."

"Sure. Are you cold?" He grabbed a crocheted blanket from a large wicker basket and placed it over her lap.

"Honey, I'm okay, really. I'm sorry I frightened you. It was just—"

"It's all right. You don't need to talk about it. I understand."

"Sweetheart … listen to me. You *don't* understand, and we *do* need to talk about it. There's a great deal we need to talk about. I haven't been open with you, and you haven't been open with me … not for a long time. I don't think we intentionally meant to hurt each other, to close one another out. But we have."

"I know." Michael sat next to her and held her hand. "I'm sorry."

"Me, too." She squeezed his hand. "And I have a lot to tell you, but I'm not sure how, and I'm not really sure what I'm feeling. If it's okay with you, could I see Dr. Allen again? I think I need some help sorting this out."

"Of course! If that's what you want. Do you want me to come? I mean, for couples' therapy or something like that? I will if you want me to."

She reached over and touched his face. "I think that would be a good thing for us, sweetheart … eventually. But I need to figure out some things in my own head first. Is that okay?"

"Of course it's okay. Whatever you want. I don't want to lose you, Susan." He put his arm around her and pulled her into another close embrace.

"You're not going to lose me. Don't say that." She leaned her head on his chest and in a matter of minutes began to doze off, waking when Michael shifted his weight.

"Oh my, was I sleeping long?" She sat up, trying to get her bearings.

"Just a couple of minutes. How about we get you back to bed for a little nap before dinner?"

"I guess I am kind of tired. Loretta made me walk around the kitchen a few times after my bath, threatened me within an inch of my life." She laughed, but he could see on her face that she had used up every particle of energy in her body.

"It's all right," he said, unable to keep back a smile. "We've got all the time in the world to talk. And I promise you—we will."

Chapter 38

"Michael just called," Lily said to Ryan when he and Tina arrived at the office later that afternoon.

"I told Tina what happened," Ryan said to Lily. "Didn't think it was right to keep her in the dark."

"You can trust me," Tina added. "I won't say a thing. How is she?"

"Much better, apparently. Seems Loretta worked a miracle while she sat with Susan this morning."

"Thank God," Tina breathed.

"Exactly." Lily clasped her hands.

Ryan looked down. "She must hate me."

"She doesn't hate you at all. Your father, on the other hand …"

"She can join a long line of people for that," he muttered. "I wasn't sure I'd ever see the inside of this place again."

"Don't be silly." Lily put her hands on her slim hips. "We've got a job to do, and we're going to get on with it, regardless of what your father does."

Ryan frowned. "You don't know my old man. When I dropped him off at the airport this morning, he assured me we'd be hearing from his attorney soon."

"Well, until we do, I say we proceed as scheduled." She cocked her head. "Unless you'd rather bow out?"

He flushed. "No! I don't want to bow out. Do you still want me? Considering …?"

"Considering what? That your father is a … troublemaker?"

He laughed. "That's a nice word choice."

"Men have been trying to intimidate me for a very long time. It's going to take a whole lot more than your father to dampen my spirits."

"What about Susan and her husband?" Ryan said quietly. "Do you think they're going to want to continue the project … especially with me?"

"Michael was here earlier today and I spoke with him about the project. He assured me he is on board a hundred percent with business as usual at the White Elephant."

"But this isn't business as usual. My father isn't just making idle threats."

"That's precisely why I've called you. The records Susan has are sparse at best, and if what your father said is true, he has receipts for everything. We're going to have to make a case for every single item. So, considering the circumstances, I think it's now more vital than ever to get everything inventoried and cataloged. The movers delivered everything this morning, and I don't want us to waste another minute getting started."

"I can start right now," Tina said.

"Excellent. Your computer equipment was also delivered early this morning. This has been a busy place." Lily smiled and put her arm around Tina as they walked toward the door. "The tech crew should be arriving any minute to get things set up. If you don't have everything you need, be sure to let me know. And we'll talk tomorrow about hiring you some help to expedite things."

"Sounds good—you can depend on me." Tina headed out the door.

"I know I can, dear," Lily said, holding Ryan back from following her.

"Don't let her go crazy in there opening cartons and lifting things," she whispered to him. "She looks a little off to me these days. Are you sure she's all right?"

"She's fine, just ticked off with her boss. Can't say I blame her."

"Maybe so, but keep your eyes on her."

He agreed to do just that and jaunted down the steps after her just as Michael pulled into the parking lot.

~~~

"It's like night and day. She's up sitting on the sofa, watching TV."

"Praise God!" Lily said. "So what are you doing back here?"

"I'm not here." Michael grinned. "I'm picking up takeout from Sushi Sam's."

"Ah, I see."

"She had a taste for it, and I was happy to oblige. I only have a few minutes. I've been thinking about our talk this morning."

"It's good to reflect." She rocked slowly in her chair.

"I'm not sure why I never stopped by here before." He walked to the bookshelf and began looking at the disco items interspersed between the books and binders. "I think maybe a part of me didn't want to know all the details ... or get involved. I've been living with this disco stuff for years." He picked up an item from the bookshelf and waved it at Lily before returning it to the shelf. "But it's not me.

I never got it. I thought it was time I got to live my dream. You know what I mean?"

"I do. That is very understandable."

"Susan said she was ready to give it all up for me and the ranch house."

"I'm sure she meant it."

"But I suggested a compromise. I suggested we go ahead with both projects."

"An admirable compromise, to be commended."

"In a pig's eye!" Lily jumped at his response. "I didn't compromise at all. She was doing everything. Working at the salon, here, the ranch house office, and taking care of me and the house … taking care of everything but herself. And I couldn't even manage to get my sorry butt over here one time to see what she was doing … to tell her how proud I was of her."

"We all make mistakes, Michael. No one is perfect."

"Yeah, well, I'm not even close."

She smiled. "You're closer than you were a few days ago."

He wandered around the office looking at things and stopped at the wall of blueprints. "This really is a major undertaking."

"Yes, it is." Lily walked up behind him and peered over his shoulder.

"Why didn't she try to make me understand? She should have dragged me down here and forced me to get a clue."

"Oh, I'm certain that tactic would have worked well." She patted his shoulder and grinned. "You're not saying it's her fault for not being more forceful with you?"

Michael turned, looked at Lily, and shook his head slowly. "Ever thought of being a shrink? You could make a pretty penny doling out advice."

"I have more than enough pretty pennies." She winked. "Plus, I like giving out free advice."

"Susan wants to start seeing Dr. Allen. Thanks for recommending him. They obviously made a connection."

"Good! He's the one with insight."

Michael picked up the snow globe that sat on his wife's desk. "I wonder what the whole story is behind this. The water's all gone." He upended the glass orb, watching the dry glitter drop back over Westminster Abbey. "Seems there's a story behind most of this stuff. I should have asked."

"Don't beat yourself up. It's not all your fault."

"It's not? My wife couldn't tell me what all of this really meant to her." He waved the snow globe. "And it's not my fault? Whose fault is it then?"

"Michael, I'm an old woman, but I have learned a thing or two in my life, especially when it comes to marriage. Things are never black and white. Life usually takes place in the gray areas—at least the life worth living. It's not about being right or wrong, who's at fault and who isn't. It's about compromise and commitment. It's about fixing the broken things instead of throwing them away."

"Do you think I can fix this?" Michael sat in his wife's chair and put his head in his hands.

"No, Michael. I don't think you can fix it."

He looked up at her, startled.

"It's not up to you to fix it—it's up to *both* of you. You're both going to have to make different choices … truthful choices … this time around."

"Easier said than done." He breathed a sigh that turned into a yawn.

"Isn't everything?" Lily smiled. "Now, I'm sure your sushi order is ready by now. You need to go home and get yourself some sleep, young man." She wagged a finger at him. "You'll be no good to Susan if you end up sick."

"Yes, ma'am!" He saluted.

"You are welcome to come by anytime for more free advice." She took his hand. "But before you head out, let me show you something."

They moved to Ryan's office to look at the bank of security camera screens, focusing on the storage building, where literally hundreds of boxes and crates were stacked and a team of tech gurus was busy setting up Tina's computer system.

"I don't know what kind of game Gene Power is playing or what kind of records he actually has, but to fight him we need a detailed inventory of everything in that building." Lily tapped on the screen. "And those two young people are going to get it done."

They watched Tina and Ryan as they worked with the tech crew.

"Are they a couple?"

"Why do you ask?" Lily rested a finger against her cheek and watched the screen.

"I'm not blind. Look at that body language."

"You know," she mused, "I think you're right." Then she surprised him by clapping her hands loudly and shouting, "Hallelujah! Young love!" She grabbed Michael and spun him around.

He laughed at her energy. "Take it easy. I'm not as young as you."

"It's good to see you laughing." Lily clapped again. "I can't help it. I always get excited when God-cidences turn into what God had planned. A few weeks ago those two didn't know the other existed—and now look." They watched the images from the security camera and smiled. "Life can change on a dime, Michael. We never know what may trigger a new journey."

"You can say that again."

"So, what do you think?"

"About what?" Michael walked toward the door as Lily followed.

"About the new Disco Diva. We could use you here, Michael. Susan could use you here. But you have the power to shut down the entire operation. I'm not sure I'd blame you considering what's transpired."

"Yeah, right. Like I have any power."

Lily picked up a silver framed photo of Susan and Michael on their wedding day from a nearby bookshelf.

"Susan told me how you two met. Kind of like those young people over there." She pointed out the window toward the adjacent storage building. "Think about it, Michael. That was another God-cidence, I'd say, especially knowing what we know now. And now you've been together for twenty-five years. Susan loves you very much, and I would hazard to guess she's beginning to see the part she played in making choices separate from you. If you insist she pull the plug on this operation, I can guarantee she won't choose this over you."

Michael nodded as he looked out the window toward the White

Elephant. "Don't think I ever realized how big it was. All the years I've driven by." Lily walked to the window and peered over his shoulder as he continued. "It really is a great location for what you have in mind, I'll grant you that. But it's going to cost a fortune."

"Dear boy, I *have* a fortune." She patted his arm and grinned.

"Then, if it's okay with Susan, I'll help you spend it—count me in." He extended his hand, and Lily pulled him into a hearty embrace.

"What about the Henderson ranch?" She pulled back, keeping her hands planted firmly on his arms.

"We haven't broken ground yet. That dirt's been sitting there a mighty long time. It can sit awhile longer."

"It's a big commitment. Is this a truthful choice you can be happy with?"

"It is. And thank you, Lily, for the opportunity to make it."

She walked him out to his car, making plans and discussing possibilities that increased their excitement with every breath. His internal dialogue, however, was anything but pleasant.

You're barking up the wrong tree, Mr. Jean-Claude Slimeball, if you think you're going to take away one iota of Susan's collection. Just try it.

~~~

From: Susan Anderson (boomerbabesusan@boomerbabesrock.com)

Sent: Monday, June 5, 6:36 p.m.

To: Patricia Davies; Mary Johnson; Lisa Taylor; Linda Jones; Sharon Wilson

Subject: i really am fine

dear boomer babe sisters:

michael went to get me a california roll at sushi sam's—yum. Told me he let you know I would be taking some time off to rest. That's true—i do need to rest. But mostly I need to do some heavy-duty spring cleaning with the help of a professional. Not just dusting and cobweb removal, but the deep-cleaning stuff like going through boxes that have been packed for years, deciding what to toss and keep ... and trying to figure out why I saved it in the first place. gotta make room in my house for new stuff, good stuff, fresh stuff, time for the oldie and moldy to go. it's not easy, in fact it's downright painful on many levels and I'm finding it very hard to process a great deal of it. but I trust God will make a way.

i most likely won't be online for a time. love you all so much. suze

From: Patricia Davies (boomerbabepat@boomerbabesrock. com)

Sent: Monday, June 5, 10:54 p.m.

To: Mary Johnson; Lisa Taylor; Linda Jones; Sharon Wilson

Subject: Pray and Send Cards and Letters

Dear Boomer Babes:

Just spoke with Michael Anderson on the phone. We were right to assume that Susan's cryptic e-mail meant so much more than she disclosed. The "professional" she alluded to is a psychiatrist she's going to start seeing. Seems a man from her past showed up unexpectedly a couple of days ago and opened some old wounds. Plus, she was worn down already from overworking and not eating right, so it really hit her hard. But we know our Suzie-Q. She'll pull through this.

Michael said he will tell her he told us the truth and we should feel free to send cards and letters, but she won't be online for awhile and he asked us not to call for a few days until she gets to feeling better. I'll be talking with him in a couple of days, and I'll shoot everyone an update. Let's keeping praying for Susan and for Michael as they go through this challenging time.

Love to all, Pat

P.S.: I'm going to have some flowers sent to her from all of us. Can everyone chip in $20 or so?

Chapter 39

"I watched *Breakfast at Tiffany's* again last night and discovered something new." Susan sat down on the plush leather chair in Dr. Greg Allen's office. "You know, I might be able to get used to having furniture like this in our new home when we build it."

"Yes?" Dr. Allen crossed his legs and sat back in the chair opposite hers.

"Yes about the furniture comment or yes about the movie?" She grinned.

He raised his eyebrows and tilted his head.

"Sorry ... I still can't believe I see a counselor who recommends movies as therapy."

This was their twelfth session in six days. She'd been coming to see Dr. Allen twice daily since they met. She had convinced him she was ready, willing, and more than able to handle a concentrated level of treatment ... and she thought she was making amazing headway. But the content of their time together had surprised her.

"I don't recommend it for everyone," he told her. "But it's a good exercise when it's a good film, and *Breakfast at Tiffany's* is rife with deep psychological undertones ... very well executed. So tell me, what did you discover this time?"

"I've been whining about all of my alter egos … instead of embracing them." She tucked her legs up underneath her and leaned back.

"Do you really think you whine?"

"Okay, maybe that wasn't a good word choice. How about *lamenting*? I've been lamenting all of my alter egos instead of embracing them."

"Remember what we talked about concerning alter egos?"

"Well, I know they aren't really alter egos, per se."

"Then say what you mean, Susan," he said quietly. "Speak the truth as you know it, using truthful words."

She sighed. "I have multiple facets to who I am. Not multiple personalities … not alter egos. I'm very conscious of all the times in my life where some facets shone more brightly than other times. Ergo, I've been lamenting all my facets instead of embracing them. I'm here now because I want to blend and balance all of those facets so they come together as one big, bright, brilliant, shining diamond of a personality. How's that?" She smiled broadly.

"A bit dramatic, but generally appropriate." He nodded. "So, what did you discover from the movie?"

"When Holly Golightly looks at Doc and says, 'I'm not Lula Mae anymore,' I had a profound revelation about what we've been talking about."

"Yes?"

"Well, I've got a triple whammy against me. I'm not Susan Yoder anymore, but I'm not Susan Phillips either. And even though I pretended for almost three years, I was never Susan Perrault. When I married Michael and became Susan Anderson, I never embraced all the other Susans who came before her ... er, me. I just tried to put them behind me."

Dr. Allen was silent, so she continued.

"The first decade of my life I was Susan Yoder the free spirit, the girl who understood what it meant to be fully and unconditionally loved. I was encouraged to explore whatever interested me, and for me that meant dancing, singing, art, music, dressing up, acting. I was in my element. Then when my parents died and I went to live with the other Yoders, I spent the next eight years as Susan Yoder the repentant sinner, learning how to repress all that creativity and discover God's will for my life as they saw it."

"Only as *they* saw it?" he asked.

She looked at him with frustration. "Okay, not only as *they* saw it. I did learn that God had a plan for me, that I was fearfully and wonderfully made."

After her parents died, she had gone to live in a Mennonite community in Pennsylvania with her only living relatives, a childless couple related to her father. Though far more strict than her parents, they'd loved a good and gracious God and introduced Susan to Scripture, spiritual discipline, and the power of prayer. Susan had made a connection with God and spoken to Him often—mostly in frustration over why He would give her the desire to dance and sing and perform and then take it all from her. The second pair of Yoders hadn't thought much of her kind of artistic expression.

"I understand now, in retrospect, that a great deal of what I learned during those years was good and right and just. But Doc, how can you love a God and believe He loves you when someone is telling you the most exciting and creative component of who you are is sinful and needs to be forgotten?"

She didn't give him time to respond. "So, we have Susan Yoder the free spirit, and then Susan Yoder the good little Mennonite girl." Susan held up two fingers.

"Were you really a good little Mennonite girl?'" Dr. Allen asked. "Is that how you see yourself now when you look back on those years?"

"Well, sure. I *was* good, and I *did* try to be who they wanted me to be. But I just couldn't do it. Doc, we've talked all about this. I'm just giving you a summary so I can get to my profound revelation. So would you please let me get there?"

He smiled. "Continue."

"Thank you." She held up two fingers again. "Then we have Susan Phillips." She raised a third finger. "The aspiring dancer who wasn't as good as she thought she was."

It had been years since she'd mentioned her stage name to anyone. Not even Michael knew she had used another name all the years she was in New York. The session when she'd discussed it with Dr. Allen was quite emotional, as it eventually led to talking about her time with Jean-Claude.

"I'm sorry to interrupt. I do want you to reach your profound revelation. But I wouldn't be doing my job if I didn't address salient points as they come up."

She shifted her position in the oversized chair. "Okay. Address away."

"Is it really that you weren't as good a dancer as you thought you were? Or something else?"

"You aren't about to cut me any slack, are you?"

"That's not my job." He folded his hands. "However, allow me to make a point."

"Be my guest." She opened her palm.

"The truth is, you were a good dancer. Look at how many New York productions you were in. I'm certain you weren't hired because people felt sorry for you. It's a very competitive industry. A person has to want that life with every fiber of her being to continue up the ladder. You worked hard to get where you were. You need to give yourself credit for that."

"Okay. I'll give you that point." She licked the tip of her index finger and drew an imaginary line in the air.

"This isn't a game, Susan."

"I know. I'm sorry. Okay, so maybe I was a good dancer, and, yes, I loved to dance. But the truth is, Susan Phillips was really an impostor, a girl with a fake name and an equally fake goal."

"How so?"

"Because when I met Jean-Claude Perrault, for the first time in my life I knew in my gut what I really wanted to do."

"And that was?"

"I wanted to get married and have children. I wanted what my parents had. They were amazing together. I wanted what the other Yoders had too, without all the rules and restrictions. They loved each other deeply. And I wanted children—lots of children. I wanted to raise a houseful of amazingly talented and creative kids."

Dr. Allen smiled and nodded.

"What an idiot I was."

"Why?"

"To think Jean-Claude wanted the same thing. I was delusional."

"You were young and hopeful and perhaps not yet a very good judge of character or motive."

She thought about that a minute and nodded. "Okay, back to my profound revelation. So, when Holly says she's not Lula Mae anymore, it's a lie. She will always be Lula Mae in some sense. She can't cut that part out of her like you excise a tumor. Holly Golightly doesn't exist apart from Lula Mae Barnes. She exists in part because of Lula Mae."

The doctor smiled and let her continue.

"For years I've been saying I'm not the Susan Yoder I was when my parents were alive—or when I lived in Pennsylvania. I've been denying that the Susan Phillips I was during my time in New York ever existed, and I've tried hard to forget about the dreams I had of being Susan Perrault and living happily ever after with a passel of kids. Is it any surprise that when I became Susan Anderson I was already a certifiable mess of contradictions? How Michael has managed to put up with me for twenty-five years is beyond me." She began to cry and reached for a tissue.

He leaned forward and clasped his hands. "How on earth you have managed to become the successful, bold, creative, and loving woman you've been during the past twenty-five years while being a certifiable mess of contradictions fascinates me far more."

"Oh yeah? You need to get a life, Doc." She laughed while wiping her eyes.

"Like you've done?"

"What do you mean?" Susan blew her nose.

"I mean welcome to your life, Susan-it-doesn't-matter-what-your-last-name-is. You are absolutely correct that this is a profound revelation—another breakthrough. You are the sum total of all your experiences no matter what your name was or what choices you did or did not make. This is where the real healing process begins. Bravo!"

Susan took his extended hand and smiled, knowing she had turned a significant corner.

"You really need to work on your timing, Doc." She reached for another tissue to blow her nose again.

"Pardon me?"

"This is where 'Moon River' is supposed to start playing … a musical crescendo to signify the profound moment. I don't hear anything, do you?"

Instead of music, their laughter filled the air.

Chapter 40

Tina needed a break.

She got up from her ergonomic chair, rolled her shoulders, did a few dance stretches. Then she stood with hands on hips, gazing around her domain.

The storage building that once had housed a conglomeration of crates and boxes was now operating like an efficient machine. Looking around the vast warehouse, Tina was amazed at how much had been accomplished in such a short time.

Her wraparound work space enabled her to sit in her chair and roll back and forth from the computer to a ten-foot-long table that held the most recent batch of unpacked items. Everything she needed was at her fingertips, including a digital camera to photograph every item as it was unpacked. Nearby, a two-seat golf cart stood ready to navigate the long aisles down the length of the vast building as she brought one box after another to her work station to unpack each item, identify it and assess its condition, then number and catalog it.

"This cart is more for me than you, dear," Lily had informed her when it was delivered. "Between this building and the Elephant, I'm going to wear out these tired old bones."

Tina had laughed, wondering how Lily managed to do all she did at her age. *She needn't make any excuses for the golf cart,* Tina thought admiringly and secretly thanked her, because she was finding it more tiring than usual to walk back and forth.

Once a group of items had been cataloged, they were repackaged in color-coded bins and transferred from her station to what Ryan called the "holding room"— the far northeast corner of the building. "Display is one of the last things we'll do," he'd told her. "It's going to be awhile before we're ready to move everything into the White Elephant. But I want us to be able to put our fingers on what we need when we want it." Together they had developed a system whereby they could track the location of every item in the building once it was cataloged and transferred from her station.

"This list Susan created is actually pretty good," Tina had said to Ryan as they set up the inventory system. "But I'm finding quite a few discrepancies in what the list indicates is actually inside. Like that box." She pointed. "The list says pictures, but it's full of roller skates, and some boxes don't have any identifying markings on them at all."

Returning to work, Tina unwrapped yet another framed shot of Susan, Jean-Claude, and a well-known celebrity. It appeared to have been taken at a restaurant. Tina couldn't tell the location, so she placed the photo with a collection of items that would need further identification from Susan when she was up to it. Perhaps Ryan would recognize the place from the years he lived in New York. He was inside at the moment, meeting with Lily.

Michael would be joining the team within the next few days, and Tina hoped Susan would be returning as well. It just wasn't the same without her, and Tina was eager to show her how much they had accomplished. She was also anxious to discuss the choice she had made regarding her pregnancy.

Tina took out another framed photo, a duplicate of one she'd already seen. She entered it in her system as such and placed it in the proper bin. They'd been working on the inventory project a little more than one week, yet with Ryan's help her system was as fine-tuned as any industrial assembly line, with the added benefit of a fully air-conditioned space. The portable building was enormous, a full 60 by 160, and she couldn't imagine what it cost to keep cool, especially during a Las Vegas June. But climate control was necessary to preserve the art, fabrics, vinyl records, and a host of other priceless memorabilia.

Tina was personally grateful for the comfort as well. She had reached week twenty-four in her pregnancy and wasn't sure how much longer she could keep it a secret. She was clearly one of those lucky girls who didn't start showing until late in the pregnancy, but her svelte dancer's body was definitely changing, and wearing loose-fitting halter tops was only going to work for so long. One day she would wake up looking very pregnant indeed. She didn't have much time left to pretend otherwise.

Although at first Tina hadn't wanted to believe what Ryan's father had said about Susan having an abortion, she had to admit now that it made perfect sense. No wonder Susan had been so adamant about making Tina aware of all her options. And Tina was so glad Susan had insisted. After talking to Thelma, reading postabortion stress documents, learning about the various abortion procedures, and watching heartbreaking videos of people on adoption waiting lists who desperately wanted to be parents, Tina was convinced beyond a shadow of a doubt. She would give her baby up for adoption.

But now that she'd made that choice, she had to decide what she was going to do next. She could now afford to stay in Vegas, thanks to this full-time job Ryan had given her, but who was she kidding? It wouldn't be realistic to even consider remaining here. Once Ryan found out she was pregnant, he would drop her faster than he could spit. So be it.

Then again, maybe there really wasn't anything to drop. Maybe she was misreading their closeness. Maybe he didn't care for her as much as she had grown to care for him.

No sense thinking about that now.

Right now, she had a job to do, a job she was good at and was enjoying tremendously. She reached into the bottom of the box of photos.

"What do we have here?" She pulled out something wrapped in what appeared to be a bath towel. Unlike the inventory project at her parents' store, in which she knew beforehand what everything was, this project was like being on an archaeology dig and discovering a long-buried tomb filled with treasures. Every box contained something exciting.

She unfolded the towel to reveal a padded pink satin box. She placed the box on the table, gently opened the hinged lid, and, upon seeing the delicate nature of the items inside, put on latex gloves so she wouldn't transfer oils from her skin onto the fragile papers. She began to remove the contents, carefully placing them on the table one at a time: a crushed rosebud pressed between sheets of waxed paper; a heavy linen card with the tiny footprints of a baby in faded ink; a hospital-grade photograph of a baby's face with ringlets of blond hair, the baby's tiny eyes tightly shut; a delicate lock of the same blond hair the size of a dime, pressed between two glass squares like microscope slides from a lab; a tiny pink beaded baby bracelet with the name Y-O-D-E-R spelled out in alphabet beads.

How precious, Tina thought. *Susan's own baby box! I wonder what this is doing here?*

She opened the folded papers at the bottom of the box, fully expecting to see Susan's birth certificate. Then her heart skipped a beat.

She read and reread the documents in her hand as tears cascaded down her cheeks.

~~~

"Susan has a daughter?" Lily whispered, holding in her lap the papers that Tina had breathlessly delivered a few moments ago. "A daughter your age?"

"I knew she wouldn't have had an abortion. I just knew it." Tina clutched the satin box to her chest.

"Shh, dear." Lily placed her index finger over her lips. "Ryan's in his office. I'm not sure it's our place to tell him this information."

That he has a half sister somewhere in the world, she was thinking.

"Oh. Should I have told *you*?" Tina bit her lip. "Maybe I should have gone directly to Susan first."

"No, dear, you did right in coming to me. Susan is in a fragile place right now, and she has obviously worked very hard to keep this a secret for many years."

If things made sense to Lily before, they now took on even more crystal clarity as she began piecing together the fragments of facts from years of friendship. Susan wasn't conflicted because she'd had an abortion; she was conflicted because somewhere out there she had a daughter who was very much alive.

"Do you think she knows where she is … her daughter?" Tina whispered.

"Oh my, I wouldn't begin to guess."

"Do you think Michael knows? Should we tell him?"

"Sweetheart, I don't think we should tell anyone. It's not our place. But I am going to consult with Susan's doctor and see what he suggests. We don't want to do anything that might jeopardize her health, do we?"

"No." Tina looked down and picked at her cuticles. "Uh, Lily?"

"Yes?"

"Do you think she regretted giving her daughter up for adoption? Is that why she had a breakdown?"

"I couldn't say, dear. I'm sure Susan had a very good reason for what she did, and it's more likely she had a breakdown because that pathetic excuse for a man accused her of something she knew wasn't true."

Had he been half the man Susan must have thought he was in the first place, Lily conjectured, she most likely wouldn't have given up her child, and that seemed more than enough reason to send her over the edge. Seeing Jean-Claude had made her face the fact that she'd given up her only child because of him.

"Forgive me, Lord, for hating that man," Lily said to herself. Then she noticed that Tina had begun to weep, quietly shaking in her chair. "Sweetheart, it's okay." She walked to the other side of the desk and sat next to the troubled young woman. "It's all going to work out, don't you see? This all makes so much more sense now. Susan is getting the help she needs, and eventually everything is going to be fine."

"It's not going to be fine," Tina sobbed. She lifted a tear-streaked face toward Lily. "I'm pregnant. I planned to give my baby up for adoption. Now I don't know what to do. Please, tell me what to do."

"Oh my." Lily held the young woman and let her weep. When Tina began to compose herself, Lily stifled a giggle.

"What's funny?" Tina pulled a tissue from her pocket and blew her nose.

"I'm so sorry, honey. Nothing is funny, not in the sense that any of this is humorous. But I couldn't help but think of all those reality TV shows that are popular today. They ain't got nothin' on us." She winked.

"I suppose that's true." Tina wiped her eyes.

"Tina," Lily said more somberly, "you know how we always talk about God-cidences?" Tina shook her head affirmatively.

"I couldn't, and wouldn't, begin to tell you what to do. You are a brilliant young woman, more than capable of making a decision based on all of the rational facts available to you." She paused and looked Tina in the eye. "However, I will say this."

"Yes?" Tina whispered. "What?"

"God surely had a definitive plan when He delivered you to Susan's doorstep. Everything that is unfolding on our private reality TV show is part of His plan. And, my dear child, God-cidences are not always rational. The only thing I can tell you to do—that I feel comfortable telling you to do—is to balance your head knowledge with your heart knowledge and ask God to make His purpose clearly known."

―*mm*―

From: Susan Anderson (boomerbabesusan@
boomerbabesrock.com)

Sent: Tuesday, June 13, 7:31 p.m.

To: Patricia Davies; Mary Johnson; Lisa Taylor; Linda Jones;
Sharon Wilson

Subject: Thank you, dear friends

Thank you, sweet boomer babes, for all of your cards and letters. And the flowers were breathtaking—big enough to lie over a casket. Are you sure they sent the right order? ☺

I'm sorry I worried so many people, but I'm happy to say I'm feeling much better, on the mend for certain. I've done a lot of soul-searching, courtesy of a great psychiatrist who has more than a few interesting theories on why so many boomer babes (and boomer dudes) melt down in their fifties. Remind me to tell you about his PIES theory.

I've learned a great deal in therapy and there are some things from my past I need to discuss with Michael—things even you boomer babes don't know. As soon as I come clean with my DH, I'd like to share a bit with you boomer babes. In the meantime, I cherish your prayers and would ask that you continue being my intercessors as I prepare to journey into unknown territory with Michael.

I'll be back. Love you all more than I even realized.

Susan

P.S.: Keep the cards and letters coming. I'd forgotten how exciting it is to get "real" mail.

Chapter 41

"You look fabulous!" Lily kissed her friend on both cheeks as she walked through the Andersons' door.

"Hey, nothing like a good old-fashioned breakdown to help you get in shape."

Lily winked. "I'll have to remember that the next time I need to look ten years younger."

"Loretta just said the same thing. God forbid I've started a new beauty craze."

"You do look good, darling. Bright. Healthy. Your color is back."

"Doc says I need to gain some weight now."

"Well, you can thank me for helping you follow the good doctor's orders. I brought cream cheese muffins from Mama T's." She handed over a white bakery box secured with a gold elastic band. Susan wasted no time opening it, tearing off a bit of one of the tender cakes, and popping it into her mouth.

"Oh my," she mumbled around the crumbs, "that's even better than I remember it."

"It's good to see you like this. With an appetite, I mean—not talking with your mouth full."

"Sorry." Susan put her hand over her mouth.

"Did you go to the salon to see Loretta?" Lily led the way to the kitchen.

"No. She just left. I haven't been to the salon yet. Haven't been anywhere in two weeks except here and Doctor Allen's office ... per his orders."

"Good girl. First things first."

"Well, he's given me my walking papers now. Says it's time to get back to the real world."

"You're done seeing him?" Lily was surprised.

"Oh no—just not twice a day every day. I've graduated to twice a week, and I can start seeing folks and dealing with life ... one step at a time. That's why Loretta was here. She was giving me an update on the salon and my customers. I'm going to start back next week, but not as many hours."

"I'm glad to hear that. How's Loretta doing?"

"Loving the responsibility at the salon but bummed she can't take a more active role in our project at the White Elephant."

"Well, I don't blame her. It is rather exciting. But her time will come. There will be more than enough for her to do when we move into the new facility." Lily placed muffins on two small plates, sliding one in front of Susan. "Can I get you anything else, dear?" she asked.

"You've done more than enough." Susan reached into her sweater pocket for a tissue. "I don't know how to thank you for the past two weeks. Michael told me what you did—what you've been doing ..."

"Oh, nonsense! I haven't done a thing. It's that superman hubby of yours who's done the most. He's quite a guy."

"That he is." She looked down, her eyes filling with tears. "I'm sorry, Lily, for causing so much trouble."

"Oh, sweetheart, you didn't cause trouble. It was—" She stopped herself before saying more.

"It's okay. You can say his name … Jean-Claude. At least that was his name when I knew him. Jean-Claude Perrault. I'm not sure when he changed it to Gene Power."

"Ryan figures it must have been before he was born, because his birth certificate lists his father as Gene Power."

"How is Ryan, by the way? I feel bad for him."

"Don't. Their relationship was strained long before this, so don't carry that weight on your already overburdened shoulders." Lily took a sip of coffee. "And Ryan is doing fine."

"Tina? Is she … okay?"

"She's pregnant, and you know it," Lily said quietly.

"She told you?"

"Yes, only a few days ago. What an imbecile I was not to have noticed. I can't believe how some young women today don't show until very late in their pregnancy. Must be all that dancing—keeps the muscles tight."

"Did Tina tell you anything else … if you don't mind my asking?"

"Not much. She's a mighty confused young woman. I know she's anxious to see you."

"I'm going to call her." Susan picked at the muffin on her plate. "Does Ryan know?"

"She hasn't told him. I'm not even sure they've admitted to each other how smitten they are. But they sure work well together."

"I'm glad to hear that. Hope it lasts."

"So what do you think about having Michael work with us? I know he asked you."

"I have mixed feelings." Susan pushed some crumbs around on her plate. "Please don't misunderstand me, Lily. I would love to work with him on the new Disco Diva—that's not it. But Michael and I still have so much to work through. We're taking it one step at a time. For now it's good to have him involved. We'll see how things work out."

"I understand, dear. So, has Michael told you what we're doing now?"

"Yes. You're conducting a thorough inventory in preparation for what Jean-Claude is going to do next."

"You do know what he's saying … about your collection?"

"Of course—that I stole it from him. It's not true. He did pay for a lot of it, but he gave it all to me. He wasn't even that interested in the stuff."

"I never for a moment believed him," Lily said. "What do you think he'll do next?"

"I imagine he'll try to sue us. Slap us with an injunction or a cease and desist order. Anything to hold up our progress and throw his weight around." Susan walked to the refrigerator and took out a bottle of drinking water. "I wouldn't put anything past him. Water?"

"No, thank you. I have my attorney on high alert—we're ready and waiting."

"Actually, I need to tell you something about that. But first— about the other thing he said …"

"Sweetheart, you don't owe me an explanation for anything. All that's important is that you're getting better. Do you like Greg? He's a fine doctor, isn't he?"

"He's amazing." Susan sat and gulped water directly from the bottle. "I should have seen someone, talked to someone, years ago."

"Ah, retrospective wisdom. If only we could go back."

"I'm not sure I want to go back, but I do wish I'd done things differently."

Lily nodded and took a bite of muffin as they sat in comfortable silence.

"Lily, I asked you to come over because I have something I need to tell Michael, and I would like your guidance. You've always been like a mother to me … and I'm having a really hard time with this."

"What is it, dear?" Lily leaned forward.

Susan drew in a deep breath, then blurted it out. "Jean-Claude was wrong. I didn't have an abortion. He thinks I did because that's what he wanted me to do, that's what he paid me to do. And that's what I wanted him to believe. But the truth is, I had a baby girl and gave her up for adoption. They never even let me see her. All I have is a baby photo. Or rather *had*—I don't even know where that is anymore. I lost the box years ago."

Tears spilled down Susan's cheeks as Lily stroked the back of her hand like a beloved kitten. "I tried to tell Michael when we first met, but all I could hear was the voice of one of the nurses at the hospital who said it was better to forget it ever happened, to get on with my life. Except now when I look at things, I can see that I never did get on with my life, did I? Not really."

She took another deep breath and straightened her shoulders. "But that's about to stop. Doc Allen has me on a new journey—a journey of truth on many levels. My next step is to tell the truth to Michael about my daughter. But I'm afraid of what he might say. We've been married for a long time, but I'm beginning to realize that I never really let him in to see the real me. What if he discovers the truth about me and decides he doesn't love me? I mean, intellectually I don't think he will. But emotionally ..."

"Oh, honey, I understand completely." Lily tilted her head. "But how can I help?"

"Role-play with me. Give me every possible scenario, every response imaginable, so I can be prepared. Help me to find the right words. Please?"

"I can do that. But first I'd like to help you find something else. Excuse me for one moment." She pulled her cell phone from her cherry red Chanel handbag and stood while pressing speed dial.

"Franco, can you please bring me the black velvet bag in the trunk? I'll meet you at the front door. Thank you." She flipped the phone closed and walked to Susan's front door, where she waited less than a minute for Franco to bring the bag to her. Then she returned to the kitchen. "Tina found this a few days ago during her inventory project. I believe you've been looking for it."

Lily placed the velvet bag in front of Susan, who gasped as she removed the padded pink satin box. "Where was it?" she whispered, tears gently falling down her cheeks as she rubbed her hand over the soft fabric. She opened the lid slowly, staring down at the pieces of her heart she thought she'd lost.

"At the bottom of a box of photos, wrapped in a bath towel."

"I looked everywhere. I thought it had been thrown away by mistake. Oh, Lily ..." She picked up the baby photo and held it to her chest, weeping. "Thank you. Thank you."

"It's Tina you have to thank."

"I will. Oh, I will—"

Chapter 42

After dozens of dry-run rehearsals with Lily, Susan felt well prepared to disclose her information to Michael when he came home later that day. But she hadn't anticipated this latest occurrence, which tossed a monkey wrench into her plans.

"Settle down, Michael," she yelled. "You'll have a heart attack!"

"I don't want to settle down. I should have punched him in the face when I had a chance. The lowlife son of a—"

"Michael, please. It's going to be okay!"

"It's not okay! Did you actually read this?" He waved a sheaf of papers.

"I had a breakdown, Michael—I didn't go blind. Yes, I read them."

The documents had been delivered to the White Elephant construction site office while Lily was role-playing with Susan. Michael had been there and signed for them. He'd arrived home, livid, about five minutes after Lily left.

"How does someone have documentation for every single thing he bought more than two decades ago?"

"I told you, honey, he was a trust-fund baby. He never had money, only unlimited funds via a checkbook. His family had a team of accountants whose only job was to keep track of what he spent. Not that it mattered. There wasn't any limit on his spending."

Michael sat on the edge of his La-Z-Boy and paged through the stack of documents, shaking his head.

"I don't know what we're going to do. Lily will call her legal team as soon as we tell her, but at this point it's his word against yours, and he has all this." He waved the papers again. "All we have are a few insurance appraisals and twenty-five years of payments on two storage units in east Las Vegas."

"And my things … we have my collection."

Her husband rubbed his chin and shook his head.

"Michael, do you believe me?"

"Of course I do. You wouldn't steal, and you surely wouldn't have blatantly displayed your things all of these years if you had something to hide. I can't figure out why he didn't find you sooner. It's not like you and your stuff aren't easily recognizable!"

"I don't think he was looking."

"He claims he was."

"Michael, think about it. Disco Diva has been all over the news for years. If he wanted to find me, he could have."

"Yeah, but he's been living in Paris."

"They have cable TV in Paris." She smiled. "And Internet."

"This isn't a joke, Susan. We could lose everything. I don't know how you can be so calm."

"We? I never thought you cared much about any of this." She waved her arm. "Especially that." She pointed at the huge nine-panel Andy Warhol portrait of her twenty-two-year-old face.

"Yeah, well, that was before I learned it was worth more than my car."

"Ah, the truth comes out. It's all about the money, huh?" She sat on the arm of his recliner and playfully pinched his shoulder.

"Can you prove that was a gift?" He looked at the multicolored portrait. "You should at least be able to keep that."

"I can keep all of it—we can keep all of it." She stood and put out her hand. "Come sit next to me on the sofa. I have something I want to show you."

He sat next to her as she opened the drawer of the coffee table and took out an envelope. She clutched it in her hand as she spoke quietly. "Michael, I know beyond a shadow of a doubt that he didn't find me because he wasn't looking for me. This recent escapade of his is nothing more than an elaborate bluff. Well planned and executed—I'll grant him that—but a bluff nonetheless, and he's banking on the slight chance I won't be able to call him on it. But I can, and I will."

"Go on," Michael said.

"I need to tell you a little story," she said. "It was New Year's Eve, 1979. The Studio was closing, and a new decade was beginning. And I was pregnant—I guess you know that much by now."

He nodded, and she continued. "I'd known for at least a month, but I waited until that night to tell Jean-Claude. I wanted to have all the hoopla to accompany my grand announcement. We'd been living together for more than two years by that point. He'd said we were going to get married, and I believed him."

She took a drink of water from a glass on the table.

"He said he was excited. He even looked excited. I remember

he picked me up and twirled me around the dance floor. I was sad because it was the last time we would dance together at Studio 54, but I was envisioning our lives as parents. Picturing all of the adventures we would have with a child. Michael, living with Jean-Claude was unlike anything I'd ever experienced. We flew to Europe on a whim, ate out almost every night. And, yes, we bought whatever we wanted. Collecting disco memorabilia was my idea, contrary to what he says, and he was like a kid every time he found something for me.

"I imagined things would change a little with the baby, but we could afford a live-in nanny, and there was plenty of room at the Sherry. A couple of his friends had children, and he seemed to enjoy them. I honestly thought we were going to be fine."

Throughout the account, she kept her eyes fixed on his, fearful of turning away and losing her nerve.

"Nine days later I woke up to find him gone. I think he put a sleeping pill in my tea before I went to bed so I wouldn't hear him pack his things during the night. He took all of his clothing, toiletries, a few framed photographs, and his mother's pearl necklace, which he had given me. He left this on the dresser."

She held out the envelope she'd unconsciously been rolling into a cylinder.

"Read it," she said, taking another drink of water. "This is my trump card. I think he's hoping I destroyed it or lost it years ago."

Michael unrolled the document and scanned the handwritten letter.

Dear One:

I trust in time you will come to understand my motives for departing in such a hasty fashion. Given the circumstances, I felt it was the best thing to do for us both. I'm returning home to work in the family business, a place I've always known was my true calling. Consider everything in the penthouse and in our storage facility yours, including Marilyn, whom you know is currently garaged at the Plaza. The collection bug has always been yours and, frankly, disco never was my thing ... but it was a playful adventure nonetheless. You are welcome to stay here at the Sherry until the lease is up in March. I trust also that the generous gift I've left will see you through the speedy handling of your current situation so as not to cause either of us undue shame and responsibility. You have been a joy to know, and I wish you great happiness in your future endeavors.

Respectfully and lovingly yours,

Jean-Claude

The second page was a faded photocopy of a bank check made out to Susan Phillips in the amount of one hundred thousand dollars and signed by Jean-Claude Perrault.

Michael stared. "He gave you one hundred thousand dollars?"

"For an abortion," she said quietly. "Guess he didn't know you could get one in the City for under a thousand. I used some of it to move here, get an apartment, and put my things in storage."

Michael looked at her as tears filled his eyes.

"It's true then. You did have an …" He couldn't bring himself to say it. "Sweetheart, I'm so sorry, I'm so—" He reached for her hand as she abruptly pulled it back.

"No, I'm the one who's sorry. I should have told you all this years ago. I should have told you so many things, but I guess I just got in the habit of sweeping things under the rug. I don't know—maybe I was afraid you'd leave me too. I guess I didn't trust anyone back then, not even myself." She took a deep breath. "Michael, I didn't have an abortion. I boxed everything up, put it in storage in New York for a short time, and lived in a home for unwed mothers in Ithaca, where I placed my daughter for adoption. I was twenty-four years old when she was born. I never saw her. Somewhere in the world, I have a beautiful daughter whose birthday I celebrate every year alone. She'll be twenty-six years old this year."

She took a deep breath, amazed that she had gotten through the confession without tears. After the past two weeks, apparently, she was all cried out.

Her husband, however, was not. He put his head in his hands and wept like a baby.

Chapter 43

"Thank you for meeting me." Susan and Tina embraced in the Starbucks parking lot as they got out of their cars.

"I've missed you!" Tina said, squeezing her friend tighter.

"Oh my!" Susan placed her hand gently on Tina's tummy. "I can feel a little baby bump ... at last. If you hug Ryan that close, he's an imbecile if he doesn't notice."

Tina's lower lip began to quiver.

"Oh honey, I'm sorry. Let's go inside where it's cool and talk."

After getting their drinks, they opted to sit outside in Susan's car, preferring the quiet privacy to the busy Saturday rush at Starbucks. The air conditioner blew the gentle scent of vanilla and gardenia from Susan's clip-on air freshener.

"Lily gave me the box you found. Thank you."

"You're welcome." Tina played with the cardboard sleeve around her cup of decaf.

"I'm sorry I didn't tell you about the adoption," Susan added.

"I understand. It's okay."

"No, it's not okay. Considering what you're going through—trying to make the same decision yourself, or not, I should have said something," Susan said quietly. "But I just ... couldn't. It's still hard. I ... I ..."

"Please don't." Tina placed her hand on top of Susan's. "I really do understand."

Susan let out a long breath and nodded. "So, tell me what's happening at the White Elephant." She took a sip of her coffee. "I hear you've got your corner of the world running like a well-oiled machine."

"Things are progressing quickly, that's for sure. But it hasn't been the same without you. I'm glad you're feeling better. We all are."

"Thank you. Me too. It's been a long two weeks." They sipped their coffee and watched silently as a young mother unloaded a baby carrier from the back of her Lexus SUV.

"So how are you feeling?" Susan asked.

"Me?"

"Yes, dear, you. You do know that one morning very soon you're going to wake up with a far more discernible baby bump than that little pooch you've got now, and then what? Have you told Ryan yet?"

Tina shook her head. "No."

"Do you think it will get easier the longer you wait?" Susan placed her coffee in the dashboard cup holder and reached for a tissue to blow her nose.

"I don't know what I think. But I've gained almost sixteen pounds. You'd think Ryan would notice on his own and say something."

"Well, don't hold your breath, honey. Guys aren't always the most observant of God's creatures."

Tina laughed. "Tell me about it. He thinks I look great—even with sixteen added pounds. Although he doesn't know that's how much I've gained. He still thinks I'm trying to lose weight so I can go back to work."

"Hmm. Only sixteen pounds. Is that healthy?"

"My doctor says I'm exactly on track. But I'm afraid you're right about waking up one day and having the surprise of my life. I'm about to start my third trimester, and this little one isn't going to stay little for too much longer."

Susan cleared her throat. "You know, I've learned a lot—remembered a lot—the past few weeks." She swallowed. "I used to think that if Michael really loved me, he would somehow sense when something was wrong and ..."

"Come to your rescue?" Tina said, smiling.

"Exactly! Like he was supposed to read my mind. When we were first married, there were so many things in my past I should have shared with him, but it was painful."

"I know what you mean." Tina picked at a cuticle.

"Not just painful. I felt guilty and ashamed of many of my choices. I was afraid to tell him."

"Because you thought he wouldn't understand?"

"Yes. I was an emotional mess. And I figured when Michael didn't ask what was wrong during times when something was clearly wrong, either he didn't want to know or he didn't care. So I just kept things to myself."

Tina was silent.

"Hey," Susan said, "that's your cue to ask me Dr. Phil's famous question."

Tina grinned. "So how did that work for you?"

"It didn't. The more I kept things to myself, the more out of balance my PIES got."

"Pardon?"

"Sorry. That's Dr. Allen's theory about my breakdown." She explained the PIES theory to Tina, who listened raptly.

"That makes perfect sense," Tina finally said. "And you're telling me all this because you think I need to tell Ryan everything, right?"

"I'm telling you this because I don't want you to make the mistakes I did. Twenty-five years of marriage, and we've been strangers much of the time—all because I was too proud, or too afraid, or too ashamed, to be truthful with my husband. Scripture tells us that the truth will set you free. And truth, Tina, comes in many levels, at many stages."

Tina was fighting back tears as she whispered, "Susan, I need to ask you something personal. But I don't want to hurt you …"

"It's okay, honey. I think I know. You want to ask if I regret giving up my daughter for adoption. Right?"

"Y-yes."

"Sweetheart—" Susan took Tina's hand in hers—"at the time, it was the wisest decision I could have made. I wasn't prepared to be a mother or a single parent. If my PIES are unbalanced now, you should have seen them back then!"

They laughed and Susan took a deep breath. "I pray every day that my daughter grew up with two stable parents who were able to love and care for her during those formative years and beyond. I'm afraid I would have done her great emotional harm had I been in her life when mine was a such a mess. But I won't lie to you. The older I got, the more I wondered about her." Susan reached over and brushed a stray piece of hair behind Tina's ear. "And with every baby I lost, it got worse … the emptiness I felt in my heart as a mother grew."

She let the tears fall unashamedly down her cheeks. "It never crossed my mind that I would be unable to have more children. I don't regret giving her up, but a day doesn't go by that I don't think about her."

Tina wrapped her arms around Susan, and they cried together.

Early Monday morning, Lily and Michael showed up at her attorney's office, brandishing copies of the documents that proved Jean-Claude had indeed given ownership of everything to Susan, including a considerable amount of money. Her legal team was ecstatic.

"You have to wonder, did he forget about the note?" Lily said to Michael as they sat alone in the law firm's conference room. The lawyers had returned to their offices to start filing their response to Jean-Claude's false accusations.

"Either that or he figured Susan wouldn't have kept it. He had to know she was a collector, for crying out loud. She doesn't throw out a thing. I'm sure she has her own baby teeth in a drawer somewhere."

"Most likely."

"Speaking of baby mementos, Susan showed me the box you brought over to the house. She told me about her daughter. She also told me how you helped her rehearse what she would say to me. Thanks for being there for her—for us."

"Nonsense. I didn't do anything," Lily said quietly. "I'm glad she finally told you, though. That's a heavy weight to carry alone for so many years."

He nodded. "We've talked a lot about that, and I can kind of understand now where she was coming from."

"How so?" Lily asked.

"Well, she felt really guilty, for one thing. She couldn't believe anyone would ever love her if they found out what she'd done. And she'd been hurt so badly when Jean-Claude left her. So she spent years hiding her true feelings from me—afraid to let me see the real Susan. Afraid I'd leave her like that no-good piece of garbage did."

"That makes sense. The poor child."

"I still can't believe I was so stupid, that I never figured it out. All those years …"

"Oh, sweetheart," Lily said, "how could you possibly have known? Besides, God always had a plan for her. Look how the experience changed her life. So much makes better sense now, doesn't it?"

They both knew that Susan had come to know the Lord shortly before moving to Las Vegas. Knowing she had given birth the same year she herself was born anew gave them a deeper sense of what Susan must have gone through so long ago.

"Susan wants to tell Ryan herself on Thursday when she goes back to work," Michael said. "So don't tell him about any of this, okay?"

"I wouldn't think of it. He'll be thankful to hear it's a fraudulent lawsuit, though. Knowing that his own father is suing us has turned the boy inside out."

"Wonder what he'll think of the fact that he has a half sister out there somewhere."

"Hmm. Michael, did Susan say if she ever tried to look for her daughter?"

"After every miscarriage she considered it. But each time, she got afraid and changed her mind."

"Afraid?"

"Yeah, like what if the adoptive parents had elected not to tell her—what if she didn't know? Susan said she couldn't do that to her daughter no matter how much she wanted to know how she'd turned out. Then there was the other side of the coin. What if her daughter had had a bad life—if things hadn't gone well for her? Susan was afraid she'd feel even guiltier. She's still really torn. I can tell she wants to find her, but I think she'll go to her grave before causing any trouble."

"But what if her daughter is looking for her? It's not an impossibility. Michael, did you look at all the items in the pink box?"

"She showed me the photo, and I could see some other things—the baby bracelet, a little piece of hair …"

"At the very bottom of that box are the adoption papers. Just in case you wanted to know."

No fanfare marked Susan's first day back to work at the White Elephant. That was exactly how she wanted it. What happened three weeks earlier had been dramatic and humiliating. Now she was eager for a little low-key normalcy … or at least the positive drama of being at a high-energy workplace.

A great deal had been accomplished in her absence, including the addition of another desk in Ryan's office for Michael. That arrangement, she'd been assured, was more than acceptable to both men. "They actually get along famously," Lily had told her during a recent visit. Susan had smiled at that, remembering her husband's initial jealous reaction to the young man months ago and his feelings about him after having met his father. Things had changed.

A lot of things had changed, in fact. Her talks with Dr. Allen were helping her come to terms with the past, and Michael had started attending sessions with her to work out some of their issues. She was relieved to finally be on the same page with him and eager to start fresh.

Susan's next concern at this point was Tina. She didn't know what would happen between her and Ryan, but Susan was prepared to stand by the young woman as she prepared for the adoption of her child.

"Is that the boss lady's car I see in ye olde parking lot?" Ryan yelled from the entrance.

"You bet your sweet bippy it is, boss man," she called loudly from her office. "Time to shape up or ship out."

They embraced warmly when he came inside. "Nice to have you back," he said.

"Just in time, I'd say." She stepped back, looking him over. "What is this—casual Thursday?"

She'd only seen him in Hugo Boss or Armani, always the epitome of casual chic. Now he wore old khaki trousers with paint spatters and holes in the knees and an untucked, rather shopworn, cherry red Ralph Lauren polo shirt with spots on the front.

"Are those Converse high-tops?" She pointed to his shoes.

"Yes, ma'am. You like?" He pulled up his pant leg to show off canvas shoes that were easily ten years old. "From the looks of you, I guess you don't know what's on the agenda today." He playfully punched her shoulder. "Otherwise you wouldn't be looking like a fashion model—a young fashion model, if you don't mind my saying so."

She smiled. "Therapy agrees with me."

"Rest agrees with you."

She had taken extra care in dressing that morning. Excited to be back at the White Elephant, she'd selected a sleeveless Diane von Furstenberg wraparound dress with platform wedge shoes she'd recently found at Banana Republic. Although most of her clothing was vintage, she occasionally strayed off the purist path as long as the look didn't clash. Her hair was pulled into a French twist, and a single strand of pearls complemented the look.

"So what's on the agenda?" she inquired as they drifted toward his office. "Dumpster diving?"

"Very funny. First of all, we're moving the next stack of cartons for Tina to sort. Did you know she's already gone through more than twelve of the really big crates? Have you been over there yet?" He stuck his thumb out toward the adjacent building.

"Not yet. Just got here. Give me some time." She smiled.

"Anyway, after the boxes comes the really dirty job. Mighty Mike and I are venturing into the crawl spaces in the Elephant."

"Mighty Mike? He lets you call him Mike?"

"Sure. Is that a problem?"

She shook her head. No one *ever* called Michael by the slang for his name. Until now, apparently.

"But why the crawl spaces?" She shivered at the thought of what they might find.

"Because we can. Is the old man in?"

"Not yet. Lily says you guys are doing okay …"

"We're having a blast. I've never had much experience being around someone like him. I guess he's kind of what they mean by a 'man's man,' you know? I can't believe how much he knows about electric, plumbing, landscaping, pretty much everything. But he never comes on too strong, always defers to me like I'm his boss or something."

"Well, technically you are." She grinned. "I'm glad it's working out. The dynamics around here have changed, haven't they?"

"For the better, I'd say," he said.

"I'm glad you're back at Cedar Ridge."

"Yeah, me, too. The Palace Station wasn't quite the same. But, Susan, I'm glad you're back too—here. Are you doing okay? I mean … are we okay? I wanted to come see you, but Mike said to give you some breathing room. I still can't believe my old man is suing—no, that's not really true. I *can* believe it. I'd do something if I thought I could, but he couldn't care less about anything I have to say."

"I'm sorry for that, Ryan. He's missing out on a wonderful relationship with a fine young man."

"Aw, shucks, ma'am." He comically scuffed his toe on the ground and swung his arms around like a little kid, but the blush on his face revealed the truth.

"Ryan, do you have a few minutes before you get started? I need to talk with you about something."

"Sure. What's up?"

She closed the door of his office and proceeded to tell him the truth about how his father had abandoned her, the note he left, and the fact that somewhere in the world he had a half sister a year older than he was.

Chapter 44

"Ryan, please. You need to keep your voice down." Tina put her index finger to her lips. "These walls are like paper, and my landlord lives next door."

"I'm sorry." He paced around her small but tidy living room. "But I can't believe it. Well, that's not true. I can believe it. I always knew he was a coward, but this takes the cake."

"I'm sorry."

"Why? What do you have to be sorry for? He's the no-good piece of trash who abandoned her when she was pregnant."

"Don't, Ryan," she said softly. "He's still your father."

"I don't care. He paid her off like she was a gambling debt or something. That's all his own kid was worth—one hundred thousand. He makes me want to puke."

"But we don't know the entire story. It was a long time ago, he was a different man, the circumstances were different. You don't know what was going on in his mind. Not really."

"You're sticking up for him?"

"I'm just saying that he's your father—and he brought you up, didn't he?"

"My mother brought me up. He wasn't around much."

"Well, anyway, the thing with Susan was a long time ago. They

were both different people. And we still don't have all the facts. Didn't
you tell me your father said there was a chance the child wasn't his?"

"I can't believe you said that."

"Why?"

"So now Susan is a tramp?"

"I didn't say that—you know I would never say that." Her lip
trembled and tears welled up in her eyes.

"Tina, are you crying?" he asked, baffled. "What's the matter?"

"What's the *matter?* Look, I know you're angry with him, and
you have every right to be. But what if it wasn't his child?"

"It shouldn't have made a difference—if he loved her, which he
obviously didn't. He had no intention of marrying her."

"Again, you don't know that."

"The letter he wrote speaks for itself, don't you think?"

"So it's that clear cut for you?"

"What?"

"That if he loved her he would have married her, whether the
child was his or not?"

"Absolutely."

"But things aren't always that simple."

"They should be."

She gazed at him for a long minute, her eyes unblinking. Then
she said softly, "I just don't want you to hate him. Because you're his
son. And hating him means hating yourself a little too."

"You confound me, woman," he said, reaching to pull her close.
But she pulled away from him—again.

Why did she keep doing that? She was driving him crazy. It
wasn't that she was playing him—he didn't think that for a minute.

He knew there was a genuine connection between them. Was it that she didn't trust herself enough to let him get close?

Then again, he knew she had been deeply hurt by the decision of the artistic director at the Tropicana. Ryan was still mad about that, but now he realized his reaction was nothing compared to what Tina must have felt. Had the suspension made her question her own attractiveness, causing her to pull away from him when he touched her? Why hadn't he seen that before? He needed to be more understanding.

It had been a little over a month since her suspension. He knew this because he was keeping track of the time before he would lose her again. He couldn't tell if she had lost enough weight to go back, and he surely wouldn't ask her. But how could he get her to see that he found her more attractive than ever? And that the more he got to know the person she was on the inside, the less concerned he was with the outside? He felt as though he'd always known her—couldn't remember what his life had been like without her in it.

The next realization hit him like a two-by-four. He was in love. No question about it. But did she feel the same?

They ate dinner in relative silence, comfortably talking yet not feeling the need to fill up the space with mindless chatter. He loved that. It was so unlike his previous dating relationships. It gave him time to gather courage for what he needed to do.

"Tina?" he asked while rinsing off their dinner plates.

"Yes?" She scooped gelato into glass ice cream dishes.

"I love you."

She hesitated just an instant. "I love you, too."

"I'm so glad you said that." He wiped his hands on the dish

towel and leaned back against the sink. "It could have been very awkward otherwise."

She nodded solemnly and held out a dish of gelato. "It's pineapple coconut, your favorite."

They stood toe-to-toe, staring into each other's eyes, eating frozen dessert and knowing their lives had suddenly turned a corner.

—*mm*—

"Can we talk?" Ryan walked slowly into Susan's office the next day.

"Sure." Susan nodded to a chair. "Sit."

"I just got off the phone with Gene's attorney."

Susan was sad that Ryan had ceased to refer to Jean-Claude as his father in any way, not even using the slang "old man" that used to drive Lily crazy. These days, it was always Gene.

"He's formally dropping all charges."

"Thank God."

"We knew he didn't stand a chance, but he could have held up our plans for a long time just to be—well, just because."

"Why the sudden change of heart, do you think?"

"For one thing, they authenticated his signature on the letter and check, so he really didn't have a legal claim. But there's something else."

"Yes?"

"He didn't change his name because he wanted to make it easier for folks to pronounce."

Susan crossed her legs and leaned back.

"He changed it because he was in trouble."

"With the law?"

"With a husband."

It didn't take long for his words to register.

"I see. Any idea who? Never mind. I don't want to know."

"The lawyer didn't say who, and frankly I didn't ask. Apparently Gene had an affair with the wife of a very important man—someone involved in, shall we say, less than honest pursuits?" He held an index finger alongside his nose, indicating mob involvement. "If you get my drift."

"Oh my."

"The guy hired a private investigator and got photos, receipts, the whole nine yards. Gave Gene forty-eight hours to get out of town."

"I see." She leaned forward. "Did the attorney say when this affair took place?"

"Do you really want to know?"

"Yes."

"It went on for two years—1978 and '79."

Silence. Susan stood, walked over to the window, then turned back to him, her face unreadable.

"I'm sorry, Susan."

"Don't be. I'm not surprised. But he eventually brought you and your mother back to the City to live again. Even with a new name, I'm sure a man that connected would still be a threat."

"You'd think so, huh? But ol' Gene's still alive and kicking. Unfortunately."

"Don't say that, Ryan. He's still your father. And if it wasn't for him, I wouldn't have Michael, my collection, or Disco Diva. You wouldn't be here, you would never have met Tina, and, well, everything would be different."

"How can you be so optimistic?" He shook his head.

She gave him a crooked smile. "Hey, it's no secret I've been in therapy since my breakdown."

"Yeah, we all know the boss lady is crazy as a loon."

"You got all this information from Jean-Claude's attorney? Isn't he bound by some kind of confidentiality clause or something like that?"

"Yeah, he is. He's also the father of one of my best friends. I asked, he told me. He trusts me not to get him disbarred."

"I won't say anything."

"I know you won't." His cheeks dimpled. "You're not that crazy."

"At least not as crazy as I was. I'm getting things sorted out, Ryan. It feels good, and in a way I have your father to thank for that."

"But—"

"I'm serious, Ryan. I'm not sure my marriage would have survived if a major change hadn't occurred. I don't think either of us was ready, willing, or able, quite frankly, to do what needed to be done. We needed a kick in the pants, and Jean-Claude did nothing if not that."

"So things really are better for you?" he asked. "I felt so …"

"Guilty?"

"Yeah. I did."

"I know all about guilt. Trust me, it's highly corrosive. It'll eat away at your soul if you don't get rid of it."

"Easier said than done."

"Not true, my dear. It's a choice you can make. Do you think I'm lying to you when I say it's not your fault?"

"No."

"Then if you choose to hang on to your guilt, I have to wonder why."

He smiled. "Sounds like I should be visiting Doc Allen."

"I have his card if you'd like one." She stood up and stretched out her arms. "Come here." They hugged warmly. Then she quickly pulled away and looked at her watch. "Now, I have an appointment with a vendor. And Michael and Tina should be here any minute."

"Well now, wasn't that a subtle change of subject."

"Not subtle at all." She put her hands on her hips. "Now, you listen to me. We are going to be A-OK—you, me, and Disco Diva. We can put Gene Power, guilt, and secrets behind us and move on. It's a new day, a new journey, and I, for one, intend to have the time of my life enjoying it! So get your little behind out of my office and get to work. I'm sure you can find something productive to do."

"Uh, Susan?"

"Yes?"

"Could I talk to you about Tina?"

A look of pained concern came over her face. But before she could respond, they heard the door open and the sound of Michael and Tina coming in.

"Oh, sweetie, I really do have to go," she whispered. "After this appointment I'm heading over to Doc Allen's, and I won't be in at all this weekend. Can we talk at Michael's birthday party on Monday?"

"Uh, sure. Okay."

"Whatever it is, I'm sure it's going to be fine." She kissed him on the cheek and walked out, leaving him thoroughly confused.

Chapter 45

"… Happy birthday, dear Michael, happy birthday to you!"

Everyone clapped and cheered as he blew out the trick candles one more time.

"Gonna start a forest fire there, old man." Ryan slapped him on the back. "Need help?"

Michael laughed. "Leave my candles alone!"

"There won't be any icing left after that heat melts it," Tina teased.

"Oh, great, we have two wiseacres in the house. Franco!" Michael called. "Can you bounce these thugs out on their tails?"

"If Miss Lily wishes," Franco replied with a nod.

"What Miss Lily wishes is to propose a toast," Lily said. "If we don't burn down the house first. How is one supposed to extinguish these perpetual candles?" She tilted her head as everyone laughed.

"You should have told me to bring my spritzer bottle from the salon," Loretta joked.

"This will work," Susan said. "Help me out, dear." She and Michael began blowing out the sixty candles a few at a time, dropping them into a bowl of water before they could ignite again.

"I had to go to two separate stores to find sixty of these," she said.

"Ouch. You know how to hurt a guy." He kissed her forehead.

"Now, our toast!" Lily held up her glass as Franco poured sparkling cider for everyone. "Here's to sixty years of wholesome living, Mr. Michael ... and to my new family ... and to Suite 494!"

Everybody cheered.

The name Suite 494 was a recent development. After months of calling the project "the new Disco Diva," or "the White Elephant," the team had finally agreed on a name for the entertainment complex—based simply on its street address.

"That's how they named Studio 54—it was at 254 West Fifty-fourth Street," Susan had casually remarked one day, and a collective bulb had lit up over everyone's heads. With feedback from the team, Susan had decided to retain the name Disco Diva for the salon and call the spa facility the Diva Day Spa. The retail arm of the development would be Boutique 494. The bulk of Susan's collection would be housed in the Disco Hall of Fame and Museum, while the dance club, restaurant, and banquet facilities would fall under the auspices of Club 494. And all these various identities contained under one roof would collectively be known as Suite 494.

"I knew when the time was right we would be given the perfect name for the complex." Lily held the plates as Michael dished up the birthday cake and Susan passed it around the table.

"Where's Franco? Did he get a piece of cake?" Susan asked. Lily shrugged.

"Has it only been a few months?" Loretta licked icing off her pinky finger. "It seems like much longer."

"Ryan only arrived April 1." Lily sipped her sparkling drink.

"Seems like years," Ryan said.

"What does that mean?" Tina took another bite of cake. "This is really good."

"It means I feel like part of a family, like I've been here for ages. It means I can't believe I get paid to have this much fun!" He raised his glass. "Here's to a long and happy project."

"Happy, yes—long, no." Lily wagged her finger. "I'm not getting any younger. I'd sure like to see opening day before I check out."

"Yeah, well, that's not gonna be for awhile." Michael gave her a hug. "You'll outlast all of us."

They took time to enjoy the cake and ice cream. Tina went back for a second helping of both, passing Susan with her second slice. Susan winked at her before declaring it was time for Michael to open his gifts. He plowed happily through the pile of presents—some rather nice but most of them jokes about the six decades he had lived. When he was finished, he stood up.

"I've got a gift to give too." He grinned at Susan. "Two gifts, actually."

"Uh-oh." She laughed. "He's going to pay me back for the candles."

"I'm not very good at speeches, but you all know it's been a rocky few months. For all of us, but especially for my wife."

The room got quiet as he continued.

"I know the friendship of everyone in this room has been vital to her—to both of us. But Susan also has a special friendship that some of you may not know about—a long-distance cyberspace friendship with a woman who's helping us develop Boutique 494. Her name is Patricia Davies."

"We all know Pat," Ryan said. "She's one of our paid consultants, remember? We've been conducting video conferencing with her for some time."

"Then you also know that she and Susan have never met. But as soon as Franco returns from the airport, that will be rectified."

"Pat's coming here?" Susan cried. "Tonight?"

"Yes, ma'am. She'll be staying here at Miss Lily's for a few days, and she'll be working with you two." He pointed at Susan and Ryan. "You know, to give you professional recommendations for the store so that when you meet with the architect you can tell him what we'll need."

"Oh, Michael!" Susan jumped up to hug her husband. "It's your birthday—you're not supposed to give *me* a present. But thank you! I can't believe I'm finally going to meet her."

The women were abuzz with talk when Michael loudly cleared his throat.

"I said there were two gifts. Here's the other."

He handed a small gold-ribboned box to Susan, who looked at him quizzically.

"What's this about?"

"Well, I'm afraid I let your fiftieth go by without the fanfare it deserved, and I hope this makes up for it. Open the box."

She untied the ribbon and lifted the lid. An airline envelope lay nestled among shredded tissue paper.

"Oh goody, a trip," Loretta said. "Where to? Come on, don't just sit there like a bump on a log." She nudged her friend. "Open it."

"I'll give you a clue," Michael teased. "Think flea market. A really big flea—"

"No way!" Ryan shouted.

"New York?" Susan squealed. "We're going to New York?"

"Oh, man, I am so jealous!" Ryan whined like a baby when Michael nodded. "Lily, I really think you need to send me. Puh-leeze? To scout out possible additions to the project?"

"No way, José." Michael laughed. "That's what *we're* going to do."

Billed as the World's Biggest Flea Market, the annual event in upper New York was supposedly a collector's dream. It had begun shortly after Susan moved to Nevada. She had always wanted to attend, but she'd never been back to the state once she had left.

"Well, we could use a few more mirrored balls," she said, hugging her husband.

"Who knows what we'll find?" Michael swung her around, equally excited.

Ryan stood and held up his hands to calm the room. "Since everyone's in such a good mood, I have an announcement to make as well."

"Oh, sure, steal my thunder." Michael laughed.

"It's not really an announcement, per se." He looked at Tina, who got very quiet as all eyes turned toward her. "More like a question."

He moved to where Tina sat on the edge of an overstuffed ottoman and got down on one knee.

"Tina Deitman," he said, "I love you. I know you love me. I can't imagine any part of my future that doesn't include you. Will you marry me?" He pulled a velvet ring box from his pocket and handed it to her. She gazed at the pear-shaped diamond for a few moments before bolting from the room—reaching the hall bath in time to lose the birthday cake she had just eaten. Ryan followed and stood close by, holding her head.

"Well, now." Loretta shook her head. "That's a proposal reaction for the books."

"Should we call a doctor?" Michael asked.

"Oh, Tina's been seeing a doctor." Susan fell back into a plush side chair next to her husband. "She'll be fine."

"I agree." Lily smiled.

Loretta quickly comprehended the situation and joined the two women in a knowing smile, but Michael cocked his head in confusion, still wondering what was going on.

"Don't worry, dear." Susan patted him on the knee and giggled. "You're sixty. Give yourself time to catch up."

———

Franco returned from the airport with Pat a few minutes after Ryan had taken Tina home.

"I can't believe it's you! You're even prettier in person!" Pat embraced Susan in a tight bear hug.

"And you're stronger in person." Susan laughed. "I can't breathe!"

"Sorry." She held Susan at arm's length. "I was aching to tell you! But your loved one over there"—she nodded at Michael—"who I must say looks much more handsome than the photos I've seen, would have had my head if I'd let the cat out of the bag."

"You're darn right. Thanks for coming." Michael extended his hand to Pat, who promptly ignored it and wrapped him in a bear hug as well. He introduced her to the others as more hugs and laughter followed.

"My flight was a nightmare," Pat said. "But seeing Franco with my name on that little signboard and then seeing my mode of transportation from the airport made up for it. I can't believe I'm here!"

"That is a fabulous haircut," Loretta said, peering closely at Pat's coif.

Lily handed Pat a goblet of sparkling cider. "It's nonalcoholic," she said.

"Too bad. I could use a drink after that flight." Pat giggled. "Do you really like my hair?" she asked Loretta. "I've never worn it this short, but I was having a kind of midlife crisis and got carried away."

Pat's hair was thick, wavy, and jet black with a streak of gray running through the front. It was about an inch and a half long all over and spiked with a firming gel. Her olive complexion hinted at an Italian heritage. With a zaftig shape that kept her busy from time to time as a plus-size model with an agency in Los Angeles, she was a stunning woman—the polar opposite of Susan in shape and coloring.

Pat looked around. "I was really hoping to meet Ryan and Tina. We talk so often I feel like I know them—thank you, Lily." She took the plate of cake that Lily handed her and sat down at the table to eat it.

"They were here," Susan told her, "but she got sick and he took her home."

"You missed quite an event, actually," Michael informed her. "Ryan proposed, then Tina promptly tossed her cookies."

"Michael!" Susan admonished. "That's not very nice."

"But true." Loretta nodded and winked at Michael.

They discussed the proposal and the fact that no one had suspected how involved the pair really was. The conversation eventually traveled to Suite 494, and at Susan's request, Lily gave a rather thorough progress review. It was an hour later when Michael stood and stretched.

"If you gals don't mind, I think I'm going to bow out gracefully and leave you to visit."

"But it's your party!" Susan protested.

"Yeah, and you know what they say," he replied, using his best Elvis impersonation: "It's my party and I'll leave if I want to, leave if I want to, leave if I want to ..." He waved at the four women seated around the table, who applauded his rendition of the song made famous by Lesley Gore in 1963.

"Very good, Elvis ... er, Lesley." Susan reached up on tiptoe and kissed him.

"Thank you. Uh, thank you very much. And thank you for hosting my party." He bowed in Lily's direction. "But it's time for me to go. Way too much estrogen in this room." He hugged his wife. "I'll see you at home later."

"Why don't we all move into the family room?" Lily suggested after Michael departed. "I'll have Franco make us some decaf." They followed her through Lily's palatial home, with Pat oohing and aahing all the way.

"When did Michael plan this visit?" Susan asked Pat as she settled onto a plush leather sofa. "He's been online a whole lot the past few days. I figured something was up, just didn't know what."

"Well, we've talked quite a bit since ..."

"You can say it, Pat—it's okay. Since my breakdown."

"Whatever." She stuck out her tongue playfully. "You know I wanted to come to see you. And Michael said now was the time that you really needed me."

Susan nodded. With Ryan about to begin meetings with the architect they had selected, it was imperative that Susan make some firm decisions about Boutique 494. As someone who ran a successful retail shop with a unique theme and equally unique clientele, Pat was already an invaluable resource, but it would be more than helpful for her to see the physical space of the White Elephant and give her recommendations.

"Did you bring my earrings, dear?" Lily picked off an invisible piece of lint from her sea green cashmere sweater and set it on the saucer next to her.

"Of course. I also brought you something else, for hosting me at your lovely home." She pulled a small box from her purse and handed it to Lily.

"How lovely! Thank you."

"That's right!" Loretta cried. "You're the jewelry designer!"

"You know that deep blue dichroic glass set I wear all the time?" Susan winked at Loretta. "That's one of Pat's."

"Really? I want one, but in shades of brown, gold, and black. Do you make custom pieces?"

They all talked over one another, placing their orders and discussing some of the famous customers who frequented Glitter and Bling.

"Tell them whose clothes you just took in on consignment." Susan grinned.

Pat leaned forward conspiratorially. "Annette Bening! John was in the shop when she came by, and he went totally gaga over her." She laughed. "You'd have thought he was thirteen."

"Your husband works at Glitter and Bling with you?" Lily asked.

"He used to work full time for the California Department of Transportation, but he's on a temporary leave of absence. He helps out with maintenance things at the shop from time to time." She sighed. "It's an old building. Seems lately something is always going wrong."

"Thank God for handy husbands!" Susan and Pat toasted with their coffee mugs.

The four women stayed up talking for hours, but Loretta finally stood and stretched. "I'd best hit the road," she said. "I have a beauty salon to open in the morning."

"I can't wait to see Disco Diva!" Pat clasped her hands.

"You'll get the full fifty-cent tour of the whole shebang tomorrow." Susan followed Loretta's lead, hugged Pat and Lily good-bye, and left exhausted but excited.

Chapter 46

The temperature had already topped one hundred by nine o'clock the next morning. Lily was sleeping in, but Franco delivered Pat to the White Elephant, where Susan greeted her with iced chai tea and fresh muffins from Mama T's. It was a pleasantly cool seventy-two degrees inside the office.

"So, what time did you get to sleep last night?" Susan asked.

"Not long after you two left. Lily gave me a tour of Cedar Ridge, but I think I was in bed by one. I was out like a light. Michael told me I'd be staying with a family friend, but I had no idea he was talking about Lily. Or that your friend Lily was, well—man, oh, Manischewitz, I had no idea." Pat whistled. "That's quite a place. Does she really live there all alone?"

"In the main house, yes, but Franco has a suite above the garage, and Ryan is living temporarily in the guest quarters off the pool."

"I can't wait to meet Ryan," Pat said, shaking her head. "Poor guy—to have a father like that."

"I know," Susan said sadly. "It's amazing that someone like Jean-Claude could raise someone like Ryan. His mother must have been quite a person." She shook her head and stood up quickly. "Now, we're more than overdue for your site tour."

"Hey, I'm ready when you are."

Susan escorted her friend around the grounds, going from the office to the temporary storage building, where they spent almost a full hour exploring a bit of the collection and looking at what Tina had accomplished during the past few weeks. Pat sat inside Marilyn and playfully mimicked a Hollywood starlet driving down the Pacific Coast Highway.

"I can't believe you have this much stuff," she said over her shoulder.

"Apparently it's not enough. Michael and I are heading to New York for a shopping expedition in a few weeks."

"Girlfriend, are you crazy?" Pat clicked her tongue. "Going shopping with your husband is like fishing with the game warden!"

"Oh, I think it'll be fun." Susan got behind the wheel of the golf cart. "Hop in."

Pat remained inside the Shelby. "I'd rather take this, if you don't mind."

"Yeah, you and everyone else around here." She grinned as Pat stuck out her lower lip and climbed into the golf cart. They drove through the baking sunshine to the main site, where Susan delighted in making a grand entrance from the recently repaired service elevator. It opened at the west end of each floor, granting an expansive view of every level.

"I had no idea you had this much space to work with." Pat skipped like a schoolgirl around the upper level of the White Elephant.

"I told you it was twenty-five thousand square feet."

"I thought that was all three floors combined—not on every floor. You have seventy-five thousand square feet—this is mind-boggling real estate!" She went from window to window, inspecting the views.

"I can't believe this whole thing—this building, your office, the plans you have, your collection. Boomer babe, you have been blessed!"

"That I have." Susan nodded. "So where do you think the boutique should go? The main floor will house the salon, day spa, and retail space. We've estimated fifteen thousand square feet for the salon and five thousand each for the spa and store."

"Are you serious? Five thousand square feet? Now it's me who's green with envy. Glitter and Bling is crammed into a hair less than twenty-five hundred square feet. This is amazing!" Pat fanned herself with a magazine she picked up from the floor of the golf cart. "So is this heat. Can we go back to the office and talk? I've got a lot of ideas."

They returned to the comfort of Susan's air-conditioned office, where they talked for hours, sketching out floor plans, discussing display options, and volleying ideas for ways to make Boutique 494 as unique as Susan's collection. As she had suspected, the ideas Pat came up with far surpassed anything Susan had initially dreamed of, and the more Pat described the possibilities, the more excited Susan became.

"This entire disco theme is fabulous, but I'm more of a Motown girl myself. Give me the Temptations, the Supremes, the Four Tops—now that's music!"

They playfully argued musical tastes as they continued to discuss possibilities for the space. They were so engrossed in their conversation that neither of them heard Ryan when he came into the office around lunchtime. They jumped when he spoke.

"Ah! The renowned Patricia Davies." Ryan extended his manicured hand. "Sorry. Didn't mean to scare you."

"Renowned?" Pat raised her eyebrows and laughed. "More renowned than you?"

"We didn't hear you come in," Susan said. "Is Tina with you?"

"No, she's staying home today."

"Hope she's feeling better ..." Susan ventured, not yet knowing how much Ryan knew.

"Much."

"Seems I just missed you two last night," Pat said.

"Yeah, we passed the Rolls on our way out. Sorry we weren't here to greet you."

"Pat knows what happened," Susan said. "That you proposed and Tina got sick."

"Oh, now that's a nice way to put it."

"Sorry. I didn't mean it to sound like that. I just meant you took her by surprise. That was some announcement you sprung on all of us."

"Well, first of all, I didn't spring it on you as a group. I was only proposing to Tina, not the entire clan." He grinned. "As much as I love all of you."

Susan leaned forward. "So what happened? What did she say?"

"We can talk about that later, young lady." He pointed a finger at Susan. "Business before pleasure—I'd like to hear what Pat thinks of our space."

The smile that followed his mock reprimand made Susan's heart jump. She hoped Tina had at last disclosed her pregnancy to him. *Please, God,* she prayed, *let them be okay.*

"So what do we have here?" Ryan reached for one of the drawings as they launched back into an animated discussion of design possibilities for Boutique 494.

"I hadn't thought about raised platform areas and staircases." Susan picked up one of the sketches. "This is brilliant. I've been seeing everything on one level. Duh." She smacked the palm of her hand on her forehead.

"I'm sure the architect would have suggested it. The loft spaces just make sense with those high ceilings." Pat pointed to a section of the current blueprint for the building. "Especially here in this area."

They were all talking at once about architectural possibilities when Susan's cell phone began to play its digitized version of "We Are Family" by Sister Sledge. "That's Lily. Be right back." Susan excused herself and walked to the other side of the room, where the conversation was brief.

"Well, that woman is sure spoiling our sorry selves," she said impishly. "She's having lunch delivered to Cedar Ridge from somewhere in Chinatown." She looked at her watch. "Franco will be here in a few minutes to pick all of us up." She began collecting the notes they'd made that morning while Ryan straightened the chairs around the conference room table. "Let's take all of these drawings with us and run some of these ideas by Lily and Michael."

"Michael's joining us?" Pat said. "Oh, good. I didn't have much time last night to visit with him."

"Seems everyone's joining us, including Tina." Susan looked at Ryan. "Did you know about this?"

"Don't look at me." His grin revealed his dimples.

"Yeah, like I'd ever want to do that, you ugly thing." Susan gently smacked him with the stack of papers she had in her hand just as they heard the crunch of gravel indicating Franco had pulled the Rolls-Royce into the lot.

"I could get used to this." Pat gazed dreamily out the window at the Rolls.

"Well, then, let's enjoy it while we can. Ladies …" Ryan crooked both of his elbows. Susan took his left arm, Pat took his right, and he escorted them from the building into the waiting limo.

Chapter 47

The smell of spicy Asian food greeted their nostrils as they entered Lily's house, and a grand buffet met their eyes in the dining room. Dishes of chow mein, dumplings, spicy shrimp, beef and broccoli, and a variety of other dishes were luxuriously displayed on a beautiful brocade tablecloth. Linen napkins were encircled with sterling silver rings, and Lily's Michael C. Fina utensils were lined up like expensive little sentries guarding the stack of Limoges plates.

"Oh my." Pat stared. "Is this what lunch is like every day? If so, I'm never going back."

"We're celebrating." Lily nodded to Franco, who began to pour sparkling apple cider into Waterford Crystal goblets.

Susan furrowed her brow. "Celebrating what?"

"Don't look at me." Michael came in from the kitchen with a plate of egg rolls. "I just do what I'm told."

"Ditto." Tina followed him with a crystal bowl full of fortune cookies. She set it down and extended her hand to Pat. "I'm Tina. Sorry I missed you last night."

"Don't give it a second thought. Glad to see you're feeling better."

Tina sat down next to Ryan. "Lily says you had a great time after I left."

"Like a pajama party without the pajamas." Susan joined Michael just as the front doorbell rang, followed by Loretta's shout of "Yoo-hoo, it's me!"

"We're in the dining room, dear," Lily said.

"Sorry I'm late." Loretta rushed in, dropped her Kate Spade bag and keys on a chair, and hugged everyone. "Franco let me in."

"Who's minding the salon?" Susan asked.

"Shannon. She'll be fine for an hour. So what's the occasion?" She nodded toward the loaded buffet table.

"Please join me in welcoming Pat to Las Vegas." Lily raised her glass as everyone followed suit. "Here's to our new friend—and our newest team member. Thank you for joining us and for lending your expertise to our project."

"Hear, hear." They all clinked their goblets against one another and sipped the chilled cider.

"Thank you." Pat nodded and smiled. "I'm pleased to be here."

"But that's not all we're celebrating." Lily looked at Ryan, who had wrapped his arm around Tina's shoulders. "Ladies and gentlemen, I couldn't be happier to be the first to introduce you to ..." She paused for dramatic effect. "... Mr. and Mrs. Ryan Power!"

The stunned silence was immediately broken by whoops of excitement and joy. Susan and Michael rushed to the young couple and embraced them, with Loretta close behind. Lily flipped a switch on the wall that turned on the sound system. The gentle music of a Tony Bennett love song began to play as Franco emerged from the adjoining room pushing a silver serving cart. On it sat an elegant three-tiered wedding cake done up in miniature.

"Oh, Lily ..." Tina began to cry.

"When did you—?" Susan asked.

"Last night," Tina and Ryan answered in unison.

Tina blushed. "He wouldn't take no for an answer."

"We went to the Little Church of the West," Ryan added, holding Tina's hand tightly and staring at her as though no one else existed.

"That's a wedding chapel," Susan explained to Pat. "It's a landmark—the oldest existing structure on the Las Vegas Strip. It's where Elvis Presley and Ann-Margret recited their vows in *Viva Las Vegas*." She looked at Lily. "So when did you find out about all this?"

"A few hours ago, when Ryan asked if I'd host the reception." Lily pinched Ryan's cheek in a move that was as endearing as it was playful.

"I was busting a gut all morning," Ryan said. "Couldn't wait to get you here."

"I'm deliriously happy for both of you." Susan blinked back tears.

"No, you're happy for the three of us," Ryan said quietly, pulling his wife close. "For those of you who may not know, we're going to have a baby."

"That's what you meant!" Michael suddenly realized what Susan, Lily, and Loretta had been referring to at his party the night before. "Duh."

Susan patted his back. "I knew you'd catch on eventually."

"What a blessing!" Loretta wiped her eyes. "Thank you so much for including me in this celebration, Lily."

"But of course!" Lily clapped her hands. "Michael, would you say the blessing so we can eat? And then you two"—pointed at Ryan and Tina—"can fill us in on every single detail. Don't leave anything out!"

Michael said grace, including a wedding blessing for the newlyweds. After the *amen,* everyone crowded around the table to fill their plates with food.

Lily wasted no time asking the question on everyone's mind.

"So, my dear," she asked Tina, taking an egg roll, "tell us exactly what happened when you left last evening."

Tina beamed. "Well, when we got back to my apartment, I told him I was pregnant and couldn't marry him, that I was planning to go back home, have the baby, and give her … or him … up for adoption. Do you know what he said?"

"Don't make us guess." Susan shook her head.

"Go take a shower." Tina pointed her finger and mimicked Ryan's voice.

Loretta lifted her eyebrows. "'Go take a shower'?"

Everyone began asking questions at once until the sound of clinking crystal interrupted them.

"Excuse me." Lily had gently tapped a fork against her goblet. "This cacophony is more than my old eardrums can handle. Perhaps we could let Tina and Ryan fill us in."

"She's quite a dame," Pat whispered to Susan.

"You can say that again."

"I'm serious." Tina laughed. "He said, 'Go take a shower and brush your teeth,' to be exact. Remember, I had just lost Michael's birthday dinner in a less than elegant manner."

"Man, I was so freaked out," Ryan said. "I knew she wasn't drinking, so it wasn't that. I've never seen anyone get that sick so fast."

"He thought it was a bad proposal." Tina kissed the back of his hand.

"Really bad," Michael joked.

"Don't laugh, bro—I thought she was dying. There I was kneeling on the floor holding her as she heaved her guts into the porcelain goddess, and all I could think of was 'I'm losing her. I just can't lose her.'"

"Then what?" Loretta said.

"By the time I got out of the shower, he'd gone through my closet and laid out one of my prettiest dresses. And he'd called ahead to the chapel to tell them we were on the way."

"Just like that?" Susan asked.

"Just like that," Tina echoed.

"I knew nothing was going to change how I felt about her and it seemed right. It is right." Ryan grinned.

"Glad you didn't put up a fight," Susan said to Tina.

"I tried, but he wouldn't listen to me."

"That's not true. She didn't put up a fight about marrying me. It was about the dress."

"Honey, I didn't fight about it." She looked sad. "I just couldn't fit in it. Not much fits me anymore." She turned sideways and pulled her oversized blouse close to her skin. For the first time it was quite noticeable that she was indeed pregnant.

Michael stared. "Were you that big last night?"

"Honey!" Susan poked him with her finger.

"Sorry, didn't mean anything …"

"It's okay," Tina said, laughing. "I was showing, but maybe not quite this much. It's like he, or she, suddenly sprawled out and needed more room."

"I knew she was putting on some weight, but I never had a clue."

Ryan shook his head. "Just thought those idiots at the Tropicana were off their rocker."

"Do they know she's pregnant?" Michael whispered to Susan.

"Not yet, but they will. There's a pregnancy clause in her contract. She'll be able to take a maternity leave and return to the show after the baby is born."

"If that's what she chooses to do," Michael added. "Who knows? She might not want to go back to that world."

Susan turned and looked at him, aware that a few months ago she would have thought his remark ignorant and insensitive. Not anymore. "You're right, Michael. She might not." Susan took his hand. For some showgirls, there was more to life than dancing.

"So, what did you do about a dress?" Pat asked.

"We drove to the shops at Caesars Palace—they're open late. He bought me the most beautiful gown. I put it on in the dressing room and wore it out of the store. We were walking down the aisle a half hour later."

The room was quiet as everyone looked at the couple, relishing this special moment with them as they shared the experience.

"The whole night was awesome," Ryan said. "After the getting-sick part, anyway." He kissed Tina's forehead. "I can't believe I didn't know about the baby. It just never dawned on me. I mean, at first I thought she just didn't like me. Then I thought she was playing hard to get. Then when she got sick I had visions she had some kind of terminal disease and that's why she didn't want to get involved. After all that, the idea of a baby was a cakewalk!"

"Don't say cake—" Tina said and everyone laughed.

"Anyway, when I found out, I was ecstatic. Really. I have never been more sure of anything in my life." Ryan straightened his shoulders. "This is the woman I want to spend the rest of my life with—and we are going to be awesome parents."

"You certainly are." Susan smiled as everyone applauded and more than a few dried their eyes.

"And one more thing," Tina said almost shyly. "We want you—I mean, would you and Michael consider being the baby's godparents? It would mean so much to us—"

She almost didn't get the words out because Susan had gathered them both into a huge bear hug.

"Honored, my good man. Honored." Michael embraced Ryan and then Tina.

"Are you taking a honeymoon?" Loretta asked after things quieted down.

"Not until after these lucky stiffs get back from New York." Ryan playfully stuck out his tongue at Susan and Michael. "You guys are leaving next week, remember?"

"My first scouting trip, how could I forget?" Michael put his arm around Susan.

"And kind of a second honeymoon for us, too," she added quietly.

"I'll make a toast to that!" Tina lifted up her glass as everyone toasted.

"Excuse me ... excuse me," Lily once again interrupted.

"This should be good," Loretta said quietly to Pat as they watched the joyful celebration. "She has that 'I have a surprise' look."

"She certainly enjoys this, doesn't she?" Pat whispered back. "Throwing surprises."

"You have no idea." Loretta nodded. "If only more wealthy people were as genuinely generous as she is."

"We know it's hectic at the White Elephant," Lily was saying. "That won't let up any time soon, no matter who is out of town. But, darlings, that is business, and it cannot take precedence over your life. You've fallen in love, married, and soon you'll have a precious child. Please take a few days to enjoy and celebrate the blessings God has given you."

Franco handed her an envelope that she clutched to her chest.

"Susan, I took the liberty of calling your boomer babe friend … the one who owns the travel agency."

"Mary," Susan and Pat said simultaneously.

"Yes." Lily turned back to Ryan and Tina. "And I'd like to give you a little wedding gift, if I may." She waved the envelope in front of them, clearly enjoying the suspense. "It's a three-day trip to Catalina Island. I know you both enjoy the island. And we'll be fine here while you're gone. Won't we?" she queried the others, who nodded. "You'll be staying at the Hotel Metropole, where you'll have an oceanfront VIP suite. You'll also have massages, spa services, and breakfast in bed all three days. The day spa is called A Touch of Heaven—don't you just love that?" Lily giggled like a schoolgirl. "Happy honeymoon!" With a flourish, she handed Ryan and Tina the envelope.

"You're an absolute angel!" Ryan lifted Lily up off her feet and swung her around.

Pat shook her head and smiled. "Bon voyage." She lifted her glass. "I'll be gone before you return, but I've loved meeting you, and I hope to see you again." She glanced around the room. "I wish I could stay longer than a few days. You folks are better than reality TV any day!"

Chapter 48

Ryan and Tina returned from Catalina Island late Friday night and were at the White Elephant office bright and early Saturday morning for a group meeting. Everyone was in attendance minus Lily, who was currently preoccupied with cochairing a fundraising event, and Pat, who had returned to California.

After a honeymoon update, the meeting commenced.

"We accomplished a great deal while you two were off lounging on the island," Michael joked.

"Then fill us in, old man," Ryan volleyed back.

"We've had a preliminary meeting with the architectural team—they'll present us with some conceptual designs in a few weeks. Susan is working on acquiring price quotes for the salon and spa; I'm concentrating on materials and supplies. We scheduled a meeting with the head of that company specializing in museum components, and we've hired a couple of temps to help Tina—they'll start on Monday. Thanks to your detailed project list"—Michael pointed at Ryan—"we are right on track."

Susan had to agree—they were on track. The only thing bothering her was Michael's growing preoccupation with the Internet. He seemed to spend every available hour of his workday on the computer, and he often spent time online at night as well.

"Honey, don't worry," he'd teased, "I'm not visiting any porn sites."

"Don't joke about that, Michael," she warned. "People get addicted to that stuff, you know. It can really mess up lives."

"Well, it's not going to mess up ours, honey. The most exciting things I'm looking at are price quotes on lumber, concrete, and fixtures."

"Sounds like you folks have been busy." Ryan interrupted her musing.

"We have. But I'm happy to hand the reins back over to you," Michael said, handing Ryan a file folder. "Here's the list you left, with detailed notes. Welcome back."

"Is it always this hot during the summer?" Tina fanned herself with a magazine. "It's one hundred fifteen degrees out there. Thank God Lily believes in air-conditioning." She smiled. "But the walk from my office to here is enough to take the wind out of anyone's sails, let alone a fat blimp like me."

Susan snorted. "You are hardly a fat blimp, and I don't want my godchild to hear any negative self-talk whatsoever." Tina held up her hands in mock surrender.

"Okay," Ryan said, "back to business. Let's talk about the list of things to scout for at the flea market. You know—the one I'm *not* going to." He pouted, and everyone laughed. "I've been thinking about Susan's idea to display some of her designer clothing as they do in the Smithsonian, on mannequins. That means we need … mannequins."

"Can't we buy them new?" Michael asked. "I mean, they do still make mannequins, right?"

"Yes, they do." Ryan opened a catalog to show a rather large collection. "If we need to go that route, we will. But keep your eyes open. You may find some vintage models, and you'll see the difference right away."

They discussed other display ideas—a conversation topic that never failed to come up in every meeting.

"I started working on the Studio 54 collection a few days before we left." Tina shuffled through her notes. "But there's much more than I think even you realize." She pointed her pen at Susan. "I'm going to use the same system initially to categorize it, but you folks might want to begin thinking about unique ways to display all of this. I've got a list of questions somewhere—ah, here it is." She pulled a paper from the stack in front of her. "What does 'Studio Rats' stand for?" she asked Susan. "It's been showing up on envelopes, and we just found a couple of boxes with that label."

"I haven't heard that term in awhile." Susan shook her head, smiled, and leaned back, rocking in her chair. "In the world of film, you might remember the term *Rat Pack?*" Everyone nodded. "Well, the Studio had its own Rat Pack. Along with Stevie and Ian, the Studio Rats were Truman Capote, Liza Minnelli, Bianca Jagger, Andy Warhol, Nikki Haskell, and Marc Benecke."

"Marc who?" Tina asked. "I recognize the other names, but not his."

"Marc held one of the most powerful positions at the Studio. They called him the Lord of the Door."

Susan walked to the corkboard and removed a pushpin, handing a photo to Tina.

"That's Marc, the official Studio 54 doorman. He stood on a raised platform that allowed him to see over the heads of the hundreds of people standing in line, selecting people who fit the look they wanted that particular evening. Stevie called it 'tossing a salad,' and every night the salad had a different flavor, but all the ingredients needed to blend. In retrospect, it could be a cruel and arbitrary selection process. Some folks never did get in."

Ryan looked up. "But you and, uh, Gene ... were always selected?"

"Oh, we never stood in line. We went in through the VIP entrance on the back side of the club, from Fifty-third Street."

He whistled. "What a rush."

"It was. I used to think we were permitted access because of who we were—that Stevie liked us, considered us friends. And he might have. But now I can see that your father's money was really what got us in. There was always a second tier of VIPs hovering nearby in the background, all of them very wealthy. We were in that tier."

"I think the museum needs a Studio Rat display." Ryan changed the subject, sensing that it had the potential to become uncomfortable. "In fact, here's something we haven't considered. What if we re-create the actual balcony area of Studio 54 in our museum space, using the same banquette seating and life-size figures of the Studio Rats?"

"Mannequins wouldn't work," Michael said. "At least not for the VIP balcony area. To make that work we'll need wax figures or something so they'll look like the real deal. And I guess we'd need permission from the original folks, so legal will have to be on that too, right?"

"You're right," Susan concurred. "But I like the idea, Ryan. A lot. Pat has given us a great idea of new ways to look at the space, hasn't she?"

"That she has." Ryan continued to write notes.

The four of them discussed other architectural design possibilities before returning once again to the initial reason for their present meeting—listing items for Michael and Susan to look for when they walked the acres of the World's Biggest Flea Market.

"I've been thinking about how to get your larger purchases back to Vegas." Ryan looked at his notes. "I'm going to arrange for a nearby shipping company to have a truck ready for both Friday and Saturday in case something needs to be picked up from the fairgrounds. I'll make sure they have all the billing information they need—all you'll need to do is call."

"Bless you," Susan said. "You think of everything, don't you?"

"That, boss lady, is why I get paid the big bucks." He pounded one fist on the desk, and they ended the meeting.

Susan found herself fidgeting at her desk that afternoon, surprised at how excited she was getting about visiting New York. She wasn't certain how many of her old haunts she'd want to visit with Michael, but she planned at least to take him to the Manhattan Church of Christ on East Eightieth Street, where her life had really begun. She intended to play the rest by ear.

"Are you sure you're okay with this, honey?" her husband had asked a few nights earlier when they began to talk about the trip in earnest.

"I'm fine, really. It's okay. Doc says it's one of the best things I could do right now. If you'd asked me a few months ago if I was ready to do this, I'd have run in the other direction. But I think I'm ready now—Doc thinks so too. My time in New York had such a profound effect on my life, and I'm actually kind of looking forward to sharing it with you."

"Me, too," he said quietly. "We'll be there on the tenth," he added. "Is there anything special you'd like to do?"

"Bless you for remembering." The fact they would be in the City on her daughter's birthday hadn't been lost on Susan. "I've been thinking about that."

"Perhaps this is a God-cidence, honey, like you're always saying. It's been a tough day for you for a long time, and this will be the first year you have someone to share it with. Maybe we can turn a corner together?" Michael gently brushed her cheek with his hand.

She'd moved into his arms, amazed that it was possible to fall in love with her husband all over again. And now, sitting at her desk, she marveled even more at the love that filled her life—not only the faithful love of a good man, but also the love of close friends who gave her support and were helping her build her dreams; the love of God, who made it all possible; and the love for her daughter—that was still there too. But something was different now. The love was different. And it no longer had the same hold over her.

Susan had loved her daughter enough to let her go—to give her the life of hope and promise she'd been unable to provide so long ago. And now she was willing to allow herself the same kind of life. She would never forget the daughter she never knew, but the painful parts of the memory would no longer hold her prisoner.

She had turned a corner. She was ready to move forward … in truth and in love.

Chapter 49

They arrived in New York City late Wednesday morning and checked into the Ritz Carlton Central Park. The flea market didn't start until Friday, so they had almost two full days to explore the City. They wasted no time and quickly unpacked their bags, put on walking shoes, and headed out. It was the fifth of July, and vestiges of the previous day's patriotic celebration greeted them everywhere they went.

Their first stop was Ground Zero, where Susan and Michael joined in a group prayer a visiting pastor from Minnesota was conducting. "I had dinner often at Windows on the World," Susan murmured, looking up into the empty sky where the Twin Towers had once loomed. She blinked back tears. "I'd forgotten that."

They walked a few blocks in silence before they were able to shake off the somber mood; the resilient energy of the City gradually lifted their spirits, and they were laughing and talking by the time they reached 254 West Fifty-fourth Street, the building that had housed Studio 54 and was now home to a small theater company and various office suites.

Staring at the building, they fell silent again. But only for a few minutes.

"A lot of history happened under that roof," Susan told Michael.

"Do you want to go inside?" he asked.

"No … I don't think so." She grabbed his hand and turned away. But he stood firmly in place.

"Suze, remember what Doc Allen said. He wants us to talk about things—deal with things. I don't want you to run away anymore."

She thought about that, then took a deep breath. "I'm not running away, Michael. At least I don't think so. I just don't need to see what it looks like now." She looked into his doubtful face. "I have a lot of good memories of the Studio, contrary to what you might think. I'm working on the bad ones—filtering out things." She laid a hand on his shoulder. "I really don't need to go inside. I'm okay."

"If you say so." Michael kissed her and took her hand, and they turned and walked away.

They continued to wander as morning turned into afternoon. All the way, Susan gave Michael a running commentary about places she recognized and things she had experienced over the years. It was like having a personal tour guide.

"We should have visited long before this," Michael said as they turned yet another corner.

"Yes, we should have, and I should have told you much sooner what it meant to me. But don't you see? I wasn't ready, and neither were you. Everything is happening exactly as God would have it."

He wrapped his arm around her, and she stuck a thumb in his belt loop as they continued to walk.

"Maybe we should go to Fort Worth or Dallas next," she said. "I read about some kind of annual stock show or fair or something where you can buy the kind of furnishings you envision for the Henderson ranch. You know—wrought iron, saddles, animal hides, things like that." She grinned. "We'll have to start looking for things for the ranch someday. Might as well be sooner rather than later."

Michael stopped and kissed his wife—not a gentle peck, but a long, romantic kiss. He didn't care who might see them. "Good idea," he said when they came up for air. "I think we have a storage shed we could use in the interim."

She tossed back her head and laughed as they walked on, stopping for dinner when they realized the time and their hunger.

"Good food," Michael said as they left the restaurant over an hour later.

"But of course!" Susan took his hand as they once again sauntered down the street. "It's New York."

Eventually, they found themselves in front of the Winter Garden Theater. Michael looked at the marquee and checked his watch. "Still ten minutes before curtain," he noted. "What do you say we go for it?"

They managed to snag two third-row tickets to see *Mamma Mia!* They weren't dressed for the theater, and Susan was initially aghast at the thought of what she must look like after an entire day wandering the streets of New York City. But Michael whispered in her ear as the usher pointed them toward their seats, "You are the most beautiful woman in the world. And no one here cares one iota about us or what we're wearing or not wearing. They'll forget all about us as soon as the lights go off."

He kissed her neck as they found their seats, and she slouched down in pleased embarrassment. "Tell you what," he whispered. "How about we get dressed up tomorrow night and see another show, okay? It's our vacation, after all. Let's do it up right!"

Susan's smile said it all as the lights dimmed.

After breakfast in Central Park the next morning, they spent the entire day playing tourist. Susan couldn't remember having this much fun with her husband—at least not in recent years.

The Manhattan Church of Christ was, unfortunately, closed for the day, so they opted to visit the world-renowned St. Patrick's Cathedral on Madison Avenue instead.

They passed more theaters on and off Broadway than Michael could ever hope to remember, as Susan pointed out the ones where she had worked while trying to make it as a dancer.

"So, tell me more about what it was like," he prompted her.

"Well, I usually managed to land a place in the chorus, but I never could get out from behind that back line." She sighed, and he found himself looking at her with new eyes. What must it have been like to dance on so many famous stages but never quite make it to the place she wanted to go?

They passed landmarks like Macy's, FAO Schwartz, and Barneys, and Susan continued to give him a play-by-play chronicle of their significance in her past. She steered away from places like the Sherry-Netherland, the Russian Tea Room, the Rainbow Room, and other places where she preferred not to dredge up the memories, feeling no need to open every scar. However, when she found they were standing outside the Belasco, an off-Broadway theater on West Forty-fourth with a particularly famous history, she had to stop and reminisce.

"This is where I first saw Tim Curry in the stage production of *The Rocky Horror Picture Show*. What a night that was." She crossed her arms and gazed at the marquee. "It was 1975."

Throughout the years, Michael had overheard countless discussions among Susan and her clientele about that ridiculous show. He'd walked out of the movie after twenty minutes. The show had a cult following he would never understand; Vegas was host to many a *Rocky Horror* celebration.

"I'm not sure I could handle it today." She shook her head. "But back then, it was quite the experience."

"We had a fight about that show a few years ago," he said quietly as they walked on.

"We did?" She furrowed her brow. "You remember that?"

"You don't?"

"I don't. But, Michael ..." She pulled him over to sit on an empty bus bench. "Like you said yesterday, we're supposed to talk about all the things we never talk about, remember? The things we keep stuffing down, putting aside. I'm sorry I don't recall the argument. Is there something about it that still bothers you?"

He thought for a moment, and his eyes crinkled.

"Now that I think about it, I can't remember either."

"Are you sure? I can handle it. I mean that."

"I know you can, honey. I'm not protecting you from anything. I really can't recall what we argued about. I imagine it was something pretty stupid—like the movie." She narrowed her eyes at him, and he raised his arms in mock surrender. "Sorry! Didn't mean it ... not!" He stood, grabbed her hand, and pulled her down the street. At the next intersection they took a right turn, laughing and talking like teenagers in love.

"So, where should we go tonight?" She snaked her arm through his and leaned her head on his shoulder as they walked back to the hotel. They'd checked out the marquees at several theaters and discussed their options, asking almost everyone they ran into what show they recommended.

"Whatever you'd like," Michael said.

"Really?" she teased. "I can choose, and you won't whine about it later?"

"I didn't say that." He playfully knocked on her head.

"Then *you* choose. I'm serious. You make the decision."

"And *you* won't whine about it later?" He snickered.

"No, sir."

"Okay, then. Consider it done."

They ended up having dinner at Cipriani on Fifth Avenue, followed by a production of *The Phantom of the Opera* at the Majestic Theater—a perfect ending to another thoroughly enjoyable, exhausting day.

Chapter 50

"Let's hit the road, darling!" Michael checked his wallet. "I've got cash and the debit card."

Susan was surprised how excited Michael was at the prospect of walking around acres and acres of booths at the flea market, and his energy was rubbing off on her as they prepared to leave for their first collecting adventure together. They set out in the Ford Explorer they'd rented for the weekend.

"There was an article on collectors in a magazine when I went to the dentist," he said once they'd cleared the city traffic. "It's a pretty cool story." He reached into his pocket and handed her several folded pages torn from a magazine. "I've been carrying it around for weeks."

"I hate folks like you who tear up waiting-room publications." She began to read.

"Joe said I could—I asked first." He feigned innocence. "The writer guy said 'irrationality reigns supreme' in collectors. That true?"

"I would hardly call myself irrational." Yet she had to admit, in thinking back, that there were times when she and Jean-Claude had been irrationally relentless in their pursuit of a certain item. Unfolding the pages, she noticed that several sections were highlighted in yellow.

"He says that collectors, people who pursue certain objects with a passion, are often so single-minded in their pursuit that they can't imagine why anyone would be interested in collecting anything else. Scientists think there may even be a collecting gene."

"Really? So it's in my DNA?"

"According to them." He nodded at the article.

"I'm not sure I agree. I think people collect things because they hold special meaning to them. Our pharmacist for example—Jess Carter—he collects Rexall drugstore memorabilia. Lily collects porcelain dolls, and Loretta collects cat things."

"Including cats," Michael added, and they both laughed.

"So why do they do it?" He accelerated onto the freeway on-ramp.

"Well, Jess remembers going to the drugstore when he was a kid and getting the Rexall magazine. He says that's when he first realized he wanted to be a pharmacist. Lily's parents traveled a great deal when she was young, and her dolls became her children. She mothered them the way she wished she had been mothered. And Loretta just flat-out loves cats. Their motivations are different. Personal."

"What about you?" Michael asked as she refolded the article. "I mean, what really got you started?"

"Well, contrary to what Jean-Claude said, I started collecting disco memorabilia years before I met him. I just picked up things I thought were interesting and fun. I didn't have the sense that anything had cultural value until I met Andy years later. He had a way of looking at things that changed the way *I* looked at them." She shook her head. "Then I met Jean-Claude, and he was kind of like Lily, but without the heart. He liked to spend money and buy people presents. Our collecting adventures were reasons to travel, scout, and have fun."

"By Andy you mean Warhol, right? The soup-can guy with the

weird—hey, is that our exit coming up? You're supposed to be watching the map, girl."

She checked the directions and looked at the road signs. "Yep. That's our exit. And I wish you'd quit talking about Andy that way."

"I'll try. Can't promise you." He turned the car. "Continue."

"That's about it. I know Doc says keeping the disco era alive has somehow kept my daughter present in my life, and I guess maybe that's part of it. But I'm not sure it's the main reason. I think I've continued to collect over the years because it's fun. It's thrilling to find something I don't have or to make a find that adds value to the collection. It's exciting to think I have a hand in preserving an era. I guess it's a matter of taste, too—and happy memories. I happen to love the music, the fashion, the *flair*."

"So you're saying it's love?"

"Well, yeah, kind of. Sure. I do love it. Is there anything wrong with that?"

"No, sweetheart, there's nothing wrong with that. Look!" He pointed to a sign that read, "World's Biggest Flea Market—5 Miles."

Susan quickly grabbed her cell phone and snapped a picture of the sign.

"I'm going to e-mail this to Ryan." She giggled.

"Rubbing salt into the wound?"

"Not at all. Well, maybe a little. He's young. His time will come."

Michael slowed down to join the line of vehicles pulling into the fairgrounds.

"Make way, folks, we have some serious collecting to do!"

—*ww*—

The next two days were filled with more fun than either of them had imagined. They wandered the fairgrounds, sifting through countless items on table after table, looking at collections of OPJ—Michael's tongue-in-cheek acronym for "other people's junk"—and celebrating the thrill of the kill when they managed to negotiate a great price on something they wanted. They'd actually found five vintage mannequins as well as a considerable amount of clothing, accessories, and jewelry.

"You have a keen eye for quality," one vendor said as Susan sat on the ground and sorted through shoeboxes filled with costume jewelry. Michael had to agree. Susan knew exactly what she was looking for. More importantly, she was a whiz at the fine art of bargaining with vendors. She seemed to know just what to offer, how far to negotiate, and when to walk away—or pretend to.

"A poker face is vital, Michael," she'd instructed him before they got out of the car that first day. "You lose your bargaining power as soon as they know they have something you want." The trouble was, her poker face fooled Michael, too. He could never guess by looking at her if something was a five-star find or just another thing she might or might not want. So after a few hours of this cat-and-mouse game, they'd developed their own secret language.

"I need a piece of gum," she now said to Michael as she nonchalantly flipped through old vinyl records in a cardboard box that was falling apart at the seams. That was their code for striking gold. He had to believe she knew what she was doing, although he wondered. Few of the records had covers. Some, in fact, looked homemade, without labels. They were all twelve-inch, full-size LPs. Also in the box were several old reel-to-reel tapes still inside faded cardboard sleeves.

Susan moved on to sift through a box of belts as he handed her a stick of gum and she asked the young woman sitting under the nearby tarp what she wanted for the records.

"Twenty-five bucks for the lot," she said.

"I'll give you twenty," Susan responded nonchalantly.

"Twenty-two." The woman crossed her arms.

"Sold." Susan nodded to Michael, who handed over the cash and picked up the tattered box. They had walked a good fifty feet from the booth when Susan sat down on a park bench and put her head between her knees.

"Oh my gosh! Oh my gosh! Oh my gosh!" she repeated quietly as she opened her cell phone and punched a speed-dial number. He knew without asking that she was calling Ryan.

"We're sitting on a bench," she said into the phone, "and Michael has a box of records in his lap that we just picked up for twenty-two dollars. I'm going to have him read something to you, okay?"

She held the phone to Michael's ear. "Read him the names on some of the labels," she whispered.

He strained to see what names had made his wife almost hyperventilate, yet none of them were familiar.

"Yo, Ryan." Michael took the phone from Susan, whose eyes were bulging with excitement. "Okay, dude, it looks like some of these belonged to a guy named Tom Moulton, and others say G. Moroder. That mean anything to you?"

Susan caught the phone before it fell to the ground as Michael's reflexes responded to Ryan's high-decibel yell. She stood and paced, talking animatedly to Ryan for a few minutes before returning the phone to the rhinestone pouch clipped to her belt.

"The *G* stands for Giorgio," she explained as they walked to the car to unload their recent acquisition. "He was the Italian producer who introduced the world to the four-on-the-floor dance beat—and to Donna Summer. I have a few of his original dance mixes in Plexiglas shadow boxes on the wall at Disco Diva. Tom Moulton was the legendary remixer, the guy responsible for taking short songs and blending them to make forty-five-minute dance mixes.

She stopped walking and looked him in the eye. "Michael, I know the twelve-inch singles are originals, and if I'm right, so are the tapes. The vinyl alone is worth a fortune, but the tapes …" She shook her head and ran her hand through her hair. "If they're the real deal, we have just acquired a priceless piece of history. Whether or not they're in any condition to play."

They found countless treasures during the two-day event, including a cache of clothing that included more spandex, glitter, and macramé than Michael had seen in years. Susan bought every item from that particular vendor, including bell-bottoms, Nehru jackets, caftans, halter tops, and platform-soled shoes. All told, they spent roughly ten thousand dollars on memorabilia, not counting shipping costs. True to his word, Ryan had located a nearby shipping center, and their trucks had picked up several loads throughout the weekend.

"Ryan's going to flip when he actually sees everything we found," Susan said as the last truck departed. "Having it shipped was a great idea. But these babies are going on the plane with me."

She pointed to the tattered box of vinyl records and tapes and grinned, knowing the flight attendants would think she was nuts.

Chapter 51

It was Sunday in New York, and Susan and Michael had spent the morning sleeping in, sore and exhausted from two days of walking for what seemed like miles. Then they'd called down to arrange dual massages at the hotel spa.

"I got us tickets to an off-Broadway show tonight," Michael said as they lounged side by side in the unisex sauna after their massages, Michael lying one tier above his wife. "The concierge recommended it."

"That's nice," Susan mumbled, feeling like jelly after the hour massage from someone named Helga. "Do we have to get dressed?"

"What did you have in mind, going like this?"

"I think you look good in thick white terry." She smiled without opening her eyes. "You know what I mean. Dressy or casual?"

"You're asking me? I wear what you tell me, remember?" He reached down and caressed her hand, rubbing his fingers over her soft knuckles.

"We need to get away like this more often." Susan sighed. "Not necessarily to New York, just away. Vegas is filled with day spas. We could do this once a month, then have dinner, see a show …"

"Disco Diva's going to have a day spa."

"You know I can't relax in my own place."

"Maybe you could learn?"

She squeezed his hand. "Maybe we could learn together."

He leaned down and kissed her, surprising her with the tender passion of his touch.

"I've had enough of the spa treatment," she said. "Let's go to our room."

—***—

"So where are we going?" Susan asked Michael that night as the Ritz door attendant hailed a taxi.

"I'm not really sure." He pulled the tickets from his jacket pocket. "The concierge said it was a good show. It's called *The Secret Life,* and it's at the Cook Theater."

"Seriously? I auditioned there once. Didn't make it."

A taxi pulled to the curb and the attendant opened the car door. "Thank you." Susan smiled.

"You're welcome, ma'am. Have a splendid evening."

The production turned out to be an avant-garde musical revue written by a young couple from Brazil. The intimate one-hundred-fifty-seat theater was full for the show, which would be closing that night after a six-month run.

"This must have cost a fortune to print," Susan whispered as she paged through the glossy four-color program, complete with several full-page cast photographs. "They're all babies," Susan said of the cast as she looked at their headshots and read their bios.

"Sweetheart, everyone is a baby to us these days."

"Well, they're all gorgeous—that's for certain. Look at her." She pointed to the photo of a striking African American woman. "She's stunning."

"I'm partial to blondes myself." Michael pointed to one of several young women who could have been sisters, so similar were their California-girl looks. "She's a hottie."

Susan rolled up her program and playfully smacked him on the arm just as the lights dimmed.

—*m*—

"How did this bomb last six weeks, let alone six months?" Michael said as they stretched their legs in the lobby during intermission.

"Shh, honey, not so loud."

"Do you want to head out now?" He grabbed her hand. "I don't mind—I doubt we'll be missed."

"No, I want to see how it ends. It can't be much longer."

They were ninety minutes into the production, and although Susan could understand her husband's reaction to the weak script, she also recognized that they'd witnessed some amazing feats of dance prowess, especially by the two young leads.

"You have no idea how difficult those moves are," she explained as she sipped a glass of San Pellegrino water.

"If you say so." He shrugged. "Hey, look, a restaurant." He nodded toward an adjoining room, which was being set up for what appeared to be a dinner event. Michael started to walk toward the room, but Susan grabbed his sleeve.

"Honey, it's closing night," she said. "That's most likely a private reception for the cast, crew, and their guests. Curb your hunger just a little while longer—I'm sure there's a restaurant within walking distance."

The lobby lights blinked, signaling five minutes to curtain.

"See, we'll be reading menus in no time ... hang in there, big guy." She placed her hand on his arm as he led her back to their seats.

The second half of the production was over in less than an hour, a fact that surprised and somewhat disappointed Susan. She had thoroughly enjoyed the final act.

"Now that part alone was worth the price of the ticket," she said as they shuffled slowly out of their aisle.

"Yeah, well, they should have started with it and dumped part one."

"No doubt about it—those two are going places."

"Yep, they were good." Michael peered over the crowd to see why it was taking them so long to exit. "Seems to be a bottleneck."

"They might have a receiving line." She squinted. "That would be exciting. I'd like to compliment them."

"It's not a wedding, Susan."

"I know that, dear, but off-Broadway productions often relax the tradition of performers not mingling with the patrons, especially on closing night. I'd forgotten about it."

"So we have to wait?" He craned his neck. "Can't we just find another door?"

"Michael, please. I'd really like to meet the cast and extend my gratitude for a job well done." She leaned in to whisper into his ear. "It means a lot to them to hear compliments from strangers—not just from friends and family. Humor me, okay?"

"Whatever you say, dear."

They discussed the show with a couple in front of them as they moved slowly toward the lobby. It turned out they were neighbors of the parents of the young male lead. By the time Susan and Michael reached the lobby, they'd learned a great deal about the cast and crew from this gregarious couple.

Susan complimented the writers, director, and even the costumer before reaching the cast. She had just caught the eye of the female lead, whose performance had particularly moved her, when the young woman began to cry. Clearly, the previous person in line had said something to provoke the emotional response.

"You were brilliant." Susan introduced herself to the young woman named Jackie, who was still finding it difficult to regain her composure.

"Thank you," the girl said softly, then stepped back, excusing herself as Susan and Michael continued down the line to meet and greet the other cast members.

Closing night blues, Susan thought, suddenly remembering the feeling.

"That was kind of fun," Michael said as they prepared to leave the theater. "Can we go and eat now?"

She laughed and took his hand. "Yes, dear. We can go eat now."

"You're welcome to stay and join us," a deep male voice said. They turned to see the male lead dancer. "There was supposed to be an announcement after curtain that everyone was welcome to stay for our party. It didn't happen—one last technical glitch, I guess. But there's more than enough food." He extended his hand. "My name is Kenneth Klein. I think we met in line?"

"Yes, we did." They reintroduced themselves, and Susan complimented him once again on his splendid performance. "Thank you for the invitation," she said, "but I think my husband—"

"Nonsense!" Michael practically shouted. "I say we accept the gracious invitation."

"Really?" Susan whispered. "We don't have to, honey."

"Don't you want to stay?" He raised his eyebrows. "Figured you'd get a kick out of visiting with others of your kind." He nudged her with his elbow. "I say we go for the free food—a nice change after the money we've spent this weekend. Hey, I see shrimp cocktail ..." He pulled his wife toward the banquet room like a hunting dog toward game.

—✧—

"Closing night is always emotional," Susan said to the young woman as they stood at the buffet table and dipped celery stalks into a bowl of ranch dressing. "It's Jackie, right? Are you feeling better?"

"Yes. I'm kind of embarrassed about losing my cool back there. Sorry."

"Think nothing of it." Susan reached for a carrot stick. "Those void of emotion lack depth, don't you think?"

"Are you an actress?"

"Not anymore. Not ever, really. I used to be a dancer."

"You look like an actress."

"As do you. You really were brilliant tonight—I wasn't just saying that. I've seen a great many dancers in my life, and you are definitely going places."

"Tell that to my parents." She fought back tears. "I'm sorry. You must think I'm an idiot."

"Nonsense. Your parents don't think you should pursue this lofty career?"

"Sounds rather cliché, doesn't it?" Jackie laughed. "Did your parents feel the same way?"

"My parents died when I was a kid. But I have a beauty salon in Las Vegas, and many of my customers are showgirls. The saga of parental discord is more common than one might think." She smiled. "So, too, is the eventual understanding when they realize your passion isn't something you can turn on and off. Be patient with them. I'm sure they have your best interests at heart."

"They do, but they're both doctors and they don't understand."

Susan leaned closely against the young woman's shoulder and said conspiratorially, "Sweetie, I can't say for certain, because I don't know them, but take it from someone who knows a little about this dynamic—okay? Chances are, your parents will never fully understand the creative force that flows through your body. You just need to stay true to your calling and stop trying to get them to understand. Just love them for who they are. I'm sure they love you."

"They do. I love them, too ... I couldn't ask for better parents. It's just hard sometimes."

They were deep in conversation when Michael found them.

"There you are." He handed her a glass of ice water. "I've been looking all over for you."

"I've been right here. You remember the star of the show, Michael ..."

"Yes. Great job." He extended his hand as they introduced themselves. "Don't know how you get your limbs to move that way."

"Practice," Susan and Jackie said in unison. They laughed.

"Uh-oh, here come my parents." Jackie took a deep breath.

"I'd love to meet them," Susan said. "I know just what to say."

~~~

"I don't know how you do it." Michael leaned back in the taxi and closed his eyes.

"Do what?"

"Get so involved with strangers. Ten minutes, and you're a therapist."

"I wasn't trying to be anyone's therapist."

"No?" he smirked.

"No. I just wanted them to see their daughter's passion as it relates to their passion for medicine. Sometimes it's just a matter of perspective."

"A matter of perspective?"

"Yes. That young woman was born to dance. Can you imagine trying to turn her into a doctor or lawyer or—what else did they say?"

"A professor."

"Argh! What are they thinking? A teacher? Heaven forbid!"

"Doesn't look like that's gonna happen. Did I hear she was moving?"

"I don't think she knows yet. Sounds like she's going to audition for a show on the West Coast. Los Angeles, maybe."

"Well, whatever she decides, it sounds like she's got her head screwed on straight—pretty sharp gal. They must have done something right."

"I never said they didn't. They seem like good people—they were proud of her. She just wants them to love her unconditionally, that's all. Nothing wrong with that."

"No, ma'am, nothing wrong with that," he said. "Come here, woman." He put his arm around her and pulled her to him. "Thanks for a great evening."

"You, too. Thanks for a great weekend. It's been fun."

"It's not over yet." He nibbled on her ear as she laughed.

Chapter 52

It was their last full day in New York, and they'd decided to take it easy. They would spend the day packing and relaxing, go out to dinner, then get to bed early. They would catch a seven o'clock flight out of LaGuardia the next morning.

"Good morning, gorgeous," Michael pulled his wife close as they snuggled under the feather comforter. "How are you doing?"

"Great. I love the Ritz. Can't you just feel the thread count on these sheets?" She rolled over on her back and started flailing her arms and legs as though making a snow angel.

"I'd rather feel you back here in my arms." He pulled her over to him and put his arm around her. She rested her head on his chest.

"Today's the day," he said, kissing the top of her head. "I asked how you're doing."

"Surprisingly well. I do wonder where she is right now and if she's celebrating her birthday. I don't know if her adoptive parents even kept the same birth date—I've heard that some don't."

"Hmm," Michael murmured. "Well, we're going to celebrate, but not just her birthday."

"What else, then?" Susan played with the hair on his chest.

"Ouch, that hurts."

"Sorry. What else are we celebrating?"

Michael sat up and plumped the pillows against the headboard so they could sit and talk.

"Your emancipation, our relationship rejuvenation, Suite 494, our fabulous flea market finds. We should probably make a toast to Doc Allen. And we can't forget Lily—I think we should definitely celebrate Lily. Then we have Ryan and Tina, and our godchild ..."

She fought back tears. "I guess there really is a lot to celebrate, isn't there?"

"Now, don't go getting mushy on me. This is a good day. For the first time in twenty-six years you're not facing this day alone. Now, is there anything else we want to celebrate? We'll make a day of it! What do you say?"

"I say that I love you, Michael Anderson."

"Yeah? Well, talk is cheap. Come here."

An hour later they were famished.

"I'm starving." Michael jumped up from bed. "Arise, fair maiden!" He flipped back the comforter and picked up his wife.

"Michael! Put me down, you'll drop me."

"Oh ye of little faith." He swung her around in his arms. "Not quite as graceful as those dancers, huh?" They laughed as he put her down and they kissed.

"Not quite," she said. "But the passion was there." She moved toward the bathroom.

"You can say that again." He grabbed her hand, and she playfully smacked it.

"Keep that up and we'll never get out of here. I thought you were hungry."

"I am." He raised his eyebrows suggestively.

"For food, Michael—stay focused." She laughed and walked into the bathroom. "I'll be done in a jiff. Where should we go?"

"I could go for some of that pizza again." He pulled a shirt from his suitcase, checking for wrinkles.

"Sure, we can get pizza." She stuck her head around the side of the bathroom door. "Hey, how about if we get corn dogs from a street vendor and sneak them up to the observation level of the Empire State Building?"

"You've got my vote." He joined her in the bathroom for further discussion.

—————

They spent their last day in the City like kids on summer break—darting here and there and buying junk food from almost every street vendor they passed. As planned, they ate lunch high above the City, looking out from the observation deck of the Empire State Building, sneaking bites of smuggled-in food behind the back of the security guard who walked the floor.

"Hey! I thought of something else to celebrate," Michael said later as they window-shopped along Madison Avenue. "Let's celebrate our anniversary!"

"But it's not until next month."

"I know that, Jelly-Bean."

He hadn't called her Jelly-Bean in years. It had been his pet name for her when they first met.

"Where did twenty-five years go?" She stopped to look at a display of men's watches in the window of a jewelry store. "Twenty-five years."

"It sounds like a lot, but it doesn't feel like it." He wrapped his arms around her and she leaned back into him, savoring the moment.

"I have an idea," he said, spinning her around. "This has been a pretty monumental year, wouldn't you agree?"

"Ah, yes. It has."

"Seriously monumental. You turned fifty, I turned sixty, and I retired after thirty-six years of employment with the same company. If that's not monumental, I don't know what is."

She nodded. "You've got a point."

"Then we have all the other things we talked about this morning. It's been a pretty amazing year, and it's only July!"

"I agree, but why—?"

"Look where we are, Susan." He pointed up at the name on the building.

"Tiffany's!" She looked around in wonder. "How did we get to Fifty-seventh and Fifth Avenue so quickly?"

"You were busy talking. I just kept you from walking into traffic."

"Did you know when Charles Lewis Tiffany first opened this store, the receipts for the entire day were only $4.98?"

"That's a rather obscure bit of information to retain in your memory bank."

"Yeah, I know. Not sure why I remembered that."

"Probably from the movie—you've only watched it, what, a hundred bazillion times?"

"Don't sound so appalled." She gently elbowed him. "You watched it with me the last time, remember? Anyway, that bit of trivia isn't in the film. It's in a book I have."

"Did you tell Doc you knew Truman Capote?"

"I did. He gave me a free hour session because we took up so much time talking about him. Truman wanted Marilyn Monroe to play Holly Golightly. Never could get over Paramount casting Audrey Hepburn. But she was brilliant."

"So," he continued, "can I get back to my idea? To celebrate our monumental year?"

"Sorry. Sure." She crossed her arms and leaned against the building. "Shoot."

"Well, we're at Tiffany's, and we've kind of been playing like Holly and Paul all day, running around doing things we've never done before—at least not together."

She was impressed that he recalled the characters' names from the film.

"What's the name of that other girly movie you've made me watch a gazillion times over the years? The one where that millionaire falls in love with the hooker."

"*Pretty Woman?*"

"Yeah, that one. Let's do that thing."

"Michael, what are you talking about? What *thing* do you want to do?"

"Let's start here." He grabbed her hand and pulled her toward the entrance to Tiffany's.

"Whoa. Slow down. You mean the shopping thing?"

"Bingo!"

"But we're almost packed. We're leaving tomorrow."

"So? We don't need to buy an entire wardrobe, just one outfit for each of us and maybe a little bling on the side. We're going somewhere nice for dinner to celebrate all the milestones of the past year. And we have the money, remember? So come on—let's do something wild and crazy while we're still able to enjoy it!"

"Wait," she teased. "Am I supposed to be the hooker?"

"Not at all. We're both the millionaires!" He looked at her with such joy, it about broke her heart.

"God bless you, sweet man." She kissed him on the lips, squeezed his hand, and pointed toward the door. "Lead the way. I'm about to have a serious bling fling."

Chapter 53

The only thing lacking five hours later, as they left their hotel room and walked to the elevator, was the music that played when Richard Gere and Julia Roberts departed for the opera.

Michael wore a handsome rich chocolate brown Giorgio Armani suit, a perfect complement to Susan's floor-length rich cream Monique Lhuillier chiffon gown. Her blond hair was twisted into a chignon secured by a vintage diamond hairpin they'd found at a little shop in Ithaca on their way back from the flea market. On her finger was a two-carat blue sapphire ring surrounded by diamonds from Tiffany's. At nearly fifteen thousand dollars, it was by far the most expensive piece of jewelry she'd ever owned. It had taken more than a little convincing on Michael's part before she agreed to the extravagant purchase.

"Susan," Michael had said, "when are you going to realize we have money? We *are* millionaires, not pretending to be millionaires. Our Henderson land is a gold mine."

"I know. But that doesn't mean we have to lose common sense." She was adamant about not buying the fifty-five-thousand-dollar diamond Michael originally selected. But she fell in love with the stunning sapphire.

"I feel like a princess," she whispered as they walked through the lobby that evening, pretending not to notice the way people stared.

"You are a princess," he said proudly, nodding at the concierge as they passed his ornate desk.

"No taxi tonight," he declared as they slid into the backseat of a chauffeured limousine.

"My, my," Susan said. "You've thought of everything."

She wondered if he'd secretly bought tickets to the opera, the place to which Richard Gere had whisked his Pretty Woman. She rather hoped not, as she was looking forward to talking with her husband, something they would be unable to do at the opera.

She was elated when they pulled up to 21 West Fifty-second Street.

"Oh, Michael, this is perfect."

"Don't cry. You'll mess up that beautiful face." He kissed the back of her hand as he helped her from the car. "Now you see why I grilled you on restaurants you hadn't been to with … well, you know who."

"I figured you had an ulterior motive." She kissed him. "Bless your heart."

When she lived in New York, Jean-Claude and the manager of the famous establishment simply called "21" hadn't gotten along. There had been more than enough restaurants in the City to keep them occupied, and she could never have afforded the place on her own. It was one of the few restaurants in the heart of Manhattan she'd never been inside.

"Did you know this place is hailed as the most romantic restaurant in the City?"

"You don't say." She smiled.

"It's a historic landmark." He closed his eyes and recited what he had obviously worked hard to memorize. "Housed in a four-story town house, the elegant restaurant opened in 1929. During Prohibition, it became one of the most famous speakeasies in the City. It's filled with secret passages and fake walls, and the infamous secret liquor vault was never raided during the period. Throughout the years, several renovations have taken place, yet the elegant historic flavor has never been lost." He opened his eyes and puffed up like a peacock. "How'd I do?"

"Perfect. You did perfect."

"Amazing what you can find on the Internet." He put his arm around her. "Shall we?"

It was a picture-perfect evening. Upstairs at "21," the elegant restaurant that opened in 2002, was closed on Mondays. However, they had dinner in the famous Bar Room, where countless celebrities had been loyal patrons throughout the years. They sat at table seven, the preferred table of John Steinbeck, Ernest Hemingway, Henry Kissinger, and George and Barbara Bush. Dinner was superb. They had polished off their lobster and prime rib and were about to order dessert when Susan noticed the young couple being seated a few tables over.

"Isn't that the dancer from last night?"

Michael craned his neck to see. "Could be."

"It is. I'm sure of it. What was her name … Jackie, I think? Her date's quite handsome."

He nudged her. "Don't stare, dear."

"I'm not staring … am I?" She took a sip of water from the crystal goblet just as their waiter returned.

"May I interest you in dessert?" He clasped his hands in front of him.

"Yes. We'll have the crème brûlée for two." Michael handed back the leather-covered dessert menu.

"An excellent choice. Beverage?"

"Two coffees, decaf, no cream."

"Also an excellent choice—we've just brewed fresh Fazenda São Benedito from Brazil. You will love the nutty, sweet, and exceptional chocolate roast taste—our most popular coffee."

Susan suppressed a smile at the young man's earnest approval of a simple coffee order. She noted that Michael was equally amused as he thanked the young man for his help.

"May I suggest you take your coffee in our dessert lounge?" The waiter waved like Vanna White toward an ornate archway at the back of the restaurant.

"Pardon me?" Michael stifled a laugh.

"Our dessert lounge, sir," he repeated as though addressing a rather dense young child.

"Oh, yes! The dessert lounge." Susan stood and nodded to her husband. "Thank you. We'll take our coffee and dessert in the dessert lounge. Shall we, dear?" She winked as Michael stood and took her hand.

"Absolutely. Excellent idea, darling. Most excellent." They did their best not to double over in laughter as the waiter exited the room and they walked behind him into what they assumed was the most excellent dessert lounge.

"Actually, this is lovely!" Susan observed when they passed under the archway. The exquisite room resembled what she assumed the library of an exclusive men's club would look like. Deep hues of burgundy and green, mahogany wainscoting, and plush leather furniture in intimate groupings around tables, ottomans, and bookshelves gave the room the appearance of wealth. Other than a solitary couple at the far corner of the room, they had the place to themselves.

"We should have a room like this in our restaurant." Michael led her toward a nearby chair.

She smiled as she sat. "This look isn't quite the same era, honey."

"I'm talking about the concept—a dessert lounge. It's a good idea for clearing out table space in the dining room. Folks can mingle back here with coffee and dessert. I like it. Our dessert lounge would have a decidedly different flair, but it could work."

"I like how you say 'our dessert lounge.' Thank you, Michael, for making Suite 494 yours as well. It wouldn't be the same without you."

"Susan ..."

He had that tone of voice that always made Susan just a tad fearful.

"Yes?"

They were interrupted by a new waiter, who wheeled a delicate, ornate silver serving cart to where they sat. He poured coffee from a sterling silver carafe and placed silver spoons directly into the bubbling crock of crème brûlée.

"Oh my." Susan inhaled deeply. "That smells delicious."

"Will there be anything else?" the waiter asked.

"Not right now, thank you." Michael nodded his head as the young man bowed at the waist and departed.

"They sure are formal here." He handed a cup and saucer to his wife.

"Thank you." She took a sip. "Excellent." She winked as she mimicked the first waiter.

He picked up the other cup. "We're going to celebrate your daughter's birthday every year from now on, along with all of our monumental occasions." Michael raised his coffee cup in a toast. "What do you say we make this the celebration date for everything we have to be thankful for?"

Susan could only smile, overwhelmed with love for this gentle man who was working so hard to understand her—and himself.

"Doc would be proud of you—of us." Michael put down his cup and took her hand. "Honey, I have a question for you. I can understand why you've never searched for your daughter. But what if she's been searching for you? Have you ever thought of that?"

"If that were the case I would welcome her with open arms. I told you that back home. It would be a God-cidence of the miraculous kind." She took another sip of hot coffee. "Oh my, this is good. Maybe we were too hard on young Emilio's effusive recommendations."

"But you don't think it's likely?" Michael said quietly.

"What? That she's looking for me?"

"Yes."

"It could be. But I've had so many last names, and, well, quite frankly I never wanted to get my hopes up."

"Oh, Suze." He squeezed her hand. "I can hear your pain. I'm sorry I never asked why you'd get melancholy at this same time every year. I'm sorry I didn't pay attention. Dr. Allen is right—we can't just talk about the tough stuff of life; we have to listen, too. I think we're doing a great job at both now, don't you?"

She touched his face. "I think we agreed not to continually apologize, didn't we?"

"We did. But some things need an apology." He looked down. "I did something, Susan. I hope it wasn't the wrong thing to do."

"What?" She sat up, startled. "What did you do?"

"I went online to an adoption search site and posted your information—all your names and dates—just in case she's looking for you."

She leaned forward. "Have you heard anything?"

He shifted in his chair and coughed into his hand. "Not like I'd hoped."

"That's okay. I love you for trying." She set down her cup and took Michael's hand. "Thank you for this—for all of this. This night … this weekend … the past twenty-five years. Thank you."

They were kissing when they heard the sound of heels on the hardwood floor and looked up to see Jackie and the young man walking toward them.

"Are we interrupting?" the dancer asked shyly.

"Oh, goodness no," Susan said.

"Oh, goodness, yes," Michael said, "but it's probably for the best—before they ask us to leave." He chuckled. "We thought that was you." Michael stood and extended his hand to the young man as Jackie introduced them.

"This is Craig Carnegie."

"Any relation to *the* Carnegies?" Michael joked. The young man looked down and sighed.

"You are? Oops. Sorry."

"No problem."

There was a moment of awkward silence before the young man spoke again.

"I was about to head to the Wine Cellar." He pointed toward the dining room. "They have a wonderful cigar bar. Would you care to join me?"

"Don't mind if I do. Thanks for the invite." Michael followed the young man and called out over his shoulder as they walked away. "Be right back, ladies. Have a nice visit."

"But you don't smoke," Susan protested as they walked briskly from the room. "That was totally weird. I have no idea what that was about." She leaned back. "Hmm ... oh, well." She straightened up and crossed her legs. "Would you care to join me until they return?" She noticed that the couple in the back had left. "There's plenty of room. We seem to have the place to ourselves."

The young woman declined coffee as she sat in the chair next to Susan.

"You look beautiful. That's a gorgeous dress, and your hair is ... perfect. Can you do that yourself?"

"I own a salon, remember. It's part of the job." Susan smiled. "But thanks for the compliment. My sweet husband took me on a rather unexpected shopping trip today. We're celebrating twenty-five years of marriage."

"Tonight?" Jackie asked. "I mean, is your anniversary today?"

"No, next month. You look rather fetching yourself—as does the young gentleman. Is he really one of *the* Carnegies, or was he yanking Michael's chain?"

"Yes, he's really one of them."

"Wow," said Susan. "A Carnegie."

Jackie shrugged. "Well, he's a nice guy."

"So, what brings you to '21'?" Susan took a sip of coffee. "It's not like this is your run-of-the-mill Monday night dinner house." She placed her cup back on the table.

"I'm celebrating something too." Jackie swallowed. "Two things, actually."

"Really?" Susan leaned forward.

The young woman straightened her shoulders and took a deep breath.

"It's my twenty-sixth birthday," she said as tears filled her eyes, "and I'm meeting my birth mother for the very first time."

It took Susan a few moments to process what she had heard. Then she sat back and gasped.

"Oh, please don't be upset." Jackie quickly moved to the ottoman between them and sat on it. "Are you okay? Michael said he was sure you would be okay—that you'd be happy. We had a signal for me to come over if the coast was clear. I heard him give it—his cough ..."

"Michael?" Susan looked up to see her husband striding toward her.

"Honey, take a breath." He was grinning from ear to ear.

"Is it true?" she asked in hushed tones. She stared from her husband to the beautiful young woman, who was now biting her lower lip and gripping her beaded clutch bag like a lifeline.

"I told you I posted your information online."

"You told me five minutes ago." She blinked back tears. "And you said it hadn't worked out like you'd hoped."

"That's because it worked out better than I'd hoped! I got an e-mail forty-eight hours after I posted."

"I've been looking for you for years," Jackie whispered, tears falling.

"Honey, it's true. Trust me. We've confirmed everything. There's no doubt about it—this is your daughter." Michael beamed.

Jackie wiped her eyes. "Thank you, Mr. Anderson."

"It's Michael, and you are most welcome, dear. Happy birthday." He could no longer fight back his own tears as he watched the truth sink into his wife's heart.

Susan cupped the young woman's face in her hands and stared into her eyes. Then she pulled her gently to her chest and enveloped her in an embrace that shook with emotion.

Chapter 54

Michael had orchestrated everything in advance. From the moment Jackie crossed the threshold into the dessert lounge, the room had been officially closed to the public. An informed wait staff kept the reunion private and continued to respect the unique situation by keeping a polite distance as they delivered a refreshment cart filled with beverages and desserts.

No one was thinking about food. Michael, who quickly assessed the situation, grabbed two linen napkins off the dessert cart and handed one to each woman.

"Forget protocol." He smiled as they wiped their eyes and blew their noses.

"And you've really been looking for me?" Susan said.

"For a long time," Jackie whispered.

"You knew the entire weekend?" Susan looked at her husband as tears filled her eyes again.

"I've known for weeks—we've been planning this for ages."

"The trip?"

"Planned."

"Closing night? The theater?"

"Planned. All of it was planned."

Jackie sniffled. "When I saw you in the receiving line I couldn't breathe. That's why I turned away. I'm sorry."

"Sorry? Oh my … I don't know what to say …" Susan's voice trailed off as she continued to stare at the young woman.

"That's a first—my wife speechless." Michael unbuttoned his jacket and sat down.

"Do your parents know?" Susan asked. "When we met at the theater, did they know?"

"Not then. But they do now. They understand, really. I love them … I just wanted to meet you—to know you. Please tell me you're not upset." Jackie looked down at the mascara-stained napkin in her hand. "I wasn't sure about doing it this way, but Michael said—"

"Oh, no!" Susan interrupted, shaking her head. "Please, don't think that. I've just imagined this for years, and it was never quite like this."

"Me, too!" Jackie grinned.

"How did you picture it?" Susan whispered.

"You'll think I'm a nut case." Jackie demurely blew her nose.

"No, I won't. I promise."

"Well, it's all rather … old Hollywood. If you know what I mean."

"Oh well, not like she can relate to that!" Michael grinned like a Cheshire cat. "She's not all that dramatic—rather bland, actually."

Susan smiled. "He's pulling your leg."

"I never figured you'd be this … beautiful."

"Sweetheart, it's you who are beautiful." They started crying again.

"So what did you imagine I would say?" Susan dabbed at her eyes. "You first."

"I don't know, really. Something perfect, I guess." Jackie looked down again.

"Jackie?" Susan said. "This is probably more than you want to hear right now, and I'm not sure what Michael has already told you. But we've been married for twenty-five years, and for a great many of those years we said things to one another that started with those same words—'Oh, I don't know'—when the truth of the matter was that we did know, but for some reason we chose not to share our feelings."

"Or to listen when the other person did, for that matter," Michael added.

"I had a little trouble as a result of that—"

"*We* had trouble," Michael interrupted. "It wasn't just you, Susan."

"Okay, we had trouble. But anyway, now I'm trying—we're trying—not to say 'I don't know' if that really isn't the case."

"I see," Jackie said quietly.

"I mean, if you really don't know, that's totally fine. But somehow I think that if you've imagined this moment in dramatic detail for years, you probably have an idea what 'perfect something' I would say."

Jackie looked at her mother as tears once again cascaded down her cheeks.

"Well, you asked for it." She took a deep breath. "There's always a musical soundtrack in the background, playing something amazing."

"Please." Michael laughed. "Not disco."

"No, not disco. More like John Barry-esque."

"And then?" Susan inquired, her eyes glowing.

"Then you'd see me in the distance and start to run toward me, kind of like those slow-motion scenes out of an old movie. It all had a kind of ethereal feeling to it. Kind of hokey, you know?"

"I'm following right there with you." Susan grinned as Jackie continued.

"And when we met, you'd look at me and say …"

"Yes? What would I say?"

"You'd say something like, 'I'm sorry for the choice I made. I thought I was doing the right thing, but a day hasn't gone by that I don't think of you, and I love you more than you could possibly know, and I'm so sorry. Please let me make it up to you. Please let me love you …"

Jackie's lip quivered, and her voice trailed off toward the end as she tried to stifle the continuing flow of tears.

"Well," Susan said, "I'm sorry there's no music. And I think if I stand right now my legs wouldn't hold me, so I'm afraid the slo-mo running scenario won't happen. But, sweetheart, look at me. Please." Susan held her daughter's hands and through tears said, "I did think I was doing the right thing at the time—I still do. But I haven't gone a day without thinking of you. I love you so much, more than you could possibly know, and I'm sorry if my decision hurt you. Please let me make it up to you. Please let me love you."

When at last they were able to compose themselves, Michael interrupted.

"You have no idea how much I wanted to tell you." He gazed at his wife. "Especially when you thought all of my online activity was, uh, less than noble."

"Oh my gosh!" Susan exclaimed. "That's what you've been doing online!"

"Guilty as charged."

Jackie blew her nose again, this time less daintily. "I almost came to Vegas—"

"But when I learned about the flea market and saw the dates, I got this idea instead. It was just like what you call things like this ... a God-cidence."

"A God-cidence?" Jackie raised her eyebrows.

"Coincidences that aren't coincidences." He removed the thoroughly damp faux handkerchiefs they were both holding and handed them each another dry dinner napkin. "That's pretty much everything in Susan's world."

"Start at the beginning." Susan swallowed as she wiped her face and smiled broadly. "Tell me everything. I can't believe this—that you're here." Her heart swelled as she grabbed her daughter's hand and held on for dear life. "Is it really you?"

They talked for over an hour before the manager interrupted them. "I'm sorry, but we need to close."

"We understand." Michael stood. "Thank you for everything."

"It was truly our pleasure." He smiled at the women, who were still holding hands and staring at one another. "If I may be so bold ..." He cleared his throat and stood erect. "It was our honor to participate in this ... special occasion ... and I speak for all of us." He waved at the small group of employees who stood by the service door, smiling and applauding. "We wish you every good thing."

"Thank you." Susan beamed, and Jackie nodded as they stood. "I'm afraid we ruined quite a few of your linens."

"Think nothing of it," he assured her. "A very small price to pay for such joy."

"Time to go, ladies." Michael extended both his hands.

"But ... we can't go yet," Susan stammered. "There's so much more I need to say—to know. We have to change our flight, Michael. We can't leave tomorrow. Where's your cell phone? Call the airlines."

"I'm sorry," Jackie said quietly, "but I have to leave in the morning."

"B-b-but ..." Susan stuttered.

"I'm starting rehearsals for a new job," she continued. "The casting director was in town last week and offered me the job the next day."

"Oh, honey, that's fabulous." Susan's lip quivered. "But when can I see you again? Where is the show? I mean, when can we—?"

"Ladies," Michael interrupted, "we really have to go. The manager will be hoarse tomorrow if he clears his throat one more time. Let's continue this outside." He led the women out of the restaurant to where the limousine waited, parked next to a sleek red Ferrari. The chauffeur and Craig Carnegie were leaning against the building.

"Oh my." Susan put her hand over her mouth. "I forgot all about your young man."

"Don't worry. He's not my young man. He's the son of our producer—just doing me a favor. I couldn't come alone." Craig tipped an imaginary hat at Susan, who smiled.

"Is he really a Carnegie?"

Jackie giggled. "That part was true."

"So, this is good-bye for now?" Susan bit her lip, fighting tears. "I'm ..."

"Oh, heck, Suzie-Q, don't look like that," Michael said. "Maybe we should tell her?" He put his arm around Jackie's shoulder and smirked.

She nodded. "I think that would be a good idea."

"Oh, please, my heart can't stand much more of this." Susan wagged her finger at them. "What do you two have up your sleeve now?"

"The show I'm doing?" Jackie leaned in. "It's a pretty big break for me. I got the job because one of their performers is on maternity leave." She used her hand to cover her laugh. "And because someone named Lily suggested to the artistic director that they give me an audition."

"But she didn't get you the job." Michael wagged his finger at her. "Your talent did. Susan, say hello to the Tropicana's newest dancer," he said proudly. "They couldn't find one person to fill Tina's shoes, so they hired both a singer and a dancer. Our girl here is the dancer."

"I'd love to sing." Jackie shook her head. "But it's not my gift."

"I can't believe this …" Susan leaned into her husband, who braced her as he pulled an envelope out of his jacket breast pocket.

"Two first-class tickets on the seven a.m. out of LaGuardia to McClaren, for you two." He handed her the envelope. "First class was full, so I'm flying coach, thank you very—hey, we don't have any more napkins. You two really have to stop that," he said as Susan and Jackie fell back into a tearful embrace.

―✐―

From: Susan Anderson (boomerbabesusan@
              boomerbabesrock.com)
Sent: Tuesday, July 11, 2:25 a.m.
To: Patricia Davies; Mary Johnson; Lisa Taylor; Linda Jones;
              Sharon Wilson
Subject: An EPIC discovery ... story to come later

You can see by the time stamp that it's well after two in the morning. Couldn't sleep. Still in the hotel, using business center computer. Flying back home on the 7 a.m.

Had a successful shopping trip—found lots of treasures at the World's Biggest Flea Market. But I also found something else far more valuable. Words can't describe it, so I won't try. I'm bringing it back with me on the plane, and I'll have Ryan set up one of those video conference calls when I get back. So stay tuned.

I love you all so much.

Suze

P.S.: You are NEVER going to believe this!

~~~~~

None of them had slept, but they were as alert as a trio of watchdogs when they met up again. Jackie appeared just as the plane was beginning to board its first-class passengers.

"That was close." She breathed deeply. "Didn't expect so much traffic this early in the morning."

Michael gave her a hug. "I knew you'd make it."

"I was afraid …" Susan started, then paused.

"Of what—that I'd changed my mind? I've been looking too long to let you go now." Jackie smiled and handed her boarding pass to the agent.

"This is where I stop," Michael said. "You two go ahead. I have to lag back with the huddled masses in coach." He handed his wife her rolling bag and gave her a peck on the cheek.

"Is that as heavy as it looks?" Jackie pointed to the bag as Susan pulled it down the ramp.

"Yes, it is. But this doesn't leave my side—and neither do you." She touched her daughter's cheek. "It'll slide under the seat. I'll tell you all about it when we get settled in."

They were buckled in, drinking diet soda, and talking like old friends by the time Michael boarded the plane and walked by, playfully pinching his wife on the arm as he passed.

She startled the passengers behind him when in one deft movement she unlocked her belt, stood abruptly, and planted a kiss directly on his lips. "I love you. Thank you," she whispered in his ear and quickly sat back down.

Michael grinned. "Must be the aftershave," he said to the astonished people in line as he proceeded down the aisle to his seat.

It was a smooth takeoff. Susan watched her daughter's face as she gazed out the window. Sunlight streamed in brilliant vertical beams through the billowing clouds.

"God light," she whispered.

"It's beautiful," Jackie whispered back.

The plane broke through the clouds, and suddenly they were immersed in an infinite sea of azure blue sky. Susan smiled as she squeezed her daughter's hand, and they both stared dreamily out the window.

"I can't think of a better place for us to begin our journey of discovery," Susan said quietly. "Close to heaven ... close to God."

Epilogue

Once more, Lily Peyton had made the front page of the *Las Vegas Sun*—and she loved it. She laughed out loud as Ryan read the article aloud to the group.

"We can well expect the grand dame of special events to pull out all stops for tonight's gala grand opening of Suite 494. After maintaining a high level of security throughout the two-year development, Mrs. Peyton and her partners will at last allow a glimpse inside what the local community has always referred to as the White Elephant."

"They won't be calling it that for long." Susan opened another carton of tissue paper to refill the supply that was running low on the goody bag assembly line. They'd been stuffing bags for two days now.

Susan was first in the assembly line, assigned with the task of opening the elegant gold foil shopping bags and inserting sheets of silver tissue paper watermarked with the Suite 494 logo. Next in line was Pat Davies, who had flown out from California early to help with the gala, followed by Michael and Jackie. PM&J, as they'd dubbed themselves, were a trio working in tandem, stuffing the bags with the vast assortment of expensive goodies each guest would receive that night. Jackie was adding final touches of gold and silver metallic ribbon tied to the shopping bag handles.

Lily didn't have an assignment, per se, other than to sit back and enjoy the culmination of a project that, if not for her, would never have come to fruition. Ryan's task was to oversee all aspects of the gala event—that is, when he wasn't reading the newspaper to the goody bag assembly line.

"May I continue?" He waved the paper dramatically as the group nodded.

"The parasitic pachyderm that once sheltered addicts and pushers is now home to what is being billed as the world's largest collection of disco music and memorabilia. With three full floors of disco-era entertainment, Suite 494 will open to the public on Tuesday. But coveted invitations to the gala grand opening tonight were reserved for Vegas elite—celebrities, politicians, prominent members of the business community, and distinguished religious figures."

"Did he really say that?" Michael furrowed his brow. "Religious figures? Like we've invited John the Baptist … or the pope?"

"No. This is good," Lily interrupted. "The media typically leave out any references to religion, or they spin things way out of proportion."

Attending as personal favors to Lily, several guests were, indeed, very prominent members of the evangelical Christian community. And they were eager to come. A celebration of this magnitude without alcohol was truly a historic event in Las Vegas.

"I'm rather impressed with the parasitic pachyderm reference." Pat inserted a Disco Diva coffee mug into her bag and passed it down to Michael.

"Yeah, that's a great choice of words." Michael carefully placed a custom-made snow globe into the bag and passed it on to Jackie. "Only in the *Las Vegas Sun* could 'parasitic pachyderm' and 'religious figures' occur in the same paragraph."

Everyone laughed as the door to the construction-site office swung open. In ran a cherubic two-year-old, followed by his very pregnant mother. The curly-headed boy made a beeline for Lily and wrapped his arms around her legs. "Up … up …"

With little arms still holding fast to her legs, Lily shuffled to a nearby chair and sat, reaching down to help Harrison Oliver Power climb up on her lap.

"How's my little Harry?" She kissed his chubby cheek. "Did you come to help Mommy and Daddy stuff pretty bags for our guests?"

"I don't see Ryan stuffing anything." Jackie waved a roll of ribbon in the air. "Other than the air with his words." She stuck out her tongue at her half brother, who responded in kind.

"I was reading, dear," he said to his wife, grabbing the twelve pack of soda she was carrying.

"Sorry. Please continue." Tina walked to the counter to drop her purse. Then she grabbed a bottle of water from the cooler and sat down heavily.

"I swear, Ryan," Lily said, "this young man looks more like you every day!"

"Yeah, kind of amazing, isn't it?" Though Harry wasn't Ryan's biological son, they shared the same deep dimples and coloring. Even their eyes matched.

"I don't know," Tina said. "Harry's much more handsome, don't you think?"

Ryan pretended to pout and Tina laughed, holding her hand over her bulging tummy. "I can tell you one thing, this one's a lot more active. I've never felt a baby kick so much."

"May I feel?" Jackie put down the ribbon and scissors.

"Sure." Tina placed Jackie's hand over her stomach.

Jackie waited, then jumped. "That is so amazing!"

"Um, aren't we supposed to be working?" Pat chimed in. "I mean, I appreciate the wonders of mother nature and all myself, but we still have bags to stuff."

Susan winked. "Slave driver."

"Yeah, well, if that's what it takes. I want to get out of here and back to the hotel before Lisa and Mary get here, and we've still got a lot to do. Can someone take this next batch over so we have room?" She pointed to dozens of stuffed bags sitting on the floor, tissue paper rising from inside like petals bursting forth from a vase.

"Jackie, how about if you make the next run?" Ryan suggested.

"Sure, boss, no problem." She began to pick up the bags.

"The cart's at the bottom of the stairs, dear," Lily said, gently rocking Harry in her lap.

"Great." Jackie took a load of bags outside to the cart for transport, declining Susan's offer to help. "I'm fine, Mom—you've got enough to handle. But thanks anyway."

When Jackie walked out with the last of the bags for what appeared to be the next-to-the-last run, Ryan tapped his Montblanc pen against the table to capture the attention of the group.

"Okay, while Jackie's taking over the last of the bags ..."

Susan interrupted. "I know Lily would like you to finish reading the article for us, Ryan, but first—has anyone seen Loretta and Bob? Maybe someone should take a break and see how they're doing."

Loretta Wells had become Loretta Hutchings in a quiet ceremony at Cedar Ridge last year when she married Doctor Robert Hutchings— her veterinarian. She'd jumped at Susan's offer to serve as general manager for the new Disco Diva Salon and Diva Day Spa—especially when she discovered she could hire a full-time assistant and still see clients several days a week. With Dr. Bob's help, she was now putting the last touches on the new salon, located on the main floor next to Boutique 494, the retail shop. The social hour this evening would be taking place on the main floor, so guests would be able to circulate through the salon, spa, and boutique. Loretta was adamant that their first glimpse of the new Disco Diva be perfect in every way.

After the social hour, appetizers would be served on the third floor in the Disco Hall of Fame and Museum, with dinner and the program taking place in the big second-floor banquet room. Dancing and special entertainment would close out the event in Club 494. The entire evening had been well orchestrated, starting with the red-carpet entrance.

"I'm done here. I'll go see how Loretta and Bob are doing." Susan stood and stretched.

"Give me a minute, and I think I'll head over with you." Ryan blew a kiss to his wife as he put down his feet, sat up straight, and flipped pages on his clipboard. "In fact, once the last of these bags is taken over to the parasitic pachyderm"—he winked at Susan—"there really isn't anything left to do except go get ready and meet back here in …" He checked his Piaget watch. "… three hours."

"Is it already one o'clock?" Tina asked.

Ryan nodded. "Yes, ma'am."

"No wonder he's asleep." She looked over at Harry and whispered, "He's not the only one."

"Lily's been sleeping for awhile." Pat, her task accomplished, had begun to straighten the worktable.

"I'm not sleeping." Lily opened her eyes and shifted slowly so as not to wake Harry.

"Yeah, right," Michael teased. "Do you always drool when you're awake?"

"Michael!" Susan admonished.

"It's okay, dear. I understand your husband's humor. Now, Ryan, are you ever going to finish reading our article?"

Ryan picked up the newspaper, preparing to read, just as Jackie returned.

"Things are surprisingly calm over there … looks like everything is being handled. Loretta and Bob said they'd be over in a few minutes."

"Oh good." Susan sat down next to Pat. "You saved me a trip."

"Looks like the guys are here with the searchlights." Michael looked over at Ryan from his place by the window. "I know where you want them placed—want me to handle it?" Ryan nodded, and Michael headed for the door. "Be back in a jiff."

"Finish reading, dear," Lily said.

"This is the end—won't take long. 'With a full calendar of exciting events and an amazing array of exhibits filled with painstakingly preserved and creatively displayed artifacts, Suite 494 is the ultimate place to learn about an era that is experiencing a renaissance. Young and old will delight in the extensive private collection of Susan Anderson and the exact replica of the famous balcony at Studio 54. Peyton's Pavarotti-sized hunger for perfection and personal touch on tonight's gala celebration is certain to make this the social event of the season.'"

Ryan bowed as everyone applauded, then began to talk at once.

The excitement was palpable as they discussed events leading up to this night.

"The lights are in place." Michael closed the door behind him. "What did I miss?"

"Nothing much," Pat said. "Just Lily's Pavarotti-sized hunger for perfection."

"We're all heading out." Susan tossed her Beijo bag over her shoulder just as Loretta and Bob walked in.

Ryan cleared his throat. "Before anyone goes, since you're all here, I'd like to say something. It's been my honor to work with all of you these past two years. This project has clearly been a God-cidence of the most epic proportions, and my life has been irrevocably changed for the better because of it." He reached for Tina's hand. "We've talked it over, and we'll accept your offer to stay on."

Michael's holler was the loudest as he slapped Ryan on the back and the others cheered.

"You'll make an amazing executive manager." Susan grabbed him in a firm embrace. "Thank you for everything."

Hours later, everyone was sitting around the conference table dressed to the nines. The men looked dashing in Armani tuxedos, and the women glowed in designer apparel, some on loan from Saks Fifth Avenue. Courtesy of surveillance cameras that gave them a bird's-eye view, they were all watching guests walk the red carpet. It was like watching an Oscar night telecast.

"Those are some mighty well-dressed folks." Doc Bob whistled.

"And you're right up there with them, honey." Loretta kissed her husband. "We need to go to more soirees like this so you can wear a tuxedo more often. You look yummy."

"So do you," said Susan. She gestured around the circle at her friends in their designer finery. "So does everybody. Your dress is stunning, Lily."

"Thank you, dear. It's Badgley Mischka," she said matter-of-factly, folding her hands in her lap. A brilliant shade of jade green, the satin-and-chiffon custom gown was encrusted with crystals. She wore green diamond Harry Winston studs in her ears and looked like royalty.

"I'm wearing Versace." Jackie stood and twirled, revealing a gold metallic gown that clung to her curves. She stepped back and motioned to Pat, who also stood.

"This is vintage Oscar de la Renta. I can't tell you which of my regular customers brought it to Glitter and Bling on consignment, but her mother wore ruby slippers in some obscure film years ago." Pat batted her eyelashes and slowly turned, showcasing her cobalt blue sequin gown with a plunging back. "Mary and Lisa are wearing Oscar as well."

Their fellow Boomer Babes Rock cyberfriends were already inside Suite 494. They'd wanted to mingle with the celebrities as they arrived.

"Your turn." Pat stepped back next to Jackie and pointed to Loretta, who followed suit and stood.

"Ladies and gentlemen, I am sporting Vera Wang, and Saks is never going to get this back!" She spun around several times, allowing the diaphanous material to float around her legs. A one-sleeved Grecian design, the off-white material and gold braiding accents made her look like a bronze goddess.

Loretta leaned down and kissed her husband, then moved back to stand next to Pat. "You're on, little mama," she said to Tina.

"I can't believe they make dresses like this for whales." Tina stood.

"You are not a whale, dear." Lily wagged her finger. "That is a breathtaking maternity gown!"

"It should be—it's the one Mariska Hargitay wore to the Screen Actors Guild Awards." Pat beamed. "As soon as it came in to the shop, I pulled it for Tina. It's perfect!"

"Honey, you look incredible." Ryan applauded as Tina turned slowly in her white satin Carolina Herrera gown with crystal-embellished neckline. She stepped back, stood next to Loretta, and nodded at Susan, who stood and spun dramatically.

Jackie shook her head. "Mom, that is the most amazing dress I have ever seen."

"It's probably older than Susan is," Michael said, laughing. "Am I right?"

"Almost. It was designed in 1960 by Hubert de Givenchy for Audrey Hepburn to wear in *Breakfast at Tiffany's*. They decided on the black version instead. I've had it in cold storage for years, waiting for the right event."

An exact replica of the dress worn in the opening scene of the classic movie, Susan's version was a deep shade of burnt sienna, accented by vintage canary yellow Weiss earrings. Once again, she'd fashioned her hair into an elegant French twist ending high on her head, a diamond Tiffany's hairpin secured in the center like a tiny glistening tiara. The entire look whispered expensive elegance.

Susan walked with an overly dramatic flair to stand at the end of the line of women and turned. The three men in attendance applauded like patrons at a haute couture fashion show, oblivious to Lily, who had stood quietly and walked to the stereo system.

"Hit it!" Susan said, surprising the men as Lily flipped the switch. The room filled with the sound of Sister Sledge singing "We Are Family," and the five elegantly dressed women launched into an obviously choreographed disco dance that sent the men into hoots and hollers. As the song ended, the women bowed deeply and embraced each other in joy.

"We did it!" Pat said.

"Of course we did." Jackie put her arm around Tina. "The Tropicana didn't hire us because we clean up good." She giggled.

"They didn't hire me to be a baby machine, either." Tina took a drink of water. "I am so out of shape."

"Thank you, ladies. That was certainly a fine way to usher us into the party," Lily said. "Now, what do you say we greet our guests and"— they all shouted together—"let's get this party started!"

Susan held back as everyone filed out of the building, crossing the short distance from the office to the red-carpet entrance of Suite 494.

"I'll be right over, Michael," she said as they reached the bottom of the office stairs.

"Everything okay?"

"Everything is more than okay. I just want to take a minute. Promise."

"Sure. I understand. You did it, babe. You did it."

"We did it." She held his hand as they both stared at the searchlights puncturing the night sky with light. "I'll be right behind you." She kissed him before he walked away into the cool October evening.

It was a bittersweet moment—the end of one dream and the start of another. Susan stretched out her arms as if to gather hopes, dreams, and possibilities as she stood and watched her family walk down the red carpet. They really were all family, every last one of the group who had helped make this dream come true. And she loved them all. With all her heart.

She looked out over the vast property to the shining lights in the distance, and beyond that to the stars that twinkled reassuringly in the autumn sky. And she smiled.

Tonight, history was coming to life while at the same time being put to rest.

Acknowledging the truth about her past had set her free.

But it was love that made the freedom worthwhile.

... a little more ...

When a delightful concert comes to an end,

the orchestra might offer an encore.

When a fine meal comes to an end,

it's always nice to savor a bit of dessert.

When a great story comes to an end,

we think you may want to linger.

And so, we offer ...

AfterWords—just a little something more after you

have finished a David C. Cook novel.

We invite you to stay awhile in the story.

Thanks for reading!

Turn the page for ...

- **Discussion Questions**

Discussion Questions

You Make Me Feel Like Dancing is the first of three novels in the Va Va Va Boom series. The "boom" refers to the baby boomers, people born between 1946 and 1964. Baby boomers today, of which approximately 38 million are women, represent 28 percent of the U.S. population. Boomer women are some of the healthiest, wealthiest, and best-educated women ever to hit midlife. Identified by the *National Association of Baby Boomer Women* as "faithful, loving, and hardworking women who multitask to survive," members of this powerful sisterhood hail from various backgrounds and carry different baggage, but most share the desire to make a difference. It is for this stalwart demographic of vibrant women who want to make a difference that the author has written the Va Va Va Boom series. She welcomes you to discuss the questions below in your book clubs and to communicate directly with her via e-mail at AB@AllisonBottke.com.

1. What are some of the major themes of the book? Did the author effectively develop these themes? If so, how?

2. Is there anything in this story to which you can personally relate? Did you find yourself identifying with a particular character or characters? (You don't need to be a baby boomer to enjoy the story!) Are there any ideas or advice you can apply to your own life?

3. Brought together in an online community known as Boomer Babes Rock, Susan, Patricia, Mary, and others form fast friendships even though they live in different parts of the country and lead completely different lives. Do you believe the close online friendships the author has described are likely or possible? What kinds of benefits or problems could stem from this special kind of relationship?

4. How important is the setting to the story? Did the setting of the novel detract or add to your enjoyment of the story? Did it raise any questions or concerns?

5. How effectively does the author portray the presence of spirituality in the characters' everyday lives? Has she succeeded in presenting faith in a way that feels relevant and relatable? Are there specific characters whose beliefs resonate with yours?

6. One of the issues Susan faces in parts of this book is the tension of living "in the world" but not being "of the world"—that is, living in her culture without compromising her beliefs and being a credible witness to those who might not share those beliefs. Her particular "world" is flashy Las Vegas and the glitzy disco culture. Do you think she did a good job of living out her faith in that world? In what ways have you felt a tension between your faith and the culture you live in?

7. At several points in the novel, we see Susan wrestling with the ability to communicate openly with her husband. How does this issue apply to the story? How does it apply to your life?

8. Susan had the opportunity to fulfill one of her most important dreams, yet she was prepared to sacrifice that dream to save her marriage. Have you ever been called to sacrifice a cherished dream? Describe the experience and what (if anything) you learned from it.

9. The first three books in the Va Va Va Boom series feature Susan, Patricia, and Mary—three baby boomer women who are living, loving, and enjoying making a difference in their world. From what you have read so far, where do you think the author will take these women in subsequent books? What aspects of their experience are specifically "boomer" and what are more universal?

10. Each lead character in the Va Va Va Boom series owns her own business, representing a unique generation of women who have made choices to survive and thrive in sometimes difficult circumstances. Discuss some of the challenges Susan faced as a business owner and Loretta experienced as an employee.

11. Money plays a significant role—both positive and negative—in this book. What are some of the money issues that arise between Susan and Loretta, Susan and Michael, Susan and Lily, Ryan and his father, and others? How have money issues affected your own life and relationships and your spiritual journey?

12. Susan is a passionate, loving, faithful, trustworthy individual who, at midlife, is suddenly faced with making a choice destined to send her on an unexpected journey. What other choices could she have made? Have you ever been faced with the need to make a life-changing choice?

13. Susan had a painful secret in her past that held her prisoner for years. How would things have been different if she had fully disclosed everything to Michael years before? How can secrets hurt a relationship? Is there ever a time when maintaining a secret is the best thing to do?

14. What are your thoughts about Susan's decision to not look for her daughter and about Michael's choice to find her?

15. Story lines within the Va Va Va Boom series will address timely issues of special interest to the baby boomer demographic such as empty nesting, aging parents, menopause, divorce, widowhood,

retirement, sexuality, Alzheimer's, drug-addicted adult children, grandparenting, adoption, sexual abuse, bankruptcy, adultery, health, post-abortion stress syndrome, and more. Which of these issues would you most like to see the author address in subsequent books? Why?

16. What did you like or dislike about the book that hasn't been discussed already? Were you glad you read this book? Would you recommend it to a friend? Do you want to read more works by this author? Why or why not?

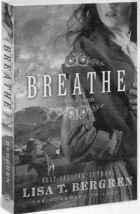

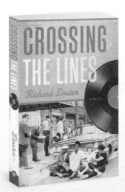